REPARATION
&
AN OUNCE OF DISCRETION

-SHEILA SMITH-

i

Previous books by Sheila Smith

Valley of Stone
Rural Haven
Restitution
Aftermath
Demons and Daffodils
Mother Goddess
Synergy
The Whispering Tarn
The Hermit of Hesperia
Retouched
Stormy Paradise
Free Zone
Golden Triangle

REPARATION
&
AN OUNCE OF DISCRETION

ISBN 978-09569349-7-0

First Published 2014 Sheila Smith

Printed by CreateSpace

REPARATION

After a traumatic childhood, the main characters are against marriage, because of past events.

Despite being left to fend for herself at sixteen, Bethany Browne manages to get the education she desires and becomes an Accountant with the help of a friend she met in nursery school.

James Castleton also despite a very troublesome childhood, without the help of grandparents who care only for themselves manages to get on in the world, as he cares for his brother who was badly injured in a road accident.

AN OUNCE OF DISCRETION

A family story set in the English Lake District, including changes of circumstance, misunderstandings, indiscretions and danger in the rock climbing world.

I dedicate Reparation to my son Dr Duncan Smith, with thanks for his patience, encouragement, and attention to detail.

Front: Loughrigg Tarn and Langdale Pikes.
Back: Derwentwater.

REPARATION

CHAPTER ONE

James Castleton, pulled his black overcoat around his tall frame, and looked across at the three ancient yew trees, surrounding the dug out grave, and the earth hidden by a synthetic green simulated grass cover with the two identical wreaths of white lilies waiting to adorn this final resting place. It was a good day for a funeral, cold, dark and miserable as the fine rain covered everything, and the cobwebs glistened in the electric light from the ancient Crosthwaite Parish Church porch in the distance. The Church was quite well known in the Keswick, Cumbria area, as there had been a church on this site since St. Kentigern (named in Scotland as St. Mungo) came from West Scotland and set up a cross in this place in 553AD. There were not many people left to say goodbye to the old gentleman in the coffin, he had outlived most of his friends and relatives, and the two young relatives remaining, looked on without any deep sorrow for his passing. However, their grandfather was in good company, this being the place where Sir Thomas of Eskhead was the Vicar whose famous nephew was one Fletcher Christian. In the Church were memorials to Robert Southey the poet, and also Canon Rawnsley one of the founders of the National Trust, and he had been Vicar for thirty four years from 1883.

The deceased, James Castleton senior had always been a Church goer, but also an embittered man after the death of his only son caused by a cancerous brain tumour. He had not helped either his son's wife or his own wife (the mother of his son) to come to terms with their loss and because of his cynical beliefs it turned out that both grandparents were selfish in their grief. They had both stood back and left their son's widow Mary to cope with her loss alone, except for her two young sons James and Joss. Mary had been five years younger than her husband, a husband that she had looked up to and left to deal with everything of a monetary nature, and even as far as suggesting how *she* should go about bringing up their two boys. She had relied on her husband for everything, and that had made his loss very difficult to come to terms with.

Now James looked at the funeral director blankly as he held a bag of soil before him, and he realised he must take a handful of the soil and then throw it down onto the coffin of his grandfather after whom he had been named. This he did, and then he moved his brother's wheelchair nearer to the grave so that he might do the same. Joss did not acknowledge the fact that James had assisted, neither did he glance at his older brother as he threw in a handful of soil in an almost disdainful manner.

Jasmine, the daughter of James's next door neighbours made a thing of throwing in some soil with a smile towards James which *she* thought was both sympathetic and beguiling, and the clergyman droned on completing the service. James knew that he would be expected to invite his neighbours back to the house, for the drinks and food that was already awaiting them. He stared back at Jasmine enigmatically, as he realised that she had no idea that her arch looks and posing moves left him cold. After today he need not see her or her parents again. Since he had qualified as a solicitor she had made a point of calling to ask how his grandfather was, but now she had no excuse, and he had every intention of doing some alterations on the ground floor of Willow Trees the home he and his brother would now inherit, and he would have a very good excuse not to invite anyone inside. Hopefully after this funeral he would be able to put aside all his cynical and derogatory ideas about everyone around him, and put his mind to helping his clients to the best of his ability, that was why he had decided on this career and due in part to his mother's experiences, although he found most of the time he had to do this in Court!

The funeral director was moving around, and James realised that he was waiting to start the filling in of the grave, and he started to get hold of Joss's wheelchair. The wheelchair jerked, and with difficulty on the uneven grass his brother moved off slowly, declining any help from his elder brother.

James glanced into the grave for the last time, and hoped that his grandparents would at last have a peaceful rest. It was eighteen months since his grandmother had been buried and now her husband had joined her. As far as James could

3

tell they had done nothing but bicker with each other since he had moved in with them when he was fifteen. They had both requested burial rather than cremation, and James believed that in the future, both he and Joss would be cremated, and their ashes buried here in the family plot with their parents. God, he was being particularly morbid today.

Willow Trees was only three hundred metres away from the church yard, and James had walked along behind Joss in his wheelchair for the service. He did the same now on the way back, and couldn't wait for the guests to eat and drink, socialise for a while uttering meaningless platitudes, and then make their way homeward! Perhaps a few of the older mourners could remember a time when the family Castleton were a happy family, as James could with difficulty, as so much had happened since then which had detracted from those happy memories.

It was quite a struggle to get the wheelchair up the temporary ramp to the front door, and Joss could not do this without his brother's help, and he looked really upset and disagreeable by the time he was in the building.

Two hours later when everyone had gone home except Henry Clarkson, their grandfather's solicitor, the Will was read. Except for a few small bequests the house Willow Trees had been left (the solicitor paused with a quick glance towards James Castleton who quickly nodded) to them both, as had the money remaining, which came to a sum of approximately fifty five thousand pounds. This was a surprise to Henry Clarkson, but not to the two young men. The grandparents had preferred to have Joss looked after in Blackstone Hall, which had been a Home for Disabled Children when he was sent there, and was now a home for all ages of the disabled, and this had made a big dent in the family's finances.

James had never forgiven his grandfather for placing Joss in Blackstone Hall when he was ten years old - James had insisted that they could look after him at home, but he had been overruled, what did a fifteen year old boy know? He would never forget the way Joss had reached out to him in desperation, but his grandfather had pulled James into the car, and after that James had only been allowed to visit his brother once a week. Two hours on Sundays James had spent with his young brother, which was very hard to bear as for the previous five years he had seemed to bring Joss up single-handedly whilst their mother was ill. On Wednesday evenings after going to the gym, he sometimes managed to visit his brother, but that visit was brief and only served to upset Joss and the grandparents were unaware of this visit. James remembered almost every despairing minute.

Both the boys had missed their father after he died in hospital, but they had already become accustomed to having just mother at home, and that had continued and their mother had made a big fuss of them at first.

Money had not seemed to be a problem, as their mother had provided them with good food, and as far as James at eleven years knew, the bills for running the house had been paid. In fact, for part of the time their mother was very cheerful and playful, but over the months this had changed as she consumed more and more of the bottles she bought along with the groceries. One day James had tasted it, and had spit what was in his mouth into the sink. It was horrible, and it was doing strange things to his mother. Then he found that he had to put the alarm clock in his own room, and get his brother up and ready for school. He would go into his mother's bedroom, and ask for money for their bus fares and school lunches. She invariably pointed to her purse on the bedside table, and he would help himself to what was needed for them both.

Not many months later, he decided that they should walk to school, and take a sandwich for their lunch. It was much easier that way, as his mother started to accuse him of emptying her purse to buy none essentials. He soon grasped the fact that the *essentials* were the numerous bottles of wine she bought at the supermarket. This she sometimes supplemented with bottles of spirits.

James soon found out the day that their mother withdrew money from the bank, and he made it his business to take some of it, and hide it, tied in a plastic bag, inserted into the box of detergent in the utility room. His mother rarely did any laundry these days, and he started to gather up some of her clothes for washing with his own and his brother's clothes. He had once tried to iron a shirt, and had burnt it, and since then he put everything into the dryer, and always remembered to take them out as soon as the cycle stopped, and folded them carefully. Not one person at school had noticed any difference in their appearance, and he felt quite pleased with his efforts.

The main problem he had was managing to get clothes to fit him as he kept growing out of them. His clothes he kept for Joss to grow into. When he or Josh had a birthday coming up, James would arrange for them to visit their grandparents where, suffering a deep embarrassment, he would ask if they could have sports clothes for school as a birthday present, as their mother was not interested in sport

6

and always forgot to provide them! That way the extras needed for school, and longer trousers were usually covered.

Eighteen months or so after their father's death, James decided that the money must be running out, as he found it difficult to get enough from his mother's purse to feed them. He arranged to do a newspaper round in the mornings when he knew that his mother would stay in bed. He was always home in time to make sure that Joss was ready for school, and the money he made each week he made last as long as possible. He dare not go out in the evenings to work, as their mother was becoming very abusive. She would rant and rave at them, as she was so depressed, and not managing to buy enough to drink.

One weekend James tried to talk to his grandmother about this, and was told that "Mary will get over it soon, time is a great healer. She should get herself out of the house and get a small job and meet people." James gave up asking his grandparents for help!

One morning he arrived home from his paper round to find the house in uproar, his mother was slapping Joss around the head, because he wouldn't hand over the money she had heard jingling in his pocket.

"Mum stop, I gave Joss that from my newspaper money, as it is for his bus fare, it's raining and he hasn't got a decent coat." James put his arms around his mother to trap her arms, and she stared towards her youngest son in surprise. "Joss hasn't got a coat, why not?" She sounded really shocked.

"Because you spend all the money on your bottles of wine," James told her angrily. He was really upset when she pushed him away from her, and sat down at the kitchen table with her head in her hands, and started to cry.

James sent Joss off to school, and watched his mother with a kind of relief. It seemed to be sinking into her addled brain the realisation of their true circumstances.

"James I miss your dad every day, and I can't manage without him," his mother said brokenly.

"I have to go to school now mum, so we'll talk about it tonight."

"I haven't any money left James, what will we do?"

"You always get money from the bank, but don't you get Family Allowance for us?" James asked. He had heard the boys at school talking about it.

His mother looked interested, and moved over to the pile of post on the table, and started to look through it, she was very upset. "You go to school now James, and we'll talk about it tonight. I have been very stupid and selfish, and together we can manage things I'm sure."

That night after school the boys arrived home, to find the house warm and quiet. There was a plastic shopping bag on the table, and they found beans and eggs, bread and milk, and James put slices of fresh bread in the toaster. They were going to have a feast, as their mother must have found the Family Allowance books or found out which bank account the money had been going into over the months. James thought he must find out about this, and maybe, they could discuss some way of managing things much better.

They enjoyed their meal, and Joss went off to watch television, with a reminder from James that he should be getting on with his homework!

James went into his room to do his own homework, on an old laptop computer that he had borrowed from his best friend at school. If things were better with his mother and the money situation, he would start to save up to buy one of his own with the newspaper delivery money he earned. In fact, he might see about getting another paper round in the evenings, now that his mother had accepted the fact that she needed help with managing the money. Maybe he could start going to football training in the evenings, and possibly Josh would like that too. He might be able to get them both some decent trainers to wear!

An hour later, James began to worry about his mother. If she had money, she was probably out there somewhere, drinking. It was unlike her these days as she seemed to have lost her friends and so she drank at home, and made his and Josh's life a misery. Suddenly he ran towards her bedroom, and shouted that he was coming inside to pick up any washing she had to go into the washing machine.

He pushed open the bedroom door, and stood for a moment in shock. His mother was on the bed with one arm hanging limply over the side of the bed, and the other arm across her forehead as if to keep out the light from her eyes. For a moment he thought that she was not breathing, and then he saw a slight movement, and went to place his fingers against the side of her throat as he had seen people do on the television. He shook her gently then with more force, as she didn't wake up. He hated to think how long she might have been like this. It was *his* fault, as he had thought she intended to start looking after them, as she had been shopping for food. Instead she had been in her bedroom all the time, consuming the alcohol she had also bought, and he had ignored her! He looked at her closely and realised she had lost a lot of weight, no wonder she was ill, he should have stayed home from school just for the day.

He went into the hallway, and picked up the telephone. There was no dialling tone - the 'phone had been cut off again! He ran out of the house and up the next door drive and hammered on the door.

"What's going on James, what do you want in such a hurry?" Mr Walker asked angrily when he answered the door. His wife came to stand beside him her eyebrows raised questioningly.

"Can you please ring for an ambulance Mr Walker, our 'phone has been cut off," James asked, near to tears, and wondering what he could say to Josh when he got back to the house. Some boys at school had a mobile 'phone and James had never coveted one, until now!

"Has your mum fallen over again with the drink?" Mr Walker asked in a resigned voice.

James was taken aback, and wondered if the whole area knew their business. He wanted to hit out at Mr. Walker, but he wanted his help more, he would have to put up with his pitying look.

"I can't get her to waken up, she might have been like that most of the day," James said and hurried back down the drive, followed by Mrs Walker. *Why* had his dad had to die, and why couldn't his mother cope without him? He and Joss had to, and why couldn't they be a normal family? What could he tell Josh, their mother might be a waste of space, but they loved her, and if she got better they would make a better job of looking after her!

A paramedic arrived, followed shortly by the ambulance, and James wanted to go in the ambulance, but they said he was too young, and Mrs Walker whom James had not had much time for, volunteered to go to the hospital with their mother, if James would go and tell her husband.

James went into the bathroom, and had a little cry, and when he could manage it he stopped crying, and washed his

10

face. He went to tell Mr Walker about his wife going with his mother to the hospital, and he was surprised when Mr Walker was not angry and shouting at him, but asked if the boys would like to spend the evening in his house? James was very surprised and thanked Mr Walker very kindly, but he and Josh would wait at home until Mrs Walker came back, hopefully with their mother?

James asked Josh to help him clear away all the bottles from their mother's bedroom. They had collected them all, and James had made the bed with clean sheets, when the doorbell rang, and they rushed to the door in the hope that it was their mother.

There was a young woman on the doorstep looking very much like a teacher, and she showed James a card. She was from Social Services.

"How old are you James," she asked, looking very calm, but interested.

He added six months to his age it seemed a good idea, as he had added at least a year to his age for the news vendor to get a job! "Fourteen Miss Sinclair," he answered looking at her card. He kicked Josh with his foot on his shin, when he opened his mouth to speak, and Joss swallowed and was silent.

"I'm sorry, but we must find you somewhere to stay for the night. At least until we hear how your mother is coping," Miss Sinclair said regretfully.

The grandparents were a last resort, as they always looked upon the boy's mother as someone who had married their son, but *she* had *lived* rather than their son. James couldn't think of anything, but he knew that he wanted to be here when their mother returned, as return she must!

"Mr. Walker might let us stay with him," James said hopefully, as Mr Walker walked up the drive, towards the young social worker.

Mr Walker paused and thought a moment, and then he smiled ruefully, remembering what his wife had just said to him on the telephone. "Well, yes the boys can stay next door for a night or two, until their mother comes out of hospital. My wife just rang and your mother, after having her stomach...., well after treatment she seems to be doing quite well. My wife says I should put the boys in the spare room, and she will be home from the hospital shortly, by taxi."

Miss Sinclair looked thoughtful, and James could have hugged Mr Walker, he was much nicer than he would ever have believed. How many times had he complained about having to throw back their football from the other side of the hedge, yet he wasn't so bad after all! Also Mrs Walker had gone to the hospital with their mother and that was great!

The boys were wonderfully well behaved, and after two nights in hospital their mother did come home, full of determination, and with a leaflet that James read, which gave the address of the local Alcoholics Anonymous group. Their mother promised to visit this group, and to give up the 'demon drink' (her words) and both boys thought it would be easy for their mother, but Mrs Walker talked to them, and said it would be very hard and they should be as good as they possibly could be, as their mother would go through a hard time. She also said that their mother would have a telephone number for a friend from the AA group, and if things got very bad, then their mother could ring that friend for help.

When their mother had arrived home from the hospital, she made lots of promises of how things would change, and told them how much she loved them, and was going to look after them. James was amazed, when his mother had been drinking then part of the time she had been quite amusing and happy. However, they were not prepared for how miserable and bad tempered she could be as she walked from room to room in the house, and moaned and grumbled. James was there for her, and Joss looked on hopefully. Sometimes just to see *them*, and to know that they were both still living with her was a help, but sometimes she couldn't stand the sight of them.

Twice James had rung the supposedly secret number that their mother had for the friend from the AA Group, and twice that man named Michael, had arrived to visit them and their mother had seemed to manage to get through to the next day without screaming and shouting and threatening them with her tongue. James now learned words that he would never have dreamt could come out of his mother's mouth. Afterwards, she was always sorry, but it hurt him, really hurt him, and when those bad times occurred Joss had usually gone to his room and switched on the television at James's suggestion. One particularly difficult day James watched his mother bang her head against the living room wall in her anguish, and when she realised what she had done, and how upset James was, she agreed when he pleaded with her to see her doctor at the local surgery. The doctor gave her some pills, only on a temporary basis he said, and after that she seemed to cope much better, but she was sensible enough to give the pills to James to look after, and he gave her one at the prescribed times.

After about eight months in this see-saw world, when they never knew what to expect when they came home from school, they slowly got back to an almost normal family life.

Their mother was very loving, and she cooked, cleaned and washed their clothes and had money to purchase whatever they needed. She frequently saw Michael, and both Josh and James liked him very much.

There was one problem - she put the house up for sale, and said they would 'downsize' and she would find it much easier to cope with a smaller house, and she was also trying to get a job, something she had never had, as she had married their dad straight from college, as he had a very good job, and within three months she had been expecting James.

James took his mother to meet the proprietor of the newsagent for whom he delivered newspapers still, and his mother was offered a job in the Post Office alongside the newsagent.

Their mother, who now looked really attractive with her blonde hair shining and soft with her blue eyes mellow and happy, and she often saw Michael and also included James and Joss, and both boys were hoping that something would come of that relationship, in fact, for the next two years although their mother never married Michael, they all enjoyed a very happy time together. Something that James supposed was a *normal* life, and at fifteen he was proud of his younger brother Joss, who was doing well academically at school, and who was becoming very popular as he appeared to be a good athlete and represented the school.

James was also proud of his mother, who had battled with the 'demon drink,' and finally she seemed to accept that she had to live without the husband she had loved, the loss of whom had been the cause of her deep depression, and with the added help of her mentor and friend Michael and her two sons she had come out the other side and deserved every moment of her new found happiness. However, the childhood of her two sons had been irreparably damaged.

CHAPTER TWO

Bethany Browne hurried along the street towards her shared flat, and was surprised by the friendly looks she received from people she was passing. She had no idea how attractive she looked with her 5'4" slim figure, and shoulder length hazel coloured hair, and striking blue eyes with dark lashes to die for. She suddenly realised that every now and again she skipped, and was swinging her shoulder bag dangerously. Also she couldn't stop smiling. Today she had received the news that she had achieved a First Class Honours Bachelor of Science Degree in Applied Accounting from Oxford Brookes University in association with the Association of Chartered Certified Accountants. Her work wasn't over yet, and she would have to change her job to get the necessary experience before she could become chartered. It had not been easy to get her qualifications, and she had done it alone and from home in Keswick in the English Lake District, working long and hard into the night over the last four years. The books required had been very expensive, and she had not been able to join the expensive weekends with other students to get tuition and help with anything she found difficult to understand. Unfortunately, with so much studying taking up her time she had lost touch with some of her friends, who were mostly occupied with their boyfriends or husbands. However, she was looking forward to sharing her news with her flatmate, Nathanial Dixon, he would be really pleased for her, knowing how much time and effort she had expended in the last four years, and how often he had been asked to turn down the music 'just a little bit.' The other reason for her good humour was the sunny bright day, and the wonderful mountains surrounding the town, behind her was Skiddaw looking proud and quite green, and across behind Derwentwater the mountain ranges looked every shade of blue, and the shapes were as always fascinating to gaze upon, and even better to walk upon!

Bethany and Nathanial (Nat) had started pre-school together, and afterwards had shared their school years, until Nat had gone to teacher training college, and she to a night class at secretarial school, whilst working as a junior in an accountancy practise. Unfortunately, although they were happy to keep her on working for them, she was now over-qualified, and would need experience in different areas of accountancy to eventually become chartered.

She slowed her jaunty walk as she looked forward, as there was some sort of commotion on the pavement. She watched in dismay slowly drawing nearer, as she saw a man in a wheelchair being harassed. Three youths wearing hooded tops, were placing a piece of tree branch which must have fallen from the trees in the park onto the pavement in

17

front of the wheelchair, whichever way the man in the wheelchair tried to pass. Twice Bethany watched as he managed to lift the front wheels over the obstacle, but was in danger of turning over the wheelchair, as he was obviously tiring. Seeing this was so unexpected in this holiday town, she was almost blindingly angry as the three youths continued their harassment, and without much thought she took out her mobile telephone, and marched towards them intent on putting a stop to their vicious and unkind manipulation of the young man in the wheelchair.

Bethany swung her heavy handbag which hit one of the youths on the seat of his jeans, to get their attention, and all three turned towards her menacingly. She almost stopped breathing for a second, and then ostentatiously used her mobile 'phone. Two of the youths decided to make a run for it, but the third stared at her angrily, his eyes were narrowed and his nostrils seemed to flare over his thin angry lips, and she wondered if she had made a big mistake in trying to help the young man in the wheelchair! The hooded youth rambled on about 'people who were born with a silver spoon in their mouths, and he and his Uncle Silas were as good as anyone around here.' He stopped ranting and looked up and down Bethany's small frame, and his eyes were full of hate and anger. The stare they shared silently was filled with animosity, and Bethany's heart started to beat fast as she was determined not to look away from those green tinged eyes filled with hate. If she looked away first she would appear to be submissive, and she stared back angrily. The ringing tone stopped and she thankfully head a voice, and she spoke into the 'phone.

"I need your help, I'm outside at the corner, by the traffic lights," she said to Nat as he answered the 'phone.

"I'm coming now," was all he replied, but she still held her 'phone to her ear, not wanting the young man to know the call had been ended.

She could tell that the young man was undecided, and probably thought she had called the police, the only trouble with that was that she would very likely need help in the next few seconds and Nat was, hopefully, in their flat a few yards away.

Bethany was amazed that the young man in the wheelchair who could easily have made his get-away, slowly moved his chair to her side, this she noticed in her peripheral vision, as the hateful green eyes of the youth tried to dominate her.

Her eyes were still locked with those of her adversary, and although he didn't take his eyes from hers, he gave out a torrent of abuse, his words disgusting in the extreme. Bethany was feeling rather faint as she watched Nat come up behind the young man and put his muscular arm around his neck, forcing the man's arm up his back, as his martial arts and teacher training probably now being fully utilized for the very first time. The youth still spouted abuse, drawing a large crowd of interested people around them. They seemed interested in what was going on but not interested enough to help so they were probably visitors to the area! The youth was being held fast, but was unhurt.

Bethany sighed and stumbled against the wheelchair, and knew that if it had not been there she would have fallen, how stupid was she to feel so weak now that Nat was here and had the youth in his grip. However, Nat let go of the youth as he realised that she might fall and upset the wheelchair and injure one or both of them. The youth took to his heels, and made rude and menacing gestures as he ran down the street. Nat held the wheelchair firmly and had a supporting arm around Bethany, and the crowd started to disperse now that the excitement was over. Nat received a nod of approval from an elderly man as he passed them by.

The young man in the wheelchair looked up at Bethany, his face a picture of dismay tinged with gratitude, and when his glance continued towards Nat he looked embarrassed and angry, probably because he felt so utterly useless.

"Thank you both for your help, nothing like this has ever happened to me before, in all the years I've spent in this damned wheelchair." His voice showed that he meant his thanks, but his eyes filled with weak tears, as he strived to appear fully controlled.

Bethany tried not to show the pity that she felt. Had he not been in his wheelchair he would have been about six foot tall, and was handsome enough to attract any young woman.

"Where do you live?" Nat asked suddenly, looking slightly uncomfortable as Bethany kissed his cheek in thanks and moved away from his steadying arm.

"Willow Trees, just around the corner, near to the park gates. I can manage, thank you. I am Joss Castleton." Joss held out his hand, and Bethany shook it, and glanced at Nat.

"I am Bethany Browne, and this is Nathanial Dixon, we share a second floor flat in this next building. We are pleased to meet you Joss, but would have preferred better circumstances," she said regretfully.

Nat quickly shook Joss's hand. "Now, I'll give you a push home, you must be a bit tired after all that carry on," Nat said, and started to push the wheelchair forward before Joss could object. "Willow Trees you said, that's rather grand."

For a moment Bethany thought that Joss was going to object to being pushed home, but he must have realised that he was pretty well shaken up.

"Very grand indeed, my brother and I have just inherited it from our grandparents, and we are having it made wheelchair friendly but it isn't quite finished yet, so I would appreciate your company back to the house, the temporary ramp is a bit difficult," Joss said. Bethany looked at his handsome face closely – he did look rather pale and most definitely upset, and probably hated the idea of being escorted home by two people and one of them a girl, whom he had just met in very difficult circumstances.

Nat negotiated the wheelchair easily, and Bethany walked alongside feeling rather awkward, wondering what would have happened if she hadn't interfered. A fine sweat dewed her temples, as she realised that a different situation might so easily have arisen. They crossed the street and moved up the drive to an imposing house, with a ramp that looked very unstable. Nat pushed the wheelchair up the ramp, and Joss could only just reach the keyhole with his key because of how the temporary ramp was situated, and Bethany noticed he seemed to have a little feeling in his upper legs, and he had lifted his torso slightly with the effort he took to reach the keyhole.

"Is there anyone in the house," Bethany asked worriedly.

"Not at the moment, but please come inside, I'm sure you could do with a strong coffee, I know I could." Joss said feelingly. "I *am capable* of making coffee." He finished speaking, and Bethany realised that if they allowed him to do this, it would somehow compensate for the fact that he had needed their help.

21

"Thank you that would be great," Nat said, with a smile at Bethany, and she was pleased that they were on the same wavelength. Nat closed the front door behind them, and he and Bethany followed Joss across the imposing tiled hall, passing four tall mahogany or pitch-pine, closed doorways towards the back of the house, and into a very spacious kitchen. Joss switched on the kettle, and pulled out mugs from one of the lower cupboards. He spooned ground coffee into a café filtre, and when the kettle boiled, carefully poured water into the container. Bethany had stepped forward to help automatically, but Nat restrained her with his hand on her elbow, and so she continued to move forward and passed Joss and looked out through the large sliding glass doors which opened into a conservatory overlooking the back of the house.

"You have a rather splendid garden out here, may I take a look?" She glanced at Joss, and he nodded ruefully, and she realised that not much that happened escaped his eye, although it was on a lower level at the moment!

She unlocked the door and moved out onto the stone terrace, and looked with awe at the lovely grounds. All this space, how lovely, and she gazed with pleasure at the tall weeping willow trees just beyond a pond, and a backdrop of splendid trees and mountains.

Probably because she had just recovered from a very worrying experience, and also because she was still high from learning that she now had a BSc Degree, she ran down the three steps to the green lawn, and did a forward somersault landing on her feet, just as Nat had shown her last Sunday in the park. She straightened her skirt and pulled down her shirt, and looked with dismay at the two indentations in the lawn where her feet had landed, showing plainly the shape of her shoes as the low heels on her shoes had dug into the lawn surface.

"Oh dear, what have I done?" she muttered as she picked up her shoulder bag, scooped into it her bits and bobs, and straightened up to look a long way up into disdainful grey eyes in a very arrogant and angry face.

"Yes indeed, what *have* you done?" His voice was well spoken, but very angry as he too looked at the indentations in the lawn, which were actually slowly returning to the normal level as they watched, except for the low heel puncture marks.

"A forward somersault, but it wasn't very good, I have done better." She said literally, and he looked even more annoyed.

"I quite agree," Nat said with a laugh from the patio surrounding the conservatory, where he stood beside Joss in his wheelchair.

"Perhaps you would be kind enough to introduce me to your friends Joss?" The tall, grey eyed man said with raised eyebrows, as Bethany looked at him, and realised he was wearing a smart suit, was carrying a briefcase, and looked as though he belonged here. She felt her face going red, which was really very annoying - she hadn't blushed like a schoolgirl for years!

What an idiot was she, today was turning into a nightmare of epic proportions, she had already been on a high, after receiving wonderful news she had faced-out three hoodlums, experienced so many new emotions, and now let herself down in front of this arrogant authoritarian, who was probably Joss's brother! His mouth was compressed in anger, and a muscle flicked in his autocratic jaw, as he stared at her in disbelief. She gulped suddenly, then realised that she was, in fact, wearing quite sensible panties but no tights (not a thong thank goodness) and she doubted that Nat and Joss had seen anything from the kitchen, but this cool eyed stranger she had *not seen* approaching, or from what angle? Many days she wore smart trousers to work, why not today, when she had let herself down acting in a juvenile way, which was definitely out of character?

Joss wheeled himself forward, and glanced at Bethany and Nat with a gleeful smile, and it was good to see, after seeing him so upset earlier when the yobs had been harassing him. However, his glance at his brother was not exactly friendly. "These are my new friends Bethany Browne and Nathanial Dixon, we just met today. We are about to have coffee, would you care to join us?" He glanced from Bethany who was wearing a very chagrined expression on her pretty face on which there was still an embarrassed blush, towards Nat. "This is my older brother James Castleton. I don't suppose he expected me to be entertaining friends."

Bethany thought that Joss's invitation to join them for coffee to his brother could have been more welcoming, also why did he think his brother should assume that he didn't have any friends?

James firmly shook hands with Nat, and turned to Bethany with a slight frown, but offered his hand, which she took. He didn't only take her hand he took her breath away, and she moved quickly through the conservatory into the kitchen and sat down on a chair at the kitchen table slowly drawing in a reviving breath of air, and was slowly joined by the others.

She glanced at James Castleton, and found him looking at her with narrowed eyes, as if he was trying to sum her up!

She really ought to apologise for jumping on his pristine lawn, even though it probably showed no signs of her physical exuberance now!

"I'm very sorry you must think I'm rather strange, all I can say is that I apologise for jumping on your lawn. I have no excuse, but there are extenuating circumstances, as I heard today that I have a Degree, after four years hard work, *and* we also met your brother!"

James Castleton looked vaguely surprised, Joss smiled with pleasure, and Nat jumped up and lifted her off her chair, and kissed her on both cheeks before placing her back on her chair, where she blushed again for the second time today.

Nat sat down at the table and smiled at her happily. "Your somersault was not the *best*, your feet were not quite together on landing, but your Degree is wonderful news, and quite a relief, but not by any means a surprise after the way you have worked. Now I might be allowed to play my music a bit more often and louder."

"Nat, you didn't see the somersault, just the aftermath," Bethany said with a worried smile.

"Well, maybe not, but I did see you working alone, and really hard for nearly four years, congratulations."

"Perhaps we should be having something a bit stronger than coffee," Joss said surprisingly.

"Congratulations Bethany on achieving your goal," James said and she was annoyed as he looked around his large kitchen, and then back to her, as though it was an every day occurrence to get a Degree! "However, nothing stronger for me Joss, coffee will do nicely. I have some work that needs my urgent attention." James said briskly, picking up a mug of coffee off the table and moving through the door into the hallway. He glanced back. "Nice to meet you both, I'll leave you to get better acquainted with my brother." He smiled at Nat, and gave Bethany a very enigmatic look. She would have loved to know what he was thinking, nothing good she was sure.

Bethany screwed up her nose, as she couldn't have made a much worse impression on James Castleton, just when she had decided to have a word with Nat about Joss too, as perhaps all he needed was encouragement to make his life much better!

"When will the work be finished?" Nat asked Joss.

"It will take a week or two, the builders have quite a lot to do to make this place wheelchair friendly, they have almost finished the ramp to the back patio so that I can use the back entrance, and there are one or two changes to the downstairs bathroom to be made. It is a nice change to have my own space, but can be a little bit lonely after living at Blackstone Hall."

"I have a couple of books that might interest you Joss, can I call tomorrow at about this time," Nat said as he placed his and Bethany's mugs into the sink, and pushed the chairs back under the table. He decided not to wash up the mugs - that would look as though they thought Joss couldn't manage.

Joss looked surprised but nodded his head. "Do you have to go already?" He would have liked them both to stay longer, and that was a surprise to him.

"Yes, I'm taking Bethany out for a meal to celebrate her success. I'll see you tomorrow Joss."

"Oh are you really, that's nice," Bethany said, and quickly kissed Joss on the cheek, (receiving a surprised look for her trouble) and gave a little wave as she and Nat walked together to the front door to let themselves out of the house. She glanced back as they walked down the drive, she felt as though they were being watched, and that could only be the bossy older brother. Serve him right if she leap-frogged onto Nat's back for a lift home, as she often did in the park (but of course suitably dressed! She walked beside Nat nice and sensibly - Mr James Castleton already thought she was an idiot, maybe he was right and it was time to grow up!

"What do you have planned for tomorrow?" she asked Nat as they walked out of the drive to Willow Trees.

"I thought you would be more interested in where I intend to take you tonight. That is if you haven't already got a date?"

"No Nat, I haven't got a date. Everything fizzled out between John and me, when I refused to go out with him a couple of times because I had too much studying to do. It wasn't really working out anyway, not after he insisted that all *accountants* must be boring," she couldn't help but smile herself as Nat burst out into laughter.

"Oh, I'm sorry to hear that, I quite liked John, and I know at least *one* accountant who isn't at all boring."

Bethany smiled. She was aware that James and Joss probably thought of her and Nat as a couple. That was all well and good, she and Nat had been the best of friends for all their school years, and not once had they wanted to take things any further. They were very happy living in the same flat, they got on very well, neither of them wanted a serious relationship, and as far as Bethany was concerned she had no intention of ever marrying, not after the fiasco that her parents had made of their marriage! She knew that neither of her parents had been happily married, neither had they had a particularly happy divorce! However, she could hardly tell new acquaintances at a first meeting that the man she shared a flat with and spent most of her time with outside the flat, were only good friends, they might wonder why she wanted to make that clear to them. Nat was a wonderful friend and had been since they started school together, but over the last five years he had surpassed himself in the friendship stakes!

CHAPTER THREE

When they arrived at Flat 24, Cat Bells Mansions, Bethany looked around the flat which she had made as cosy as possible under dire circumstances, she wondered who had thought up that name, someone with delusions of grandeur. As soon as she was sixteen she had left the home with her mother where she had been brought up. Her mother's new husband was nice as pie to Bethany when her mother was around, but it became clear to Bethany that she was not welcome. It seemed that Ronald Wood, her stepfather, wanted his wife to himself, and he made it plain that Bethany was an unwanted third in the household. He had even given Bethany five hundred pounds to find herself a flat, provided she didn't tell his wife! Bethany had always assumed that she would be able to go into further education, but since the divorce her father had bought a small flat for himself, a few miles way from Keswick. He had believed that a daughter should be with her mother in the marital home, in particular, because of the circumstances of the divorce.

Nat had not hesitated in suggesting that she should share his flat, and she had realised then what a truly good person he was, and she was lucky to have him as her friend. She had since realised that the five hundred pounds handed to her by her stepfather would not have secured any other accommodation, and her wages at sixteen didn't go very far. Now she was nearly twenty one, and things were slightly easier.

There were two double bedrooms, bathroom, and a reasonably sized room which was both lounge and kitchen. The cosiness that she had managed to suggest, were a few table lamps, cushions, and plants. Nat had provided a large HD television, and music centre, which were his pride and joy. Being a physical education teacher he loved sport, the best of which he enjoyed on his widescreen television. Every evening Bethany was allowed to watch any programmes of her choice as long as they didn't clash with his sport, just as Nat was allowed to make use of her reasonably new computer when she wasn't using it.

As usual after a day teaching sport, Nat went to take a shower. Unusually, Bethany awaited her turn in the bathroom, as she usually prepared their evening meal. Today was different as Nat was taking her out for a meal to celebrate her newly acquired First Class Honours BSc Degree.

She stared out of the second floor window towards the park, feeling rather sad. She rarely saw her parents, and wondered if they would be even mildly interested if she rang to tell them her news! She felt that this degree belonged to her and her alone, as she had acquired it *despite* her parents, rather than because of them! However, it would have been nice to ring around giving the good news, as the rest of the distance learning students must be doing!

She absently watched a group of young boys in colourful football strips, as they kicked a ball around in a specific area of the park. She was very lucky to have her friend Nat with her, but that would not last forever. He had suffered a break-up with Janette, the girl he had been planning to marry, and as a number of months had passed, Bethany wondered how long it would be before he met someone else. She had thought that he and Janette would be together again quickly, but that hadn't happened. If it had then she would be looking for somewhere else to live! Nat had some quiet times when she wondered if he was pining for Janette, and realised that she would rather have to find somewhere else to live, than that he was unhappy. He had a great body as he worked out a lot, and was quite good looking although he had one blue eye and one brown, which was very individual, but he and Janette had looked as if they were meant to be together. She suddenly realised that *she* might be the blot on Nat's landscape, surely not? They had never been anything but very good friends, surely Janette had been aware of that, whenever Janette had been around Bethany had always made it a priority to go out, but unfortunately had usually come home too early she now realised, but she had nowhere else to go. She would have a word with Nat - he would be straight with her, wouldn't he?

Her mind than turned to Joss and James Castleton. She had definitely seen some movement in Joss's upper legs, and she wondered if something could be done to help him recover the use of his legs. Her intention was to talk with Nat when he got out of the shower. She wondered if Joss had always been in a wheelchair, or if it was due to an accident. The latter seemed more probable, she had definitely seen movement in his upper thighs. As for the other brother James, no doubt, he would be full of himself and have a very good job and a beautiful girlfriend hanging on his every word! She wondered if the reason she felt such antipathy towards him was because he had witnessed her giving in to her feelings so unexpectedly, and he was possibly the only male that had seen her knickers, at least whilst they were being worn!

Nat came out of the bathroom, as usual, fully dressed, but still rubbing his hair with a towel.

"Nat, I wanted a word with you about Joss. When he put his key in the lock he had to reach up, I'm sure there was a bit of movement in his legs."

"There you go again Bethany, rushing in where angels fear to tread, just as you did with those louts who were harassing Joss earlier. You could have got yourself into deep trouble wading in like that, I think we should continue with your self-defence lessons, and forget about the somersaults." He finished with a laugh. "Don't worry, Joss and I didn't see your underwear, but the look on James's face was worth seeing. He was completely dumbfounded. I nearly burst out laughing when he asked you what you thought you were doing, and you answered '*a forward somersault*.'"

"Never mind about *James,* I was concerned about Joss."

"As you know, I'm calling on him tomorrow, I have a book or two he might like to read, and also I was going to mention my mate Barry Stansfield, who is an excellent physiotherapist. I think you should come too, as Joss will be just a bit less likely to create a fuss and tell me to mind my own business if you are there. I'm sure everything has been done for him in the past, but things change, and maybe something could be done for him now. You saw how upset he was at having a let us help him, maybe now is the time for him to try again."

"You are a lovely man Nat, and of course I'll come with you but let's make it a bit earlier than yesterday, before the 'big brother' arrives home."

"Why he seemed alright to me, but I guess he ruffled *your* feathers a bit," he smiled with a wicked glint in his blue eye, but quite possibly both eyes!

"Nonsense, he just seemed very bossy and arrogant, I bet he doesn't do anything spontaneously. Everything will have to be perfectly worked out and studied."

"Well not somersaults anyway," he laughed out loud, and she couldn't help but smile back. "Although he did look very fit and I wonder which gym he goes to, or perhaps he runs, there's certainly plenty of places to go running around here. I wonder where he works-out?"

Bethany showered and washed her hair, and put on her best little black dress. She turned in front of the mirror, wearing slightly higher heels than earlier - she didn't look too bad! Maybe she shouldn't have an ice-cream every time she went to the park with Nat, her bust looked a little bit more rounded than she remembered, but her waist and hips looked as trim as ever.

Nat took her to a very nice Italian Restaurant, and they both enjoyed their meal, and when it was time to pay they had the usual argument. However this time Bethany gave in graciously. They were both surprised when the waiter came to the table with two glasses of champagne. He placed them carefully on the table, and smiled at Bethany. "These are from the gentleman in the corner, with his compliments."

They both turned and peered into the dim recesses of the dimly lit restaurant, and Bethany saw glinting in the candlelight an ice bucket in which was a bottle of champagne, and she recognised the proud bearing of James Castleton. She realised he was not alone, and would have liked to see more clearly the blonde haired woman sitting opposite him. Definitely out of a bottle she thought waspishly, then curbed her ill-humour, was she jealous of the bright hair? Her own hazel locks had highlights in the candlelight, she had noticed them in the mirror behind Nat (how vain was she?) She was satisfied with those.

"That was very kind of James, they must be having a celebration of their own," he remarked, and lifted his glass in thanks, which James acknowledged with a nod of his head. Belatedly Bethany did the same, but his companion was leaning across the table demanding his close attention, with her talons on his hand. When did well manicured red painted fingernails become talons? Bethany looked at her own hands with clear varnish, and fingernails suitable for the use of a computer! Shortly afterwards they walked home in high spirits arm in arm, enjoying the usual night sounds and gazing at the dark blue shapes of the nearby fells, and the almost quiet streets.

It was when she was about to put out her light, after reading a book which was meant to help her sleep, that she realised that she hadn't mentioned to Nat the fact that she was worried that it was because of her living in his flat, that had helped to break up his engagement to Janette. She lifted up her head and could not see any rim of light around the door which indicated that the lounge light was out, and Nat must have already gone to bed. She would remember to speak to him tomorrow, without fail as both he and Janette were so nice that they really deserved to be together.

The next day Bethany's immediate boss, asked her into her office for a brief meeting. Bethany was told that they were pleased with her success in getting her degree, but told her she was now overqualified for the work she was doing, but they would be pleased for her to stay with them until she found something suitable. Bethany was relieved although this had been intimated before she had received her results, without her monthly wage she could not manage to live. However, it would be easier now that she had no further tuition fees, or books to buy, and they would be reasonable if she needed time off for interviews.

After work Bethany rushed home to accompany Nat to see Joss. He made them welcome, shaking Nat's hand happily, and Bethany kissed his cheek as he held her hand. However, when Nat mentioned his physiotherapist friend Barry, he seemed to clam up. However, Bethany asked Joss how long he had been in a wheelchair, and he informed them since he was about ten years old, and then he went silent. Bethany changed the subject, thinking he would probably mull over this idea in the next few days. She told them both she would be looking for another job, and how difficult that might be. Joss told them he was looking for a job also. He had found the computer course he had just finished very interesting, but he wasn't very good at the technical side of fixing up the computer he had bought since receiving his inheritance.

"I put my own together when I bought it, but wonder if I should have just bought a lap-top," Bethany said. "I can help you put it together, and help you install your software," she offered.

"I would appreciate someone being here," Joss said, and seemed to cheer up, and she decided when she came to help him, she would allow him to do most of it with maybe just a little help and she might find out more about why he was in a wheelchair.

"Since yesterday, when Bethany decided to throw her weight about, I've decided she needs some more self-defence classes. We go to the park, to have fun mostly, why don't you come along?" Nat asked Joss, looking as if the idea had just popped into his head. Bethany, of course, knew differently! "You could get some fresh air, and probably get a bit of amusement out of watching Bethany make a mess of things."

"I would like more fresh air, and I would definitely like to watch Bethany training, and I bet she doesn't make a mess of things," Joss smiled, and Bethany grinned back at him. Nat went a little quiet, things appeared to be going well, but he didn't want Joss to get any ideas about Bethany, he didn't want either of them to be hurt. Bethany was surprisingly outgoing and got on very well with almost everyone. It took a great leap of faith after what she had been through in her earlier years. She was definitely against marriage, in fact, anything except friendship.

"Are you going to the park today?" Joss asked, and seemed quite keen to join them.

"Unfortunately no, I have football training at six o'clock at the school, but tomorrow we will be going, after I have done some marking," Nat said, and seemed really pleased that Joss had agreed to join them.

"If you are not doing anything, I can come back in about an hour, and help you set up your computer," Bethany offered. "We are only having a salad for tea, as Nat doesn't want much before football training."

"Thank you I would like that. I haven't had the use of a computer since I left Blackstone Hall, where I used one when it was available. It will be nice to have one all to myself." Joss said, and glanced at Nat who looked a bit preoccupied.

Joss wondered if Nat did not approve of him using Bethany's time, however, she had offered, and Nat would be otherwise engaged.

"Where are you going to have your computer, here in the kitchen," Bethany asked with eyes raised.

"No, if I want any privacy I guess I should have it in my sitting room, maybe we should have a look and decide where it would be best placed."

"OK, we'd better do that before we leave, just in case we need to move anything, we might as well make good use of Nat's muscles." Bethany replied.

Joss didn't reply, just wheeled himself out of the kitchen, and across to one of the mahogany doors in the hall. They followed Joss into the room, and Bethany was not surprised to see lovely antique furniture, shown to perfection in a room with tall windows which let in a lot of light, and a high ceiling beautifully decorated with intricate mouldings. She walked over to one of the tall windows and looked out into the garden.

"You lucky thing Joss, what a beautiful view, what could be better than that to look out on whilst you are working. Nat do you think we could move that kneehole desk in front of the window? Look at all these lovely drawers for all your papers and things." She glanced at Joss who looked interested, and noticed his wheelchair. "We'll have to see if it is the right height for your wheelchair." She stopped suddenly, wondering if she had said the wrong thing.

"I guess we could move the desk, but it looks very heavy," Nat said quickly. "But you are forgetting the basics Bethany, are there any electric plugs handy, we don't want to spoil this wonderful room with wires going all over the place?"

Bethany sank down onto her knees, and moved the curtain to one side. "There is a double plug here, but I don't think we could move the desk very far Nat, it looks very solid."

"I think Nat and I could do that between us," a voice said from just inside the doorway, and Bethany looked up from where she was sitting on the floor. Why had James had to arrive just then, she felt at a definite disadvantage yet *again*!

"Don't bother, I'll buy a lighter modern one," Joss said sharply.

Bethany jumped up and looked at him closely, how could he possibly want a nice modern one when he had such a splendid one already in the room?

"Nonsense Joss, it will only take a while to move, and if you don't like it you can change it later." She said, wondering if he didn't *want* his brother's help. "I'll go and get our meal prepared, and be back in about an hour to help with the computer."

She moved towards the doorway, and inevitably James. He raised his eyebrows questioningly, but she glared back at him, she believed he was well aware that his brother was behaving oddly because he had arrived, and she was determined to ignore Joss's petty behaviour, even though she couldn't understand it!

When Nat arrived home she had their meal on the table, and she had showered and changed – definitely not because James Castleton might be around. She sat down at the table and looked across at Nat, who looked as though he had something on his mind.

"Did you manage to move the desk into the right position?"

"Yes, but something is bugging Joss. He is in a very odd mood. I get the impression that he doesn't like his brother, or rather his brother's help."

"I know. It seems that they live completely separate lives, one upstairs and the other down."

"Well, for a very good reason, unless they put in a lift then Joss has to stay on the ground floor." Nat said briskly. "You are getting too involved Bethany, you might end up taking sides, and that wouldn't help anyone. Besides, you should be very careful with Joss, I think he is starting to like you a little too much. I don't think he is used to women who are as friendly as you." Nat said with a warning note in his voice.

"What rubbish Nat, why would he do that? I haven't given him that impression, just because I helped him when those yobs were having a go at him. Besides, you were the one that scared them away."

"I don't know about that Bethany. You can be quite scary at times." He managed to catch the stainless steel salt pot, and placed it carefully on the table.

"That reminds me Nat. I was going to ask you about Janette, and the reason that you broke up ..."

"Sorry Beth, I have to get to football training. See you later," Nat said and pulled on his tracksuit jacket, and she realised he didn't want to discuss his private affairs or his ex

39

fiancé. He looked back as he reached the door. "Besides you have to get over to Willow Trees, Josh will be waiting."

Bethany fumed, he really was aggravating, but she loved him. Why couldn't they love each other as more than friends, they were so suitable! But so was Janette, and she hadn't been near for weeks, but Nat was obviously missing her.

CHAPTER FOUR

Bethany was about to ring the doorbell of Willow Trees, when the door opened and she came face to face with James Castleton, obviously on his way out. He stood back ceremoniously, holding the door for her.

"Back again I see. I trust you won't upset Joss, he is not used to modern young women chasing him." He stared into her shocked eyes for a moment, hesitated slightly as if wondering if he had made a mistake, and then moved on down the drive, leaving her to close the door.

"Insufferable pig," she said after him, and when he hesitated again having heard her, she stopped breathing for a second - she thought he was coming back, but he carried on. She watched as he started to run. He was wearing a pair of comfortably old track suit bottoms and a white well-washed T-shirt which did not detract from his taught shapely body. However, his training shoes looked very expensive. He did appear to be extremely fit, was that what Joss held against him?

"Joss," Bethany called along the hallway. "It's me Bethany, your brother was on his way out and let me in."

"In here Bethany, come and see the desk. It looks really good, and I now realise why you wanted it moving a bit. The light from outside won't be able to reflect on the screen of the monitor, but I will be able to look out into the garden."

Bethany joined him, and looked at the leather top of the desk, it was dark blue, and looked to be of excellent quality. "Do you think we should cover the desk with a cloth or something," she asked worriedly.

"It's in my room so I guess it is mine, and I like the blue leather," Joss replied moving his wheelchair to the kneehole. "Maybe the desk is just a little bit high."

"You won't be able to tell until we have put everything together. Anyway, if it is too high for you to sit in your wheelchair, you'll have to get a proper office chair, which can be moved to whatever height you want," Bethany said briskly. "I'll start unpacking the computer they pack them so carefully with all this hard foam, and plastic. It's fun popping the plastic though." She laughed and started to unpack the boxes. Joss had not said anything since she had suggested he get a 'proper office chair.' She hoped he was thinking about it seriously, it had obviously never occurred to him before!

When he remained quiet, she wondered if his condition meant that he would never get any better. However, until he tried he wouldn't know that for certain. She handed him the instruction books. "Can you read these, and then when I get stuck you will be able to tell me what to do." She glanced at Joss when he didn't say anything.

"Come on, I can't do everything Joss," she said briskly.

"You are a bit bossy Bethany, but because you look so pretty in that dress which is the colour of your eyes, I guess I'll put up with it," Joss said. She noticed the beginning of a wry smile.

"Look all you want Joss, but don't get any silly ideas. I intend to be a happy old maid. Marriage or serious relationships are *out* as far as I'm concerned."

"Why is that Bethany, a lovely girl like you?"

"I remember every day my parent's splitting up, and divorce - there is no way that *I* will go through that."

"So you and Nat are not a pair?" Joss asked in pleased surprise.

"Of course, we are a very happy pair of friends since nursery school. Nothing will alter that." She paused for a moment. Maybe, Janette should have that pointed out to her once more!

She had unpacked the base system, and placed it on the desk to the right side, then started unpacking the monitor and keyboard. Joss wheeled himself around the side of the desk and was sorting out where to plug in the various leads, and Bethany lifted the monitor and keyboard onto the desk, together with the printer and let him carry on. She found the speakers and plugged them in for him, and opened up the pack containing the operating system and application software. The printer didn't seem to be plugged in correctly, and Bethany read the instructions and changed it, and everything seemed to be alright.

Bethany handed to Joss the software packages, and he moved to the kneehole in the desk, and she had to adjust the base system so that he could easily reach it. He seemed to be engrossed in what he was doing, and she tidied up the boxes and packaging.

"Where shall I put this out of the way Joss, you had better keep it for a little while just in case anything has to be sent back."

"Yes I suppose I should. Would you mind taking it through the cloakroom next to the kitchen, there is a little utility room just inside the back door, the boxes and packaging could go in there for now." He didn't take his eye of the screen, and she was pleased to see how well he was managing now that the system was all in place, within easy reach.

"Are you getting broadband Joss," she asked as she set off with the boxes and packaging.

"Yes it should be delivered in the next couple of days. If you give me a note of your email address I'll test it out as soon as it's installed. And thank you for helping me set up everything I would have found it a bit difficult on my own."

"No problem," Bethany smiled, and tried to get the boxes to fit into each other but that was not possible. She picked up what she could carry and set off for the utility room. She had to go through the doors backwards with the bulky boxes, and was relieved to arrive at the utility room door, which she backed through, and fell as she turned forward landing on the biggest of the boxes. The corner of the biggest box just missed her eye as it was deflected by her cheekbone, and it was very painful.

"Damn, damn, damn," she said angrily.

"Sorry, you tripped over my trainers, can I help you up," James said worriedly.

"No you can't, what a stupid place to put your trainers in the middle of the floor."

James handed her a tissue, and knelt down beside her, moving her hand away to inspect the already red eye. "Oh dear I bet that will be black and bloodshot by morning," he said regretfully. "And by the way I always remove my muddy trainers in here before I go upstairs."

He was looking into her eye closely, and she could see the patterns of the iris of his grey enigmatic eyes, and the long lashes, and she was very conscious of his hand holding her wrist. What was *he* thinking? Probably how bloodshot and black her eye would be by morning!

He moved around her, and lifted her under her arms onto the bench seat where he must have been just removing his trainers when she pushed her way backwards into the room.

"Before we meet again Beth, I would like some warning. You never do anything by half whether it is a somersault, or fall. I'm hot and sweaty from my run, I'll just take a quick shower, then I'm taking you to the local hospital for someone to look at that eye, you can't be too careful. Can you see alright?"

"Not at the moment, it's watering too much to tell. I'm not crying you know," she assured him.

"I know you're not Beth, but you are probably in shock, you have started to shiver a bit." He pulled a thick red fleece from a peg on the wall, and wrapped it around her shoulders, moving the arms so that she could slip hers into them, and then he zipped it up, and she thought it probably smelled of him, and surprisingly it wasn't unpleasant!

"Five minutes for my shower, and I'll be back to take you to the hospital."

45

"No, it's alright I can manage. Stop laying down the law to me, who do you think you are? You don't even know me." she said belligerently, as her head was beginning to ache.

"I suppose laying down the law comes easily to me, I am a solicitor."

"I *wasn't* thinking of suing you, but you've put the idea in my head now," she snapped. "Joss never said you were a solicitor."

"Why should he, my occupation is of no interest to him," James said resignedly, and Bethany thought he seemed hurt by this thought. "How did you first meet Joss? His only friends would appear to still live at Blackstone Hall where he was living until the grandparents died."

Her head was really starting to ache, and she put her head back against the wall, and wrapped her fleece clad arms around her to try to stop shivering.

"We wouldn't have met except for the threatening behaviour of...." She stopped suddenly. Although nothing had been said she had assumed that Joss would not like his brother to know what had happened.

"Hold it there Beth, you need to get to hospital to be checked over, and I need a quick shower. You can tell me everything about how you met when we are travelling in the car." James said, and she knew he would not let the matter drop. She sighed and opened her good eye, as he put his hand on her forehead, and sighed. "Don't move, Beth. I will be back in a few minutes."

She decided to stay where she was, not because *he* said so, but because she didn't feel like moving. She would close her eyes again and rest, just until she felt a little less shivery. She quite liked the way James Castleton said her name, it seemed to roll off his tongue easily except, of course, when there was a threat or disapproval in his tone of voice which seemed to be most of the time. She rested for a while, and then realised that she had better tell Joss what was happening. She made it as far as the hallway, when James came down the stairs, took her arm, and directed her out to his car on the driveway and sat her in the front seat. He then went back into the house, presumably to inform Joss.

"You got as far as *threatening* behaviour," James reminded her harshly as they drove towards the hospital. So much for hoping he might forget!

"Why don't you ask Joss about it, if he wants you to know anything he'll tell you," she replied, not wanting to start telling tales.

"If there has been *threatening behaviour* with regard to my brother, then I need to know about it, particularly in *his* situation. Surely you are aware of that?"

"I suppose so," Bethany agreed reluctantly. "Surely if Joss wanted you to know about what happened he would have already told you?"

"I am sure that you have realised that Joss has one or two hang ups, and I appear not to be his favourite person. However, I do need to look out for him as I am his only kin."

She was silent for a while, and then realised that what he said was true, whatever Joss thought about the matter.

"Well, I was walking home from work, and came across Joss who was being teased by three boys, who were putting branches which had fallen from a tree in front of his wheels, making him keep turning from side to side, and back and forward, to try and get away from them. I told them to stop,

47

and switched on my mobile, hoping they would think I was ringing the police. However, I rang Nat as we were quite near to our flat, and he came along. Two of them ran away, but one stopped and was coming towards me, he had the most hateful determined stare I've ever seen, and was ranting and raving something about his uncle and himself being as good as anyone else, he had a real chip on his shoulder. Joss wheeled his chair beside me, and Nat came up behind the youth and grabbed him, but so as not to hurt him. Nat saw me stumble and thought I was going to topple the wheelchair, and let *him* go to help *me* and the young man got away. We decided to wheel Joss home as he seemed quite shaken up."

"Beth you might have been hurt, or at least taken on more than you could manage." James said worriedly.

"I guess subconsciously, I thought some of the people around would help me and Joss, but that wasn't the case. I was surprised that nobody came to our aid, as the youth was getting really agitated, rambling about his Uncle Silas. At least when Nat arrived they all disappeared. Don't tell Joss I told you about it, I think he feels inadequate as it is." Bethany said, and looked at James as the car swerved somewhat and he quickly righted it – he was silent for a while, and she was beginning to think he wasn't going to answer her!

"I have been trying to get Joss to get reassessed, but he thinks I'm doing it just for my own benefit. I don't really know what he has against me, except that I am well and he is not." James said, and Bethany looked at his worried face and the hurt showing in his eyes. She guessed there was much more to it than that! She glanced at James and his eyes had turned a very cold and steely grey.

"Don't worry, Nat has a little plan to get Joss to meet a physiotherapist friend of his, and also Joss has decided to join us in the park some evenings, to watch Nat giving me self-defence lessons. Also I have dropped a hint that I think he could manage a 'proper' office chair, and I think he might be mulling that idea over." Bethany said, wondering if James was going to object to their interfering, as he might see it!

"Well I hope it works, as Joss has had a chip on his shoulder for a number of years, and I can understand that, but it doesn't help. You were both lucky to have Nat to call upon, he seems very capable. How long have you lived together?

"Since I was sixteen," she was about to continue her explanation when she saw the look of disapproval on his face as he stared forward into the traffic. She was furiously angry when she realised that he thought that Nat had been taking advantage of her for all those years. Just when he had stated that she was lucky to have Nat to call upon! He was no judge of character that was for sure, what was wrong with the man - perhaps he had a chip on his shoulder as well?

"Can we get to the hospital please, my eye is starting to hurt quite badly, and I don't want to take any pain killers until someone has looked at it." Bethany said impatiently. How dare James Castleton make assumptions, just because he was a solicitor and assumed that he knew best!

"As fast as the traffic will allow us to get there within the law," he replied and she was aware that she had angered him once again, but she wasn't about to forgive him or set him right, when he made such assumptions about her best friend! As if Nat would take advantage of a sixteen year old girl, or any girl for that matter!

They arrived in Accident and Emergency, and he walked up to the desk, and gave her name and address, and she was surprised that he knew it!

"You will be seen as soon as possible Mrs Browne, eye injuries need urgent attention. Perhaps your husband will find a seat and I'll come and get you." The sister said with a sympathetic smile. Going quite coy and she glanced at James.

"I don't have a husband sister, nor do I intend to ever get married," Bethany said and immediately regretted it, seeing a wedding ring on the sister's left hand. "Sorry, that's just me, I'm sure you are happily married."

"Yes Ms Browne I am happily married. Perhaps your *friend* could find you both seats, and I will come and get you as soon as possible." the sister said with a rueful smile, and moved on to assess the next patient.

James took Bethany's arm none too gently, and walked beside her to two armless plastic covered seats.

"I got you all wrong Beth, I thought you were nice and bubbly and maybe just a little too friendly. I got that wrong. You needn't take it out on the sister, just because you and I can't see eye to eye. How is your eye by the way?" He looked into her eyes, noticing that the right one was now almost closed because of the swelling, and was quite bruised. "As for being married, you should try harder, maybe Nat will come around some time soon and ask you to marry him. From what you said, you have been living together long enough!"

"Why don't you go home James, I can get a taxi home." Bethany said with a deep antipathy running through her veins, which he was surely aware of, how dare he just assume things about her and Nat- he had only just met them!

She was surprised and a bit hurt when he stood up and stared at her with a dark and impenetrable gaze, and then shook his head. He walked out of the hospital, and her heart dropped into her shoes, as she knew she was going to have to ring Nat to come and get her, if James was going to leave her!

She was surprised again later when she walked out of hospital to find James waiting. Nothing was said, but he took her arm and walked her towards his car, and both her eyes started to water just a little bit. Although he appeared furiously angry still, he had waited for her! He couldn't be all bad.

"They are sending you home so I guess there is no lasting damage." He said, placing her in the front seat, and closing the door on her with a thud. They drove back to her flat in silence.

James parked the car outside the block of flats, and came around to open the door for her. She climbed out and shook her head.

"You've got the wrong idea about Nathanial Dixon, he is one of the nicest people I know, and he has been wonderful and supportive to me over the last few years, just as he now wants to help Joss if he can."

"I see. Then Nat is *not* the one taking *advantage*." James said, and looked down into her bruised face, and felt a heel. He wasn't usually so unpleasant, but she seemed like a burr under his skin and he wasn't used to the feeling. "I'll come up to your flat with you." He offered belatedly.

"Please don't bother James, as it seems I've been more than enough trouble to you for one day." She said proudly, and he watched her walk away from him.

He started up the car, and drove around passed the park, and into the drive of Willow Trees, and saw Joss waiting anxiously at the window for his return with news of Bethany! James sighed, and slammed the car door shut with a clunk. Joss was no longer the young boy that had looked to his older brother for care and advice, and he was getting too involved with his feelings for Bethany, and there was nothing that James could do about it that wouldn't make the gulf between them still wider! Besides that, James had enough to think about for the moment.

James stuck his head around the door and looked as his brother turned the wheelchair towards him.

"How is Bethany, James?" Joss asked anxiously.

"No lasting damage to her eye, thank goodness. However, she was not in the best of moods when I left her." James replied, knowing *he* was the cause of her bad temper rather than the inconvenient accident she had suffered. Why that should be he didn't know, it was obvious that Bethany believed it was alright to live in sin with her boyfriend, and nobody should disagree!

"Oh dear, I hope she hasn't to have time off work because of me. I should never have agreed to her helping me set up my computer."

"Probably not as it was Nat and myself who moved the furniture, and I guess you could have done the rest of it yourself?"

"That may be true James, but she is certainly nice to have around." Joss said with a grin, and watched his brother leave the room banging the door shut behind him.

Joss looked after his brother with narrowed eyes, as he heard yet another door bang as James arrived in his own apartment upstairs. Bethany seemed to have rubbed his brother up the wrong way, and it was almost unheard of for James to get annoyed, if he did he certainly never showed it. Joss remembered the unstinting way James had looked after both their mother and himself over many years, and thrust this to the back of his mind. He also remembered the accident, and felt a deep anger in his heart. Why had he been the one to suffer so terribly? What had he done in his short life that he should have been injured and have to have a wheelchair for the rest of his life!

Joss doubted very much that Bethany would change her mind about staying single, as Nat had suggested when he had told Joss not to get fond of her or he could be hurt. She was a very pretty and friendly girl, and Joss thought he might as well play on her sensitivity, especially as it would certainly annoy his older brother! Bethany was a big girl, really nice and he didn't believe that she would be hurt as he knew from Nat that she didn't want to become involved. He might get hurt himself, as he really did like her, but there was nothing new about that, he would cope as he always did!

His mind had been taken back to the time of the accident, and he closed his eyes to try and dispel the graphic images that haunted him, whenever he was reminded of that horrific day. He thumped his fist on the desk, ten years had passed and it was still haunting him!

CHAPTER FIVE

During the next three weeks Nat visited Joss three times, and managed to get him to agree to at least meeting his friend Barry Stansfield the physiotherapist. When Joss arrived at the park to meet up with Nat a couple of weeks later, and Bethany's face was no longer black and blue and she had resumed her self defence instruction with Nat, Joss informed them that he had started an exercise regime with Barry. In time he thought that it might help him regain more movement in his legs. Nat shook his hand to show his pleasure at this turn of events, and Bethany kissed Joss on both cheeks.

None of them noticed James Castleton in his running attire complete his second tour of the Park. He looked towards them pleased to see his brother was managing to get out of the house, until he saw his brother being saluted by a kiss on both cheeks. What was Bethany doing, she should keep her distance from Joss, he had not met many young women except in Blackstone Hall, and it would all end in tears if Joss became fond of her, which he most likely would! James hoped that she had informed Joss of her belief that marriage didn't work, which happened to agree with his own views. Anyway, she was already in a longstanding relationship with Nat! Whom she had already told him was a wonderful man.

During the next three months, Joss improved every month, and it became a ritual to try to encourage him at the end of the month. This time Nat shook his hand in congratulations, and Bethany moved over to kiss his cheeks, but he bashfully received a kiss on the cheek from Bethany, but quickly moved his face at the last minute to receive the second kiss on his mouth. Bethany laughed with him, it was a good joke, but in future she too would shake his hand! Neither Nat nor Bethany had again seen James in the distance, but *Joss had* and felt quite pleased with himself, that would give his brother something to think about!

Bethany had not yet found herself a job commensurate with her qualifications. She needed experience to become a fully qualified practising accountant, but she needed a good job to get experience.

In one week she had two interviews, the first being a large building firm, but she received a very definite impression that if she was kind to the man in charge, then she would definitely get the job. This was a definite reminder of her manipulative stepfather, Ronald Wood, and she turned down the job. She castigated herself for so doing. She should have more backbone, as she could have reported him if he stepped out of line. However, she didn't want the hassle and unpleasantness that would entail.

With regard to the second job interview, she didn't think she would stand a chance, as it was a quite local firm of solicitors, Ashcroft, Castleton & Edmondson. She was determined to try for the job, but was certain that if James Castleton *was* as she suspected one of the partners then she would not stand a chance.

She wore her best black suit, with a snowy white blouse, and went into the waiting room where two other candidates were waiting. One woman was possibly in her fifties, obviously full of experience, and the second was in her thirties, and had the top two buttons of her blouse undone, and Bethany wasn't quite sure what *her experience* entailed. However, she was aware that she herself had none! Bethany was the third candidate to go in to meet the partners, and was really pleased when she met only Mr Ashcroft and Mrs Edmondson, who both seemed very nice. Unfortunately, Mrs Edmondson was the women she had seen in the Italian restaurant with James Castleton many weeks ago. They apologised for the fact that their third partner was in Court today, and then settled down to the interview, which took about twenty minutes, just as the previous two had done. It transpired that their accountant was about to retire in two months time, and Bethany wondered if that information meant that she stood a good chance of acquiring the job, at least for two months she could learn the ropes so to speak. She was asked to wait outside with the other women, whilst the partners discussed the matter.

She returned to the waiting room, and the other two women seemed very confident, and Bethany tried not to look too desperate. Was she desperate to work here, she wasn't sure?

The door from reception opened and James Castleton walked through the room, and did a double take when he saw Bethany. She felt her nerves tighten up, as she returned his surprised glance. He did not acknowledge her, but closed the door behind him, and joined his partners. Well, that was that, she might as well leave now, she could well imagine what he was telling his colleagues. She walked to the water cooler and half filled a paper cup, and took a couple of sips of the cooling liquid. Should she leave the office now, it might be less embarrassing than waiting! She straightened her shoulders and lifted her head. She wondered if James was hoping she might do that – if that was the case she wouldn't give him the satisfaction. She returned to her seat and tried to look as confident as the other two candidates. If they gave her the job, would she get the experience that she required to become chartered? She had been informed that it was a large practise, in addition to the three partners, there were three other junior solicitors. The woman with the undone buttons, was asked into the inner office, and came out quite quickly, leaving the door into reception open behind her as she left. Then the woman in her fifties was called in, and she returned smiling, and nodded to Bethany as she left the office. Well that seemed to be that.

Mrs Edmondson, dressed impeccably for the office, came to the door and indicated that Bethany should follow her. Bethany did and sat down opposite to the partners with a sigh. She noticed that the male partners were also smartly suited and booted too. She couldn't meet James Castleton's eyes, which didn't matter as the men left everything to the practical and professional Mrs Edmondson.

"Now Miss Browne," Mrs Edmondson said pleasantly, "We would like to offer you the job. We understand that you need experience in a number of areas, and as Mrs Woodhouse, who has just been in to see us, only wants a job for six months, we thought we would ask you *both* to join us. She is very experienced and should be a great help to you, as will our present accountant for the next two months. We understand from Mr Castleton that you are reliable and eager to learn, and after the six months you should be able to take over from Mrs Woodhouse. What do you think?"

Bethany was in a state of shock. Mrs Edmondson's blonde hair was no longer obviously dyed, and her fingernails no longer looked like talons, and as for James Castleton she could kiss him – well maybe not! She pulled her surprised thoughts back to some semblance of order.

"Thank you I know I would like that, but I will need to give my present employer's two weeks notice."

"Wonderful Miss Browne, we will be writing to you to confirm our offer, and we will see you in just over two week's time." Mrs Edmondson said with a smile, and stood and shook Bethany by the hand across the desk. The partners got up from their chairs and filed out of the room followed slowly by Bethany.

James was waiting in the outer office, and stared back at her with raised eyebrows. "Reliable and eager to learn I told my colleagues. Bethany, don't let me down. When you have inwardly digested the fact you have a good job where you can gain experience, and a quite substantial salary to help you get your own flat, please let me know where and when you intend to do your somersaults?" He watched her expressive face, as she took in *all* that he had said she looked really angry, and then blushed becomingly. He turned away with a sigh.

"You are not my 'boss' yet James Castleton," she murmured so that only he could hear. He walked away, and she was furious that he should suggest that she move out of Nat's flat, but on the other hand she was surprised to find that he must have a smattering of a sense of humour.

James stood at his office window, waiting for her to vacate the building just below him. She did, and surprised him by walking jauntily back towards her present work-place. She looked as if she could jump up and side kick her smart shoes to the side at any moment - he imagined that most young women would have taken the rest of the day off! She was certainly a very interesting and intrepid young woman, and it was his aim to keep her safely out of *harm's* way - similarly, his brother Joss and the likeable Nathanial Dixon. He took his seat and swung round from the window with a look of keen determination, and picked up the telephone.

Bethany reached her office and gave her immediate boss the good news. Everyone was pleased for her, but insisted that she would have to pop back in to tell them all about her new job every now and again. She should keep in touch, and she was very touched by their insistence that she should not lose touch. She felt really happy as she realised that she did have good friends in addition to Nat, Joss, and just possibly the impossible James Castleton. She picked up the telephone thoughtfully. She would ring her mother and give her the good news, as she was bound to be pleased at her daughter's success.

"Hello mum, I rang to tell you I have got my *degree*, and also a very good new job."

"That's wonderful Bethany, congratulations. I'm sorry, but there's the doorbell, and your stepfather is waiting for someone to call. I'll ring you back as soon as I can." The telephone went dead, as did Bethany's heart. She replaced the 'phone, and sighed. She knew that her mother had *meant* 'congratulations' but as usual her stepfather had to be the centre of her universe. Bethany felt quite mean feeling upset, and hurt because her mother had no idea how difficult it had been to get where she was today! Also she could not have done it without the help of her good friend Nat providing a roof over her head, and encouragement at every turn.

There was a leaving party in the office for her after two weeks, and she had a wonderful time, and was worried that her new work colleagues would not be nearly so friendly. She had consumed only two glasses of wine, but it would be soaked up as she had also enjoyed a couple of sandwiches and a piece of her leaving cake. She was very sad to leave her friendly colleagues, and it would have been much easier just to stay there where she was known, but she must move on and use her newly gained qualifications. She left for home rather late after staying to help clear up the office after the surprise party. She was carrying a cardboard box holding all the personal things that she had accumulated in her desk, together with a rather splendid pen in a presentation box which was a leaving present, and the remnants of her leaving cake. Her feelings were very mixed, and she decided she would not look upon working in the same offices as James Castleton as something to worry about, but rather as a challenge! It could turn out to be a challenge to stay friendly with both the Castleton brothers, as they didn't seem to have much in common, and it might be too easy to take sides!

She was within two blocks of home, when she heard the footsteps immediately behind her, she felt the hair on the back of her neck stand up, and she gave a little shiver. She slowly speeded up, and the footsteps still followed, then she slowed down again, and they were still there! She thought the person must be wearing trainers or something similar, as they were difficult to distinguish from her own footsteps as she was wearing soft leather sandals. He was quite close it seemed and he was trying to frighten her as he speeded up when she did and also slowed when she did, and she both wanted to ignore the foot steps, but was also getting quite keen to see her stalker, because that was what it felt like!

She was nearing the park and felt an adrenaline rush, but decided against taking a short cut that way, and was really glad when she heard muttered oaths following her, and when they turned into words she could recognise, such as 'silver spoon' and 'uncle,' she knew without a shadow of doubt the identity of her stalker! She thought he must be alone, and decided that when she came under the next lamp-post she would turn and throw her filled cardboard box at him, and make a run for it. She felt so uptight that she wondered where all these thoughts were coming from!

She wound her hand around the strap of her shoulder bag a couple of times, and turned quickly. She threw the box which unfortunately just glanced his shoulder, and then swung her bag as hard as she could, which he grabbed. She must have shouted something, because she heard footsteps running towards them. Her attacker pulled on her bag which was still wrapped around her hand a couple of times. She was swung right off her feet, and felt herself falling with a thump, and she stared up from the hard pavement into the hateful green tinged eyes of the youth who had been harassing Joss a few months ago, when she had intervened. She saw him raise his fist to hit her face, and rolled to one side, and heard his breath draw in quickly as the pain shot up his arm from his clenched fist as it glanced off her shoulder and hit the pavement. The youth was hauled away from her and thrown to one side, as James Castleton knelt down beside her, breathing very heavily.

He was wearing his track suit bottoms and a T-shirt, and so he must have been out for a run, and she wondered if the youth had been hurt, or was he still intent on doing harm, probably to both of them now!

"Beth," he said hoarsely as he realised it was her, "Just in time, the youth is running off."

"A couple of minutes earlier would have been good," she said trying to lift her aching body off the pavement. He slipped his arm under her shoulders, and raised her to a sitting position, and shook his head as he realised what she had just said!

"Are you badly injured Beth, where does it hurt?" His free hand, he was running up and down her arms, and then her legs. At some other time that might have been quite pleasant, but now the shock was getting to her, and she started to tremble and weak tears ran down her cheeks. She quickly pulled herself together, lifting a stiff arm to wipe the tears from her cheeks with the back of her hand. This was the second time she had appeared to be a wimp, who cried at the least little thing!

"Would you mind helping me get home, I threw my box of belongings at him, they are of no real value, but we can't leave them here." Bethany said getting to her knees and slowly standing. She swayed slightly, and felt James arms around her, and for a while she rested her head against his shoulder. She glanced up into his worried eyes, and was glad it was not full daylight. He bent down and kissed her forehead gently, as if she were a child.

"Can you stand alright Beth, whilst I pick up your goods and chattels?" James asked, and upon her nod he moved her to where she could hold on to the lamp-post, and picked up her belongings, putting them into the misshapen box. He glanced at the one photograph which must be of her and her parents at a very early age. It was the only photograph in fact, and he thought there was very little to go back into the box for a woman of her age! "I think we will leave the cake for the birds," he said. She still had her shoulder bag with the strap wrapped around her wrist, and he unravelled it and placed it on his own shoulder and the box under his arm.

"Can you manage to walk back home, with the help of my one arm?" He asked, and she quickly moved against his comforting warmth, as they slowly walked towards her block of flats. When they arrived he very gently sat her on a low wall, and ran up the stairs with her belongings, and she felt bereft. However, he was soon back and lifted her into his arms and carried her up the stairs. She seemed a long way up from the stairs, and besides that she didn't know where to look, so she tucked her head in the side of his neck, and felt his pulse working overtime. She didn't think she was *that heavy*!

James kicked his foot against the door, and when Nat opened it he walked into the flat and placed Bethany carefully onto the settee, and sat down beside her to get back his breath. Bethany sat exactly where James had placed her, and felt a need to touch his dishevelled dark hair, but realised her fingers were still shaking with shock.

Nat looked really concerned, and noticing the box and her shoulder bag on the floor outside the flat he brought them in, placing them on the table. Both James and Bethany were slowly regaining their breath, and James was staring worriedly at Bethany, who looked embarrassed and almost shy.

"What is going on James, what has happened to Bethany?" Nat stood with his hands on his hips, as if in readiness to defend her.

"She was being mugged, and I managed to get there, but he got away," James said angrily. He was furious with himself, as soon as he had realised the victim was Beth then he had let the perpetrator get away!

"I wasn't being mugged James, I think I was being stalked," Bethany said. "Can you put the kettle on Nat please I need a cup of tea."

"Why do you say *stalked*?" James asked quickly.

"It was the youth who was harassing Joss, when I stepped in and called for Nat to come and help. I will always remember his hate-filled eyes, as his eyes were the only things I could see."

"Are you certain it was him?" Nat asked bluntly.

Bethany started to get up from the settee, and glared at both men.

"Where are you going, you have had a bad shock?" James asked worriedly.

"To put the blasted kettle on, have a cup of tea, and then an aspirin. Then I'm going to have a hot shower and get into bed, and you two can discuss this matter all you want, I'm going to bed." She was now standing, if a little unsteadily.

"I'll put the kettle on," Nat said and rushed into the kitchen area.

"I could help get you into the shower room, that is, if Nat doesn't object?" James said with raised eyebrows. She now looked really angry, and he walked her to the door she indicated, opened it, and helped her inside. He was about to say something, and she pushed him outside and closed the door.

"Don't lock the door Beth, or we might have to break it down if you suffer some sort of reaction to your ordeal." James said with authority. He heard two thumps and assumed they were her sandals hitting the tiled wall, and he hoped she had now vented her anger, not sure it was with her stalker or her knight in shining armour, it didn't really matter he was determined to find out more. He then listened as the shower started hissing busily, and decided he would be better employed listening to Nat in the kitchen area.

Nat arrived with a pot of tea, milk, sugar, three mugs, on a tray and a packet of chocolate biscuits.

"Where's Bethany?" he asked in surprise.

"She's taking a shower." James said, just a little bit embarrassed as he assumed that Bethany and Nat shared in every sense of the word! Just then Bethany opened the door and glided through to a bedroom door, she was covered from head to toe in a white towelling robe. She joined them five minutes later, in pyjamas and a long dressing gown, looking beautiful and very young, and smelling like an angel. James now knew why Nat had not been able to resist her, living with her in his flat. The fact that James liked Nat very much didn't stop the ache in his heart, which he assumed was jealousy.

"We should ring the police," James said angrily, "as you know who it was who attacked you."

"No, James. I'm alright, and I have no proof it was him, and also if it was I have no idea who he is, it was only the expression in his eyes I recognised."

"They will be able to show you photographs, you could probably pick him out." James said starting to get annoyed with her.

"He has had his revenge, leave it alone both of you." She poured herself a mug of tea, and glanced at the packet of chocolate biscuits, and decided against them. She made her way to her bedroom door, and turned belatedly. "Thank you James for coming to help me, all I want to do is put it behind me, and get on with my life. I will probably see you in your Office next week, when I start work."

Nat restrained James as he started to speak to Bethany, as the door closed behind her. "She is far too stubborn to listen to you James. Sit down and I'll get us a drink a bit stronger than tea." He moved towards another door, and James saw it was another bedroom, with a pair of large trainers tucked under the side of the bed, and Nat brought out a bottle of brandy, and two glasses.

James suddenly felt much better, and waited by the settee as Nat poured them both a drink. It was very late when James left, after having a very interesting long talk with Nat.

CHAPTER SIX

Mrs Woodhouse started work at the same time as Bethany, and soon grasped what was needed in the Office. She was a great help to Bethany, and put her to work right away, explaining everything in detail. She also asked her to call her by her given name Elaine. For two months Elaine was the go between with the retiring accountant to Ashcroft, Castleton & Edmondson, and Bethany, and they all worked together very well. However, Bethany was just a little bit disappointed that she never saw James at all for the first two weeks and afterwards only occasionally, and realised that he spent much of his time in Court.

Bethany was happy in her work and very much aware that she was earning a much higher salary. She, therefore, approached Nat about where she should live.

"I thought I might try to get a flat of my own Nat, as I think you are missing Janette, and she might come back to you if I was out of the way." She had decided to state matters as she saw them, and not as James Castleton had suggested.

"What nonsense Bethany. If she had wanted to, Janette could have come back at any time. I won't hear of you moving out, not for that reason anyway," Nat said, and seemed quite upset by the very idea.

"For what reason would you consider it a good idea Nathanial?" Bethany asked. As she had used his full name he realised that she really meant what she was suggesting, and she was surprised by Nat's adamant refusal to even think about it!

"I guess the only reason would be if you really wanted a place of your very own. Maybe I am in *your way*? Maybe you now want to bring someone home with you, to stay overnight, you are over twenty one, and not sixteen as you were when you moved in here?" Nat said looking at her closely.

"Well I never allowed John to stay over did I," she said angrily. "I was just thinking of you Nat, you are nearly a year older than me. Maybe *you* should be out and about enjoying yourself more."

"Forget it for now Bethany. When and if you change your mind, let me know." Nat said, and picked up his trainers, and forgot to ask Bethany if she wanted to join him and Joss in the park.

Bethany felt quite put out, she hadn't wanted to upset Nat, but she knew that Nat had not been out with anyone since Janette has disappeared off the scene. She had been thinking of *Nat* hadn't she, she banished the thought of arrogant grey eyes, with long dark lashes. That would never happen!

When Nat returned it was with news that Joss had secured himself a job. He would be working with the local Social Services Department. He would be mostly working on his computer, and some of his work he would be able to do at home. However, for the first month he would be full time in the Office. He had also amazed Nat when he had brought a stick from behind his wheelchair, and had taken a few steps, but was adamant that nothing should be said to his brother James. Bethany felt hurt on James's behalf, surely Joss was aware that James would have been overjoyed had he been there to see his brother walk, even just a few steps!

That evening Bethany was surprised when she was reading in bed, and picked up her mobile. "Hello."

"Bethany love, it's your Dad. I understand you should be congratulated. Well done love, it's wonderful that you have your degree, also a new job. Tell me all about it."

She almost burst into tears, it was so unexpected. She had been told not to ring her Dad when he was working, and she never had. Neither had she rung him in the evening, in fact, she didn't have his telephone number. After being so upset when her mother had seemed to brush her aside, because she was too busy looking after her second husband, Bethany had not felt she could deal with the same from her Dad!

She was very pleased but also shocked as she realised that the only way her Dad could know about her good fortune, was from her mother. Bethany had no idea that they kept in touch with each other! She explained in detail about her degree, and also her new job, all the while waiting for him to end the call, but he didn't and she enjoyed getting up to date with him, and felt a little distressed that she hadn't found the time to try and see him.

He appeared to be really pleased for her and proud of her! He went on to tell her a little about his job, which was in a rehab centre, where young alcoholics lived until they managed to conquer their addiction. This was a revelation for Bethany, at first he had been working with underprivileged children in connection with a local Church, when his marriage had broken up and he had left his well paid job as an insurance assessor. She began to give serious thought to the fact that maybe she was the one to blame and not her parents for their long estrangement. When her dad terminated the call, she immediately rang one four seven one to get his number.

He must also have been given her number, by her mother, and she began to wish she had given him her mobile number. It was very late when she eventually managed to get to sleep.

The next morning she was late getting up, and although she went without breakfast she was late when she arrived at the office. She missed her normal bus, and decided to walk the three quarters of a mile. She had walked about ten minutes when it started to rain, and because she was late she hadn't collected either an umbrella, or her raincoat, and arrived looking very damp and bedraggled. Normally, she would have apologised to Elaine and made up her time at lunchtime, but the first person she met in the office was James! She pushed back from her forehead her wet hair, and met his disapproving grey eyes. He looked immaculate, of course, and she hoped he was on his way to Court! She clutched her briefcase before her, and stared back at him dolefully.

"Before you say 'reliable and eager to learn,' I'm sorry I'm late, it won't happen again, but I had an unsettled night, and I'll make up the time in my lunch hour." She glared back at him, and noticed that he looked taken aback by her tirade.

"I was merely going to suggest that you made yourself a cup of coffee or tea, and took off your damp jacket. If you do make a cup, I could do with one, as I have just come into the office myself." He moved off towards his own office, and didn't wait for a reply.

Bethany closed her eyes in dismay, there she was running off at the mouth, and saying more than she should.

Ten minutes later she tapped lightly on James's office door, and upon hearing his reply of 'come,' she moved inside. She quietly placed his cup of coffee on his right side, and paused.

"Sorry I went on a bit before," she said and lifted up the small tray with her own coffee cup.

"You might as well have your coffee in here Bethany, whilst you calm yourself down." He indicated the chair on the other side of his desk, with a nod of his head. He picked up his cup, and took a drink. "Sit down Bethany, and tell me how you are settling in here. I have only heard good comments from my partners and Elaine Woodhouse, she is confident that you will be able to take over entirely when she leaves us." He sat back in his chair and raised his eyebrows in enquiry.

Bethany did sit down, but felt a little uncomfortable, as she had not given James a chance to speak to her when she arrived in the office late and rather damp. She had just assumed that whatever he did say would not have been very complimentary.

"Thank you Mr Castleton, for telling me what Elaine and the partners said. I am very happy here and find the work varied and interesting."

"Bethany, you have no need to call me 'Mr Castleton' you are not one of the office juniors, you are soon to be our accountant, and you have always called me James previously." He sounded rather aggrieved, and she felt a little odd.

"Sorry, er James."

"So why did you have an unsettled night Bethany? Did Nat upset you?"

"No, of course not, well no - not really." She paused, and he caught her eye, and she rushed into speech, wondering why he didn't start work on the many files piled up on his desk. "My dad rang me and I was surprised, and realised that he could only have heard about my degree and new job from my mother, and I didn't think they had been in touch since the divorce. I didn't ring him because I'm not supposed to go and see him as he works in a rehab centre, and I didn't have a number for him." He nodded sagely, and now that she had started talking it was hard to stop. "He came home slightly inebriated one night when I was quite little, and they had an awful row and he hit mother, because she went on and on at him. I was on the stairs and I saw and heard it all. She, of course, ordered him out of the house, and he went. I didn't see him again for years, because when he left he took the car and there was an accident, and a woman was hurt. Mum divorced him, although it came out in court that he had just found out he had cancer, you know men's type of cancer. He had also stopped smoking, and she still divorced him."

"As you spoke to him last night, he obviously recovered from the cancer."

"Yes he did, but she wouldn't let me see him."

"You could see him anytime you like now, Bethany."

"Yes, I could." She glanced across at him, and was shocked that she had poured out her family's embarrassing history.

"Is that why you are against marriage Beth?"

"I suppose so, I'm very sorry I went on like I did, I'll go and get on with my work," Bethany said, picking up the coffee cups and placing them on the tray hurriedly.

"Beth, how did Nat *'no, not really'* upset you?"

Bethany put down the tray on his desk. "Is that what *you* do in Court James, and when you have meetings with your client's? You never forget anything they say?"

"Maybe, I haven't thought about it," he replied. "How did Nat upset you?" He started to take a file from the pile on his desk, and opened it, as if whatever she said was only mildly interesting.

"I asked him if I should get a flat of my own (you sowed a seed in my mind about that if you remember) and he said there was no hurry. Now I can't remember what I told you about Nat and why I moved in with him, no doubt *you* can *remember*. Just in case you haven't got it straight, Nat is good and kind, and has been a good friend to me all my life, or at least as much as I can remember. My stepfather gave me some money to leave home, because he wanted me out, and to have my mother all to him self! There wasn't enough for a returnable deposit and a month's rent, so Nat insisted I shared with him. Shared as in *flat* only, not what you obviously thought."

"I am aware of that Beth, I saw his trainers under the bed in the second bedroom, and besides he would never take advantage of a young girl. I don't see why you were upset when he said there was no hurry, he is quite right, there is no need to hurry." He started to read his file.

"That isn't what you suggested when I got this job," Bethany said angrily, and picked up the tray balancing it in one hand, as she opened the door, and banged the door very satisfactorily behind her. She had walked a couple of steps when the door opened quietly, and she glanced back to see James in the doorway. She wondered if banging doors after telling your boss you had a miserable childhood was a sacking offence. She suddenly realised that she felt better than she had for years, just by talking to someone, and she was a little surprised that that 'someone' was James.

"Bethany, don't bang my door like that again." James said quietly. "I hope doing it helped with your obvious frustration."

Bethany walked back towards him and handed him the tray, which he placed on a chair in the hallway, and looked at her questioningly.

"Thank you James, I feel so very much better, I've never told anyone, even Nat, everything I have told you, and thank you for listening - you will have to send me a bill. Thank you again." Bethany said feeling almost euphoric. So, of course, she stood on tiptoe, and kissed his cheeks with her hands on his shoulders, and then made the mistake of catching a glance from his steel grey eyes. Suddenly they were back in his office, and his lips were on hers and they seemed to cling. She felt helpless, and not only because her feet were not reaching the floor! James lowered her slowly, and seemed surprised and a bit shocked at what had just happened.

"Beth," he murmured, and she had never seen him lost for words.

"I'm sorry James, I shouldn't have done that." She looked down at the floor in embarrassment.

"I'm not sorry you did Beth, except that it was in the wrong setting. You also kiss my brother on both cheeks I've noticed."

"But that's just because he needs encouragement to keep on with his..." She stopped speaking suddenly, realising that Joss didn't want James to know about his continuing hard work with the physiotherapist.

"From what I've seen in the park he certainly gets plenty of encouragement. I don't want my brother hurt. I think you should go and start work Bethany," James said looking at his watch. When he looked up she had gone, and he sighed deeply, rubbing his hand through his usually immaculate hair. She had only kissed him on both cheeks - he was the one to take advantage of the situation, and unfortunately, he now knew what it was like to kiss Bethany!

Bethany rushed into the accounts office, and apologised to Elaine for being late. She switched on her computer, and realised that she couldn't make much sense of the items on the screen. She couldn't think why she had told him most of her life story, they certainly didn't get on very well, but he was still easy to talk to. She should never have kissed him on the cheeks like she did Joss. Why had he taken things further, and kissed her on the lips? He had burst her bubble of happiness as she realised how much better she had felt after unburdening her memories of her troubled early years, but now she knew the truth.

She relived the moment when he had kissed her on the mouth, and was shocked at her heated reaction and the fact that she wanted so much more! She had been drawn to him at their very first meeting when she had also been feeling on top of the world because of her success at getting her degree, and she had learned about jealousy when she had seen him in the Italian restaurant with is partner, Mrs Edmondson. It was just as well that she was against marriage, as it was quite ridiculous to fall in love with someone so unsuitable. She would strive to get her feelings for James under full control, it would never do for him to guess how she felt, besides she loved her job and she didn't see him very often did she? She also decided to stay with Nat in the flat, she would need her best friend in the months ahead, and for some strange reason James now appeared to approve of that scenario!

She managed to keep out of James's way during the next few weeks, and Nat seemed to have forgotten that she had suggested moving out.

CHAPTER SEVEN

It was the half year end, and Elaine and Bethany stayed late at the office to get ready the accounts for presentation to the Partners the next morning. It was the first time that Bethany had been asked to stay later than five o'clock, and it so happened that it was also the end of the month, and she knew that Nat and Joss had arranged to meet in the park at seven o'clock. Bethany was just a little bit disappointed that she wouldn't be there to see how much Joss had improved. She hurried towards the park thinking she might just call there on her way home from work as it was only seven twenty. She was surprised when James came up behind her and jogged slowly beside her as she walked briskly.

"You're late home Bethany," he stated, "Are we working you too hard?" He was still jogging almost on the spot and she wished he would stop, which he did when he didn't get an immediate reply. He took her breath away in his immaculate suits, and she now discovered that the same thing happened when he was wearing his running clothes, she was much too aware of his tall well honed body at the moment.

"No everything is up to date James, you have nothing to worry about. We had a visit from the VAT man today, and everything is fine. However, it did make us a little late getting out the accounts for the half year end. We want them for the partner's meeting tomorrow morning."

They were nearing the park, and she could see Nat and Joss through the trees lining the Park. As usual there were a number of young boys joining in with Nat's exercises. She stopped and gazed through the trees, there was nothing she could do about James's sudden arrival there was no way that she could have known that he would suddenly arrive and stop to talk with her. As she stopped, so did James.

"Something seems to have caught your interest. Oh, I see Nat is there, you are usually with him, and Joss. She felt his hands resting on her shoulders as he stood behind her to peer into the park through the trees. Well, she hadn't arranged this she thought, knowing that she was pleased that James had joined her just at this particular moment!

"You should stay a few seconds longer James," she said as he was about to move away, and she was aware of the slightest increase in pressure of his hands. They both watched in silence, as Nat finished his exercises and walked towards Joss. Bethany drew in a deep breath as Joss, pulled a stick from behind the wheelchair, and slowly stood and walked towards Nat, and Bethany realised how much more confident Joss was in his movement since last month. The hands resting on her shoulders gripped just a little harder and she was aware of James behind her watching his brother. He didn't seem to breathe again until Joss was safely sitting in his wheelchair, and Nat had shaken Joss by the hand. James then turned her around to face him.

"If you had been there you would have kissed him on both cheeks – you and Nat have been encouraging him to try to walk again. It's wonderful, Joss is doing really well." James stared into her worried blue eyes, and then kissed her on both cheeks, and he felt the tension that was growing between them, and although he wanted to kiss her on the lips, this was not the time or the place, and he stood back from her reluctantly. "I won't advise Joss that I know about his improving mobility Bethany, don't look so worried. I assume this is due to Nat's friend the physiotherapist and the encouragement from yourself and Nat. Thank you, Beth. I appreciate what you just did."

Bethany watched as his tall frame walked away from her towards Willow Trees, and realised that at the moment there was a definite lift in her heart, but wondered that later she might regret the fact that she had allowed James to watch his brother and know his secret. For two weeks she wondered if Joss would have reason to be upset that she had allowed James to find out about his improved mobility. However, Joss seemed much as usual, except that he was getting very preoccupied with his job, which she knew was a very good thing.

On the following Friday afternoon whilst at work she received a very worrying telephone call from the school where Nat worked. Nat had been taken by ambulance to the local hospital with a suspected broken leg.

Seconds later Bethany tapped on Elaine's office door, and went in. She was surprised to see James with a sheaf of papers in his hand.

"Whatever is wrong Bethany, you look very pale," Elaine said worriedly.

"I have just had a telephone call from the school where Nat teaches. It appears he has had some sort of accident and he has been taken to the hospital in an ambulance. I must go to the hospital to see how Nat is, and if he needs anything from home. I'll make up the time lost tomorrow." She promised, with a distracted look towards James. Surely he wouldn't object.

"Bethany, take a deep breath and then go and get your jacket and handbag. I'll have my car at the front of the building in a couple of minutes, and I'll drive you to the hospital." James said adamantly, and pushed the sheaf of papers onto Elaine's desk.

Bethany ran back to her office, and collected her things after closing down the computer. Why did it seem to take so long to close down?

James was outside with the car when she closed the office door behind her, and she climbed into the front passenger seat with a feeling of relief. James started the car and set off slowly, having made sure that Bethany had fastened her safety belt.

"What did the school tell you about the accident?" James asked as he negotiated the heavy traffic.

"They think he has a broken leg," she said miserably.

"Well, a broken leg can mend. Don't look so worried or I really will think that you and Nat are more than flatmates." James said sounding exasperated.

"How do you think he broke his leg James? I can't help thinking about the boy that was stalking me, he wasn't very pleased when Nat caught him and put him in a headlock, and Nat only let go of him because he thought I was falling onto the wheelchair and could have knocked Joss out of it. I shouldn't have rung Nat I should have rung the police." She answered miserably.

James indicated and stopped the car in the nearest parking place. He turned to Bethany, and put his hand on hers to stop them pulling at a paper handkerchief.

"Look at me Beth, and stop worrying. When are we allowed to see Nat all will become clear, there is no point in speculating just yet."

"He was quite a young man James. He could even be a pupil at Nat's school, as some of them don't leave until they are eighteen or nineteen."

"If you will let me drive you to the hospital Beth, then we can find out, and worry about it then, OK?" He looked into the expressive eyes, and wondered at her feelings for her long-time friend. Suddenly he kissed her on the lips, and turned back to the steering wheel as she stared at him in surprise. If she interrupted their journey again, then he might have to kiss hcr again, and he felt surprisingly disappointed when she was silent! They pulled into the car park, and before James could switch off the engine she was running towards the entrance, and when he had paid the car park fee, and rushed in behind her she was waiting in a queue, where he joined her.

In Accident and Emergency James strolled up to the desk followed by Bethany, and the sister looked at Bethany closely.

"Hello, I remember you Miss Browne, *and friend* I believe. Can I help you?"

James glanced at Bethany and she caught him smiling at the sister.

"We have come to find out about Nathanial Dixon, he is Miss Browne's flatmate, and we understand he has been brought here from the school where he teaches. He doesn't have any relatives in this area."

Bethany looked at James in surprise, how did he know that? She didn't like the fact that both the sister and James were both amused with regard to their last visit when she had damaged her eye! She knew that she was the one at fault, but for the life of her she couldn't smile, not until she found out about Nat.

"Mr Dixon has just come back from X-ray, and he definitely has a broken leg, but we can't get it plastered until he has been in traction for a short while, and the wound caused by the broken bone has healed. When we have got him settled in the ward you will be able to see him for a while. He is in a lot of pain, and we have given him a painkiller, so he may not have very much to say. Perhaps you would like to get a drink or something, and come back in about half an hour?"

"Thank you sister, we will be back in about half an hour as you suggest." James said and smiled at her again, which seemed to take her mind off what she was doing, and Bethany was fully aware that sister was a married woman!

James took Bethany's elbow, and directed her to the lift, and they went down to the restaurant on the lowest floor. He sat her at a table for two, and went to get two coffees. He also brought a ham and an egg sandwich. He settled himself opposite her.

"I thought we might have half of each, unless you are vegetarian?"

"No I'm not vegetarian, but I don't feel very hungry James. I wonder how Nat is now, he must be very upset about his leg, he has always been so fit and well," Bethany said shaking her head.

"You had better eat something Beth it could be a long time before we can see Nat. You do realise that they will have to keep him in for a few days before they can plaster his leg, and then he won't be able to manage the stairs to your flat?"

"Oh, I hadn't thought of that. What will we do?" Bethany said, quite distressed at the thought. Nat would need a lot of help.

"Eat your sandwiches Beth, we can sort all that out with Nat when we see him." James said briskly, making a note of the fact that she had said 'we', did she mean her and Nat, or was he included?

Bethany managed half the egg sandwich, and James ate the rest, and they each managed two cups of coffee.

When they arrived at Accident and Emergency, they were told that James had been moved to the ward and wanted to see them. They were shown into a side ward, where Bethany moved carefully around the contraption holding Nat's leg, and worriedly put her hand on his as she sat down.

"Janette," Nat said sounding very dazed.

"No Nat, it's me Bethany, and James is here too, he was kind enough to drive me here. How are you feeling, and what happened to you?" Bethany was intrigued by the idea that Nat had been thinking of Janette!

"Bethany, can you ask the nurse if I can have some water please?" Nat asked with a sigh.

"Of course, I'll only be a minute." Bethany said, and went to find a nurse. "I'll ask her what I should bring in for you while I'm there."

As she left the side ward she was wondering whether she should get in touch with Janette, Nat was obviously a bit befuddled, but his first thought had been for Janette. Janette's telephone number must be on Nat's mobile telephone, or in the small file beside the house telephone!

Bethany received quite a shock when she arrived back in the side ward, everything had already been arranged, for two men that was something she found hard to believe.

"Nat has agreed that it would be a good idea if you both moved in to Willow Trees for the foreseeable future," James said and gazed out of the window rather than look at Bethany.

"Whatever for?" Bethany asked absolutely flummoxed by this strange solution to their immediate problems. She stared at James in dismay.

"Well there is an en suite room on the ground floor that I'm sure Joss would have offered if he had been here, for Nat." James stated firmly.

"But he will need a certain amount of care, which I doubt that Joss could give him." Bethany said with disdain.

"That's where you will come in Bethany, I know you will help all you can. There is another en suite room upstairs for you." Nat said wearily. "You can go now, I think the painkillers are really kicking in and I'm about to fall asleep."

Bethany looked dumbfounded, and stared at James, who raised his eyebrows for a moment, and then picked up her handbag and handed it to her.

"Bethany will be in to see you tomorrow, and I might come too, if everything goes well at Court, that is where I shall be for most of the day." James said to Nat, and shook his hand.

"Thank you both," Nat said and closed his eyes, and if he hadn't looked so tired Bethany would have given him a good shake!

The drive home was accomplished in silence, until James drew up outside Bethany and Nat's flat.

"Promise me you won't answer the door to anyone unless you are sure that you know them." James instructed quickly.

"Of course not James! I don't see why I need to move in to Willow Trees, I can come and help Nat when he needs me." She said angrily.

"The stipulation that you should come too was Nat's. He won't come if you don't agree. Don't be selfish Beth, at least let Joss do something for you both after all that you have done for him. Don't worry I haven't said anything to him." James said, and drove away and she only had just enough time to close the door of the car!

She stood on the pavement and watched him drive around the corner to Willow Trees. What would Elaine Woodhouse and his partners think in the office?

She was even more embarrassed by the situation when she discovered from a remark from Elaine, that Mrs Edmondson and James were dining with clients the next evening, and Elaine wondered if there was something special between the two partners, as it was nearly two years since Mrs Edmondson had been divorced!

That evening after much debating with herself, Bethany rang the number for Janette in the book by the telephone. The answer-machine came on and she left a brief message, all the time wondering if she was doing the right thing.

Four days later Nat arrived at Willow Trees by ambulance. Joss was really pleased that he had agreed to move in for at least a few weeks. Bethany tried to get out of moving in at the same time, but Nat said he might need her help, as he didn't intend being a nuisance to Joss, who was still using his wheel chair. Bethany could not get over the fact that Nat had agreed to this arrangement without any fuss, and she wondered if he was really uncomfortable with his injury but just wouldn't admit it. She began to think she had done the wrong thing in ringing Janette and telling her about his accident, four days and they hadn't heard from her! It transpired, however, that she had been away working, and the moment she got back she came around to Willow Trees, after ringing the flat and hearing a recorded message regarding their temporary new address.

Joss was the one who answered the door to her, and he invited her inside, and indicated Nat's door. She tapped on the door, and when Nat called "Come in Bethany," she opened the door and went inside. Joss waited for a few minutes, then shrugged and went into the kitchen to put on the kettle. He had seen Bethany leave the garden wearing her running gear, and he wished with all his might that he could have joined her! He had not decided whether he intended to carry on with his idea that he would make James think there was something between him and Bethany. He felt rather uncomfortable about the way he had been treating his older brother, as James over the last few days had done everything he could to make things easy for him and his friends Bethany and Nat.

He now had a strong incline himself how it was to feel jealousy. He couldn't understand it, but two of his colleagues at work seemed really close, and he didn't like to see the way that Roger was always putting his hand on Marianne's shoulder, or taking her hand to help her. She only had an iron on her leg, she didn't need Roger's help at all, and anyway he was nearly old enough to be her father! A lovely girl like Marianne could have anyone she wanted she was so attractive, and a really good person. He liked the way she was always laughing and was willing to help anyone, a lot like Bethany he suddenly realised.

After about half an hour Joss went and tapped on Nat's door. Janette opened the door and introduced herself to him properly, and she thanked him for his offer of tea and suggested that he come inside, and she would bring the tea from the kitchen, which she did. Joss watched both Nat and Janette closely, and realised that it looked like a new beginning for them. Neither of them seemed to be taking anything for granted, and after drinking his tea Joss decided to leave them to it.

Joss was wheeling his way across the hallway to his lounge, when the door to the utility room opened and a bare footed Bethany joined him.

"Don't go and disturb Nathanial, he has a visitor, named Janette. I guess he has you to thank for that?" Joss said and watched pleasure light up Bethany's face.

"Oh good, I'll go and get my trainers, and go upstairs," she said with a smile. She went into the utility room and bumped into James, who had just removed his trainers and was now pulling off his sweatshirt. There was nothing pasty-white about his torso and she wondered when he had time to sunbathe. They bent down together to pick up their trainers, and she was knocked off balance. He put out his hands to save her, and she smiled up at him.

"What is the smile for Beth? Is Nat settled down for the night?"

"Nat has a visitor, Janette, his ex girlfriend. I'm going for a shower, as I don't want to disturb them."

"You don't mind her visiting Nat?"

"Of course not, *I rang her* saying he had been in an accident, she obviously cares enough to visit him, she was never jealous of me, she knows I never intend to get married."

"Don't you Beth? You might change your mind, as most women want to get married. I don't believe in it, but then a lot of men don't. It doesn't mean that I wouldn't like to share a shower with you, you know, save on our carbon footprint!"

Bethany was breathless with shock, but he had put into her head the idea of being wet and close to his beautiful body and she blushed wildly. Suddenly he pulled her towards him, and after the slightest pause, he put his lips to hers. She slid her arms over his bare shoulders, and he lifted her slightly and held her against him, and she wished she was also without her sweatshirt. Suddenly he took her arms from around his neck and put her firmly onto her feet.

"Beth, I think you had better go now, whilst you still can. I want you so much, and I think you want me."

She ran upstairs and stood with her back against her bedroom door. God, he was right she did want him. He had said he also wanted her, was she prepared to do something about that?

She went into the bathroom, and put the shower on cold.

CHAPTER EIGHT

A couple of days later Bethany arrived at Willow Trees after finishing work, and was almost knocked over in the large hallway.

"What is going on here," she demanded in disgust.

Joss and Nat where each in a wheelchair playing some sort of exhausting game with a large ball - on the exquisitely tiled hall floor!

"Stop it both of you." Bethany demanded. "One of you will be hurt, probably you Nat as a wheelchair is new to you! Anyway you are supposed to be trying to walk with your crutches."

Joss turned his wheelchair on a sixpence, and threw the ball at Nat, and it hit him on his broken leg. He was in some pain and was trying not to show it when the doorbell rang.

"Saved by the bell! Behave yourselves it might be your physiotherapist Nat." Bethany said in disgust, and went to answer the door.

"Thank goodness, it's Janette." Bethany said, and held the door open for Janette to enter. "Reinforcements are just what I need Janette. These two are being particularly difficult tonight. Look at their faces neither of them are at all repentant, and Nat has just had his leg bumped, and you can tell he's in considerable pain."

Janette walked over to Nat and kissed his cheek, and could tell from his eyes that he was in some discomfort. She took hold of his wheelchair and turned towards his room.

"Just a minute ladies I've just had a brilliant idea," Joss said excitedly. "It's my birthday in three days, and we should have a party. I'll ask a couple of people from work, and maybe a couple from Blackstone Hall, seeing as we are wheelchair friendly here, and you may all bring a guest, including James." James was standing in the open doorway. He had come to the front door because it was wide open, but normally he went around the back, where he had caught Bethany doing somersaults some months ago. He remembered how disapproving and shocked he had been, since then he seemed to have mellowed considerable as far as she was concerned, as she was so happy and caring with everyone. Everyone except himself, of course! He was well aware that there was a definite frisson between them, something that was very difficult to control!

"An excellent idea Joss, we should celebrate your twenty fifth birthday. My contribution will be to get a caterer in to do the necessary." James offered, and noticed with pleasure a pleased smile on his brother's face. He had not seen his brother so happy since before the horrendous accident! Besides that, he noticed a definite expression of approval on Beth's pleased face.

Bethany immediately started to plan. Which room would be best for the party? It would have to be Joss's lounge on the ground floor of course. It was a lovely room, and with a little rearranging it would be perfect. Perhaps some flowers and a few decorative lights would make it really nice, and the best thing of all would be if it brought the brothers to a better understanding!

"Janette, come and see Joss's lounge, and see what you think? I thought some flowers and maybe a few lights." The two girls moved off, and James watched them go, wondering who Bethany would ask to the party. He shrugged and moved upstairs, who was *he* going to invite?

At the office the next day James asked Mara Edmondson if she could recommend a firm to do the catering for Joss's birthday, as it was rather short notice.

"Certainly James, I have a business card in my top drawer," she sorted out a business card and handed it to him. "These people have done a good job for me in the past. Are you inviting any of the partners, or is it just family?"

"Joss has requested that everyone in the house ask a friend. Would you care to join us Mara?" He glanced at his watch. "It will be in two days which makes it Friday evening."

"I would love to come for a couple of hours. If you remember I will be going away on the Saturday for two weeks to the South of France? Would you like me to ring the caterers, they owe me a favour?"

"Thank you Mara, that would be a great help," James said thoughtfully as he handed back the business card. That seemed to be that. As usual his partner was proving to be extremely efficient.

Bethany had decided to ask Barry Stansfield to the party. Barry had been such a help to Joss over the months, and was now helping Nat with his own problems. However, she was too late as he had already been asked by Nat and Janette. In the end she decided to ask Elaine Woodhouse, she had been really kind to her, and Bethany was aware that at present she lived alone, but was very young at heart. In a couple of months Elaine would be moving into a granny flat with her son, where she would see more of her grandchildren, and hopefully would be a help to her son and wife who were both still working full time. Elaine was really pleased to be asked, and decided that she would come home with Bethany from the office, and change there, and then they could share a taxi. Being a very good accountant she was not in the habit of spending money unnecessarily!

When Elaine and Bethany arrived at Willow Trees, Joss met them at the door.

"Thank goodness Bethany, the caterers have only been here for an hour, we will never be ready in time. I have been expecting them to put in an appearance all day, that's why I have been working from home today."

"Joss let me introduce you to Elaine Woodhouse, she is my guest tonight, and she has come home with me as she works in the Office."

"Welcome Elaine, I hope you will enjoy the party, that is if the caterers get on with it," Joss said shaking Elaine's hand, but looking rather harassed.

"Bethany, you go and have your shower and make yourself look even prettier," Elaine said thoughtfully. "Now why don't I go and have a word with the caterers for you Joss? You are a handsome young man, just like your brother.

Now I brought you a small birthday present. Perhaps you should go into the lovely looking room through that impressive door over there, and make a place to put your presents in case there are more, whilst I attend to the caterers?"

"Thank you Elaine I will, you must be someone's mother to be so caring," Joss said in surprise.

"Not only someone's mother, but a grandmother too," Elaine replied with a laugh.

"In that case Bethany, do you think we could adopt her?"

Bethany smiled her thanks at Elaine as she made her way towards the large kitchen, and Joss wheeled himself into the lounge, and made a place for his presents on a small table. He wheeled himself to the window and stared out. It was the first time since the accident that he had been able to talk to a woman who was around his mother's age, and not feel bitter and twisted inside. It had taken him to the age of twenty five to learn to accept, and yes, maybe to forgive!

It transpired that the caterers had brought everything already prepared, and it was only a case of warming or cooling various items, and arranging a very nice buffet on the large kitchen table, where there was ample room for wheelchairs to circumnavigate the table. However, Elaine was very useful in the kitchen, and enjoying herself immensely. There was also a smart young man to preside over the drinks for the partygoers.

Bethany who had not been to too many parties over the years, had decided to treat herself to a dress, and a pair of shoes she loved. The shoes were higher than normal and open toed, and felt quite comfortable, and she hoped she would not have to change them during the evening, because they matched the dress to perfection. She felt cool and slim in her dress, and knew it picked up the colour of her blue eyes, if only she could manage the lovely shoes! She walked down the stairs just as James and Mara Edmondson arrived in the hallway.

James stared towards the stairs and took a breath as he saw Bethany in all her finery. Mara Edmondson followed his eyes, and smiled warmly at Bethany.

"Goodness me Bethany, it's just as well you don't look like that at work, or the men wouldn't be able to get any work done. You must tell me later where you bought that lovely dress." Mara Edmondson said, and suddenly she saw Elaine, and turned towards her. "Elaine, how nice to see you here too, it must be quite a gathering."

Elaine smiled at Mara and James, and stared at Bethany.

"You look really lovely, Bethany. I've come to tell you that Joss's friends have arrived and he wants to introduce you. We are in the lounge."

Bethany could feel James's eyes on her, and dare not look in case he disapproved. She glanced at Mrs Edmondson who seemed to be in a very good mood, and very friendly tonight.

"Lead on Elaine, we should all go and meet Joss's guests." Bethany said briskly, and followed Elaine.

Joss met his guests with a smile, and accepted the small presents and cards with a flourish placing them on the small table, with a wink for Elaine. Both Bethany and James looked at him with surprise.

Bethany felt James's eyes on her, and glanced at him, and quickly looked away. His eyes seems to like what he saw, and for a second Bethany felt really close to him realising they had both been surprised by Joss's unusually light hearted behaviour.

"Now let me introduce my friends in the wheelchairs first, this is John and Mike, and those standing are Marianne and Roger, with whom I work. I also work with Barry but in a different way, look." He suddenly stood up and walked four steps away from his wheelchair, and four steps back, with one hand on the nearest bookcase. When he was again in his wheelchair, John and Mike moved their wheelchairs across the room to shake his hand, talking excitedly. James and Mara, followed by Marianne and Roger, had to wait their turn to congratulate Joss.

"Bethany, you usually kiss me on both cheeks when I prove I have been working hard," Joss said cheekily.

"Not tonight Joss, you are too full of yourself," Bethany said with a laugh, and briefly shook his hand. She moved out of the room, and returned with a tray of half filled glasses of champagne. She made sure that everyone had a glass, and looked at James. After a slight pause, he proposed a toast for Joss's birthday, and his improved mobility. After which everyone seemed to be talking at once, and Bethany slipped out to find out if the buffet was ready, whilst Nat asked Barry to switch on the music.

An hour later, Bethany walked into the room with a plate of food, and noticed that everyone seemed to be enjoying the evening. She was surprised when Mara Edmondson indicated that she should take the third chair in front of a small table, where she and James were sitting.

"You seem to have a flair for organising," Mara smiled at Bethany. "That could be really useful in the office."

"No Mrs Edmondson I didn't do anything, you and James arranged the catering, and Elaine is wonderful looking after everyone. It is really nice to see everyone enjoying themselves." Bethany said, and was surprised when Barry came and asked her to dance, saying it was easy to dance in the hallway, Nat and Janette at least were finding it so. Nat in his wheelchair and Janette dancing around him!

James and Mara Edmondson walked into the hallway to see what was going on, and three wheelchairs were moving back and forward to the music, and Nat was laughing up at Janette dancing around him in his wheelchair. Barry and Bethany joined the dancers, and after a few minutes Mara and James joined in. When the music stopped Mara Edmondson said goodbye to Joss and to the room in general, and James followed her to drive her home.

Later Nat discarded the wheelchair, and with the help of one crutch and Janette he managed to dance on the spot. Joss applauded him, and asked Marianne to dance with him. He moved away from his chair with the aid of a stick, and with Marianne's help he managed a few steps. Roger had danced firstly with Marianne, and then Elaine. Now he headed for Bethany, and tapped Barry on the shoulder. Barry gave way with a grimace, and as Bethany and Roger danced, in ones and twos the rest of the party departed into the lounge.

"I think we should follow the others into the lounge," Bethany suggested to Roger, and he twirled her around with a flourish to the end of the music.

"Thank you Bethany," Roger said with a slight bow, and paused when the record turned to a waltz.

"My turn I think," James said from behind Bethany, and she realised he must have come in through the utility room as he did when he had been running. He turned her and waltzed her around the hallway. She was quite breathless when the music stopped once more, and it was not from the dancing.

"Who is your guest Bethany, Roger or Barry, you seem to be in great demand," James said coolly.

"Shall we join the others in the lounge James?" Her voice showed how much she was hurt and angry by his remark. "Actually, my guest was Elaine, and I'm not sure that she would want to dance bust to bust. If so, she might have asked Mara Edmondson to dance, they are quite near in age." Bethany realised what she had said and felt ashamed, Mara had been very nice to her tonight, and was probably only in her late forties. She moved quickly into the lounge, to find Elaine with her coat on, and Marianne and Roger also, as they had offered Elaine a lift home. Joss's friends in wheel chairs were being helped into a special taxi at the front door. James, Joss and Bethany went to the door to see them off.

Joss looked a little disgruntled, but said goodnight pleasantly enough, saying he would see Marianne and Roger on Monday. He turned back into the hall, and suggested a card game to finish off the night, to which Nat, Janette and Barry agreed.

"Good, I'll do a little clearing up, before I go up to bed, the wine must have made me tired," Bethany said briskly. She collected empty glasses, and what was left of the nibbles and serviettes, and took them into the kitchen. The kitchen was spotless - the caterers had done a wonderful job, and she placed the glasses and dishes in the dishwasher. It seemed the birthday party had been a big success, and she was very pleased for Joss.

She moved into the hallway closing the kitchen door behind her, and jumped when a hand gripped her arm, just hard enough to stop her getting away.

"Why were you so bitchy about Elaine and Mara? It's not like you Beth." James asked holding her with his grey eyes.

"Why were you so nasty about Roger and Barry? We were only dancing, and they are both fine young men."

"I think we might be getting 'bitchy,' and 'nasty,' for the same reason, don't you Beth?" James answered, his grey eyes never leaving hers, and there was a taught stretched out moment, when she thought he was going to kiss her, and she willed him to do just that.

"James, are you and Bethany making some tea or coffee or not?" Joss shouted from the lounge.

"Yes, tea I think, it is much too late for coffee," James replied, taking Bethany by the arm and pushing open the kitchen door.

CHAPTER NINE

James put on the kettle to boil, and Bethany found a tray and put five mugs on it together with a sugar bowl and a small jug of milk and teaspoons. She reached for the teapot the same time as James, and his hand covered hers. Smokey grey eyes stared into blue, and he pulled her towards him. When she didn't resist he slid his arms around her, and slowly placed his lips on hers in a gentle but searching kiss.

Bethany felt a strange curling sensation below her stomach, and she strained towards him, and was shocked at her wanton passionate feelings. She suddenly felt ashamed and dragged herself away from him moving backwards towards the kitchen door.

"Beth, what's wrong, I know that you feel the way I do?" James said looking very hurt and yet surprised.

"I always thought that a man was supposed to take home the woman he brought to the party. Well you've done that, I am not being used as a substitute. Perhaps you will be kind enough to tell the others that I was tired, and have gone to bed. As usual, alone," she finished angrily. She was mortified as she felt a tear roll down her cheek, she was well aware that she really wanted, needed, and loved him, but she wasn't prepared to do anything underhand. For heavens sake, he had only just returned from taking Mara Edmondson home! If she let her feelings rule her head she would not be able to face anyone in the offices of Ashcroft, Castleton & Edmondson. She would be no better than her mother, who had thrown out her father when he needed her most, and later she had married the obnoxious Ronald Wood.

Bethany cried herself to sleep, feeling hurt and ashamed, and she belatedly realised that she was afraid of her own feelings. No doubt, James would have everything under control, he usually did! She couldn't get out of her mind the look of hurt surprise in his expressive grey eyes when she had pushed him away.

For the next fortnight she didn't see anything of James. No doubt, he was keeping out of her way, and who could blame him!

On the Monday a couple of weeks later, all the employees were asked into the staff room for coffee at the same time. Mrs Mara Edmondson was home from her holiday, and wanted a word with the staff. All the staff were talking quietly, each wondering what new plans were in the pipeline, and if it would affect anyone. Mrs Edmondson came into the room with her partners and smiled at the assembled staff.

She seemed very well and definitely happy, after her two weeks away. "There is nothing to worry about, everything will be continuing as normal, except that I wanted to put you

100

in the picture before the local newspaper goes to print. I am now engaged to be married, and that will take place in six weeks, but the name on the letter heading will stay the same." She paused and received congratulations from many of the staff, who wanted to look at her engagement ring, which was a large solitaire square cut diamond. Bethany looked fixedly at the wall clock behind Mara Edmondson, this was what she had been dreading, James and Mara were going to be married in six weeks. She schooled her features as well as she could so as not to show her true feelings, and Mara continued. "You will all be getting wedding invitations in due course, and George and I hope you will be able to attend." She extended her hand, and George Ashcroft took it and kissed the back of it with a flourish, and then kissed her on the lips, to the cheers from the staff.

To say that Bethany felt dumbfounded would be an understatement. She felt quite shivery with the shock of it all, and then a weight seemed to lift from her, and she noticed James standing before her with raised eyebrows.

"I was not at liberty to divulge my partner's plans Bethany. Although, now I am aware of the doubtful traits that you seem to find in my character, I hope you will stay on at Willow Trees until Nat is well enough to go back to the flat." James said coldly, and without waiting for a reply he moved forward to shake the hand of George, and kiss Mara on both cheeks.

Bethany was mortified, and didn't blame James for the way he felt. However, she would have liked the opportunity to apologise, but realised now was not the time. When she returned to the accountant's office, Elaine was full of the day's events. Like Bethany she had not been aware of any association other than friends and colleagues between Mr

Ashcroft and Mrs Edmondson. She was, however, looking forward to the wedding, and already planning what she would wear!

During the afternoon, Bethany could not concentrate on her work, and decided to write a note of apology to James. That done, she settled down to work, but was glad when it came to five o'clock, and she hurried back to Willow Trees, to check up on Nat, and ask when he thought they would be able to move back into the flat.

James's car was not anywhere around the property, and she slipped her letter into the letter box, knowing that James always collected his post every day.

She was talking with Nat in his room, and he seemed particularly evasive when she asked how soon they could move back into the flat, and she wondered if Janette was at last going to move in with him. Then she heard her mobile ring, she had left it in her bedroom. She ran upstairs thinking whoever it was ringing her, was certainly persistent.

"Hello."

It was her mother, stating almost as a matter of fact, that her husband Ronald had died during the day of a heart attack, which was unfortunate as he had been waiting for a heart operation.

"Mum, I'm really sorry, are *you* alright?"

"Yes Bethany, I am getting everything arranged. I hope you can manage to come to the Crematorium on Friday at two in the afternoon? I didn't want to bother you at work."

"Mum, of course I will. I'll come over right now and I'll just ring for a taxi."

"Are you sure Bethany, I *seem* to be coping alright."

"I'll be with you soon mum." Bethany said and put down the receiver. She was pleased that her mother wanted her there, and suddenly felt the tears running down her face. She felt rotten, going over all the uncharitable things she had thought about Ronald over the years. She sighed suddenly and gulped, poor Ronald must have been suffering for quite a while, maybe even when Bethany had rung her mother to acquaint her with her good news with regard to her degree, and new job, she had felt very hurt when her mother had seemed distracted because Ronald was awaiting a visitor – maybe it had been the doctor! She put on her jacket, picked up her purse and mobile 'phone, and bumped into James as he reached the top of the stairs.

James steadied her and gazed into her wan tear-stained face.

"Bethany, whatever is wrong?" He sounded very kind and really concerned, and it made her feel even worse, she had imagined he would cut her dead when next he met her, after his coolness in the office today.

"My mother just rang me because her husband died this afternoon of a heart attack, and I'm crying because for once she needs me, and because of all the uncharitable things I've said about Ronald Wood, even to you."

"Beth, none of it is your fault, don't beat yourself up so," James said and pulled her towards him, and she rested her face against his strong chest and was glad of the handkerchief he placed in her hand. She felt the steady beat of his heart against her cheek, and didn't feel like moving, even less so as he stroked her unruly hair. Eventually she mopped her eyes, and straightened up.

"Sorry James, I told mum I would go and see her. I'll try not to waken anyone when I come home."

103

"Wait Beth, I'll run you over there, you needn't go by bus or taxi, as it might be late when you want to come home."

"I'll be fine, as it just feels good to think that mum wants to see me."

"Nonsense Beth, I'm coming with you," James said adamantly. "Just tell Nat where we are going, and I'll tell Joss, as soon as I've changed into something a little less formal."

Ten minutes later James drove into the drive of a rather nice detached house which must have wonderful views over the valley to the village of Rosthwaite, after receiving Bethany's direction. It was a good house, and he wondered why Ronald Wood had wanted the sixteen year old Bethany to move out, there was plenty of room. Bethany's mother greeted Bethany with a hug, and was very impressed with James when he was introduced. Bethany was also impressed with James when she returned to the lounge with a tray of tea, to find that all the many questions she had heard her mother asking James, had been answered, and she was now convinced she could cope with the funeral arrangements, and legal details that were necessary.

They were just finishing their tea, and preparing to leave, when the doorbell rang.

"Goodness it is rather late in the evening, and I thought I had rung everyone that needed to know about today's happenings." She said rather warily.

"I'll answer the door Mum, you just wait there," Bethany said, and when she opened the door the man there wrapped his arms around her, and kissed her on the cheek.

"Mum, it's Dad, he heard in town what has happened."

"Oh Jeremy, what a surprise, do come inside." She was obviously surprised and seemed a little flustered.

James was introduced, and after fifteen minutes of catching up with each other, there was a slight pause in the conversation, and James suggested that he and Bethany should leave, as they intended to get something to eat on the way home.

Bethany looked at James in surprise, and thought quite rightly that he was allowing her parents time alone, as it was rather an awkward situation for everyone! So she promised to call on her mother the next afternoon, and kissed both her parents before leaving. How strange that seemed, and she caught James looking at her bemused expression.

"Where would you like to eat Bethany, or do you want to get a take-away," James asked, wondering what was now going through her active mind.

"A take-away please, when I go out for a meal I like to look forward to it, and plan what to wear, although I haven't much to choose from, and I don't feel very hungry after all this upset." She paused. "It was a surprise Dad turning up like that, although I guess he and Mum must have kept in touch, as she told him about my degree and new job, and thank you for putting her mind at rest about all the arrangements, certificates and legal matters."

"Bethany stop worrying so, and tell me what you want to eat, we could take a bit extra back to Willow Trees, in case Joss and Nat haven't eaten yet.

"Chinese I think just a vegetable curry and fried rice please. James, Nat doesn't seem to want to move back into the flat yet, but I'm sure he could soon manage the stairs, do you think he and Janette may be thinking of moving in together?"

The car stopped suddenly, and Bethany looked out at the coloured lights proclaiming the availability of Chinese food. James kissed her on the lips, "Now keep those shut until I come out with the food and stop worrying, we can do that together when we get home." He climbed out of the car and walked purposefully into the building. Together and home, sounded wonderful! Bethany was surprised when he walked out with bags of food in only fifteen minutes. She had much longer to wait than that! She was also still touching her lips where his had briefly touched. If he wanted to distract her, then he certainly knew how to do it, and why else would he want to kiss her. Perhaps Nat really liked living at Willow Trees, rather than in a small flat with his old school friend!

When they arrived at Willow Trees, Joss and Nat were very pleased with their inclusion in the meal, and soon the table was arranged with two food heaters sporting short candles to keep the food hot, and they each had a warmed plate with tools and a serviette.

Bethany was pleasantly surprised when Joss brought out new sets of chopsticks from the drawer, and handed them around.

"Oh dear, can't we use a fork?" Nat asked in dismay.

"Not until you've tried to eat with the chopsticks," Joss replied with a grin, "I could do with a good laugh."

Bethany rather enjoyed being taught how to hold and manipulate the sticks by James. However, Nat soon resorted to the fork. "I enjoy my food hot, and believe half an hour is long enough to spend on eating a plate of food." He said and after a few minutes Bethany joined him by using her fork.

"I will learn to use them cleanly some time when I am alone," Bethany said wiping her chin.

"Is your mother coping alright?" Nat asked when they had finished eating.

"Yes thanks Nat, James was able to put her mind at rest about what should be done legally, and it appears that Ronald had been suffering health problems for some time. Maybe if I had rung Mum more often she might have told me." Bethany said looking upset.

"I don't think so knowing that pair," Nat said briskly. "Who else sent out a sixteen year old girl to fend for herself?"

"That isn't fair Nat, it wasn't mother's fault. However, it does mean that she will be living alone, so perhaps she would like me to move back home. It is a very large house to cope with alone."

"I think you should leave it for now," James said starting to clear the table of cartons and plastic. Automatically Bethany started to help.

"You provided the meal James, we can do the clearing up," Bethany said bossily.

"Clear up by all means, Beth." He changed the subject with a quick glance at Nat. "When someone dies is not the time to make new plans, there should be a time for thinking everything over carefully, and by the way, I am speaking from experience both personally and professionally."

"Nothing need be done in a hurry James. I was thinking of when Nat is ready to return to the flat. Maybe he would prefer to live there alone, or with Janette." Bethany said, and began to wish she hadn't started this conversation.

"Janette and I will let you know our plans when we make them Bethany, there's no hurry. Besides that, you are now in your twenties, rather late in life to be moving back with parents." Nat said with his mind on the young Bethany who had been relieved to receive his help when it was most needed. People, even parents, don't change so suddenly.

"I agree with Nat, it would seem to be a retrograde step moving in with your mother. In any case, she might enjoy the freedom in a few months, and start travelling, or find other interests. Have you asked her about her plans?" James asked.

"No, of course I haven't, you were there the whole time."

"Well there is no hurry to make any decisions," James aid briskly. "You are both welcome to stay at Willow Trees as long as you want, Janette too, if that suits them both." James offered. "Do you agree Joss?"

Joss looked at James, and regretted all the underhand things he had done, like pretending he and Bethany were more than friends, because he was aware that James was upset by this thought. Yet now James was deferring to him, or at least letting him have his say over his portion of Willow Trees. This man was his brother, the brother that he had treated very badly over the years, just because he was a jealous swine who wanted everything his own way. James had never failed him, but his *grandparents* had. He suddenly thought of his mother and watched James's face closely. He realised that they were waiting for him to reply.

"Of course I do James. Bethany, Nat and Janette are welcome as long as they want." He grinned suddenly, "Do you think we could entice the delectable Marianne to join us, I miss her sometimes when I work from home, and some days I just decide to work in the office to be near her!"

"You sly old fox, I wonder if she knows," Nat said, glad of a change of topic.

"Of course she doesn't its early days yet. However, if she doesn't show Roger any encouragement, and I try hard, she might even notice *me*." Joss replied with a deprecating laugh. "I think of Marianne when I do my exercises, and it's amazing how much longer I can do them!"

"Marianne did come here for your birthday celebrations, and I for one didn't notice anything between her and Roger, so keep trying Joss. She is a really nice person," Bethany said thoughtfully. "If you are going to talk about girls, I'm going to bed, and you two can finish clearing up the kitchen."

She was surprised when James closed the kitchen door behind them both, and looked at her searchingly.

"Thank you for coming with me to see my mother this evening. Today has given me so much to think about, Mum and Dad and where I fit in, Nat and Janette, and both you and Joss putting up with us in your home. We should give you something towards expenses."

"You have all the expenses to pay on Nat's flat, although you are not living in it. Nat and I will discuss that if you have to be here for very much longer, if you would feel happier." James said and sounded extremely annoyed. "Perhaps you would be happier if you had a more formal arrangement? And yet you have never bothered about your informal arrangement with Nat."

"You have been very kind to me, and I am only trying to sort out the rest of my life! I am only here to help Nat until he is moving well enough to negotiate the stairs, which I think he is." Bethany said equally angrily, but sorry she had hurt his feelings. She was trying to do what was best for all of them, why couldn't he see that?

"Promise me you won't do anything in hast?" he asked, "Like leaving Willow Trees, and your very good friends."

"I won't James you have been so very kind." She reached up on her toes and kissed him on the cheek, and it felt too intimate as his cheek was slightly rough with it being the end of the day, as he had not had any time after leaving work to wash and shave - because of finding her in distress at her mother's surprising news. She realised she wanted to be much closer to him, and only him. She blushed, and moved away from him abruptly feeling embarrassed at the rush of strong feeling which had overcome her – she rushed into speech.

"The first thing I shall do is have a good talk with my mother. When I was little she used to say she wished she had more time to do her watercolour painting. It is very sad to think that over the last few years I have no idea what she has been doing, except for looking after her husband."

James watched her as she slowly moved up the stairs. She would have been surprised had she turned and seen his worried expression.

CHAPTER TEN

Bethany had very little sleep that night, her mind was turning over as much as she tossed and turned in her bed. It upset her to realise how little she knew of her mother, and her father. Her father had his own cross to bear when his wife had asked him to leave the marital home after he had raised his hand to her. Upon his leaving he had driven away forgetting he had been drinking with his mind on what had just occurred, something that he would never have done under normal circumstances. The fact that he had just learned that he had cancer, and just stopped smoking, was not sufficient excuse to alleviate how dreadful he was feeling after raising his hand to his wife. And then to cause an accident where another woman had been injured had been the last straw! His spirits had never felt lower, and he didn't believe that he should contest his wife's request for a divorce, neither did he consider himself fit to have a hand in the bringing up of his young daughter. All this Bethany had only lately been made aware of. She was still a bit mystified that both her parents appeared to have kept in touch with each other!

Bethany later wondered about her mother, perhaps she would soon make plans that did not include her daughter intruding in her life. She was determined to speak to her after the funeral of her stepfather, to ascertain her mother's wishes, and vowed in the immediate future to keep in touch with her father on a regular basis!

As for James Castleton, he had been wonderful, and she now realised just how much she loved him. He was aware of her dysfunctional family, and her views on marriage, and she realised he would not look upon her as a suitable candidate to make him happy although she, in her inexperienced way was sure that there was a definite strong awareness between them whenever they met. She must make certain that she met him as little as possible, or he might guess her true feelings for him. That was going to be difficult living in the same building, and working in the same office!

Needless to say, she was up late the next morning with all her heart-searching. However, Elaine was quite amenable to her taking time off on Friday afternoon for the funeral of her stepfather, and disagreed strongly that she should make up the time by foregoing her dinner breaks!

There were not as many people at the funeral as Bethany had expected, as the age of the deceased was only fifty four. Bethany's father went to the Church Service, but did not attend the Crematorium. After the funeral tea, Bethany went back to the house with her mother, who seemed quite composed and almost relieved that it was all over.

"Have you any plans for the immediate future Mum?" Bethany asked as they drank tea at the kitchen table. She watched as her mother pondered as she sipped her tea.

"Well, my sister your aunt Milly, was unable to come to the funeral from Australia, and she has asked me to go over there for a few months. The travel agent will be getting back to me tomorrow with my travel arrangements, and I intend to close up the house, and the people next door will keep an eye on it for me, and if I remember rightly you still have a key. I'm going to do a bit of travelling over there with Milly and her husband, and I'm also going to take my watercolour paints." Julie Wood watched her daughter's face closely, as she slipped off her black court-shoes under the kitchen table, almost waiting for a reprimand from her deceased husband as she did so. She could see surprise, but no disapproval on her daughter's face.

"It will be lovely for you to spend time with your sister, I wish…"

"I know Bethany, you wish you had one, and so do I! With hindsight I guess I was too heavy on your Dad, but he didn't even bother to explain all the circumstances to me. However, I should have realised there was something bothering him, he had never lifted his hand to me all the time we were married until that day."

"I'm sorry Mum, and I wish things had worked out better for both you and Dad. I tried to like Ronald, but we never got on, he was much too pernickety and precise to have a child around, besides he was too besotted with you to have time for me."

"Don't apologise Bethany, I know what my husband was like to live with, I looked after him for nine long years. However, the solicitor rang this morning, and told me about his Will, he has left everything to me, except a bequest of £10,000 to you, his stepdaughter." Julie Wood finished with a smile, as she saw the expressions chase across Bethany's face, first shock, then disbelief, followed by a softening as she realised he had not disliked *her,* he just didn't know how to communicate with a child!

"That was very kind of him," was all that Bethany could think to say. She now wished she hadn't disliked him so much, and felt quite guilty for being so unforgiving!

"Yes it was. I think he realised what he had done when he met Nat. You never knew that Nat came around to the house, and berated him for what he had done in no uncertain terms! Nat also explained that as you had been the best of friends since nursery school, he would make sure that you came to no harm, and he was letting you have a room in his small flat. That was the only time that I have seen Ronald look ashamed of himself. However, he made a big mistake in offering Nat money and we never saw Nat here again."

Bethany didn't know what to say to her mother, as perhaps she was not aware that Ronald had already given her five hundred pounds to make herself scarce! As for Nat, Bethany was looking forward to seeing him to thank him for what he had done on her behalf. Her mother certainly had no idea of the way that Bethany had had to budget her small pay-cheque every month. Nor had she known of the extra jobs that she had done to enable her to complete her distance learning course, get her degree, and from that land a very good job!

"I was very pleased to meet James the other night, he was most helpful. I know he is one of the partners in Ashcroft, Castleton & Edmondson. He is very nice, are you sure he isn't your boyfriend as well as your boss?"

"No Mum, he is just my boss, and for the moment Nat and I are living in his and his brother's house, because Nat has a broken leg and can't manage the stairs up to the flat."

"Oh, what a shame." Her mother sounded really put out, and Bethany felt herself blush, and hoped that her mother hadn't noticed. Why should she, as she had seen very little of her daughter over the years?

That evening, Janette was visiting Nat, and Bethany went in to see Joss, as he called for her as she entered the hallway. She was pleased to note that he was sitting in his office chair, with a stick handy, but he was looking rather pale and worried. He enquired if the funeral had gone without a hitch, and asked Bethany to sit down, as he wanted a word with her. As he asked she looked at him closely, and realised that she recognised the look on his face. He was embarrassed, and she wondered why? She felt tired after a long day, and all she wanted was a long hot shower, a change of clothes, and would have liked to settle herself in for the night, before James arrived home from the Office. However, Joss seemed to have decided that what he had to say to her couldn't wait.

The doorbell rang, and Bethany had just risen from her comfortable chair when she heard Nat cross the hallway floor, with the thump of his crutch at regular intervals, and felt rather awkward as she was the fit one and should have answered the door saving Nat and Janette from being disturbed. All was quiet and she sat down and looked at Joss with raised eyebrows, was he going to take all night to get out what he wanted to say?

There were a few thumps of the crutch, and a tap at the door, which opened and Nat popped his head around it.

"Ah, there you are Joss. You have a visitor, who was turning tail and making a run for it by the time I had answered the door. Come on in Marianne, Joss is here and seems to be alright to me." Nat said with an encouraging smile. Joss looked taken aback, then shrugged his shoulders, and made him self more comfortable in his office chair, wondering if he had got things wrong, and that in the next half hour or so he would be without good friends, who meant such a lot to him. He could also have lost his chance of having the girl of his dreams in his life.

Marianne appeared in the room looking rather upset. "Joss, you didn't turn up at work today, and you were expected, I have just come by to see if you are well?" She was wearing a long skirt which almost hid the iron on her leg, and she moved quite gracefully across the room, with eyes only for Joss.

Joss smiled at her, and indicated that she should sit down in the chair next to Bethany, which she did looking relieved.

"Nat, could you open a bottle of wine and get some glasses please from the kitchen, and ask Janette to come in here? I have been building up all day to get something off my chest, and you might as well all hear it, not just Bethany as I originally intended, knowing she would try to be sympathetic. Make it two bottles."

Bethany stood and glanced from Joss to Marianne. "I'll come and help Nat you can't carry a tray and use your crutch." She followed Nat out of the room.

"You know that Janette would have helped me Bethany, are you playing cupid leaving those two alone?" Nat said when they were crossing the hall.

"I suppose I am but I can't help wondering what Joss is going to tell me and now all of us that also caused him to

116

worry about it all day. He certainly wouldn't be worrying about it if it was that he and Marianne were getting together. I have also noticed how well you are now moving, and it could be very soon that you can move back to the flat. Both you and James seem to be putting it off for some reason. I'm not stupid Nat."

"I'll get Janette," Nat said indicating that Bethany should go on to the kitchen. "Whilst you are getting out the glasses and opening the wine, just think about things Bethany. If I'm well enough to walk up the stairs to the flat, then I'm well enough to go back to work. Can you imagine what the remarks will be from the students - they will give me a really hard time. Also, the police told me this week that they think your stalker, and the boy that tripped me when I broke my leg, is a student at the school, and they think he may be one and the same."

Bethany stared back at Nat open mouthed. "Oh Nat you can't possibly go back to school to teach until you are fit and well, and that will give the police time to finish their enquiries. I'm a selfish cow, I'm sorry to be a grump, we will stay here as long as Joss and James will allow."

"Go and get the glasses and wine Beth, and don't mention this to Janette or to Joss."

Bethany worked on auto-pilot as she collected glasses, and opened the wine. Nat had known this for a while, and had not wanted to worry her, Janette, or Joss, and she had almost forced him to say something to her, and she had not yet thanked him for sticking up for her with her stepfather! Janette came into the kitchen and carried through the bottles of wine, whilst Bethany carried the tray of glasses. She noticed there were six glasses on the tray, and only five people in Joss's room. Was she subconsciously hoping that James would arrive home soon!

The glasses were filled, handed around, and everyone was seated, and four pairs of eyes looked at Joss. He gave a rather embarrassed and rueful look towards Marianne, coughed and then sat back in his chair.

"It is apology and confession time, and please don't interrupt or I might lose my courage. I want to apologise to Bethany. She bravely helped me when I was being harassed by some youths, with the help of Nat who came running. I want to apologise to her for ostentatiously flirting with her, for my own ends, when I was fully aware that she only felt friendship towards me. Both Bethany and Nat have been very good friends and I now fully appreciate that fact." He paused and took a sip of wine, and glanced at the faces around him. "Over the last few months, I have often embarrassed you my friends, with the way I have treated my only brother James. He has always looked out for me, even as a small child, he worked when he was at school and it was mostly for my benefit. He looked after our mother whilst she was ill, and made sure that I had the things that I needed. After the accident in which I was injured, and our mother was killed, he stood up to our grandparents to try and keep me at home with them. The grandparents were the ones that wanted me in an institution and out of their home where they said they were unable to cope. James said he would look after me but they insisted, and after that he visited me as regularly as he could. I was angry that I was the one who had been injured, and almost hated him for being fit and well and able to get on at school, and then University. The one thing that I hated him for the most was that he was the one who held our mother in his arms as she

118

was dying. I couldn't move and was in great pain, and I have let those feelings ruin our relationship over these many years. As you know, James has made it possible for me to live here with him, and I have appreciated that fact. He thinks I don't know that Willow Trees was left to him in its entirety, and the money that was left by our grandparents, which wasn't much, was shared between us. In other words he has made me a present of half of this house, and all he got for his kindness and brotherly feelings were a selfish, self-absorbed and unkind brother. If it is not too late I mean to change that," he paused with closed eyes, as if trying to block out graphic images from his past, and feeling so many conflicting emotions. "You as my friends, I hope, will be able to advise me what I should do?" There was a stunned silence for a few minutes.

Over the second bottle of wine, they did advise him, and Bethany accepted his apology with some misgivings. She felt really hurt on James's behalf, and realised she had no right to! Soon Janette and Nat retired to Nat's room, and Bethany left with the glasses and empty wine bottles for the kitchen.

When the others left the room Joss and Marianne sat in silence for a few moments. Suddenly, Marianne quickly kissed him on the cheek and prepared to leave, reiterating the advice of his friends, that he should speak with his brother and try to make it up to him in the future. He was definitely distracted by the touch of her lips, and it was a mesmerizing moment as he realised she was not disgusted with him, and if Roger wasn't her choice, then there might be a chance for him Joss, the very bad brother who didn't really deserve such a wonderful young woman, and he was determined to do exactly as he had promised his new and most definitely good friends!

Bethany came out of the kitchen after putting the glasses in the dishwasher, and found Marianne in the hallway. There were tears in her eyes.

"You will come and see Joss soon?" Bethany asked worried about Joss.

"I told him I will call and see him in a couple of days, because there is a lot to think about, for both of us." Marianne said, and Bethany gave her a long comforting hug.

"Goodnight Marianne, I would just like to say that Joss is really a very nice person, when he gives himself a chance, and he didn't have to tell us all about his bad feelings for his brother. That was very brave, and he seems determined to put matters right if he can." Bethany said, hoping Marianne *would* come back in a couple of days! Joss would be devastated if she didn't.

Bethany opened the door for Marianne, who quickly said goodnight, just as James swerved from his route to the back of the house and walked in through the front door, carrying his briefcase and a stack of files.

"Marianne seems upset?" He said to Bethany, who quickly wiped a tear from her eye, thinking there was no time like the present, and should she interfere?"

"James, go in and see Joss, I think he is a bit upset too." Bethany said, and watched as he walked towards Joss's door, as she made her way upstairs thoughtfully. Joss had bared his sole to his friends, could he do the same for his brother? Would Joss's burst of contrition last long enough for him to be honest with his brother, and could James forgive him for all these years of unhappiness? She was certain that he could! Bethany prepared for bed, now her tiredness had disappeared as she waited for James's footsteps coming up the stairs. Almost an hour passed and she heard his slow steps.

She opened her bedroom door, and met James on the landing.

"Are you alright James?" she asked hurriedly, searching his grey eyes.

He stopped and stared at her then gave a bemused grin. "I'm very well, thank you Beth." She stood on tiptoe and kissed his cheek, and he gave her a long hug his arms holding her tightly against him, as she felt a sharp pain in her chest. The combination of his previous pain and happy bemusement she found difficult to withstand.

"Good night Beth, see you tomorrow." He said, and walked into his room as if in a daze, leaving her feeling both hurt and bereft. She might be feeling hurt and bereft, but James must have a lot on his mind, mostly a better understanding of his only brother.

CHAPTER ELEVEN

During the next few weeks there was a definite lightening of the atmosphere in Willow Trees, Joss and James seemed much happier, and it rubbed off on the other occupants of the house. Bethany didn't see much of James in those weeks, as there was much to do in the office, in order that both of his partners could take time off for a honeymoon after the wedding. He went off early to the office, and came home late.

The bride and groom had arranged for a private Blessing in the Church, after a wedding ceremony in the hotel at which the reception was to take place. James was to be the best man, and there was to be one bridesmaid. All this Bethany learned from Elaine Woodhouse, who was the fountain of all knowledge in the office, and a mother figure to most of the young men and women. She would be sadly missed when she left the office, but Bethany was now quite confident that she could manage the accountancy side of the business herself after spending almost six months with Elaine in charge. Elaine went on to tell Bethany that she should choose anything but deep pink and white, as the bride and bridesmaid would be wearing those colours, and Elaine herself had decided on navy and white. Bethany didn't think it would matter what she wore, but was pleasantly surprised when her mother decided to go shopping with her and insisted on buying her outfit for her, therefore, she hoped that Bethany could keep her inheritance money intact, to put towards a deposit on a flat in due course.

The mother and daughter shopping expedition was a great success, as Julie Wood acquired a new wardrobe for her trip to Australia, and she found for her daughter a beautiful georgette dress the colour of her eyes, together with a bag, shoes and fascinator of the same colour.

On the morning of the wedding Julie Wood called on her daughter at Willow Trees for the very first time, bringing with her two beautiful white roses, one to wear on her dress and the other to fasten to her bag.

Bethany's heart thumped as she watched from her window. James was leaving Willow Trees in his well fitted morning suit, and he was obviously on his way to pick up the groom and looked absolutely fantastic. She had difficulty in schooling her features before she turned to her mother's interested eyes.

Joss had been invited to the wedding but had declined, saying he had to work on that Saturday. Bethany and James were both aware that he preferred to spend the day with Marianne. Elaine and Bethany were to share a taxi with two of the junior partners, and when the taxi arrived Bethany kissed her mother goodbye, as she was leaving that evening for her trip to Australia to visit her sister. Since the death of Ronald Wood, both Bethany and her mother had enjoyed seeing each other quite often, and Bethany felt a deep sadness as she waved goodbye to her mother. Still it would only be for a few months.

The Wedding was a very nice occasion at a hotel overlooking Derwentwater and the spectacular mountains surrounding it. Everyone seemed very happy, and after the official ceremony, the main wedding party left for the Church, but were back in about half an hour. The guests in the meantime had enjoyed themselves, and the wedding breakfast and short speeches took place in a very convivial atmosphere.

The bride and groom started the dancing, and were soon joined by the best man and bridesmaid. Bethany was surprised when Elaine said the bridesmaid was only seventeen, as she was an amazingly pretty girl and full of confidence. In fact, James was kept on the floor for the next dance too. When they had arrived James had been on his way to the car to fetch the bridesmaid's handbag, he complimented Elaine on her appearance, and had seemed stunned as he looked at Bethany. As he had parted from them, he had whispered to Bethany, that he would claim her for a dance later, and she waited for quite a long time, before he claimed her.

"Are you enjoying the wedding," he asked looking down on her lowered eyes, and seemed fascinated by her fascinator. "You look beautiful Beth, please try to keep another dance free for *me*. I notice you are never off the floor, I also notice at work that the male junior partners keep finding it necessary to go to the accountants office, and I don't think it is to see Elaine on every occasion."

Bethany managed to nod in reply, and strived to keep the office workers around her from realising the uncomfortable pounding in her breast, and the fine sweat dewing her temples, just because she was dancing with James. When the dance finished, James seemed to be waiting for the music to start again. However, he was pulled by the arm towards the doorway, by the young bridesmaid, as she wanted to introduce him to her grandmother. He managed to whisper sorry, as he was drawn away, and Bethany thought she needed some fresh air, and headed for the garden.

She sat on a garden seat and calmed her breathing, hoping that James was not aware of the effect he had on her whilst dancing. She wished that Nat and Janette or even Joss were at the wedding. Elaine was a good companion, but was forever moving around the different groups. Bethany suddenly realised that she had not made much effort to get to know the secretaries, mostly girls, who worked in the main office, nor did she know the one female junior solicitor, whom she knew was married with children, and was always very busy, working hours that suited her busy life. She decided she should rejoin the party, and stood up from her solitary reflections, and stared dumbfounded through a large rose bush. She could see someone kissing the seventeen year old bridesmaid, and was shocked beyond measure when she saw the man was James! As Bethany stared in disbelief there was a scuffle beyond the roses, and the girl strode off in high dudgeon, towards the ladies powder room. James wiped bright pink lipstick off his lips with his snowy white handkerchief, and lifted his eyes, and met those of Bethany beyond the rose bushes. He looked shocked and very angry, and she saw and heard him swear. However, she was inside the hotel and then out the other side, walking home, within minutes. She had caught a glimpse of him as he came into the room, but he was stopped by an elderly lady, who moved off towards the ladies powder room, seemingly at his urgent suggestion.

As Bethany neared Willow Trees, feeling desperately unhappy, and almost disbelieving what she had witnessed, the beautiful blue/grey high heeled shoes were killing her. She met Barry in the driveway and he stopped to look at her in wonder.

"Bethany you look rather splendid, how about coming out with me for a drink, I thought I had a physio date with Joss, but Nat tells me he has gone off with his girlfriend?"

"Why not, can you wait until I've changed, as I'm not used to all this wedding finery." She decided she should make an effort and go out, to stop her going over and over in her mind the sight of James and the bridesmaid kissing – a seventeen year old girl, and she felt quite sick.

"Good, I'll wait with Nat, he said he was alone because Janette has gone out shopping." Barry said with a pleased smile, and he walked back into the house with her.

Bethany quickly threw off her outer clothing, pulled on designer jeans and a T-shirt, and comfortable sandals, and joined Barry in Nat's room.

"I thought you would be staying on for the night do," Nat said in surprise.

"Not in my line Nat, I'd rather spend the evening with Barry, see you later."

She and Barry did enjoy themselves with Barry's friends in a public house that seemed to be very well used by a lot of young people, and Bethany decided that she should do something about herself, make the effort to get out and about now that she was no longer studying all the time.

Although she felt an underlying ache every time she thought of James and the young girl, she had at least spent a couple of hours with people of her own age, and might in time really learn to enjoy herself! When they arrived back at Willow Trees, the porch light came on, and Barry quietly asked if he could kiss her goodnight. She nodded, and he did very gently but thoroughly.

She stared at him for a moment in dismay, and he pulled a rueful face.

"It's not working is it Bethany, no fireworks. I guess your mind is on someone else," Barry said kindly, and kissed her quickly on the mouth once more, and walked back down the drive, with just one backward glance to see that she was going into the house. He then carried on thoughtfully.

James had witnessed Barry and Bethany coming up the drive, and the light going on, and the goodnight kiss from his vantage point at the bottom of the garden under the willow trees. He did not however, hear what was said.

He had left the evening wedding celebration as early as he decently could. The bridesmaid's grandmother had seen her granddaughter in the ladies room, and taken her to her mother for a dressing down! He had arrived home to find out from Nat that Bethany had gone out with Barry Stansfield, and he now wondered if it had been a date already arranged. He was hot and sweaty from his very energetic run through the park, and tired after a long drawn out wedding day, and an amorous bridesmaid who needed taking in hand by her immediate family!

Bethany had gone rushing off, although he had asked her to keep another dance for him, surely she had not been upset by that stupid young girl trying to kiss him. If she was upset by that, then maybe she was jealous, that needed some thinking about. He went in as usual by the back door into the utility room. Bethany was a wonderful girl, and he really liked Barry Stansfield, but that didn't *help* one little bit!

He was half way up the stairs when Bethany came into the hallway, after saying goodnight to Nat. Apparently Joss wasn't in yet, that was something he must think about soon.

"Bethany, why did you rush away from the wedding? I thought we were going to dance again. I have been pretty tied up doing best man duties all day, I missed you." He seemed very up-tight, and she assumed he was annoyed with her. Nothing like as up-tight as she felt with him!

"The wedding was over as far as I was concerned, particularly if it was going to end with men taking advantage of teenage girls," she said angrily, then realised what she had implied and she was mortified. James would never take advantage of anyone she was sure. Had he really fallen for the young girl?

"If you mean the bridesmaid deciding she should be kissed by the best man, and doing it before he realised what was going on, then you are quite right. If that is what you believe I am like, then it is a good thing that you and I both realise it. I have left it to her grandmother and mother to sort out. I note that you had already arranged a hot date with Barry, how long before he comes in with you Bethany to spend the night?" The words almost hissed from between his lips he was so angry.

For a moment Bethany was silent, then she realised that James had been watching her say goodnight to Barry. It was just as well he hadn't heard what was said between them. If he was going to go out with seventeen year olds, then she

128

didn't want anything to do with him, but she felt so hurt. Why could she not say to him that she didn't believe it of him, was it because of what he had said about Barry, poor harmless Barry, who had gone away disappointed with her!

"Barry Stansfield is a very nice man, as you have already discovered James, and he would be suitable for any young woman who is around his age, and unattached. I will give the matter some careful consideration."

"I trust you and your vicious mind will have a good night's rest Bethany. I'll say goodnight, as you are probably very tired after a hot date with the wonderful Barry. Just bear in mind Bethany, that the bridesmaid was Mara's seventeen year old daughter, whom I have known for a number of years, and if you believe I would take advantage of her teenage crush, then you are very much mistaken, and not the sensitive women I had mistakenly come to believe you were."

His bedroom door thudded shut, followed shortly by hers.

Bethany quickly undressed and slipped into bed, what had promised to be a wonderful day had turned into something she wanted to forget. Just at the moment she believed that James would not forgive her for her erroneous assumptions, and she did not even deserve that he should!

CHAPTER TWELVE

That night Bethany cried herself to sleep. Her mind seemed to be going around in circles. She was aware that she should apologise to James, for her vicious attack on his character, whilst knowing all the time that he was too good a person to take advantage of anyone. She had to work in the same office and was terrified that he would now consider her as gauche and naïve as the delectable bridesmaid, but she didn't want him to know she had irrevocably fallen in love with him. If he did believe that she had a crush on him, perhaps he would wait until her mother returned from Australia to sort out *her* daughter! She had recently realised that living in the same house with James, was both a pleasure and the cause of much heartache, didn't she stand at the window waiting for his car to come home most nights! She would be better away from here, but dreaded the thought of living alone in her own little flat. However, she couldn't forever stay with Nat, he had Janette to think about, and was too nice a guy to mention that to her. If she moved into her mother's house, then there would have to be a lot of discussion with the neighbours, who would be aware that her mother did not expect that to happen. She eventually decided to ring her Dad in the morning, and ask if she could call on him.

The next evening Bethany climbed off the bus, and walked along the street looking for the house made into four flats where her dad was living. She eventually found it and pressed his bell. He answered it, and opened the main door for her. She climbed up a flight of stairs to his flat.

"Lovely to see you Bethany, I've brought in a take-away for us to share. Just wait a moment and I'll move things around a bit so that we can eat." Jeremy Browne said happily. He was really pleased that Bethany had asked to visit him, as he had something he wished to discuss with her.

"I came to tell you I'm thinking of getting my own flat. Not to buy, but to rent until I know what area I would like to live in," Bethany said as she took her place at the small table.

"That sounds an excellent idea Bethany. It's a pity this flat isn't bigger, we could have shared," he finished with a smile looking around his cramped quarters. "Your mother said you were very comfortable in Willow Trees, and how nice the Castleton boys are. She also said that Nathanial was there too. Why do you want to move?"

"It was only a temporary measure, living there, until Nat could again manage the stairs up to his flat. He is almost well again, and I think Janette, his girlfriend, will be moving in with him, so I guess it is time for me to strike out on my own."

"Well you do have a very good job now Bethany, and I believe that Ronald Wood left you a small inheritance, I'm afraid I *won't* be able to match that and you are *my* daughter. However, it should help you to make it nice and to your own taste. If you would like to come here until you get your flat ready, you would be welcome. I could sleep in the living room."

"Thank you Dad, but I couldn't put you out of your bedroom. I'll let you know when I get somewhere." She paused and looked at her Dad with her head slightly to one side, just as his was, and smiled. "How did you know about the ten thousand, did Mum tell you?"

"Yes she did. Have you had a card or letter from her recently?"

"Yes a brief note to say she had arrived, and had received a very nice welcome from Aunt Milly and her husband."

Jeremy put out his hand, without leaving his chair, and lifted a card from the bookcase. "This is the latest card I got."

Bethany recognised her mother's neat handwriting, read the card, and returned it to him. "So, you keep in touch, you and Mum." She stated, watching her Dad's pleased smile, as he placed his knife and fork on his plate carefully.

"I am pleased you decided to call on me Bethany, because I wanted to tell you that I have always loved and needed your mother, and intend to get her back, after a suitable time has elapsed." He watched the joyful smile on his daughter's face with a feeling of relief. Perhaps it would be possible!

"I hope you manage it Dad, she has become a very independent women since Ronald died."

"I always thought she was Bethany," her Dad replied with a rueful smile.

As she left her Dad's home, she realised that she had enjoyed seeing him, and intended to do so more often. However, she also felt very lonely. She was happy that there was a possibility of her parents getting back together in the future, but she felt she was not needed by anyone. It was time she stood on her own two feet, without relying on her friends, and she started looking for a small flat in earnest.

She saw very little of James over the next three weeks, either in the office or at Willow Trees and she began to wonder if he was avoiding her, just as she was avoiding him! The truth probably was that he was at the Crown Court and was staying in Carlisle. She should be able to catch him at Willow Trees, so why couldn't she just apologise to him as she knew she should and get it over with?

In actual fact James was feeling just the same. He knew when she left the office, and wondered how she filled in her evenings as she was seldom in her room, or with Nat or Josh for that matter. He wasn't about to ask either Joss or Nat, as it would make it known to them that there was something wrong between them!

The very next evening, James arrived home to find a sealed but unstamped letter in his post. He recognised her handwriting and tore it open, and read the contents with a glower of disappointment. It was a letter from Bethany telling him that she would be leaving Willow Trees, and finished with her grateful thanks for all the kindnesses she had received during her stay!

He strode up the stairs and into her bedroom, but everything looked as it always had, and there was not a sign of her having occupied the room. He rushed down the stairs and into Nat's room, apologising for not knocking.

"Bethany has moved out, do you know anything about it?" He demanded roughly.

Nat looked aghast, and walked over to the table where his unread post lay. He had not limped or thumped across on his crutches, as he was only with James! He tore open an envelope and read the contents. "Yes, she says she is moving out, and thanks me for looking after her over the years since she was sixteen." He grimaced, and thumped the table with his fist. "It doesn't give a forwarding address, or say exactly when she intends to move out." He glanced at James. "You can get her new address through the office."

"Yes of course," he said pulling out a small diary and thumbing through until he found the telephone number he wanted. "I'll have to speak to our PAYE clerk at home, I trust she won't mind."

Ten minutes later, they were no nearer in finding out Bethany's new address. The clerk had not minded being disturbed by one of the partners, but said that Bethany had taken a couple of days off, and would supply them with her new details upon her return to the office.

"Don't you have Bethany's mobile number?" James asked Nat.

"Yes, I did, but she has a new 'phone, that was her little treat to herself after getting left a little money by Ronald Wood, she gave the old one to a Charity shop. I'll try it now." Nat tried a couple of times, and then closed his mobile. It says she is not available, but I'll keep trying just in case. This was and maybe still is her number James," Nat said with a worried frown, "we can both keep trying." Nat read out the number and James patted him on the shoulder and made his way upstairs, taking another look into the room that had been Beth's. He wished that she drove a car, and then he could have driven around the streets in the hope of seeing it, and from that he would at least know the area where she lived. He was well aware that the population of Keswick was just under five thousand, so it couldn't be too difficult to find where she had moved, as it wouldn't be so far away, as she had to walk to work most days. The other problem was that it was the tourist season, so there would be thousands of extra souls in the town and thereabouts.

Bethany looked around her new abode. It could be better and, in fact, it would be when she had managed to place around her few personal items. However, except for making up the bed, she was doing nothing with the filled black bags, and few boxes that the taxi driver had helped her to carry into the small flat. The flat had been painted in a muted white right through before her tenancy, and the only splash of colour were the dark red cushions and curtains. Tomorrow she would buy a couple of rugs for the floor, a picture and a mirror, together with a few kitchen utensils. She checked that the door was truly locked a couple of times, switched off the lights except for that beside her bed, and crawled into the newly made up bed. Tomorrow would be soon enough to try the small shower in the small bathroom, and it wouldn't have seemed so very small if she hadn't just moved out of Willow Trees! It was good to feel tired enough to sleep instead of wondering and worrying most of the night.

The next day she spent making her few purchases, and again had to get a taxi back to the flat. The following day, she placed around her few personal belongings that James had retrieved from the pavement the night she had been attacked by her stalker. Thinking of James made her wonder what she was doing here, why had she left, already she felt lonely without her friends around her? Tomorrow when she would be back at work, then she would see the office staff, and maybe a quick sighting of James if he wasn't at Court all day, or staying in Carlisle if he was at the Crown Court. She could always get in touch with Nat and Janette and ask them to come around now that she was settled in, and maybe they would have now decided to move in together! Joss seemed to be spending most of his free time with Marianne, and also part of his working day. She had been asked once or twice to join the junior partners and secretaries for a drink after work, but she had always been rushing home to see if Nat or Joss wanted anything! She sighed and admitted to herself, she missed the times she had watched for James coming home to Willow Trees, and the satisfaction of knowing that he was safely home.

She went to the local Chinese for a take-away meal, and hurried home to her empty flat, thinking how pleasant the time was when she and James had brought home a take-away and shared it with Joss, Nat and Janette. Also how quickly James had managed to get served with enough to feed four of them, whereas she had waited about the same time for enough for one, and she would probably take two days to finish it! Going up the stairs she stopped and turned back, she had a strange feeling in her gut but there was nobody there, and she felt a fool. She had to get used to living alone, if she couldn't have James then she didn't want anybody, so lonely she would be.

She reached her flat doorway and noticed that she had forgotten to lock it, then realised that she had checked twice to make sure that it was locked before leaving the building. She stood back suddenly perhaps someone *was* in there waiting for her. It could not be a friend or the door would not have been forced open. She almost ran down the stairs, and then pulled herself together. If she was to live alone, then she had to stop relying on other people. She dialled nine, nine, nine and slowly opened the door, after requesting the police. Her heart was beating madly, as she glanced around the small flat. All the doors were open, and every room had been ransacked, but there was no sign of an intruder. Whoever had done this had left the premises. The voice on the end of the telephone asked what the trouble was, and she told them. They asked if anyone was still in the flat, and when she replied 'No' they said she should ring a friend to be with her, as it could be a while before they could be there, but they would get there as soon as they possibly could. She closed her phone, and looked around her. Every cushion had been split open and the filling strewn about. There was black paint on the walls and floor, and everything breakable seemed to have been smashed. She wondered dismally how this could have been done in the time she had been out to get her take-a-way, had this been random vandalism, or had *she* been the target? She opened her phone and dialled the house phone at Willow Trees, where else would she phone, or could she as her mother was in Australia.

"Beth, is that you," the voice asked on picking up the 'phone.

"Yes," she replied weakly, relieved to hear James's voice.

"Don't put the 'phone down Beth, tell me your address."

She did, wondering why he had expected it to be *her,* and he hadn't even asked what the problem was?

"I'll be with you in five minutes, don't go out," he said briskly and put the 'phone down.

She started to cry quietly, he didn't even know what had happened, but he was coming over anyway! He must be annoyed with her for just leaving a note, but it was time for her to stand on her own two feet and stop relying on James and Nat, well she *had* thought that, but now she felt really sick and violated. She looked around her small flat rented for six months, and cried even harder, she had felt dreadful when she had been caught by her stalker, but now she felt violated, unable to understand 'why her' was she such a bad person and did she deserve this? Who could have done such a dreadful thing?

Ten minutes later James found the right road, and felt his heart sink as he saw a police car with blue lights flashing, and made directly for it. He saw two officers leave the car and make for the flats, and followed, leaving the lights still blazing on his car and with the door left wide open. The two police personnel a man and a woman checked the flat number and hurried up the stairs with James hard on their heels.

Bethany wiped her eyes and stood up with a feeling of relief as the police entered her flat. The policewoman stood beside Bethany as the other Officer walked through the small flat.

"Bethany!" James said in a soothing voice, and she turned towards him, and found herself held comfortingly against his broad chest. "What has happened here?"

"I don't know James, I just came back with my supper, and found the flat like this," she spread one arm indicating the mess.

"Mr Castleton, if you will stay with the young lady I'll help my colleague, and contact the station." The police woman said acknowledging him. At first Bethany was surprised that they knew him, but then realised James would be known to both the police and many miscreants on the *other* side of the law!

Bethany was asked to look around the flat to see if anything was missing. She had taken her purse with her, and her handbag had been emptied out in the flat, but everything seemed to be there. Nor could she think of anything that was missing, as everything had been trashed it was hard to tell, but there was nothing there of value anyway!

Both of the officers returned to the living room, and the policewoman suggested that having taken Bethany's name it was in order for her to leave with Mr Castleton, as Bethany was very pale and had now started to shiver with shock.

"I would suggest a cup of sweet tea, but even if there are any whole cups left then we don't want anything touched, until the room has been photographed, and we may find some fingerprints."

"We have a pretty good idea who could have done this," the male officer said, and on catching a direct stare from James he became silent. Then he coughed, and suggested that they were waiting for more officers, and perhaps Bethany should leave with Mr Castleton. Bethany couldn't wait to get out of there!

"In *this instance* you may contact me at *home* Officers." James said as he gently turned Bethany towards the door.

James took her down the stairs with his arm around her, and soon had her tucked into the passenger seat in the front of his car.

"What did the policeman mean when he that they have a pretty good idea who could have done it?" Bethany asked James, and after a moment he replied after driving out of the street.

"I understand there have been one or two other break-ins recently," he looked stern and enigmatic. Then he glanced at her wan face, and patted her tightly clasped hands. "There is nothing to worry about Bethany, you are safe now."

"Nothing to worry about, I have just had my very first home which was entirely mine trashed, and this is only the third day! Where are you taking me, James?"

"Home to Willow Trees, where else? How could you just disappear like that, leaving only a brief note for Nat and me? We have been worried about you."

"I'm sorry you were worried, but I wanted to stand on my own two feet, and now look what has happened." They continued the rest of the journey in silence, as Bethany looked ahead without seeing anything except in her mind - she could see the unfamiliar little flat in its now vandalised state, with black paint and new red cushions torn and de-stuffed, and wondered why it was *her* flat that has been trashed? Was she such a bad person, did she deserve this, just as she was trying to move on with her life. The last thing she could imagine after this dreadful day was starting out on her own again!

CHAPTER THIRTEEN

It was a relief to arrive at Willow Trees, and it really did feel like coming home to Bethany. James let her out of the car and hesitated as he almost left the car in the drive, but then opened the door for her, and returned to take his car to the garage. She was still standing in the hallway when he returned, looking lost and worried.

"I'm sorry to be such a nuisance to you James. I took the linen from my bed to the laundry, and haven't collected it yet." She paused. "I'll have to let Nat know what has happened, he will be so cross with me."

"Forget Nat, I'll have a word with him whilst you gather some bedding from the linen store on the landing, or from the airing cupboard. You will not be going in to work tomorrow, as the police will want to interview you. I'll ask Elaine to get whatever she thinks you will need for the time being. I expect the police will let you have your handbag and credit cards back tomorrow. He gave her a wry smile.

"We should have brought your take-a-way. I'll bring you up some toast and eggs from the kitchen."

"I don't think I can face anything except a pot of tea," Bethany said realising that she now felt quite ill, but didn't want to upset either Nat or James. There was no sign of Joss and she assumed he was with Marianne.

"I'll go and put the kettle on, and have a word with Nat. He has been as worried about you as I have, as we had no idea where you had gone. Considering how he has always been there for you since you were sixteen, a short letter seems very abrupt and definitely inadequate." He looked at her distressed face and regretted his harsh condemnation particularly at this time. Suddenly she ran down the stairs, and after knocking on Nat's door, she slipped inside. James set off after her and then decided not to follow her, she had known Nat for much longer than he had known her, and perhaps she would be more forthcoming with her explanation of her sudden departure.

"God Bethany, you look dreadful, what has been happening, all James said when he was leaving was that he had your address and was going to see you." Nat said worriedly. Janette was there, and she pulled Bethany gently towards a chair, and pulled back her hair from her face, handing her a tissue. Nat watched Bethany closely, as her eyes were red and she had obviously being crying – had she and James had yet another argument?

"I thought I should strike out on my own, and I rented a flat. I know I should have discussed it with you, but I knew you would persuade me to stay. I also had a disagreement with James about something that happened at the wedding and I felt stupid and naïve, but couldn't find the words to apologise to him." She waited and surprisingly Nat didn't comment. Nat had his own ideas about the way James and Bethany always seemed to disagree.

"I rang Willow Trees after ringing the police, as my flat was trashed whilst I went out for a take-a-way for my supper, and they told me to get a friend to wait with me until they got there. It was horrible, and I don't think I can go back there." She glanced at Nat's horrified expression, and continued. "The person who broke in was no longer there, although I had been out for only twenty minutes to half an hour. I'm sorry for not discussing it with you Nat, and only leaving you a note, it was unforgivable after all you have done for me in the past."

"I think I understand better than you think Bethany, but you will stay here now just for another week or two?" He glanced at Janette, who gave him a small smile and nodded.

"You look done in, Bethany, and no wonder." Janette said, "I'll come up and help you settle in for the night. Do you need something to sleep in?"

Bethany suddenly hugged Janette, and then Nat. "I'm bushed, have you anything to spare Janette? I have to make up the bed too."

Janette went to a large cupboard, and lifted out a couple of items, and took Bethany by the elbow and the girls went towards the stairs. Bethany went with her, quite pleased that at least Janette has some of her things in Nat's room, and so she must be staying over quite regularly.

"Janette, I've made some toast and a pot of tea for Bethany. Can you manage to take it up with you?" James said from the kitchen doorway. He scrutinised Bethany's expression, and nodded to Janette as she took the tray from him. He then made his way to Nat's room, closing the door behind him.

The girls found a bottom sheet, pillow cases, and a duvet cover, and made short work of making up the bed. Janette also brought a bath and a hand towel, and placed them on the bed.

"I think I can manage some toast and certainly a cup of tea," Bethany said in surprise, and Janette sat on the bed and watched her for a few moments.

"Nat and I are not the reason you rented yourself a flat and moved out are we?" Janette asked, watching Bethany closely.

"No of course not, I always hoped you and Nat would get back together and it seems that you have," she finished with a poor attempt at a smile.

"Then the reason is James Castleton." Janette said filling up Bethany's cup from the teapot, and as she lifted her eyes from the cup she found Bethany's blue eyes staring back in consternation. "Don't worry Bethany, as I'm sure that Nat, Joss or James haven't got a clue. I know that James is a wonderful man, and I'm sure that working in his office, and living in his house must be very difficult at times, if you happen to be in love with him."

Bethany lowered her eyes in confusion, thinking what a nice person Janette was, but then she would be – Nat loved her!

"Don't bother to contradict me Bethany, when I first met him I thought he was gorgeous and a real gentleman, but happily I was already in love with Nat! I think he thinks a lot of you Bethany, and you do seem to strike sparks off each other quite regularly. Wouldn't it be better to stay around just in case there is a chance with him?" Janette said, sitting on the bed beside her young friend. Janette suddenly realised that they were probably around the same age, but

Bethany although having left home at sixteen didn't seem very worldly. She had spent time studying over the last few years although she had a full time job. Maybe she hadn't had the time, the inclination, or the money to fool around finding out about the opposite sex. Janette suddenly felt, for the first time, that her family of three siblings and happy parents were a true blessing.

"I don't know where I stand with James," Bethany admitted sorrowfully. "I was certain he and Mara Stephenson from work were an item, and then she married the other partner. I was shocked and relieved about that, but then after the wedding when I saw him kissing the bridesmaid, I was incensed and very hurt, and accused him of coming on to a seventeen year old. The bridesmaid turned out to be Mara's young daughter, who was trying to seduce *him*, and now I feel such an idiot, but if I make a point of apologising he may guess how I feel."

"Leave it for the moment Bethany, both you and James have enough to deal with at the present time. Do you think you can settle down for the night now, or would you like some medication to help you sleep?"

"No thank you Janette. You have been very kind, no wonder Nat is in love with you." Bethany smiled at Janette, and realised what a good friend she was, not *only* Nat's girlfriend.

There was a tap on the door, and Janette opened it to James. "I have spoken with the police Beth, and they want you to go down to the station in the morning at about ten thirty. Do you want me to ask Elaine to do some shopping for you?" He looked closely at them both, and Janette smiled at him.

"Why don't I come down with you to the station, I can get tomorrow off work, and then we can go shopping?" Janette asked, and looked as though she really would like a day off to go shopping.

"Thank you James, I guess Janette and I will manage tomorrow between us," Bethany said with a grateful smile at them both. "Oh, and thank you for bringing me home James, and for the tea and toast, goodnight."

As he left the room with Janette, he had a wry smile, as he was very pleased that Bethany seemed to think of Willow Trees as her '*home*.'

Bethany hurried into the shower room as she felt unclean and she relished the hot water cleansing her body, but she felt very lonely, and kept seeing flash-backs of her flat, and the few things that she had cherished such as torn family photographs, slashed cushions which she had only just chosen with such care, and liberal amounts of black paint! She had a very long hot shower, and returned to her room wearing the thick bath towel. She slipped on her borrowed nightdress which was a rather long T-shirt and hung up her clothes in the wardrobe, as they were all she had to wear for her visit to the police. She *must* feel better in the morning!

She looked at the two tablets she had taken from the shower room, they should help her sleep, and she needed to block out the graphic images of her flat that were in her head, and then she might be ready to face tomorrow.

Everything was dark, and she turned restlessly in her sleep, and she felt a hand shaking her shoulder, and she cowered away, in deep distress.

"Beth, Beth waken up, you are having a nightmare, don't be frightened it's only me," James's voice slowly soothed her as she lay shaking, and from the trapezoid light from the landing shining through the open bedroom door, she could make out his familiar frame dressed in a towelling robe, and slowly realised they were *his* hands on her shoulders, and it was *his* knee resting on her bed.

"I'm sorry I wakened you James, but it was horrible and I'm glad you woke me, and please hold me for a moment until I feel better," Bethany said, and struggled up and put her arms around his chest in desperation.

He pushed her back onto the bed, and lay down beside her, holding her close.

"It's alright now Beth, just try to take big breaths and it will all go away," he soothed, as she tried to assess the complex sensations she was feeling. She did take a deep breath, and smelled his soap and shampoo, his own particular scent, and sighed deeply, putting her head on his shoulder and holding on to him tightly.

Soon her breathing became less erratic as he stroked her from shoulder to back, and he started to ease himself away from her innocent, lithe form, which was the most difficult thing he could ever remember having to do!

"James, please don't leave me, I *need you* now more than anything." She pleaded, and put her lips to his throat, feeling him swallow quickly, she really needed the tantalising exciting things that she knew he could bring to her, as nobody else could!

"Stop it Bethany I'm not made of stone. It is not me you need, save yourself for the man you will marry one day." James whispered in a strangled voice, between deep breaths, as her slight, supple and alluring body drove him wild.

"You know I'm not going to marry anyone James. Please James don't go I need you so much." She pleaded against his ear, willing him to satisfy her in ways that she knew he could, but not knowing what they were!

"Beth you are driving me mad," he sighed, "I can pleasure you but I have no protection with me," he whispered. He did pleasure both of them, and she felt the full glow of euphoria, and a glowing, floating world built of pleasure and a need outside her understanding, and when her small hand touched his great need, it was too late, and he drove them both to the ultimate glowing sensations and euphoric satisfaction, as he strived to be gentle with her. Later they slept in each other's arms, complete and exhausted.

Sunlight lit up the room, as the curtains had been drawn back, as Bethany slowly awakened to a new day. She stretched luxuriously, and then remembered why she felt so complete and different, blushing rosily. She put one hand to her mouth in dismay (what had she done) and the other out to the pillow beside her and realised with a sinking heart that she was alone.

For the next twenty minutes she lay in bed thinking, going over every small detail in her mind. She had wantonly seduced James, and he had gone and left her alone. They had not said anything meaningful to each other, so how was she supposed to act the next time she saw him. She had not declared her love for him, thank goodness, but knowing him she was sure that he was not in the habit of irresponsible behaviour, he had said as much.

Goodness, she was anticipating with bated breath their next meeting, but was also dreading it more than her interview with the police today! Oh, and she must go to the chemist, and how embarrassing would that be as she needed

148

more than just soap and shampoo! Was James still at Willow Trees, or had he left, and would Nat and Janette be able to tell that something had happened? She looked at her watch and made for the bathroom, wondering why she didn't feel any aches or pains, and then put her sensitive face under the shower, trying to dislodge all the doubts she was feeling.

When dressed she left her room. Glancing at the door opposite she stopped to listen, but there was no sound, and she slowly went down towards Nat's room, schooling a face which didn't know whether to laugh or cry.

She went into the kitchen to put on the kettle, which was full, and had already been boiled recently. If someone had enjoyed breakfast then everything had been put away. Nat strolled in with an interrogating look. "Are you alright Bethany? Janette has popped out to the shops, and she will be back in time to accompany you to the police station. She thought you might need a lie-in."

"I'm fine Nat thank you." What was the point of a lie-in if you were alone? Goodness, she must get her mind into gear or Nat would suspect something, and also the police would think she was very strange, and she had discovered last night that Janette didn't seem to miss a thing!

"Oh, James popped in earlier. He said - not to worry about your interview this morning. He also said to remind you he is in Court for the next couple of days in Carlisle and will have to stay there, and you are not to go in to the office until you feel up to it."

It was a definite anticlimax, as she wouldn't see him today, or tomorrow, but maybe on the third day – possibly. She would be at the office, would he call in to see her, or would he wait until they were at Willow Trees, and would they be together? Last night she would never have dreamt

149

that something could happen that would put the trashing of her flat to the back of her mind! Well, she could stop wondering about James for a couple of days and get her act together, and find out what the police had found.

CHAPTER FOURTEEN

Bethany heard the front door being opened and realised it must be Janette, and she felt a driving necessity to appear calm and collected. If Janette had already picked up on her feelings for James over the last few weeks, then how much easier it would be for her to pick them up now!

Janette came into the kitchen, and glanced at Bethany. "Good you look fine, I'm glad you had a good nights sleep. It shouldn't be too bad at the police station, all you can do is tell them what you know, and then we can go shopping and get you a new wardrobe, that should be really exciting."

"I did take a couple of tablets I found in the bathroom upstairs, I think they helped me sleep." Bethany said just to put Janette's mind at rest, she didn't want her starting any kind of interrogation, as she would have liked to have a good heart to heart with Janette, but for the time being she must wait and see if James declared his feelings. She didn't believe that James would have been so involved and intent on her satisfaction, if he had not cared. However, she had read that men were capable of making love at the drop of a hat, or was that just the sex act? She was so naïve she didn't have a clue!

They had about twenty minutes to wait before the police started the interview, but there was very little she could tell them. They asked if she was insured, and she admitted that she was, of course, she was an accountant! They gave her the Crime Number, the reference for her case which the insurance people would want! They returned her handbag, and she didn't know if she really wanted it back, it seemed polluted in some way. They informed her that investigations would be ongoing, and as soon as they had anything to report, she would be the first person to know. They gave her a card with the name and address of a firm who could clean up the apartment and put it back as it had been, and a new lock on the door. She decided she would use them, and when the flat was back as it should be, she would tell the letting agents that she didn't want it, as there was no way she would move back there! She began to wonder what she should do, could she stay at Willow Trees?

That would all depend upon James in the end, but he would probably expect her to stay there until Nat and Janette moved out, which they seemed to be taking their time about arranging. However, she would only stay on at Willow Trees if he made it plain to her that she was welcome, but she also remembered that he didn't believe in marriage any more than did she! Everything was so difficult.

She and Janette had a very busy afternoon, buying the essentials, and clothes suitable for the office, but apart from that Bethany didn't want to spend too much on new clothes, she didn't know where she would be living in a few weeks time, and she said a little prayer of thanks to her stepfather for bequeathing to her a sum that would help and stop her having to worry about her finances for the time being!

The next day Bethany returned to the office, and was pleased to note that Elaine was the only person privy to the traumatic time that Bethany had suffered over the last few days. She told the PAYE clerk that she would be staying at Willow Trees for the time being, and would be looking for another flat as the one she had seen was not suitable. She had lost her month's rent, and probably the bond money, but that seemed a small price to pay just to forget about the whole upsetting business.

Bethany was just running for her bus, when James drove into the office car park, and she was pleased when he waved to her, as she climbed onto the bus. She had a quick shower as soon as she arrived at Willow Trees, and dressed in one of her new dresses, wondering if James would like it, in fact, wondering if he would even see it!

She heard him drive into the drive, and then around the back to his garage. She imagined him coming in through the utility room at the back of the property, and then she was disappointed as she heard him talking with Nat and Janette, and at the same time Joss came home from work, and she could hear Marianne's voice too. She didn't know what to do, and decided to wait in her room.

Twenty minutes later she heard James come up to his room, he then went into the bathroom, and she heard the shower. She was in an intense state of anticipation and dread, when she heard a slight tap on her door. She opened it, and yes at long last it was James.

"Bethany, are you alright?" She nodded, and he continued. "Joss and Marianne have arrived in a state of bliss. They have asked us all to accompany them to the Italian Restaurant. It seems they have some news they want to impart to us all together. Are you ready, do you need to get anything? You look really pretty tonight." He said, looking at her, fully aware of the four people waiting downstairs.

"I'm fine James, thank you, and yes I'll just get my bag." She said blandly, wanting to scream at him that she needed to talk to him, now!

She followed him down the stairs, a stair behind, and only just stopped herself from putting a hand out to smooth his hair, where it must have been resting against the headrest in the car. If he would just touch her hand, or look directly into her eyes she might know what he was thinking and feeling!

"Hello Bethany, thank goodness you are OK," Joss said quietly, as they all stood in the hallway. "Nat has been telling me what happened to you, I hope it has nothing to do with you standing up for me against those yobs, when we first met? Why did you move out anyway, I thought you were happy here?"

"Hardly Joss, leave Beth alone, she is just getting over it. Do you want me to bring the car around?" James asked in a businesslike voice.

"I thought we might walk to the Restaurant, it's not very far, and I can manage it now you know. We'll get taxi's back, and then we can *all* have a drink." Joss said briskly, wondering why his brother didn't want to talk about what had happened to Bethany, and realised that she was looking especially beautiful tonight, the new clothes that Janette had helped her choose were slightly more flamboyant than she had worn previously. Joss was aware that nothing had gone right for Bethany since their first meeting! Except, of course, that she had managed to get an excellent job with Ashcroft, Castleton, & Edmondson!

"Come on Joss, if you think you can walk it, stop mooning around, it could take us a long time," Marianne said briskly, clasping her hand in his, his other hand was holding the stick.

They paused as James locked the front door to Willow Trees, and then they moved along the pavement towards the restaurant, of necessity two by two. Bethany glanced at James, who gave her a wry smile. They were following Joss and Marianne, and Nat and Janette were following them. Bethany tucked her hand in his arm, as she knew that that was what she would have done, normally, and he didn't move away from her so she breathed easily once more.

When they were seated at a large table for six, Janette looked from Marianne to Joss impatiently. "What are we celebrating you two you can't keep us waiting all evening?"

"Well you might as well know now, Marianne has agreed to become my wife, and we thought we would do the deed as soon as possible." He glanced around the table stopping at his brother.

"Oh, so you are not rushing into anything," Janette said with a laugh, and caught Nat looking at her seriously, what she said was not a dig at Nat, but if it got him thinking that might be a good thing!

"Before anyone else says it, I know I haven't had any other serious girlfriends," Joss paused and took Marianne's hand in his. "However, I have a girlfriend now, and she is the only one I want, or will ever want."

James paused for a moment, and then stood to shake his brother's hand, and kissed Marianne on both cheeks.

"Congratulations to you both. Waiter, I think we need a bottle of champagne, and put a second in the cooler please."

When everyone had congratulated Joss and Marianne, and things settled down, Bethany glanced at James who was sitting beside her. "I guess Joss doesn't have the same beliefs as you with regard to marriage, although you both went through the same things whilst growing up."

"Hardly the same Beth, he was a number of years younger, and he was the one that suffered traumatic injuries in the car accident that killed our mother. I was the one that was taken away from him by our grandparents, I never forgave them for that, nor for the way they treated our mother when she lost her husband and us our father. I don't begrudge him any of the happiness he wants to pursue with Marianne, and who knows, it might even last!"

Bethany wished she had kept quiet, as there had been a definite cynical twist to his lips, as he stopped speaking. She had wanted to know how he was feeling, and now it seemed that she had, and it wasn't really what she had wanted to hear! She also remembered with a sinking feeling what she had said to him the other night. "You know I'm not going to marry anyone." Now she wished she could take that back, but at the time the only thing she had wanted was James to stay with her!

Bethany pulled herself together, and tried to enjoy the evening with her friends, which she did, and was pleased when they walked out to the taxi that was to take them home, that James clasped her hand in his, but less pleased when she realised he had waited to touch her until none of the party could see them! Was that for his *own* or for *her* benefit?

The taxi took them to Willow Trees, but Marianne was working the next morning, and Joss decided to go back with her. Nat and Janette shared a pot of tea with James and Bethany, and as soon as she could Bethany said a quick goodnight and went up to her room. James seemed to be blowing hot and then cold, and she couldn't make out what he intended, so she decided to leave him to make up his own mind.

She was in bed reading, when there was a tap on the door. "Yes," she said with a slight gulp, her heart was beating so fast she could hardly hear her reply!

Her heart dropped as she saw that he was fully dressed, and that he looked particularly unapproachable. He looked as if he had his solicitor's head on, and she was bitterly disappointed. He moved to the foot of the bed, and straightened his shoulders, he must look like this in his wig and gown!

"Relax James, you are not in Court now," Bethany said angrily. She was hoping for a declaration of love, and he was enigmatic and cool.

"Janette said you had a good sleep the night after your flat was trashed, she said you had taken two tablets from the upstairs bathroom cabinet."

"So what of it, James? *You know* why I had a good sleep." She was amazed when he looked uncomfortable and flushed, and she felt her cheeks go pink – what a thing to say to him! Was he trying to make excuses for their night of passion!

"I would like your reassurance that you knew what you were asking, when you '*needed me*,' and that it wasn't caused by the tablets you had taken. Sleeping pills could have made you act out of character." James said seriously

For goodness sake the man had a bee in his bonnet and wouldn't let go, of course she had wanted him, more than she intended to tell him if he didn't lighten up.

"Go to bed James, I didn't expect a prosecution interrogation on the *first time* I made love, I had hoped I'd done quite well for a first time, but then what do *I know*? I had two aspirins if you must *know* - do you suppose that made me act out of character?" She turned a page of her book, and ignored him, which was marginally better than throwing it at him, but she didn't see any of the print! He looked at her closely, then turned and moved towards the door. He looked at her face, wondering if she was going to laugh or cry, then closed the door quietly – from the outside and she thought her heart might break.

She remembered when he had seen the indentations in his beautiful lawn, and when asked what she thought she was doing, she had replied 'Somersaults,' both Joss and Nat had laughed uproariously, but not James.

She threw the book to the bottom of the bed, in disgust. She was going to have to go after him, because even if they were still against marriage, she really wanted him, but he could wait a few minutes – serve him right, he was altogether too pompous worrying about a couple of aspirins.

Five minutes later there was a knock on the door, and she heard James's voice. "You are alone, aren't you Beth?"

"Of course James, come in." She tugged at her hair to straighten it and smoothed the bedcover covering her below the waist.

She watched the door opening slowly, and James stood there in his wig and gown, and she slowly realised that that was *all* he was wearing! There was a definite twinkle in his eye, and she burst out laughing as one of his hands flashed to one side in front of him just for a second where he was holding the edges of the gown together. She almost rolled off the bed laughing. His voice came sternly, in his best Council for the Prosecution tone, "What about this cross-examination?"

"Yes please," she managed to say, as he joined her on the bed. She could hardly believe it, James had a very good sense of humour, and that she had never suspected! He was also very thoughtful, as he also had bought some protection, and this made her feel sure that he had not considered their coming together as a one off!

A considerable time later she asked him about the day she had made indentations in his lawn with her shoes, and when he asked 'what do you think you are doing' angrily, and she had answered 'Somersaults.' He smiled at her, and held her very tightly. "It was all I could do not to laugh, but I didn't know you then," he answered, "and I felt at a distinct disadvantage, having just seen your delectable pink underwear."

She was truly happy as she settled down to sleep in his arms, they did not believe in marriage but she was going to be with him as long as she possibly could. Would he tell his brother and Marianne, and Nat and Janette, or would they guess! She stopped worrying for the moment, and felt truly loved and cared for, which was quite a new sensation for Bethany.

CHAPTER FIFTEEN

They were both used to waking early, but instead of going for a run, they lay in bed and talked.

"When did you know that there was something sizzling between us," she asked quietly.

"Almost from the first day I couldn't get you out of my mind, but it was really when I saw Joss, as I thought at the time kissing you in the park. With him being my brother, and my thinking that you were with Nat had me in quite a state of turmoil as I didn't want you to be with either of them! What about you Beth?"

"It must have been from the first day for me too, but I remember being very nasty in my mind to poor Mara when I saw you out dining in the Italian restaurant, I thought you were an item then. But the time I remember most is when I opened up to you in the office and told you about my parents, and disappointing childhood – I had never told anyone before then in full, and I realised I loved you when you kissed me." She paused. "James, I must apologise to you, I didn't really think you would come-on to a seventeen year old girl, but I was shocked and really jealous when I assumed you were kissing her. I was scared to apologise because I thought you might realise how I felt about you. The last thing I wanted was for you to realise, and then treat me kindly because you felt sorry for me."

"I forgive you Beth, but your reaction had given me cause for some hope. I was a mess in Carlisle and found it hard to concentrate on the Court Case, I was worried you might have changed your mind after spending the night with me and think that I had taken advantage of you, and you might have gone off to find another flat. I do love you Beth, but after our traumatic childhood, I still worry that something will go wrong."

"I love you too, James, more than I can say, we will just have to see where life takes us. Isn't it time we got ready for work?"

That evening Nat asked James what was going on between him and Bethany, and James told him that he loved her, but that neither of them wanted to make any commitment, and they would see where things took them. For the time being they would not be broadcasting their association.

Bethany had a long conversation with Janette, admitting that she loved James and that he loved her, but that was as far as things would go. Janette immediately left Bethany to find Nat, and they both agreed that they would wait and see!

Nat was waiting for Janette to declare herself, and Janette, after having left once before, was waiting for the same from Nat!

Later that night Nat and James walked around the gardens, presumably for exercise, but they had much to talk about, in fact Bethany had fallen asleep when James finally came into the house! He didn't want to disturb her, but neither did he want to go to *his own* room. She woke as he opened the curtain slightly to look down into the garden, "What are you looking for James," she asked tiredly.

"Nothing my love, just wondering if it would disturb you if I went and got showered then slipped into bed beside you."

"It depends which way you are thinking of the word *disturb*, the answer is no, and yes I hope so!" She answered with a smile.

"Well, I was thinking of a cuddle, and it depends how you interpret that word."

"We'll see if you ever decide to stop looking at the gardens, and come to bed."

Over the next few weeks, James took her out to lunch once from the office, and she wondered if he didn't want anyone there to know of their involvement, and felt quite hurt. However, she had nothing to complain of at home, and in the company of Nat and Janette and Joss and Marianne. Joss and Marianne had decided on a Church wedding, and so they had to wait until the Banns had been called, and the Wedding Day dawned, bright and sunny.

James was to be best man, and Marianne had her niece as a bridesmaid, however, with family and friends they only had about fifty at the wedding.

Bethany could see from the attitude of the Vicar, that he had not performed such a wedding ceremony before, however, he was quite a young man. There were four wheelchairs parked in the isle, and the groom walked as well as he could with just one stick. Marianne wore a traditional white wedding dress which covered the iron on her leg, and she managed to glide down the isle on the arm of her proud father.

Bethany was on the front row of the groom's side of the Church, and was in tears as she watched Joss give his stick to James, and then he stood proudly beside his bride, and did not ask for his stick until the service was over. Not all her tears were for Joss and the beautiful and sublimely happy Marianne. She glanced at James, and sorely regretted that they had both decided not to marry. She knew that they had both reached this conclusion because of James's difficult childhood, and also because of her parent's difficult divorce. If her parents managed to get back together again, would she change her mind, or had she now changed her mind after meeting James? Perhaps, but she didn't want anyone except James, who looked particularly handsome today in his morning suit. He had never mentioned a change of mind and she had no intention of rocking the boat.

The reception at a nearby hotel went off very well, and Bethany was again reduced to tears when both Joss and James made a short speech, and she realised how well they now got on after Joss's turn of heart and lengthy explanation to his older brother, in particular about his own inability to comfort their mother, and his despair as he could only watch James!

The bride and groom only started off the dancing after the reception, and Marianne insisted the James and Bethany should take over, and soon the floor was crowded. Joss was aware that he had done a lot today, and decided to watch and smile with Marianne at his side, until it was time to get the taxi to take them off to the nearest airport. They were to have two weeks in Mara Stephenson's, (now Ashcroft) holiday home in the South of France, which was by the sea, where the terrain was quite flat around the secluded bungalow site.

Four hours later Nat, Janette, James and Bethany were gladly enjoying a quiet evening, and quite early James and Nat went out for a walk around the grounds. Bethany shook her head as she watched from her bedroom window, as far as she could see Nathanial Dixon was moving very well, well enough to be back at school teaching in her opinion. Perhaps Nat and Janette were too comfortable here at Willow Trees. She drew the curtains, and put on the light. Joss and Marianne were to return to Willow Trees to live after their honeymoon, which also seemed rather odd, as Marianne's apartment was quite near to the offices where they both worked. Joss did, however, because of James' fair-mindedness, own his own part of this house. Bethany began to wonder how long they would all be living at Willow Trees, maybe it would become a commune! She hastily stopped her train of thought, what was she thinking, wherever James was, was where she wanted to be, she didn't have to have him all to herself!

Such a family occasion as a wedding should have left her feeling happy, but for some reason her spirits were low. She picked up her mobile 'phone and dialled her father's number, he answered almost at once.

"Bethany, nice to hear from you love, it is weeks since you called on me. Have you heard from your mother recently, if I'm right she should be coming home in four or five days?"

"No dad, I just wanted to know that you are alright, and I'm sorry I haven't been in touch, but I have been busy at

164

work." She had been about to tell him of the break-in at her flat, but decided he might start to worry, and all he seemed to have on his mind was her mother, and obviously he was counting the days until her return! She promised to ring him again in a few days, and folded up her 'phone.

The next morning, it being Sunday, she awoke to find that James had already left the building. He and Nat had decided to take a brisk walk, instead of James going off on a run on his own, which seemed to confirm that Nat's leg was much better as she had already assumed last evening.

She had enjoyed a cup of coffee with Janette, and they had talked for over an hour, now she decided to take a long soak in the bath, putting on time until James returned, as he had promised a trip out in the car to find a nice place to have lunch.

An hour later she didn't know what she felt, there was both disappointment and relief, and she now assumed that she had been suffering from PMT. She checked her calendar and found that it was over six weeks since her flat had been trashed, and she had spent the night with James without any protection, and normally her cycle was quite regular. She cried for a few minutes, not knowing why, and wondered if she should tell James right away, perhaps he had been worrying, and she had been living her life to the full without a care in the world!

When James and Nat returned, it seemed that they also were slightly low in spirits, and Bethany wondered if it was the anti-climax after the wedding. It also seemed rather odd without Joss and Marianne being around.

Bethany suggested that they should ask Nat and Janette to join them for the trip out for lunch in the countryside, and was surprised when Nat said he was feeling a bit tired, and maybe Janette would take him out for a drive later. James agreed, and tucked Bethany into the front seat of the car, and opened the sun roof. They had been driving for a while, when James glanced quickly at Bethany, and suggested that she was rather quiet, was anything bothering her.

"No, I'm fine James, and looking forward to lunch," she replied with a smile, and glanced out of the window. Liar, she didn't feel at all hungry, and she had been wondering why Nat and Janette had not joined them. Should she tell him that everything was alright and she wasn't pregnant, as it should be, as she had taken a morning after pill? If they slept together tonight, then she could tell him without making it something special. Was he only going to sleep with her when he was feeling horny? She stared at the dials on the dashboard and had a brilliant idea.

"James, can you explain all these lights and dials. I think I might like to learn to drive a car, just a small car. Not like your large one, a car of my very own."

At first he looked startled, and then thought about what she had said. "Yes, of course I can, and I would be much happier if you had a car of your own to drive, rather than travelling on the bus." He pulled off the road, and instructed her as she had requested. "Do you still want to drive, Beth?"

"Yes, of course," she replied, and was put into a state of terror, as he drove off the road into a large car park, on the outskirts of a small village, stopped the engine and got out of the car. He opened the passenger door, and indicated that she should get out. "Get out Beth, and into the driving seat, and you can get a feel of everything, without even moving."

"But James I didn't mean now, this minute," she replied quickly.

"There's no time like the present," he said, as he helped her into the driving seat then adjusted the height and position of the seat, and instructed her not to touch anything, until he was in the other seat.

She looked at his splendid car, and shivered. "I said a small car, of my very own," she reminded him.

"I'm only suggesting that you *sit* in the driving seat, and I'll explain everything to you now that we have moved the seat, and you can put your feet on the pedals."

She wished she had told him what was bothering her, rather than starting this stupid idea of driving. Half an hour later she had learned what everything was for, and had pressed all the pedals and thought she could remember which was which! Her mind was humming, and she *almost* wanted to start the engine. She felt on edge, and yet exhilarated, and ten minutes later looked at the menu of the nearest public house, and thought she might enjoy her lunch! At the back of her mind was the thought that what was left of the ten thousand that Ronald Wood had left her would be sufficient to buy her first car.

That evening when she kissed James on their way upstairs, she whispered to him that they would not be able to make love fully. She wondered if he would understand what she was trying to tell him, and he stood quietly for a few seconds.

"I can still hold you, and sleep with you can't I," he said and watched her expressive face, as she smiled warmly back at him. He was a solicitor, a truly intelligent man, and he must know what she was telling him in her round about way. Maybe he was truly in love with her, she hoped so.

CHAPTER SIXTEEN

The return of Bethany's mother to the United Kingdom from her sister's in Australia was a pleasant surprise for Bethany. Her mother called at Willow Trees on her way home from the airport, bringing a selection of T-shirts for Bethany and her friends, together with a cuddly koala bear for her daughter, and a large leather outback hat for James, as a thank you for the advice he had given her on the death of her second husband. Bethany was amazed, and hoped that this signified a closer relationship between her and her parents for the future. However, her mother was full of her holiday, and said how much she liked Australia, and it had given her an appetite for travelling and she was soon to plan another trip, which just might be a cruise, as that would be the easiest way to travel, and yet she would visit many new and exciting countries.

Bethany was really pleased for her mother, but wondered if her father would be disappointed, as his plan to get back with his ex-wife seemed doomed if she was away travelling most of the time.

Over the last couple of weeks Elaine Woodhouse had gradually been handing over the reins of the accountant's office at Ashcroft, Castleton & Woodhouse to Bethany, and Bethany was looking forward to the challenge. Elaine's only worry, was would the granny flat at her son's home be ready in time? Bethany's worry was that James, who was as much out of the office as working in it, had not as yet told anyone in the office of their close relationship. Did he think of it as semi-permanent, or was he worried that it would not even last that long!

He had helped her choose a small silver Rover car in which to learn to drive, and she enjoyed her lessons with an instructor, and James often now sat with her in the evenings and weekends whilst she practised her driving. Bethany was quite pleased with her progress, she seemed to have an aptitude for driving, and she couldn't wait for the time when everything would be more automatic, and she might then stop worrying quite so much.

Joss and Marianne had also returned from their honeymoon, and they both looked tanned and extremely happy. Joss's mobility was getting better every week, and now it was Marianne who congratulated him on his progress with a kiss, and the other inhabitants of Willow Trees, shook his hand enthusiastically. The temporary ramp at the front door, was taken away, but the ramp at the utility room door, remained as this was a permanent feature. Bethany wondered if Marianne, who seemed truly happy, was thinking that it might be useful for some other form of wheeled contraption in the near future! After this thought, Bethany had to try to lift her own spirits, or James would be asking her what was worrying her as he seemed to be tuned in to her every emotion!

The next week James was in Court up to the Thursday, and on the Friday morning he surprised Bethany by offering to accompany her in to work in her car, so that she could get some driving practice. At four thirty in the afternoon he put his head around her office door, acknowledged Elaine, and apologised because he had to work late for another hour or so.

"No problem James, just come and say when you are ready to leave, I have more than enough work to be getting on with," she replied. Bethany glanced up and caught a very thoughtful glance from Elaine. However, Elaine didn't say anything, and Bethany was relieved, shuffling a handful of papers Bethany put down her head to discourage any awkward questions which she was very much aware that Elaine might like to ask!

Elaine left as usual at five o'clock, and it was six forty five before James came to collect Bethany. He took the opportunity of them being alone and kissed her very satisfactorily, and they set off for Willow Trees. The roads were not too busy, and Bethany concentrated on her driving, and was signalling to turn in to the drive at Willow Trees, when she noticed a car coming through the gateway. It was James's car, and she looked askance at James.

"Quickly, Bethany pull in front of him," James said and she did. As soon as her car stopped he sprang out of the car and opening the driving side door of his own car, and she could tell he was instructing the drive to 'get out.' Bethany was in a panic, as she heard a car shudder to a halt behind her, but she couldn't take her eyes away from James, and the man who was obviously trying to make off with his car.

The youth climbed out of the car, and slammed the open door into James, which caused him to lose balance and he fell heavily onto the pavement, hitting his head. James had obviously been stunned, and the youth sprang on top of him with fists flying.

Bethany switched off her motor, and was trying to get out of her car, when she was stopped by a policewoman. Bethany shouted and turned in her seat trying to see what was happening. The policewoman then moved aside, and Bethany got out of the car, in time to see two policemen pulling the youth off James, as they detained him. Bethany rushed to James, only to be pulled back by a policeman.

She stared in dismay as she recognised the young man who had been detained who was now in handcuffs, being held by another policeman. By now Nat and Janette were running down the drive, slowly followed by Joss who was struggling along with his stick to help him.

"Sorry Madam, please stand back, an ambulance is on its way," the policewoman said, but Bethany shrugged away from her and knelt beside James's still frame. She saw blood on the pavement where James must have hit his head, and her heart plummeted, no she couldn't lose him now, her mind screamed at her. She touched the side of his neck and could feel a pulse, and then she was lifted aside by Nat as a paramedic started to attend to James. She struggled, but Nat held her tightly against him. "I must get to James," she said in desperation.

"They will allow you to go in the ambulance with him, but for now stay here and let the paramedic do his work." Nat said calmly, and glanced at Janette who was beside him. "Please can you take care of Bethany, as I think Joss might be in need of a bit of attention as he seems very upset."

Joss had one hand gripping the gatepost, and the other gripping his stick which he was swinging around dangerously. Nat walked up to him, and taking the stick from him he supported him, and just then an unmarked police car shuddered to a stop, followed by the ambulance. A man in plain clothes got out of the unmarked police car, and spoke with a couple of the officers. He walked over to Bethany, and indicated the handcuffed youth.

"Do you know this man, Miss?" he asked quickly.

Bethany turned, and stared at the youth, and was horrified as she stared into the hate filled eyes, and she felt quite weak – was he still stalking her? "Yes, he is the man who stalked me, and threw me to the ground. If you ask the man over there, Joss Castleton, I think he might remember another occasion when we met. If you don't mind, officer, I am going in the ambulance with the other Mr Castleton." Mr Castleton, James, she had known for months that she was in love with him, but today had made her realise just how much! She drew in a deep breath, and handed her car keys to Janette, moving to try to coax the tense muscles in her body to loosen, and took a couple of reviving breaths. "Can you park my car please Janette, I must go with James."

"You go in the ambulance Bethany, and don't worry Joss, Nat and I will be following shortly." Janette said, as she kissed Bethany's pale cheek.

"Which ever of you two young ladies is Bethany, can you please get into the ambulance, we must be going, and our patient is asking for Bethany."

Bethany climbed into the ambulance, and the doors were closed behind her. She moved towards James with her heart in her mouth, and grasped his hand and kissed his forehead. "I'm here James," she said on a sob.

He seemed to quieten then, and the ambulance man nodded with satisfaction, glancing at Bethany's pale face.

"We didn't want to sedate him until he has been checked over at the hospital, talk to him quietly for a few minutes, and we'll be there."

Two hours later, James was in a single side ward, and Bethany was feeling slightly better, as now James looked much better and with the aid of sedation he was now sleeping. They intended keeping him in the hospital for at least twenty four hours, maybe longer. The ward door opened, and a haggard looking Joss appeared with an enquiring glance at Bethany.

"Come and sit here Joss," she vacated the chair next to James, and helped Joss settle himself down.

"How is he Bethany, the sister was a bit noncommittal when I enquired half an hour ago."

"I think he will be fine, he is sleeping off the sedation they gave him. His X-rays seem alright, but we can't be sure until he wakens up again. Then, of course the police will want to interview him."

"Good, I'll sit with him for a while. Janette and Nat are out there with Marianne, they wouldn't let everybody in to see him. Janette has brought you a sandwich, and there is a drinks machine. Tomorrow we will get to the bottom of what happened, it is all rather strange don't you think so Bethany?" Joss said angrily, and he could see from her face that she was at a loss to understand it all. "Never mind for now, the main thing is that James is improving." He finished, for the first time realising the full meaning of what James and Bethany meant to each other.

Bethany was glad to see their friends in the waiting room, and even managed to eat most of the sandwich that

173

Janette had provided. They waited for Joss, who was angry with himself that he couldn't do more to help James, and Bethany had decided she was going to stay with James. Bethany looked towards Nat and Janette who looked rather uncomfortable as Nat knew that she was about to start asking him awkward questions.

"We will all be getting back to Willow Trees now, Bethany. Marianne will look after Joss, and tomorrow or when James gets home, we can thrash out any worries that you are now feeling." Nat said, and looked at her meaningfully.

She didn't know what all this was about, but she had learned to trust Nat over the years, and besides the main thing troubling her was James, and she was going to stay with him here at the hospital, whatever the sister had to say!

That night Bethany slept in the chair in James's room, and in the morning when she awoke she found that someone had put a pillow behind her head, and had covered her with a blanket, she felt grateful for their thoughtfulness, and looked at James in the bed taking his hand in hers.

"Are you alright Bethany, are you hurt," James asked from the bed beside her.

"Of course not James, you were the one who was hurt, how are you feeling."

"Much better for seeing you my lovely Beth. Could you get me a drink of water please, and then kiss me?" She did both, she poured him some water and helped by lifting the glass to his lips, and then she kissed those lips – how could she not when he had called her 'my Beth.' James then appeared to relax, and then as things seemed to come back to him, he started saying how stupid he had been, to allow that youth to hit him with the car door, how could he protect her if he was so stupid, and couldn't protect himself!

Just then the doctor arrived to check on James, and the sister asked Bethany to leave, and she reluctantly went into the waiting room where the sister said she would come for her after the doctor's rounds.

Over an hour later spent reading magazines some of which were years old, she went to the sister's office. The sister looked up, and seeing Bethany, said she could now go in to see Mr Castleton, if the police had left after interviewing him.

She went to the ward door, tapped and listened. She couldn't hear any voices, and pushed her way in.

"Are you alright James, sister said the police had been to see you."

"I'm fine Beth, don't worry. If I manage to take a shower on my own, without getting the head dressing wet, the doctor says I can go home by taxi later in the day."

"Wonderful, you will be careful won't you James, I'd like nothing better than to arrange a taxi home for us."

Bethany rang Joss and gave him the good news, and as it was Saturday he was able to tell the others who had all stayed around the house, waiting for news.

James had the dressing on the wound on his head redone, and had to wait for some pills to be dispensed, and then they were on their way home. Willow Trees looked wonderful, and after a brief odd feeling coming in through the drive, Bethany felt wonderful. James was now tiring, and after being greeted by Nat, Janette, Joss and Marianne, he insisted on getting his clothes changed, checking that their briefcases had been removed from Bethany's car, before he was able to meet the others around the kitchen table, for explanations!

Bethany had been expecting to hear any explanations by herself, and was just a little bit miffed, but perhaps they were all involved! However, she would have preferred James to wait until Sunday, as he had not had time to recover from his ordeal!

They all sat around the table where they could see James, and he accepted a cup of tea from Janette, who then sat down.

"It's almost as bad as being in Court, you are all looking at me expecting something special, and I think I might disappoint you all, or at least most of you." He breathed in and smiled, presumably to put their minds at rest.

"When Beth told me in the car, when I took her to the hospital after damaging her eye on a box a few months ago, about what the youth who had been harassing Joss in his wheelchair had said, I put two and two together but hoped I was not right in my assumptions. However, when I saw her as I thought 'being mugged,' she behaved very bravely, and I unfortunately let the youth go, I began to think I was right to be worried. I told the police what I was thinking, and they had been thinking on the same lines. When Nat suffered a broken leg, it was obvious who had done that from the CCTV footage at the school playing field. The police then checked the CCTV Cameras in the street where Bethany was accosted, but nothing was very clear.

After Nat's accident, it seemed that the best way forward was to have Joss, Nat and Bethany all in one place. It was easier for the police to keep a watch on the area, and I know that Bethany has been under the impression for quite a while that Nat was well enough to move back into his flat. As nothing was happening she, unfortunately, because we had yet another disagreement, decided to go out on her own and

176

rented a flat. Her flat was trashed, and yet again CCTV footage, placed the same youth in that Street at the right time. I was relieved to be able to tell the police that she would again be living at Willow Trees, and hopefully, she would be safe here." He paused and glanced at Bethany. "I will have some further explanations for you alone Bethany, I can tell you are going to interrupt me, but please be patient."

Bethany felt embarrassment suffuse her face, she had been about to ask him if that was the only reason they had made love, to keep her in Willow Trees where it was easier for the police to keep watch on the area!

"The police have been patrolling this area, slightly more than they would have under normal circumstances, and it is just as well, or I could stupidly have let that youth get away once again." James paused and glanced at Bethany first, and saw her heightened colour, and then at Nat, and seemed happy with the expression on Nat's face.

"When I realised that Nat and Bethany were not an item, I shared my beliefs with him so that he would also be able to help me keep an eye on both Joss and Bethany. When he had his 'accident' then it was time for us all to move in here. Nat is quite well again you will be pleased to know, and he and Janette will be moving out whenever they want, although I have made it plain that they are very welcome if they decide to stay here. Janette was happy to spend time with Bethany, like going shopping with her after her flat had been trashed, without even receiving a full explanation from Nat, so don't start to interrupt me yet, please Bethany."

"As if I would dare, you seem to be able to read my mind," she said angrily, then subsided as he gave her a small smile.

"Now, the reason for all this happening, I believe, is because a Mr S Bartholomew, after five years, is being released from prison today, and that is why the police were on hand yesterday. Five years ago I was the Crown Prosecutor, and Mr S Bartholomew's family have always believed he was innocent. The young man who was intent on taking away my car yesterday, is his nephew, and he has very mistakenly, been carrying on a crusade on his uncle's behalf…"

"Uncle Silas," Bethany stated in surprise.

"Yes Bethany, the young man is the nephew of 'Uncle Silas.' Because of the behaviour of his sister's only son, and because he doesn't want his nephew to continue on the wrong side of the law, 'Uncle Silas' has given a *full confession* to the crime he committed over five years ago. The police are considering trying to get that young man into a special youth initiative, which Joss and Marianne will be aware of, and which I will explain to both Bethany and Nat." James said, and everyone in the room started talking at once, and after a few minutes James shook his head. Joss and Marianne were trying to explain to Nat, Janette and Bethany all about the youth initiative that James had mentioned, maybe it would be a good thing for the youth, but he really should be punished for what he had done!

James did not say a word, but held up his hand, and gradually everyone was silent, and looked towards him waiting.

"I want to apologise to you all, because in that youth's eyes, *I* was to blame for putting his Uncle Silas in prison, and he truly believed his uncle was not guilty. He also wanted to hurt me, through a member of my family, and that was why he started on Joss. Unfortunately, or fortunately, however you look at it, both Bethany and Nat became involved and I guess he picked up on the fact that there was something between myself and Bethany and he thought she was the easier target. Although *I* wouldn't say that, you should have seen her try to throw him, and there was no way that she wasn't going to help Joss that very first day. Luckily for the *youths*, Nat turned up just in time." James said, and everyone around the table found relief in laughter at Bethany's expense. "Thank you Nat for all you have done." James said and shook Nat's hand. Bethany stared at James, and loved him.

"Now I have one or two explanations to make to Beth in private if you don't mind," James said seriously, and he took Bethany's hand and pulled her towards the door. He didn't have to pull very hard she was going anyway!

In the hallway Bethany stopped and looked James in the eye. They were not rolling and looked quite normal. In fact they promised all sorts of things! "Are you sure you are well enough James," Bethany asked worriedly. "You have been through an awful lot that none of us realised?"

"Beth, please stop worrying. All I want to do is explain to you why I haven't been able to commit myself to you. I couldn't broadcast the fact that I loved you, until I knew *that* young troublemaker was out of the way, even in the office of Ashcroft, Castleton & Edmondson. Had I declared myself you would have been in much greater danger my love." He sighed deeply, "Do you think we could just get upstairs to one of our bedrooms?"

She walked sedately up the stairs beside him, trying not to skip, and worrying about his head wound.

He sat her down on her bed, and then moved close beside her. He took her hand and turned the palm up towards him to receive his kiss. She held her breath as a shiver of anticipation ran down her spine, God, how she loved this man.

"Will you marry me Beth as soon as possible, as I have wanted to ask you since we made love for the very first time? I have been terrified that you would think I was still against marriage, but that belief went out of the window since our first meeting, but I was forced to keep that to myself." His grey eyes looked into hers and she was happy beyond measure.

"I will marry you James, I love you more than I believed possible, and since Joss and Marianne's wedding I have been hoping you might change your mind."

"You are not going to do any somersaults or anything are you Beth? Because my head is starting to hurt, and I don't want anything to be less than wonderful, just because I've had two aspirins." James said with a blissful smile, remembering all too vividly the second night they had spent together, when he had proved to her that he *had* a sense of humour!

She did a backward role from her sitting position, and landed upside down on the bed, but he soon put that right, and joined her. Every single thing was much more than wonderfully right between them, even without the help of aspirins or a wig and gown!

James and Bethany married six months later, and Bethany was given away by her father, and as her mother was in the same country she helped to make all the arrangements and seemed to enjoy doing this very much. Bethany was hopeful of her parents getting together in the near future. Joss, who was now able to walk comfortably with just one stick, and a glowing with health Marianne, announced at the wedding breakfast that the ramp at Willow Trees would again get a lot of use, but there would be either three or four quite small wheels in action. As this was announced Nat smiled and took the hand of Janette, and a solitaire diamond sparkled on the third finger of her left hand.

AN OUNCE OF DISCRETION

CHAPTER ONE

Emma swung the garden gate shut behind her, and redistributed the weight of her shopping bag and the books in her arms. She hurried to the front door of Laurel Cottage to be met by the expected blissful whining of the black dog. He knew the sound of the Rover that she drove, as he also knew the sound of her dad's vehicle. She hardly had the door open when he squeezed out and knocked the pile of books to the floor with his ecstatic welcome. As she picked up the books from the step the dog did a quick lap around the lawn, bending the leaves of the clumps of early daffodils, and grabbing a stick to fetch to her - the tail seeming to wag the dog rather than the other way around!

"Good boy Jason. Jimmy not home yet?" To ask Jason a question was not as odd as it might appear, as he dropped his tail, and looked steadily down the road, thereby giving a perfectly clear answer. Emma held the door open with her elbow, to enable Jason to follow her inside.

The dappled afternoon sun, through the new leaves of the cherry tree outside the kitchen window, highlighted

Emma's pale gold hair as she deposited the books and shopping bag onto the table. She quickly put away the groceries and as she checked the time, saw that the time switch on the cooker was lit up. At least they would eat on time tonight she thought with satisfaction.

She was almost twenty, and taking a computer course at the local college, as well as taking care of the housekeeping and her father and brother. Her father, Robert Smyth, was a partner in a local firm of accountants, and had been looking a bit weary of late. However, he never complained, and Emma was very much aware that he still missed his wife, and mother of his children, although it was over two years since she had succumbed to cancer, after a long and brave fight. Emma spent as much time as she could with her father, but quite often he would encourage her to go out with her friends, rather than spend most of her time at home. Emma was sure this was unselfish on his part, as he wanted her to enjoy herself as much as possible in the short time she could spare from her studies. She had managed to put behind her the disappointment that she was unable to take up the offer of the degree course at this time, and from the university she had chosen. Maybe in the future that would be an option, and she would not feel any guilt at leaving her brother and dad to cope without her.

Jimmy, her seventeen year old brother, was busy studying also, for his 'A' levels, and was going through a very grumpy stage, when he wasn't silent (as in not speaking altogether)! If not studying, he was not silent, but practising on his drum kit (bought for him by his father shortly after the death of his mother) one assumed to give him something else on which to focus. The drum set, being bulky to move about, meant that usually his friends arrived

184

at Laurel Cottage most weekends together with musical instruments and sound equipment, convincing themselves that they would soon be in the money! Emma had her doubts about this, but was pleased that Jimmy had friends and interests to occupy him. Provided that she left them a pile of sandwiches and drinks, she needn't worry about Jimmy and his friends. Mrs Robinson usually came in for two hours, three days during the week, so that after the family wash whilst her father was playing golf on Saturdays, Emma had Sunday free to catch up with any small chores, and do any necessary studying.

Returning to the kitchen she prepared the vegetables, and went to have a shower. She was quite pleased with her reflection in the long mirror in the bathroom. Her slender young body was nicely rounded in all the right places, and the shoulder length pale hair had a very satisfactory sheen. She looked with some surprise into the mirror, after wiping away the haze. Yes, her eyes were probably her best feature. Her interest in her appearance was caused by the rather flattering remarks of Simon Park, her current boyfriend. Emma was not besotted with Simon, but he was good company and provided he didn't try to fondle and kiss her too much, she thought they had a very satisfactory relationship. She felt a moment of doubt, should she be going out with Simon? He didn't have the effect on her that she had read about in books, but then neither had any of her previous boyfriends. If she didn't go out with them, how could she possibly learn about them? The only boys she thought she understood were her brother Jimmy (that had taken seventeen years to learn), and Tom his best friend, who had a big crush on her at the moment. The crush, although flattering, was becoming rather wearing, and she hoped it wouldn't last too long!

She slipped into her clean underwear, and glanced at her watch as she replaced it on her wrist, it was a plain and serviceable watch, not pink and sparkly like that of her best friend Charlotte - was she going wrong somewhere? Simon was calling for her at seven, and they intended to visit the cinema. She went into her bedroom and lay on the bed for a moment or two, putting her arm across her eyes to shield them from the sun shining through the window. Suddenly the bed gave slightly, and Jason crept quietly beside her, licking her hand. She stroked him, and after a few minutes slid off the bed, reaching for her jeans, and T-shirt.

"Alright Jason, just a quick walk before we eat," she said as she quickly dressed, and then chased him downstairs to retrieve the sandal he had picked up. At the bottom of the stairs she cannoned into a hard, tall body and was steadied by two strong arms.

"Hello Joe, what can we do for you," she smiled and disentangled herself from his arms, his broad shoulders and slim torso inside his charcoal grey suit made him look very tall, and his healthy outdoor tan was shown to perfection by the white of his shirt - but this was Joe from next door, friendly, and so familiar.

Joe patted Jason, telling him to sit as he was excitedly jumping up and licking his hand. Jason sat, yet still looked hopefully towards Emma. Joe also looked at her closely, and then shrugged his shoulders, and moved off towards the lounge. Emma and a subdued Jason followed him. Joe stood in front of the patio doors, staring into the garden, his tall frame blocking out a considerable amount of sunlight, which viewed from behind made him appear introspective

186

and sombre. Damn, she knew better than to try to hurry Joe if he wanted to say something. She had known him for years, but the eight years difference between them seemed like many more to Emma. He was, undoubtedly, very attractive to women, judging by the number of girlfriends he seemed to squire around. She moved her weight from one foot to the other impatiently. "Joe?" she said impatiently, and he turned towards her.

"Your father will be a bit late home tonight, he asked me to let you know," he answered, looking with interest at her freshly scrubbed face and flowing hair.

"Oh, late again, why is it that you are never late home?" Emma said, annoyed because she wanted to be ready when Simon came to pick her up.

"Believe it or not, I am often late home. I'm on time today because I have finished the case I had to do today, and your father insisted that he wished to finish the case he was working on himself, and would not let me help. Why I'm bothering to explain to you I can't imagine," Joe finished abruptly.

He turned away and gazed out into the garden once more, his hands in the pockets of his dark suit trousers. He had dropped his jacket onto a chair, but still looked immaculate. His hair was dark, with a slight kink, and at the moment was tidily brushed. Emma preferred it at the weekends when it was attractively unruly when he returned from golfing or climbing. Joe was her father's business partner and lived next door in a similar house, which he had named Pillar Rock. Much too big for a single man in Emma's opinion but, no doubt, Joe would be married or co-habiting before too long, he was certainly a good catch, a thought that was rather depressing. She didn't fancy any more changes, everything seemed to be getting bearable after a long time of grieving. The penetrating dark lashed grey eyes turned to Emma, and he studied her impatient face, and then sighed.

"Are *you* going out again?" he asked abruptly.

Emma bristled, she didn't like his tone of voice, who was he to ask whether or not she was going out? It was none of his business! She moved into the kitchen and put the vegetables on to cook, then returned to speak to Joe.

"Simon is picking me up at seven, what has it got to do with you?" she replied impatiently, deciding not to apologise for sounding rude.

"I just thought that as your father would be tired from a long day at work you would be here to get his meal."

"His meal is almost ready, and it won't spoil even if he is late. Anyway, I don't care for you telling me what to do. Dad and Jimmy are well looked after. What do you suppose I have been doing all day Joe, sitting in the garden sunbathing? I have been to college, done the shopping, prepared a meal, and now I'm taking Jason out for his second walk, and later I shall go out with Simon. That is if you have finished interfering in our lives." She pushed back a handful of hair from her face, and glared at him, and then wondered if perhaps she was acting childishly, and schooled her features.

"Your father still misses your mother, and I would have thought *you* could at least spare a little time to spend with him." His tone of voice was both resigned, and showed his disappointment in her.

"We all miss her," Emma replied. So that he wouldn't see the tears that filled her eyes, she walked into the hall, grabbed Jason's lead from a peg and banged the door behind her and Jason. She brushed the tears from her eyes as she walked along the road, jumped over the stile, and set off through the woods, her feet rustling the dry leaves as she walked, with Jason covering twice as much ground as they progressed. Jason was scratching in the undergrowth, and Emma lifted her eyes to the central Lakeland fells across the large expanse of water which was Windermere Lake, reflecting the blue of the sky and the blue hazy mountains. Around the shoreline bright dappled spring sunshine shone with a glint of silver.

Until recently Joe had been a good friend to have around. He often played chess with her father in the evenings, and had always been good company. Now it seemed he disapproved of her, and thought she was out too much, and not looking after her father and Jimmy! She did all that she could, and quite often it was quite late when she managed to get to bed. She couldn't do any more, what did he expect? As she and Jason were quite alone in the woods, tears ran down her cheeks unchecked. She realised she was the one that had stormed out of her home, and left Joe in sole charge. Oh well, he would either lock up the house and hope she had a key, or wait until she returned.

She had always assumed that Joe liked her, and it was very hurtful to learn that he disapproved of her. Had her father complained to him? Surely not, he never complained and was always encouraging her to go out with her friends. She had always got on well with Joe, why had he suddenly turned against her? He had been a very good friend to them all, particularly since her mother had died. Emma decided she must be overtired, why else should she feel so let down and hurt by Joe's observations. It really hurt - the thought that she might be inadequate. God, she must be feeling sorry for herself, to hell with Joe, he could think what he liked!

Emma suddenly stopped, how could she be so stupid? She looked around for Jason, and she turned and set off home at a run, the tears stopped as she ran, and she was becoming breathless.

"Come on Jason, quickly," she called into the trees. How could she have forgotten the vegetables, they might have boiled dry by now, and would certainly be tasteless? She vaulted over the stile, and knocked into Joe for the second time that day. He held her steady with his hands grasping her forearms, and looked at the tear stained cheeks, an apologetic look on his face.

"Don't panic, I switched off the cooker," he gave her a rueful smile. "I'm sorry if I upset you Emma, but..."

"You didn't," she interrupted, "you just got me thinking of Mum." She shrugged away from him and continued on her way home. It was only a white lie, she had been thinking of her mother, and well as dealing with an ache which had arisen since Joe's disapproval had been made known to her! She was pathetic and getting too self absorbed. Together they turned and retraced their steps towards Laurel Cottage, and Emma murmured, "Thanks Joe." He shrugged his ample shoulders and walked through the gate towards Pillar Rock, his own house.

Later, Emma and Jimmy had almost finished their meal when she told him about Joe, and what he had said.

"Joe's OK. Maybe you *should* stay in more," he said never taking his eyes from the TV schedules he was studying. Emma kicked the long jean glad leg under the table, and pulled the paper out of his hands.

"Cheek, I'm in more than you are," she almost shouted.

"I'm always in at weekends, except when I go walking or climbing with Joe," Jimmy also raised his voice.

"Dad is out at weekends anyway, probably to get away from your noise," Emma said returning to her seat. "Whatever Joe says is always right with you," she accused.

"Well he usually is right."

"Maybe he is, and it's damned annoying," she replied.

"What's going on here," Robert Smyth's voice came from the doorway.

"Hello Dad. Emma's had a disagreement with Joe, that's all," Jimmy informed his dad, returning to his reading.

"Oh, I see." It was plain to Emma that he didn't see at all, and he too was assuming that Joe must be in the right! "I'll just have a quick wash, and be with you in a minute Emma."

Emma quietly fumed inside, someone else who thought the sun shone out of Joe. She watched her dad leave his briefcase in the hallway, before moving wearily up the stairs - perhaps Dad *was* feeling overtired, and the grey at his temples seemed to be more prominent than she remembered. Just for the moment she was feeling outnumbered by arrogant males!

By the time she had reheated her dad's plated meal in the microwave, he was sitting at the dining table reading his newspaper. He put down the paper, and smiled his thanks. "Thank you Emma, that looks really appetizing."

Emma looked at him carefully, the vegetables were slightly overdone, and his meal had been reheated which didn't help, however, she could not detect anything in his voice to show that he had meant anything but what he had said. She kissed him on his only slightly receding hairline, and made her way to the garden at the rear of the house. She intended to ring Simon on her mobile to say she couldn't meet him, as maybe she *should* stay in tonight with her dad. The best signal was received in the back garden, and she dialled and was waiting by the fence, when she heard a very familiar voice in the next door garden, answering the distinctive ring on his mobile phone.

"Hello, Mary, what can I do for you?" There was a short silence. "In about an hour I'll see you then."

Emma met Joe's thoughtful grey eyes above the fence, and turned abruptly away as Simon answered her call.

"Just checking our arrangement was for seven," she said briskly. "See you later." She clicked shut the 'phone, and glanced across the fence, to again meet Joe's speculative eyes.

"A bit brusque with the boyfriend," he stated. "Is your dad home yet?"

"Yes, he's just finishing his meal. Go in and see him if you want."

"I may just do that," he replied with a grimace at her scowling face, "You could get frown lines between your eyebrows if you don't lighten up Emma."

Emma glared back at him, disliking the twinkle in his wicked eyes, because he had no right to look at her like that when she was annoyed with him! She swung her hair as she turned away disdainfully, and made her way to the house, feeling his eyes following her. She nearly tripped over Jason as he pushed his way out through the doorway into the garden with great enthusiasm, and she heard Joe's chuckle at her misfortune. He could be most aggravating at times! She filled the dishwasher with the dinner dishes successfully, although her mind was on other things. The niggling guilt at changing her mind, and deciding not to stay in with her dad was worrying her. Also, who was Mary, Joe's latest girlfriend? His voice had been both familiar and indulgent as he had agreed to meet her!

Emma walked through the hallway, and could hear Jimmy playing music in his room, and continued to the lounge. Robert Smyth was sitting in his armchair, with the evening news on the television, and his telegraph crumpled up on his chest which was rising and falling at regular intervals as he slept. She had been about to inform him that she was going to get changed before meeting Simon, but instead went back to the telephone table in the hallway, and wrote a note to that effect. She had been toying with the idea of asking Simon in to meet her dad, but was quite relieved to find that this was not the ideal time. Simon had informed her on their last date that he had failed his first year at university, and maybe the time to meet her dad would be when he had come to a decision about whether he was going back in the autumn to either take his first year in Mechanical Engineering again, or whether he might change his Course to something more interesting! For the last six months he had been doing odd jobs around the town, and Emma thought he was possibly enjoying himself just a little too much! He always seemed to have a little money to keep him going, and also time to enjoy himself.

When she had changed into smart jeans, a skimpy top, and carrying a matching jacket she waited in the hallway. She wanted to slip out to meet Simon before he rang the doorbell and disturbed her dad. Although she had not heard Simon's car, she heard footsteps coming to the door, and quickly swung the door open.

"Oh, I wasn't expecting you," she stared at Joe.

"Sorry to disappoint you Emma, but I said I would pop in to see your dad," he replied with a wry smile. His hair was damp from a recent shower, and he looked very good in his casual clothes. No doubt, to impress Mary later in the evening, she thought waspishly.

"I was waiting to catch Simon before he rang the doorbell. Dad has fallen asleep reading his paper. Is it important, do you still want to come inside?"

He thought for a moment. "No I guess it can wait until tomorrow, or I'll call back later if I see your dad around." The grey eyes scrutinised her closely, taking in her lightly made-up face, and the blue eyes sparkling with annoyance, and her youthful figure and fashionable clothing.

"Well?" She demanded, and only just stopped herself from putting her arms akimbo, or stamping her foot!

"Well, yes you look very well, but it may be quite cold later, perhaps you should wear something a bit warmer."

"Of all the cheek, you sound just like my dad," she hissed back.

Joe looked quite annoyed by her reply, and would have answered but Robert Smyth walked from the lounge into the hallway.

"Ah Joe, did you want to see me," he asked pleasantly.

"Yes, it will only take a minute or two of your time," Joe replied, and started to follow Robert into the lounge. "I'm meeting someone at seven."

Robert glanced at his daughter and her flushed cheeks.

"It looks as though Emma too is meeting someone," he said with a smile.

"Yes Dad, I am. I left a note for you on the coffee table by your chair."

Joe's glance was disapproving as though he was thinking that she could at least tell her father she was going out, not just leave a note! His expression changed somewhat at Robert's next remark.

"Are you sure you will be warm enough Emma, your top looks a bit skimpy."

Emma chuckled, and caught Joe's rueful grin. She heard Simon draw up in his car with music blaring, as she collected her small bag. Did she really want to go out tonight she wondered, as Simon made no effort to come and meet her, but just revved the car engine which was probably keeping half the young children in the area wide awake? She sighed and closed the door firmly behind her, and then hurried towards the car.

CHAPTER TWO

Simon drove off, too fast as usual, giving a cheeky grin as Emma switched the music down a few decibels. "Do you have to have it so loud?" She demanded, and saw his young face cloud at her disapproval.

"Lighten up Emma please. You'd think you were thirty-nine not nineteen and ten months. I couldn't find a decent film to see. What do you say, should we meet the gang at the Red Lion for a drink it might cheer you up a bit?" He smiled beguilingly. As usual he was anticipating getting his own way. He purposefully swung his unkempt long blond hair - the diamond in his left ear flashing in the diminishing sunlight as he glanced at her with his eyes sparking in anticipation of her agreement. She began to wonder if he was right, was she becoming a prude and a bore, she had already been told to stop frowning once today! Maybe she was taking herself too seriously. Because circumstances had caused her to act more than her actual age, it didn't mean that she had to change.

"I've only brought ten pounds with me, as I thought that was enough for a night at the cinema, even if we finished the night off with an odd drink." They were both usually strapped for cash, particularly Simon, and they usually went 'Dutch,' which on their first date had been Emma's suggestion, a suggestion which had been applauded by Simon with a very relieved sigh of relief. Any cash he managed to hold onto for more than the odd day, usually went into his old car in the form of fuel.

"Great, don't worry, I worked today and managed to get thirty quid cash in hand, for weeding a flower bed and cutting two lawns. I would have settled for twenty, but asked for thirty, and got it." He smiled, looking really pleased with himself.

Emma wondered if he would be getting any more work from this source in the future, and didn't he ever think of saving a pound or two! Apparently his parents now dealt with the licensing of his car, since learning that he had been driving without a licence for three months – they also dealt with the insurance because it was cheaper to have it in his dad's name. Apart from that he seemed to do whatever he wanted, even with regard to his education. He had never taken Emma home to meet his parents, and she was quite pleased about this, to meet them would indicate that they were sharing more than just a friendship. She was relieved that she had not invited Simon in to meet her dad tonight, the thought that she should had been her dad's idea, and she couldn't really blame him for wanting to know the boy she was, apparently, dating.

Simon swerved into the Red Lion car park, stopped for a second, and slammed it into reverse, and parked with a flourish coming to an abrupt halt. Emma released her hands from gripping the seat of the car and the door, and decided that it might be better if *she* drove in future, even if it dented Simon's substantial ego. Her dad had kept her mother's small Rover and Emma now had the use of it – this was also the vehicle in which Jimmy was now learning to drive.

The Red Lion was a popular venue, and upon entering, they were waved over to join a group at the large table in the bay window, by one of Simon's friends. The pub was a mixture of the old and the new, around the original long bar everything was old tankards and comfortable chairs and tables, but now the pool and snooker table area of the bar had been modernised with bright colours and without seats except for tall stools, which were anything but comfortable. Emma was relieved to see Charlotte Fleming, a friend from her schooldays. Charlotte and Emma were good friends, having walked to school every day together, but Emma had been too busy just lately to keep up regular contact with her friend.

"Great to see you Emma, I was feeling a bit conspicuous thinking I might be the only girl here," Charlotte said with a laugh, as she made way on the bench seat for Emma. The bench seat followed the curve of the large bay window, and the oval table had stretchers underneath where it was possible to play footsy with the person opposite.

Emma did not believe Charlotte's declaration that she was feeling conspicuous as the only girl here. Charlotte was a pretty and lively girl, with dark shining hair cut very short. She was a little cheeky and flirtatious, but managed to get away with it, as she had two older brothers who kept a wary eye on her, and she was never at a loss in either male or female company. If anything she was a bit too friendly, but usually had one or other of her siblings around, should she need their support. She was dressed almost identically to Emma, but the message on her top, almost drew a derogatory remark from Emma. She decided to ignore it, she hadn't seen Charlotte for a few weeks, and she was relieved to have her company, and maybe she *should* 'lighten up' as Simon had suggested. Simon seemed to be pleased that Emma had someone to talk to, as he only came to the table three times with a drink for her. Charlotte chatted happily just as she had when they were at school nearly five years ago, but Emma decided she must be the one to have changed, she found the conversation light but uninteresting, and realised the responsibilities she had taken on after the death of her mother, had changed her into someone older than her years! Whenever she looked his way, Simon seemed to be in deep conversation with one of the boys, or indicating that he was slipping outside to the tented area for a smoke!

A couple of hours later Emma was ready to go home, but couldn't catch Simon's eye. Emma and Charlotte had chatted most of the evening, and the boys had got louder and louder, and Simon indicated that the forty pounds they had between them had gone, and Emma wondered how they had managed to spend it all, she had only had two lagers and one orange juice! She indicated back that she was ready to go home, and he nodded, but didn't seem at all downcast.

When they reached the car park, Simon went towards the car, but Emma insisted that they should walk, because if she had only had two lagers then he must have had considerably more! He ignored her, and she decided she would walk anyway. She was almost home when he stopped beside her, holding up the traffic, and giving two loud blasts on the horn to get her attention. She decided she had better get in or he would cause a scene, and awaken the whole neighbourhood! He had already honked twice, and she felt embarrassed and got in as quickly as she could, but he only smiled at her stern disapproving expression.

He didn't speak, and in a couple of minutes he was drawing up outside her home, when the car slipped forward and bumped the car in front. Joe's BMW! Emma closed her eyes for a moment in shock, and a deep anger with Simon, she couldn't speak to him, as she felt like screaming at him. By the time that Simon and Emma vacated the car and walked to see what damage had been done, Joe was beside them. He was an imposing figure, with keen interrogating eyes as he sized up Simon.

"What an idiot, and a drunken idiot, and that's not all judging by the dazed look in your eyes." Joe said in a cold, uncompromising voice. "Not only are you driving under the influence of drink and most likely drugs, but you had the recklessness to drive whilst carrying Emma as your passenger. Are you completely devoid of any sense whatsoever?" The tone of his voice made Emma squirm, and Simon blink his eyes a couple of times, probably to bring things into focus.

Simon looked at both cars and visibly winced. He had hit the BMW but the tow bar had protected it from all but a few scratches, however, the front of Simon's car was smashed, and there was water dripping onto the tarmac.

"I will deal with my own car, and if I see you driving and drinking again *I will call the police*. Emma has enough to be dealing with at the moment without having to give statements to the police. However, if you try to move the car before you are sober, they will be here within minutes you can be sure of that." Joe said angrily, and he seemed to pull himself together visibly, but Emma knew that he would not take Simon to task physically, however much he might want to!

A look of relief moved across Simon's face. "I'm very sorry, I don't know what happened," he said worriedly, as he pushed back his long blond hair with an agitated movement.

"That's the whole trouble, and when Emma's father hears of this he will not want you bothering his daughter again. Give me the keys to your car, because I can't trust you not to try to drive it again tonight." Joe said angrily, and held out his hand, and when the keys were safely in his hand he indicated that Simon should leave. Simon did, after giving a shamefaced look at Emma, as he set off at a quick pace along the road without a backward glance, his unsteady gait proving the state that he was in.

Emma moved towards Joe, "Joc I'm sorry..."

Before she could finish Joe interrupted her and said in a tired voice, "Get in the house Emma, before all the neighbours come out to see what's happening." He looked at her closely, and she got the feeling that she had let Joe and her father down very badly. "I can't understand why you let him drive you home, or why you seem to have missed the drunken and drugged state he was in. Go into the house now, before I say something I might regret later." Joe said angrily, and felt devastated as he saw her eyes fill with tears before she slowly turned and walked up the drive, and he could hear her fumbling, and a smothered sob, as she tried to get the key in the lock. He felt a little relief as he realised that she was definitely sober, and the fumbling was because she was so upset. However, he wasn't sure if he or Simon was the cause. He watched as her silhouette in the lighted hallway moved into the living room to let her dad know that she was home - then return to the hallway, and a few seconds later the light came on in her bedroom. He sighed deeply and moved towards Simon's car, with the keys in his hand.

Emma quickly undressed and went into the shower-room in her dressing gown, she could have a little cry under the shower and nobody would be the wiser.

Later she lay on her bed in her pyjamas staring up at the ceiling. Simon was an absolute idiot, to spend so much money he must have had some sort of drug, and she couldn't be bothered with his stupid ways. If she finished with him, Joe would say 'I told you so,' and she really didn't want that. However, if her dad thought she was with someone like that he would be very disappointed in her, and though Joe had made perfectly clear his estimation of Simon, that was really none of his business, and she couldn't bear to let him have the last word! Maybe Simon would just keep away in future, and save her the bother of deciding either way.

She moved off the bed and peeped through the curtains, wondering why the BMW had been parked on the roadside. Ah, there was a car in Joe's drive, probably his girlfriend Mary! No wonder he had been so annoyed at being disturbed.

Next morning Emma was on her way to the bathroom after a bad night, when she looked out of the front of the house to see Joe shaking hands with a smartly dressed gentleman who took some keys from Joe and, thereafter, drove away Simon's car from Joe's driveway, where Joe must have parked it overnight! Even Emma had to admit that was good of Joe considering the circumstances, particularly as his formerly pristine BMW had been slightly damaged in the incident!

Emma turned towards the bathroom, and stamped her foot in disappointment, Jimmy had managed to get there first. She stopped in front of the mirror in her room, and began to wonder. Was Jimmy interested in some girl at school, as it wasn't like him to spend a long time in the bathroom during the mornings before school? Come to think of it, he had asked her to iron one of his school shirts, usually he just grabbed one off the coat-hanger, usually before it was even dry if he could get away with it, never mind ironed. Well all this might take a little of the heat off her, as Jimmy was bound to ask Joe's advice.

The next afternoon Emma received a telephone call from Simon, apologising for getting drunk and then expecting her to get into the car with him. There was no mention of drugs, and Emma was disappointed in him, it had been obvious to Joe that he had been on something, and in this she bowed to Joe's superior knowledge. Emma accepted his apology knowing that his father had insisted he should make one, and thought she had probably seen the last of Simon, and felt only a slight regret that things had turned out so badly. She later surmised that someone had been standing beside Simon, making sure that he made the call, because she received a text stating that, for the moment, he would keep a low profile, but they would get together again soon!

The next two days she worked hard on her studies, and enjoyed two long walks with Jason, who was always pleased to see her, and particularly if there was a walk on offer. In fact he was a little fickle if anything, it didn't matter if it was her dad, Jimmy or Joe, Jason was still up for taking a long walk, his body being wagged by his tail, and his lead and collar found within seconds.

Charlotte came round to visit during the evening, and they spent the time in Emma's bedroom whilst Charlotte complained about not having a boyfriend and wondering if she could really cut it as a singer, she had received good press when she had sung in the school pantomime four years ago. Emma smiled at her friend, knowing full well that she would find herself a boyfriend very soon, as was the norm, and that she would soon decide the singing was too much like hard work, unless she had changed drastically since leaving school, and then dropping out of her secretarial course which followed.

Emma wondered if things had also gone wrong for Jimmy, as he had not rushed into the bathroom again in the morning, rather he had been instructed to get in there by their dad, who of late, had seemed a little short tempered both in the mornings and the evenings, just as he had been shortly after their mother had died. It was nearly three years ago now, and she had hoped that he would be getting over the shock of it all, if not the grief.

The next afternoon Emma arrived home late, to find Jimmy and two young friends playing music loudly in Jimmy's bedroom. This she could cope with, but in the living room Tom Bell (the second guitarist) was watching snooker, eating crisps and drinking diet coke. He had made himself quite at home, and stood up when Emma came into the room, but continued to watch the television for a few more minutes, before switching it off. Then he turned his attention to Emma, and followed her into the kitchen, and back into the living room chatting away, and trying to catch her eye with vain posturing. Tom was nearly three years younger than Emma, and it seemed much more to her, but she was getting a little fed-up with him following her back and forth as she tried to start the preparation of the evening meal. He was a nice boy, but after circulating his gangly figure a couple of times, she stood with her hands on her hips and looked him in the eye.

"What is it you want Tom?" She asked trying not to sound too belligerent.

"Well Emma, I wonder if you will...."

"No she will not," Joe's voice came coldly from the doorway. Tom turned and saw that his way out was blocked by Joe's tall frame, with a hand on each of the door jambs. Tom glanced at the back door which opened into the back garden, and sidled towards it. "Jimmy will be waiting for me, he asked me to get a drink for him," he said quickly, and slid through the door into the back garden.

"Now see what you've done Joe, Tom is Jimmy's best friend, he only wanted some drinks." Emma said angrily. She was angry because she was embarrassed, knowing full well that Tom had had a crush on her for a few months now, but she had been handling it without any help from Joe or her dad.

"You think so. Funny that. I went into the back garden to call Mary on my mobile, and heard the boys talking in Jimmy's bedroom with the window wide open, and Tom was boasting to the others that he could get you to kiss him. I'm going to have a word with Jimmy for egging him on, what was he thinking about?" Joe appeared to be angrier with Jimmy than with Tom!

"He knows that I can handle Tom. Tom's a nice boy really, there is no harm in him, and he'll get over his little crush in time. You've upset him now."

"Don't be stupid Emma, I'm going to have a word upstairs now, and nip this horsing around in the bud, whether you like it or not." Joe replied angrily as he turned, and felt an empty egg box hit him on the back. Emma turned, only slightly apprehensive, wondering what Joe would do, and wondered with surprise – when had she decided to throw something at Joe, as it hadn't been a conscious decision? She saw her dad watching from the kitchen doorway. Damn, her dad looked quite upset.

"Emma, apologise to Joe now, and behave with a little decorum in future."

She looked at her dad and then Joe. Decorum, what an old fashioned word, but she could imagine her deceased paternal grandmother using it. Her dad looked weary, and Joe seemed slightly regretful, surely that was because her *dad* was upset!

"Sorry Joe," she said knowing full well that he could see from her eyes that she didn't mean it - well it was only a cardboard egg box. His eyes went dark and impenetrable. "I'll bring you a cup of tea in a minute Dad, are you staying Joe?"

"Oh, yes thank you Emma, I'd love a cup of tea. I will have words with your Dad and later with Jimmy." Joe said, with a smile to her dad, and a pursing of his lips when he turned to look at Emma. She looked into his eyes and was annoyed that he was always so confident and usually right! She refrained from stamping her foot, but it was really extremely difficult! Damn him, he knew what she was thinking!

Whatever Joe said to the boys it seemed to do the trick, as Emma had no further bother in that department. In fact, Charlotte Fleming came to call on her, and within minutes the whole band were downstairs in the living room, and she had to almost chase them back upstairs so that she and Charlotte could have some time together, and Emma was not at all sure that Charlotte would not have preferred the company of the boys! Emma smiled at her own musings, as she could have been very upset by the way Jimmy's friends had changed their allegiance. However, she was mollified when Charlotte let slip that Simon had suggested that she should call on Emma, and see if Emma would meet him and give him another chance. Emma decided that Simon had, in fact, been chatting up Charlotte, and revelling in her sympathy, and was probably aware that this request to meet Emma would be met with a stony silence. However, Charlotte's attention was still on the young men upstairs and their music as she kept singing along with the sound, without realising it! She left Laurel Cottage a couple of hours later, without any good news for Simon, but having promised to come and sing with Jimmy's group. For the first time since Jimmy had received his drums, Emma wished that they would find somewhere else to practice. She had already made the suggestion that they should keep the windows closed, because of the noise, but Jimmy looked a little shamefaced, and she was glad he was thinking about what Joe had heard them planning. In future they would, hopefully, be more circumspect. She looked at her friend, and hoped that it was just her singing that had attracted the boys!

CHAPTER THREE

Early morning the following Saturday, Joe and Jimmy were arranging to meet. They were intending to do some fell walking and then some rock climbing if the weather stayed good.

"Why don't you come Emma, then Jason can get a good long walk?" Jimmy suggested, "It's a long time since we all went, how about you dad?"

Jimmy glanced at his dad, who looked towards Emma with raised eyebrows.

"No I can't Jimmy, I've too much washing and ironing to do, and Jason has put his muddy footprints right across the kitchen floor." Emma said quickly, with a glance towards Joe, she wasn't at all sure that this invitation came from both Joe and Jimmy, as just lately she and Joe didn't seem to see eye to eye any more!

At this assertion, Robert Smyth stared at his daughter in dismay. "Emma you can do whatever you want. Jimmy and

I will help with the washing and ironing anytime, you don't have to do it all, and if the floor doesn't get cleaned today it can wait until tomorrow, Mrs Robinson might be glad of an extra hour's pay. You should go and get yourself some fresh air and exercise. I intend watching golf on television, and getting some peace." He sounded adamant and Emma thought he would be upset if she refused, although she didn't particularly like the way Jimmy was grimacing at the thought of helping out with a few jobs. Also, she really wanted to go! She glanced at Jason and he was wagging his tail as if he knew what was being discussed, and he was looking forward to accompanying them. Without Emma to look after him, he would not be welcome as Joe and Jimmy could not have kept an eye on him whilst climbing.

Jason wagged his tail, and nudged his nose against Emma's hand. "Well Jason is keen that I should go." She patted the top of his head, and he squirmed ecstatically. "I'll make some sandwiches, while you help Joe to pack up the car Jimmy." She smiled at them both, and wondered if Joe really didn't mind if she joined them.

"Sandwiches would be a change," Jimmy said, "We normally just take a bar of chocolate and a bottle of water, when we are climbing."

"Well *you* do," Joe said succinctly, and Jimmy looked at him with a grin, knowing full well that Joe usually was well organised for most eventualities, the weather on the fells could change dramatically within minutes.

Later Emma packed the sandwiches, crisps, chocolate bars, and bananas into her rucksack, together with a few dog biscuits. She added her waterproofs, and was a bit disappointed by the weight she would be carrying. At the last moment she added her rock-climbing shoes. The flat supple shoes, with loops on the back to pull them on looked very small, and she wondered if her feet had grown in the last couple of years – it was that long since she had received any climbing lessons from Joe, many of which had been on the climbing wall on the gable end of his house next door, 'Pillar Rock.' She had no idea why those lessons which had been very enjoyable and often hilarious had stopped. It wasn't because of the death of her mother, as they had ceased a few weeks before that devastating date.

They left Windermere early, and it was around eight thirty when Joe parked the BMW under the high stone wall, below Langdale Church. Emma put an excited Jason on his lead, after pulling the rucksack onto her back, and they followed Joe and Jimmy, laden with ropes and climbing gear, along the narrow lane towards Raven Crag, where they intended to climb. The tall bracken on the fell side was still green, but in places there were tinges of yellow and brown, the harbinger of autumn colours. Within minutes they left the lane and trudged through a weighted gate onto the fell side, which closed behind them, much to Jason's surprise. Emma looked around and couldn't, for the moment, see any sheep. She unclipped Jason's lead, and he started to hunt around whilst they covered the remaining ground to the foot of Raven Crag.

"Whilst we are the only ones here, we might as well do a bit of climbing, and take a fell walk later. Is that alright with you Emma?" Joe asked, already sorting out the climbing gear.

Emma was enjoying the early morning quietness of the Langdale Valley, knowing that within a couple of hours it could well become much busier, with regard to the traffic and to the amount of walkers and climbers. Normally, Joe and Jimmy usually picked a much quieter and more solitary place to climb, but Jimmy wanted to get back to see a friend who was returning from hospital after breaking his leg playing rugby. She must have been daydreaming as she was surprised to hear Joe's voice as he spoke to Jimmy. She hadn't even heard them getting themselves and their gear ready for the start of the climb.

"Climbing," Joe said as he started to climb to the right of a holly tree at the lowest point of the crag.

Emma watched as he started to climb, and when he had reached about eleven metres, he climbed right starting to surmount an awkward bulge in the rock. She looked at the bulge, and upwards towards the top of the crag, and swallowed hard. She didn't really want to watch she decided, she felt slightly sick, and was surprised as she was well aware that the rope just below Joe was belayed, and Jimmy had a secure hold on the end of it! She had never felt that way before when she watched them climbing, and also when she had been instructed on an easy climb.

"Jimmy," she said quietly not wanting to disturb Joe as he climbed. "I'm taking Jason up around Raven Crag, and up to the top of Silverhowe, I'll be an hour or so. Then perhaps I can have a little try, if it's not too difficult. I'll leave the rucksack here."

The rope Jimmy held made a definite move, and Joe shouted from above.

"Right, I'm climbing." Jimmy shouted back. He glanced at his sister and the dog now on the lead. "See you two later, don't get lost."

Emma and Jason circumnavigated Raven Crag to the left, and made their way up onto the ridge. The views were fantastic, Elterwater Tarns to the west, Grasmere and Rydal

Water to the north, and Windermere to the south. The quarry across the valley seemed much bigger than she remembered, but then it was a long time since she had visited this valley. There were no sheep to be seen, and she began to wonder if they had already been collected, and moved into the valley for tupping time - when the rams were very busy doing what they were made for, but she was sure it was much too early in the year! The sky was blue, with just a few white clouds, and already she was passing the time of day with walkers on the ridge, it was seldom that these outdoor lovers didn't bother to speak.

She had a sneaking feeling that she should go back to check on Joe and Jimmy, but knew they would not be expecting her back for some time. She was soon on the top of Silverhowe, with spectacular views of Grasmere, and the surrounding mountains and Dunmail Raise, where the weather was known to change as soon as the pass was negotiated. Today the weather looked balmy and unchangeable, on both sides of the pass. She walked on to Yewdell Tarn, from where the distinctive shape of the Langdale Pikes looked spectacular. The tarn was not easily identifiable as the reeds and other plants, had spread considerably since her last visit, neither were there any of the black headed gulls, which must have flown off to other parts. They retraced their steps on the Langdale side of the ridge, towards Meg's Ghyll and Raven Crag, with Jason excitedly running ahead.

They met numerous walkers and a couple of friendly dogs, and Jason enjoyed the walk just as much as Emma, judging by his wagging tail, dark glowing eyes, and his interest in the biscuit that he received for being a good boy!

When they arrived back Joe and Jason were just finishing a longer climb to the left of the crag, and Emma realised she must have been away much longer than the hour she had suggested. Joe was at the bottom of the crag, and Jimmy was coming down the last fifteen metres, retrieving any safety aids that had been used on the way up.

"Where have you been all this time?" Joe asked, not taking his eyes off Jimmy. He sounded out-of-sorts, and she wondered if he was worrying about his work, or maybe his beloved Mary!

"We only went along the ridge after going to the top of Silverhowe, as far as Yewdell Tarn, I did tell Jimmy."

"According to Jimmy you said you'd be about an hour. Anything could have happened in the last hour." His voice was abrupt, and there was a pricking behind her eyes and she blinked rapidly – she always seemed to be in the wrong these days, and she had been enjoying the unexpected outing so very much!

"I hardly think so Joe, you know what you are doing and so do I, as I'm not a child. Jimmy said I could maybe have a go on the rock, I've brought my climbing shoes." If he hadn't been so bloody-minded she might have forgotten about having a climb!

"A harness and helmet too?"

"You know I haven't brought either, but maybe Jimmy's harness will adjust to fit me?" She questioned.

"They are supposed to fit nice and snugly, not move around dangerously, so I don't think so Emma." He replied briskly.

"As for helmets, you are not wearing one."

"No but I made sure Jimmy is, because today I'm responsible for him."

"Who is responsible for you Joe?" Her voice came out sounding both worried and accusing.

Her remark seemed to have given him cause for thought, and after a couple of minutes, he gave her a rueful grin. "With regard to helmets Emma, we will get you one if you are serious about climbing. Sometimes rocks fall on you. Sometimes you fall on rocks. Sometimes some idiot above might drop a carabiner or nut tool onto your head, and a helmet makes sure it doesn't go into your head too. Next time we come, we will *all* be fully kitted out Emma, and you can have your lesson." Joe promised, as Jimmy landed lightly beside him, on the uneven hillside. They both started to coil the ropes, and pack away the climbing harnesses, and additional climbing aids. Joe turned towards her, and his enigmatic grey eyes caught hers. She stared back wondering what he was thinking, and then turned way abruptly.

"Anyone for lunch, besides me and Jason?" She pulled forward the rucksack, and soon had the plastic boxes of sandwiches arranged, together with the mugs and heavy flask of water. "I only brought tea-bags."

She emptied a plastic bag of dog biscuits onto the ground for Jason, as he was staring at her expectantly, and he was only slightly distracted as she passed Jimmy a packet of crisps and a banana. Joe shook his head, and she packed away the unwanted crisps and banana.

She had thoroughly enjoyed her morning out on the hills even though she hadn't been able to rock climb. She listened to Joe and Jimmy talking about Jimmy's injured friend. It was all very companionable, but for some reason she didn't feel a part of it, and she definitely was not hungry. Rather than move the car, they then walked the length of the valley and back, watching a few climbers on the crags at Dungeon

Ghyll, namely the other Raven Crag and Middle Fell Buttress. Emma was pleasantly tired as they returned to the car.

The journey home to Windermere was accomplished in reasonable time, as the traffic was mostly travelling in the opposite direction. Joe pulled the car into his drive, and then switched off the engine, and banged the door shut as he moved back onto the road purposefully.

Jimmy turned in the back seat to look back onto the road, and shrugged.

"Emma, it looks like Simon has been waiting for you, I thought you had seen the last of that loser." He watched with interest as she climbed out of the front door of the car and rushed onto the street in pursuit of Joe.

"Come on Jason, let's go home. Emma looks like she's up for a fight with Joe again, and we know she doesn't like Simon all *that* much. I've got to see my mate who should now be out of hospital." Jimmy said as he clipped on the dog lead. He glanced at the boot of the car and decided not to bother with the climbing gear. He could already hear Emma's raised voice, and she would deal with his stuff when she had finished arguing with Joe.

"How dare you interfere in my life Joe? Simon had probably only come to apologise." Emma stood before Joe with her hands on her hips and a furious glare on her angry face, as she watched Simon's wreck of a car turn the corner at the bottom of the street, quite obviously at Joe's suggestion.

"Somebody has to *interfere*, your dad has obviously gone golfing, and Simon was supposed to have apologised to you for his drunken and drug induced stupid behaviour on the telephone if you remember."

"He did apologise, but I might have decided to forgive him for all you know," she replied, in a fine temper – not because she wanted to forgive Simon but because she couldn't stand Joe's high-handed interference, although his intervention had probably saved her a very awkward and unpleasant interview. "How dare you embarrass me in front of the neighbours, the curtains are positively waving from across the street."

"Then lets stop giving them a show to watch," Joe replied in exasperation, and tucked her under his arm, ignoring her kicking feet, and moved into his driveway to the car. He placed her onto her feet, then opened the boot and started to remove the climbing ropes.

"Here you are Emma, and it's far too heavy to swing at me," he said placing the rucksack into her hands, and then ignoring her. He heard her stamp her booted foot, but when he turned she was already opening her own front door, with some difficulty. He didn't hear it slam shut, and looked across to see Jimmy leaving the house, obviously going to see his injured friend. He then glanced at the empty drive, and realised that Robert Smyth really must have gone golfing. He sighed, should he apologise for upsetting her? That might be rather difficult as he was taking her part really, as he was aware that her dad was not coping very well at the moment, either at home or in the Office. He couldn't tell Emma or Jimmy, as it would only upset and worry them unnecessarily, if Robert managed to get his act together very soon.

Emma had soon dealt with the debris from the alfresco lunch, she tidied the kitchen and showered and changed. She fed Jason in the back garden, where he settled down in the sun for a sleep. She wished she could get to sleep easily, and

216

get the ache in her chest to disappear. She was still annoyed with Joe, and hurt to think that he must be of the opinion that she wasn't capable of choosing her own friends. He might be right about Simon, but everyone deserved a second chance! Besides, except for Simon there was only Charlotte at the moment, her other friends she saw very rarely, they either being in further education or working. She hadn't had time to make any new friends at the College, as she was always rushing back home, and the course only had a few more weeks to run.

She heard the back garden gate close, and Jason raised his eyes and went back to sleep, it must be Jimmy or her dad. She lifted the vegetable rack onto the worktop, and the kitchen seemed to darken slightly, as she started to prepare the vegetables. She knew someone was in the doorway.

"What do you want Joe?" she asked. Her wayward body had already sensed his identity.

"Did you really *not* want me to get Simon to move on?" Joe was leaning against the kitchen table, with his arms crossed and looked very much at ease. He watched as she started work on the vegetables. She looked anything but happy, and he felt he must be to blame. She didn't reply, and then she quickly wiped her eye on the hem of her T-shirt, which was the nearest thing.

"Emma, Simon is not good enough for you, but I am sorry if you think I want anything but the best for you. Please don't cry." He put his hands on her shoulders and turned her to face him, and she put her head on his chest. It felt so good, that she slipped her arms around his waist, and after a moment he held her close. She glanced up at *his* reddened grey eyes, and they suddenly stared at her closely, blinking.

"Emma, you little madam, it's only the peeled onions," he said surprised. He lifted her away from the table, and then saw the twinkle in her eyes, and he wanted to punish her. He held her fast and put his lips to hers, and knew immediately that he had made a very big mistake. He slowly lifted his head, and was glad that her eyes were closed. He moved away from her, not looking at her again. He was on his way out of the door when he spoke. The eight or nine years between them seemed like an enormous barrier!

"Sorry Emma, let that be a lesson to you, you shouldn't fool around."

CHAPTER FOUR

During the following week Emma saw very little of Joe. He came home and went to work as usual, but did not call in to see her dad very often. Maybe they saw each other at work quite often enough! Emma was pleased to keep out of Joe's way, as she was still covered with embarrassment with regard to the way she had responded to his punishing kiss! What must he think of her, he had accused her of *fooling around?* In actual fact the onion had been strong, but that was not the reason she had been crying, not at first anyway. In a way the onion had been her saviour, she preferred to have Joe think that she was just fooling around, better than letting him know how he could so easily upset her. In particular, as he had the gall to *apologise* for kissing her!

The following Friday, Emma arrived home from the college to receive a warm welcome from Jason. When she had changed into jeans and a T-shirt, Jason was on the top of the stairs with his lead in his mouth, and his dark eyes beguiling, in a way that she couldn't resist.

After arriving back from walking Jason, she found a note from her dad on the kitchen table, informing her that Joe was having a barbeque and they were all invited. Well at least she didn't have to cook, and she could pop back through the fence after a reasonable time, and catch up with some work. Jason had made the hole in the laurel fence months ago, and Emma often had to go through it to get him to come back home! When she opened the fridge to get a drink, she saw that her dad had managed to do some shopping for the barbeque, as there were some steaks and a ring of Cumberland sausage. She quickly put the sausage onto a baking tray, and put it in the oven to make sure that it was fully cooked through, when finished off on the barbeque. She decided to put in some jacket potatoes as Joe usually provided salads and bread to go with the meat.

She collected a couple of folding chairs from the garden shed, and pushed them in front of her through the small hole in the hedge. She was putting them up when Joe turned from the gas barbeque he was lighting.

"Ahh, there you are Emma. Have you any of those plastic plates I can use, they are a bit better than paper plates?" He glanced at her slim form as she finished erecting the chairs, and then she went to his garden shed to take out another three folding chairs.

"I'll fetch the plates when I come back with the sausages, as I've put them in the oven to make sure that they get cooked through. Dad has also got some steaks, is there anything else you want?" He was wearing a small cotton apron, which was back to front, and she wondered what was on the other side!

"Besides various types of meat, I've got buns, and rice and pasta salads, and green salad from the supermarket. Do you think we need some baked potatoes?" he asked hopefully.

"Already in the oven Joe," Emma replied and looked ruefully at Joe, as Jason pushed his way through the hedge, and came and sat quietly beside Joe, he obviously knew what was going on, even though as yet there were no nice smells, but he could wait and keep a low profile. She looked around, and wondered at the amount of canned beer in the shade of a tree, and the wine rack filled with bottles of red wine. He must be expecting other guests besides the Smyth's.

Her dad and Jimmy had already gone next door with the steaks, when Emma arranged the baked potatoes in a roasting tin, together with the sausages for finishing off on the barbeque, and pushed gently backwards through the hole in the hedge, without dislodging any of the food as it was covered with foil, but catching her long hair in the fence. She made a delicate manoeuvre with the goods she was carrying, and straightened up to see Joe glancing towards her, together with a very attractive and very smart woman by his side.

"Mary this is Emma Smyth, come and meet our good friend Mary Morton, Emma," Joe said, and pushed the hair back from Emma's face, before taking the warm trays of food from her, whilst Emma tried to hide her dismay at being at such a disadvantage, and wondered at the strange way that Joe had introduced Mary!

She lifted her eyes, so this was the woman that Joe was frequently talking to on his mobile in the back garden. She felt chagrined, why had she had to arrive via the fence, and not yet having changed out of her jeans and T-shirt. The two women shook hands briefly and Emma was surprised at the close look that Mary was giving her, although she smiled warmly. Mary was very smartly dressed, if a little formally for the occasion and seemed a very pleasant person. However, Emma was surprised, as Mary looked quite a number of years older than Joe's twenty nine years, and there was even a sprinkling of grey at her temples. However, she was also very attractive, confidant, and the familiarity between them made her chest ache just a little.

"Can I get you a drink Mary," Robert Smyth asked, as he handed Joe a beer. Her dad and Jimmy had obviously already been introduced to Mary, judging by her dad's familiar tone, so perhaps that why Joe had introduced Mary as, 'our friend,' not 'my girlfriend.'

"Emma, could you please get the wineglasses from the kitchen, I'm sure Mary would like a glass of red wine?" Joe asked and returned his attention to his cooking!

Emma glared at his back, and then brought the glasses from the kitchen, and poured Mary and herself a glass of wine. How dare Joe keep telling her what to do, she was supposed to be a guest, and he could look after his own girlfriend. Jimmy appeared to be quite keen to start turning over meat on the barbeque, as he clearly intended to eat quite a lot of it. If he was busy he might not get too many beers!

"Ah, Emma, that's the front doorbell, can you get it please, I'm a bit busy here," Joe said, and glanced her way, and was surprised to receive a shrivelling look, which promised harsh words later. The way his hair had felt on the back of his neck just recently, he was aware it was not the first glare he had received! He watched Emma's feet with interest, was she going to stamp her foot? Her feet looked delectable in little gold toe-post sandals. The doorbell rang once more, and she hurried off to answer it.

On the step stood a pleasant looking young man (wearing a sweater that could have come from his mother or more likely his grandmother), and clutching a bottle of white wine in his right hand which he put out to shake Emma's hand. He then swapped the wine into his left hand, and shook her hand enthusiastically. "Hello, I'm Jeremy Morton, and my mother and I have been invited by Mr Grantham, I mean Joe," the young man said, and he moved into the hallway as Emma stood aside, her surprise evident on her young face.

"Your mother is already here, please go through to the garden, I'll put the wine in the fridge." Emma said formally, feeling like the maid of the house. She was trying to work out how old Jeremy's mother must be. Joe *must* be her toy-boy! Emma went towards Joe and the group around him. "I'm just going to get the plates," she informed Joe, and walked off towards the hole in the fence with relief.

Joe watched as she moved off towards her home, and wondered why she was feeling upset yet again. Would she have wanted to get changed into something else, had she known that Mary would be here? Mary was looking smart and confident as she always did, and he rather wanted them both to make a good impression on the other!

"Who is that lovely young woman, she didn't say?" Jeremy asked breathlessly, as he watched Emma move away and slip her young and trim figure through the hedge once more. Mary Morton looked with a frown at her son, as he stared after Emma. Joe slammed the metal tray he was holding down on the side of the barbeque, and looked closely at the bemused Jeremy. However, he knew that Jeremy was very bright and very much the gentleman, the opposite to Simon Park, so there was no reason for him to be warned off! He was also a bit of an anorak with his hobbies, but it looked as though Emma had kindled new ideas in the usually shy and retiring young man. Joe looked at Emma's dad, Robert, who seemed to be oblivious to what was going on around him. Joe was pleased to see Robert looking happier than he had for many months.

"Emma Smyth, the girl next door," Joe replied belatedly, and Mary looked on thoughtfully. Jeremy, who had not previously shown any interest in girls, had to pick on Emma Smyth and this seemed to Mary to be a bit close to home. She glanced at Joe, who was banging around the metal cutlery and cooking utensils.

"I wish she was the girl next door to us," Jeremy said under his breath, with a bemused smile, not realising that both his mother and Joe had heard his comment - neither of them looked very pleased, but both *were surprised*.

By the time that Emma arrived back with the plates, the party seemed to be in full swing. A couple of Joe's long time climbing friends, together with wives had arrived, and everyone was enjoying themselves. The food was good and the company, and Mary and Jeremy in particular seemed to be enjoying themselves.

Later in the evening, Emma was tidying away the used plates and glasses, and stacking Joe's dishwasher. He joined her in the kitchen.

"Don't bother with that Emma, go and enjoy yourself I'll do it later or in the morning." Joe said, putting his hand on her wrist. He was surprised when her hand moved passed him and pulled at the tie of his apron. She looked with horror at what she had in her hand. "I would never have worn that Emma, in particular with Mary and the other ladies present. You should not have taken it off, it has only embarrassed you, you're cheeks are quite red. Your Jimmy would have laughed at it, but I don't think Jeremy would, you have been chatting with him for most of the evening, what do you think?" Joe said, feeling sorry for her. He took the kitchen scissors and started cutting the offending apron into little pieces, and put it all into the waste bin. "That was an unwanted present, but it saved getting splashed with anything off the barbeque."

"Oh I don't think Jeremy would have been too upset. He wants to take me onto the mountains overnight." She turned back to the dishwasher, but was pulled around to face Joe.

"He wants to what?" Joe demanded with a frown. "Your dad won't allow that. Not after I've had a word with him anyway."

"Well, it has to be a clear night, and we will be taking a telescope of some description. Apparently the sky at night looks wonderful when there are no street lights, or motorways or light of any description." She paused, "You do like Mary's son don't you Joe?"

"Of course I do Emma, a lot more than that Simon Park. You would be much better off with Jeremy or someone like him, but you have plenty of time yet there's no hurry surely. He is a keen twitcher as well as stargazer, and he might get you interested in that." He finished with a frown, starting to think about the habitats of birds!

"Oh I doubt I have plenty of time, I'll be twenty in a week, catching you up Joe, and Jeremy has already said he wants to take me bird-watching." She turned, and saw Mary arrive at the kitchen door.

"Joe, Jeremy brought some white wine, one of the girls would like a glass, as she has been on soda water all evening, but would like a glass of white to finish off. She is the nurse and is working tomorrow." Mary explained, and watched as Emma picked up a handful of paper serviettes and went out to the garden, after telling Joe the wine was in the fridge.

On her birthday Emma realised that her dad and Jimmy had forgotten what day it was. She was a little disappointed but understood now that her Mother wasn't around, these things could happen. She arranged to go out with Charlotte, and put on her favourite dress, and instead of the normal dog-walking shoes she wore heels with a matching handbag. They had arranged to meet a couple of friends they had known at school, at a small restaurant. The evening was spent very pleasantly, and they all enjoyed each other's company, and the meal. Emma thought that for a girly twentieth birthday it had been quite successful.

When it was almost time to go home, the waiter arrived with a bottle of champagne in a silver bucket, also champagne flutes, together with a baked Alaska, decorated with twenty candles. The four girls were amazed and delighted, and soon demolished the pudding after Emma had blown out and removed the candles.

Before leaving the restaurant, Emma went into the kitchen to thank the chef for the unexpected 'birthday cake' and champagne. She was surprised to learn that Mr Grantham and a lady had been dining there, and he had organised the special pudding and champagne, for the young ladies!

Emma wondered why she had not noticed Joe and his companion. She was usually aware of him, but tonight she must have been just a little bit self-absorbed, trying not to mind (because she did understand why) both her dad and Jimmy had forgotten her birthday!

She had showered and was ready for bed, making a hot drink for her dad, when she saw the lights of Joe's car turn into his driveway. She quickly made her way to the hole in the fence, and tramped through the wet lawn in her bare feet, pleased that her pyjama pants came to just below the knee.

She came around from his back garden, and met him at the front door. "Emma what are you doing in your nightclothes, is there something wrong - is it your dad?" Joe asked. As the light came on automatically, he put his hands on her shoulders and moved her away from the harsh glow.

"No Joe, nothing's wrong. Everything is right, I just wanted to thank you for the champagne and the lovely baked Alaska, it was a wonderful surprise, and made the evening more of a celebration." She reached up and kissed him on each cheek, but restrained herself from touching his lips, as she remembered he had been entertaining a *lady*. She looked up at him and there was a silent stretched out moment, and she wondered if he was about to berate her for rushing out on the spur of the moment, without thinking, in her pyjamas and silky dressing gown!

"Emma, your hands are cold, and your feet are wet with the dew. You'll catch cold." He said in a husky voice. He picked her up, and carried her into the drive of Laurel Cottage, where they came face to face with Robert Smyth.

"What are you doing Emma, I went into the kitchen for my drink and the kitchen door was open. Have you been through the hedge?"

Emma wanted to die, and wondered if any of the neighbours could hear this strange conversation.

"Dad I went to thank Joe," she said, and then realised that she now had to tell her dad about Joe's kindness for her birthday, and knew that he would be very upset, because he had forgotten.

"Be quiet Emma," Joe said. "Now you are off the wet grass, I can put you down, and you can get into the kitchen and dry your feet. Meanwhile, I can explain to your dad that I had at last come up with something for your birthday, when I heard you were going to the Restaurant. Your dad asked me to think of something different for him to surprise you, and I was stumped until I realised you and your girlfriends would love some champagne, and a special birthday cake."

Before he set her down she felt his hands tighten on her body warningly, and realised that he was trying to make things better for her dad.

"Thank you Dad, the champagne and birthday cake were a lovely surprise. It didn't take the four of us girls long to dispose of the lovely ice cream, cake, fruit and meringue concoction, together with the champagne." She reached up and kissed his cheek, then moved quickly into the house.

She watched from her bedroom (before putting on the light) her dad and Joe having a brief discussion. She saw her dad take Joe's hand and shake it, as he patted him on the shoulder. Her eyes filled with tears, now all three of them were happy!

CHAPTER FIVE

A few days later, Emma was pleased and surprised to find a belated birthday card from her mother's sister Marian. She said she had just arrived home from Australia, and had realised that Emma had recently had her twentieth birthday, and she enclosed a substantial cheque, with her love. This was her first time back since her sister's funeral, and she would try to get to visit the family, but she had only got three weeks in the United Kingdom. Emma kissed the cheque, and deposited it the next day. Her Aunt Marian and Uncle Mal did manage to call, but it was whilst Jimmy was at school, and Emma at the College, but they called on Robert Smyth at his office.

The next month passed uneventfully, except for a couple of invitations from Jeremy to visit the cinema. It seemed preferable, but strange, to finish off the evenings with a visit to a coffee house instead of a public house! Emma liked Jeremy, his hobbies were interesting, and she quite liked the idea of bird-watching, but Jeremy's explanations were far too technical for her with regard to photography and astronomy.

After a lot of ribbing, and being 'put down' by Jimmy about her failure to climb when they were at Raven Crag, Emma didn't bother explaining to him why Joe had not been agreeable to her doing so. With the help of her Aunt Marian's birthday present she made up her mind to go and get the necessary accoutrements, and be ready for any future opportunities. She decided she could accompany Jimmy, he was now a good climber, and it might be preferable to do this when Joe was otherwise engaged (as he always seemed to be during the last few weeks).

On the following Saturday, Emma was surprised to receive a telephone call from Jeremy, with a suggestion that she should accompany him to an exhibition of black and white photography at the Armitt Library Museum in Ambleside. She was intrigued and had accepted before giving the matter much thought. Personally she thought that she preferred coloured photographs, as taken by her digital camera, as they showed off the beauty of the Lake District, but was quite interested in seeing the exhibition.

She drove the Rover car, and they parked in the car park in the middle of town, and crossed the bridge and road to the Library in just a couple of minutes, although the pavements were thronged with visitors. She was intrigued as she glanced across passed the small Bridge House, a quaint narrow bridge with a two rooms on two levels built on top, now owned by the National Trust, and decided to visit if they had time. Later she agreed with Jeremy that in black and white some of the photographs were more atmospheric, and some of the effects of smoke, or mist and rain were strange and rather beautiful.

After a look at Bridge House, they talked amicably over a cup of coffee, and the afternoon stretched before them.

"Jeremy, do you mind if we call in at one of the climbing shops, I want to have a look around." She looked at Jeremy, and he seemed quite amenable to her suggestion.

At the first shop they visited, she was undecided what to do. The next shop looked interesting and she was met at the door by a young man, who worked in the shop.

"You are Emma I believe, Jimmy Smyth's sister. If you remember, I'm Bill Bancroft, I climb with Joe Grantham and Jimmy quite often?" He smiled warmly, and looked the complete picture of fitness, in his rock climbing clothes and shoes, and his age must be somewhere in between Jimmy's and Joe's. Emma wondered where he put his long brown hair, when wearing a climbing helmet.

"Of course I remember you, I've watched you often enough. Are you going climbing now?" She smiled as he surprised her by kissing her on both cheeks.

"No, I'm working here in the shop. Can I help you find what you're looking for?"

"I'm just looking really. Er, this is a friend of mine Jeremy Morton." She smiled warmly at both of them as they shook hands.

Half an hour later she was pleased that she had decided to wear a T-shirt and cropped jeans, as she was suspended from a large hook on the ceiling of the store, hanging around in a snug fitting climbing harness, with the waist band above her hips, and the leg loops unable to slip around. In fact she was quite comfortable.

"Jeremy, is it time for you to fetch Bill, to lower me down?"

"Not really Emma," Jeremy replied quite seriously. "He said you should hang around for five to ten minutes to make sure it fits alright. One more minute and that will make it seven and a half minutes, and that should be OK. I'll go and find him for you." He finished studying his watch, and walked off and left her suspended.

Emma smiled, dear Jeremy, he was so precise in whatever he did, and she hoped that soon he would relax and start to enjoy himself more!

A young boy looked up to her with some interest. "Hey Miss, I'm here to get some walking boots. Is that comfortable, and do you work here? Have they put you up there because you've done something wrong? I don't know what size I want yet?"

Just then Jeremy and Bill arrived with a step ladder just in case she wasn't capable of lowering herself, and Bill was able to satisfy the young boy's enquiries, even the one asking him if he 'could have a go on the hook,' as she lowered herself to the floor.

Jeremy was beside her "Gosh Emma that's really interesting lowering yourself down like that, you didn't even need the stepladder. Maybe I'll have a go at climbing." He was holding a bunch of leaflets, which he had obviously been perusing. "Do you think there are enough gear loops on the harness Bill?" He asked seriously, and Emma and Bill glanced at each other with a smile.

"Oh I think four will be sufficient," Bill replied seriously, and then smiled broadly at Emma. "Are you happy with the harness Emma?" he asked, and as she nodded he continued across the shop carrying the harness.

"Well we'll need to sort you out a helmet, but we'll leave the belay plate until you're sure you want to take it up seriously. That goes for the rest of the gear, as I know Joe and Jimmy will have more than enough."

"The thing is Bill I want to improve quite quickly, I'm tired of Joe deciding I shouldn't climb in certain conditions, and Jimmy who just thinks I'm good in the kitchen and looking after the house and his stomach, Dad, and our dog Jason." She said with a sigh, as she tried on the helmet that he passed to her. He placed it onto her head, and it was about just less than an inch above her eyebrows, and felt quite comfortable even without the chin strap fastened, and her neat nose was protected by the front of the helmet. She took it off and admired the bright yellow colour.

"Before the evenings start getting dark, Emma, if you would like to come with me onto the crags give me a ring, here's my card." Bill offered, "I often take people out who are thinking about starting to climb, nothing too difficult of course." Bill looked at Jeremy, still reading leaflets, "why don't you come along too Jeremy?"

"Really I'd like that, to watch I mean, maybe sometime I will have a try at climbing, but I'm not very keen on heights." Jeremy said. "Maybe I could do a bit of bird-watching at the same time. I believe there are quite a few skylarks, wheatears, and raptors on the mountains. I guess you see quite a lot of nests Bill?"

"Oh yes, but we don't disturb the birds, at least not on purpose. Everyone will be careful after being spit at by a fulmar on a coastal climb believe me."

Having prised Jeremy away from continually questioning Bill they left Ambleside, and Emma felt quite pleased with her day, even the photographic exhibition had been quite good, and Jeremy was certainly entertaining even when he didn't mean to be! Before she dropped him off near his home, she extracted a promise from him that he would not mention her climbing gear or Bill Bancroft, to either Joe or Jimmy.

He surprised her by saying that he wouldn't mention it to his mother either as he might be accompanying her, she didn't seem too keen on him getting involved with anyone just yet. She was a little mystified by this remark. Did his mother Mary think that she was unsuitable for her boy? Emma was damned if she would allow Mary to decide whom she should go out with or not, she already had Joe and her dad doing that! He then asked her if she would at least go bird-watching with him on Saturday, to which she agreed as she had quite enjoyed their day out.

In actual fact two Saturdays passed before Jeremy managed to find some spare time for bird-watching, as his mother had decided he should do some studying as he would be back at university in September, and he had done very little.

That Saturday morning, Joe and Jimmy were packing their gear into Joe's BMW, when Charlotte arrived to see Emma. Jimmy saw them, and came across to talk to Charlotte. He tried to get her to commit herself as to when she was coming to sing along with his band. Charlotte swung her dark straight hair beguilingly and teased him shamelessly, before agreeing to Tuesday evening.

Emma was frustrated, she needed to have strong words with her friend, not just for winding Jimmy up, but for messing up her plans to go climbing with Bill on Tuesday, she had been a few times and thought she was improving all the time! She pushed a waterproof into her rucksack, together with her mobile telephone and the binoculars she had borrowed from her dad. Together with the bottled water and a couple of sandwiches, and her light waterproof jacket, the rucksack seemed quite heavy.

Jeremy arrived, and Emma was surprised at the size of the binoculars he was carrying, together with a very substantial camera.

"Do you want to borrow a rucksack Jeremy, to hold your gear?" Emma asked.

"No thank you Emma as I need them to hand, you never know when you might see something." He patted both items lovingly.

"Where are you going," Charlotte asked with a warm smile for Jeremy. "Can I come?"

"Bird-watching I suppose you could come, but you'll have to keep quiet you know," Jeremy said seriously. Charlotte looked very put out by his seemingly uncaring words as nobody spoke to her like that, and they usually made a fuss of her!

Emma felt a little sorry for her friend. "You can't walk in those high heeled boots Charlotte. If you want to come I can lend you some trainers."

"Of course I want to come with *you* Emma, but I'll nip up to your bedroom and try on your trainers."

When Charlotte returned she strode around admiring her footwear, with a glance towards Jeremy whom she thought *must* be looking her way. He wasn't. "These look like your best trainers Emma, but the older ones didn't fit very well."

Emma sighed, her best 'go to the gym trainers,' at least they were expensive and should not fall to bits with a trip through the washing machine when Charlotte had finished with them!

"Are you ready Emma, I'd like to get going there is so much to see," Jeremy said enthusiastically, and he climbed into the front passenger seat. Charlotte looked surprised, but climbed quietly into the back of the car. Emma glanced in the mirror, and couldn't help noticing a definite pout.

"Can we go towards Coniston Emma, as I'd also like to see the Ruskin Museum?" Jeremy asked, and Emma heard a distinct sigh from the back seat.

They arrived in Coniston, and true to his word Jeremy went to the Museum, and Emma followed on. It was about fifteen minutes later that Charlotte came in, and then followed Jeremy around as he explained various things to Emma. They then drove up to the fell gate on Coniston Old Man. The few hundred metres height was a good place to start to look for raptors, particularly buzzards and peregrine falcons.

Charlotte complained that they had missed the best of the day wasting time at the Museum, as there was now a slight mist hanging over Coniston Water. However, Jeremy seemed immune to her complaints, and excitedly wandered along through the brackens and grassy areas, occasionally seeing birds, which had usually gone by the time that Emma had raised and concentrated her binoculars in the suggested direction!

Jeremy got very excited when Emma pointed out a buzzard, by the naked eye she clearly could make out the distinctive light coloured markings under the wings and on the tail. By the time he had raised his binoculars and locked on to it, it was flying into the slowly rising mist. "Gosh Emma, it's enormous I think it's the eagle from the Hawswater area." He set off at a run.

"It's a buzzard, I've seen loads Jeremy, everything looks bigger through mist, come back let's stick together." Emma replied sharply, but he became almost indistinguishable in the rising mist.

"Come on Charlotte, we must all stick together, there's a mist rolling in from the sea, it's already covered Coniston Water." Emma informed her friend briskly.

"I can't go that fast," complained Charlotte.

"Nonsense, you are the same age as me, come on." Emma said adamantly. She took Charlotte's hand and pulled her along towards Jeremy's voice, which was becoming fainter.

They struggled forward, in the now clinging mist. When they came across Jeremy, Emma realised his voice was not faint because of the distance he was away from them, but because he was absolutely *terrified*. The mist had swirled away from him for a moment, and he had seen the depth of crag below him, and the distance the rocks and grassy areas were below that, and then it closed in around them once more.

"It's hundreds of metres down, Emma. I can't move." he said hoarsely.

"It's not that far Jeremy, the mist makes everything look different," Emma said tightly. "Move back a little bit Jeremy, and crouch down with your hands on the ground, you are quite safe." She waited whilst he did this, and heard a little whimper from behind her.

"I'm getting wet and cold Emma," Charlotte complained, from a metre behind Emma on the narrow path.

Emma sighed deeply, as she didn't want either of them to panic. She took off her rucksack, and placed it on the path in front of her. She pulled out the waterproof and handed it back to Charlotte, where the path was slightly wider. She heard the zip as Charlotte put it on. Then she handed her a plastic container. "Can you take the sandwiches out of this box, Charlotte, and when I have moved passed you, you can share them with Jeremy. You'll both feel better."

"How are you going to get passed me, there isn't room," Charlotte replied worriedly. She indicated the sandwiches, "Shall we save you something?"

"I'm going to climb up a bit, and then down the other side of you. You must keep still, I've got my mobile in my pocket, but there isn't a signal here, I'll find out if the mist is likely to dissipate, as it might only be here where we are. If I want anything to eat I'll have a piece of chocolate." She prepared to climb, and glanced at Jeremy's terrified face. "Jeremy, it was *not* an eagle it was only a buzzard, and the mist makes things look different and strange, particularly in size. Can you look after Charlotte, and both sit together and don't move. I'll be back as soon as I've got a signal."

"Yes Emma," he replied, as he glanced at Charlotte, who now appeared to be dependent upon him. He closely inspected a sandwich handed to him by Charlotte, then slowly started to eat as Charlotte wasted no time in putting her head on his shoulder as she munched slowly!

The small climb that she had made, had left Emma exhausted, although she was used to her sturdy walking boots they seemed clumsy after her rock climbing rubbers which she had been wearing lately, and everything was so wet with the mist. Also she was about to try and ring either Joe or Jimmy, *the very last thing* she wanted to do! Surely this mist would lift before it was necessary to get in touch with the police and ask for the Mountain Rescue! Even if it did, she realised that she would have trouble coaxing Jeremy back along the narrow path, which he had taken in his excitement and without any thought to what was below him! As for Charlotte, she had complained of feeling cold and damp, but she had put on Emma's waterproof, and had made herself comfortable next to Jeremy! Hopefully the sandwiches and Charlotte together, might distract Jeremy from the long drop at his feet!

She took her eyes from the path, and saw that she had a signal, and quickly rang Jimmy. Hopefully, he and Joe had not travelled too far away, and he had taken note of the weather forecast before leaving Windermere.

"If it's not life or death Emma, ring Joe, I'm on an overhang, and am in danger of dropping this damned 'phone," Jimmy answered then the phone went dead.

"Damn you Jimmy," Emma said, and just refrained from attempting to stamp her foot. She didn't want to ring Joe, he would be so disapproving, and she didn't want to ring for the Mountain Rescue – a local girl doing that - it didn't bear thinking about! But she must do it!

"Emma, what's you problem, I've got your brother on the end of a rope?"

She quickly explained that there were three of them, where the car was parked, where they had walked and the position of the crag on which they appeared to be stuck until the weather changed.

"We are climbing Emma and there is no mist, so it must be local to you, just wait, I'll ring you back in a little while," his voice sounded annoyed, and then he seemed to relent slightly. "Chin up, Ems." She felt like crying as he used the name he had used when he first moved into the house next door, and she had been about fifteen years old.

Emma made her way back towards Jeremy and Charlotte, and told them everything was going to be alright, and the mist would lift soon. She kept Jeremy busy by asking all the questions she could think of with regard to bird watching and star gazing. Even Charlotte seemed to catch on, and tried to keep him occupied and asked questions about his camera. Emma watched the mist, and was worried when she realised that it was thickening rather than dispersing. She moved back to where she had a signal, after making sure Jeremy and Charlotte would not move an inch. She wasn't aware how long they waited, but it must have been half an hour. Then her 'phone rang, it sounded eerie in the now much thicker mist.

"Emma, we can now see the mist, it is already completely covering Coniston Water and is rising and we can find you, as the paths will be easy to follow downwards towards you. See you soon."

She moved back to join her friends to wait. Half an hour later she asked Jeremy and Charlotte to be quiet. She could hear voices in the distance, how could she attract them, and how far were they away? With relief she recognised Joe and Jimmy's voices, from above. They would be furious being dragged away from their climbing, as Joe had said the weather was clear!

"Don't move any of you. I'm coming down as the mist is too thick for us to find the path you are on." Joe shouted.

Jeremy was absolutely terrified, but managed to hold on to Charlotte, and she patted his back with one hand, and held on to the rock with the other. Emma managed to persuade him to part with his binoculars and camera, and she managed to fit them into her rucksack, after jamming her booted foot into a crevice in the rock, as a kind of anchor.

She watched closely above, until she saw Joe's feet, and directed him to move left, where the path was wider and curved away, she thought around a corner. He let himself down about half a metre at a time, and then landed softly, and indicated that Charlotte should move towards him. As she started to move, Jeremy started saying prayers and trying to hold on to her, and Emma. Joe took in everything at once.

"You will have to wait Charlotte, as I'd better take Jeremy first. Emma can you help me get this rope around him we've made a sort of sling? There is a second rope, and they will belay us up together, there's nothing to worry about Jeremy, it's only about twelve metres," Joe said in a calming voice. He called to the men at the top of the crag and soon he and Jeremy were out of sight.

When it was her turn, and she was told to hang on, Charlotte did so, and Joe had to ask her not to do anything, just leave it to him and the men above, as he removed her arms from around his neck. Joe looked across at Emma. "You should have been prepared Emma, *you* should know that." He took a breath and looked upwards to where the ropes disappeared into the mist. "There's quite a crowd up there Emma, someone will be down for you soon, I'm getting exhausted and it won't be safe for me to do this again for some time - Jeremy took a lot of handling."

"How did you get here so quick," Emma asked, "You said there was no mist where you were."

"We were on Dow Crags, right round the corner from here, and much higher up, the mist rolled in from the sea and we couldn't see it until we were nearly at the top of Dow Crags, as *we* were concentrating on our climbing."

"Mr Grantham, Joe, can we go now, before I do something silly like crying, I'm getting really spooked." Charlotte said, as he began to remove her arms from around his neck once more.

"Surely we can, I just needed to see Emma was alright, and to catch my breath. I bet she won't come up here again without proper preparation." Joe said, with a frown as he noticed how wet and cold Emma was, he could tell she was trying to stop her teeth chattering. He shouted that he was ready to climb, and pulled a rope, just in case they couldn't hear.

As Joe and Charlotte slowly moved through the mist and out of her sight, Emma wiped her eyes. Joe was blaming this stupid incident solely on her, and if she was to put him right then it would not show his girlfriend's son in a very good light! She was also sure that when he had time to think about what had happened, Jeremy would be devastated by his apparent lack of moral fibre, but those at the top of the crag were not aware that he was afraid of heights! She hoped that Jimmy had had the sense to let her dad know that they were alright, as they would be late home after all this upheaval. She didn't want to ring her dad herself, as now that she was all alone she didn't think she could keep from her dad the fact that she was a bit shivery and shaken up. She was certain that if everything had been as normal, she could have climbed up the crag herself if they had let down a rope!

There was a fall of bilberry bush fragments and a couple of small stones and she knew her saviour was on his way. She was relieved when she recognised the taught amply muscled body, climbing apparel, and cheeky smile as he lowered himself onto the pathway.

"Emma fancy meeting you here. You look frozen, come on lets get you up and out of this mist. It's clear above you know." Bill Bancroft said cheerfully.

"That's *one* of the things *Joe* said to me." Emma replied, and slipped the rucksack with Jeremy's camera and binoculars onto her back, securing it around her waist, and then Bill secured her safely to the second rope and belay plate, pulled on the rope, and they slowly started their way up out of the mist. Emma was climbing up the crag as well as she could manage in her walking boots.

"You could easily have climbed up on your own Emma without the mist, so don't worry it's a piece of cake."

Emma was beginning to worry about how many people were up there waiting for them. Where the rope secured her she could feel the water seeping out of her clothes, and it was running down her face from her long hair. She must look like a drowned rat!

When they arrived at the top of the crag, and were hauled the last few inches, Emma was pleased to note that she knew most of the people there. Also no one, except Joe of course, seemed to be blaming her for this unnecessary incident.

Joe was industriously freeing both Emma and Bill from the ropes and climbing gear, when she leaned forward and kissed Bill on the cheek.

"Thanks for bringing me up Bill, you did a perfect job," she smiled at her climbing teacher.

"No problem Emma, you did most of it yourself, and I was just there in case you needed me. I think you're putting on weight, and I don't mean that heavy rucksack." he said with a laugh.

Joe paused, and the stare he gave them both resembled a very stormy thundercloud, as Emma blushed becomingly, despite her wet and dirt streaked face. Jimmy rushed forward to hug his sister, which surprised her as her family were not usually demonstrative. Charlotte kissed Emma on both cheeks, and Jeremy rushed forward full of apologies and remorse, and assured her that he was getting over his dizziness, and didn't feel sick any more! Emma looked harassed, and turned away from everyone, saying distinctly, "Thank you everyone for getting us out of a sticky spot, we do appreciate it, we would have been really embarrassed if we'd had to ring for the police to get the Mountain Rescue Team! The drinks are on me when I see you again. Come on you two," she indicated Charlotte and Jeremy, "We can easily follow the path down through the mist as we know there are no further dangerous crags. Lets get ourselves down to the car, and then home."

"Just a minute Emma Smyth, you are not driving anywhere, you are coming home with your brother and me, and I'll bring you back for your car tomorrow afternoon." Joe said adamantly. Emma glanced at him, and knew there was no way that they could move him from this decision. She did feel a bit shaky, and knew that Joe was right in his decision, but it didn't make her feel any better!

Joe left Jimmy to finish packing up the gear, and brought from his rucksack a large T-shirt, and waterproof. He held up the unzipped waterproof shielding Emma, and turned his eyes away. "Thanks for your help lads, the shows over now."

Bill sketched a wave to Emma, and turned away and started to pack up his climbing gear, with his climbing partner Jed Black.

"Get that wet stuff off now Emma, put on the T-shirt and my waterproof." Her wet fleece and T-shirt were pulled over her head by Charlotte, and she felt much better when she was dressed again, in a dry T-shirt and Joe's waterproof.

Bill came across with a woollen hat, and put it on her wet head when she had twisted up her long wet hair. She then pulled up the hood on Joe's waterproof. Slowly she was feeling much better, especially when Jed, Bill's climbing partner, came forward with a cup of hot tea out of his flask.

Emma passed the cup of tea to Charlotte, who took a couple of mouthfuls, but Jeremy refused, and Emma finished it off, with grateful thanks to Jed who had been climbing a couple of times when Emma had joined Bill in the evenings.

In half an hour they were back at the car park near the fell gate. Emma checked her car, and then slowly moved across to Joe's BMW, where Joe relegated Jimmy to the back seat with Charlotte and Jeremy. Jimmy didn't mind one bit, and as there wasn't much room, put his arm across the back seat. Charlotte looking extremely tired, and rested her head on his shoulder.

"I'll put the heater on in a couple of minutes," Joe promised as he pushed his hand through his unruly hair, spraying drops of water over his shoulders. They drove through the fell gate, and it was Bill who smiled happily at them as he held the gate for all the other cars to come through. Emma gave him a grateful wave, and Joe nodded his head in acknowledgement. Apart from Jimmy making the odd remark, the rest of the journey to Windermere was made in silence, every one of them with plenty to think about!

Joe pulled the car up outside his own home, and everyone started to alight.

"Stay where you are Charlotte, and you Jeremy. I'm just dropping Emma and Jimmy off before taking you both to your homes. I think your parents will need some sort of explanation, for us all being this late home. I'll see you later," he finished speaking, but looked directly at Emma.

Not if I see you first, Emma promised herself. How dare he assume that she was to blame for everything that had happened? How had *she* conjured up the mist for instance, and *she* had not mistaken a buzzard for an eagle!

"Come on in love," Robert Smyth said to his daughter, and then helped her to take off Joe's waterproof. Then he removed the plastic bag containing her wet clothing, and pulled the rucksack to one side in the hallway. "You'd better have a long soak in the bath Emma. Jimmy can wait, or use the shower room. It looks as though Jason is determined to come with you." Jason was already on the first stair, with his tail wagging, not taking his eyes off Emma.

"I hope you haven't been worried Dad since I rang, Emma had told us exactly where they were, and everything went according to plan, as it usually does for Joe." Jimmy said. His mind was still on Charlotte, and how nice it had been to come back home in the back of Joe's car. Also he was amazed at her calmness when Joe had arrived at the top of the crag with her, particularly after seeing Jeremy's ashen face, and trembling body when *he* arrived at the top of the crag! Poor guy, he had been in a bit of a mess, in fact, really stressed out. He wondered briefly what Joe would say to Mary Morton, when he got her son safely home to her? Joe had been spending quite a bit of time with Mary lately, obviously there wasn't a Mr Morton around and it surprised Jimmy that Joe should spend so much time with her, as judging by Jeremy's age she must be quite a bit older than Joe. He glanced at his damp and miserable looking sister, as she had looked after both her friends very well, with a little help from *her* friends too! Jeremy was 'different' and obviously quite intelligent, but Jimmy wasn't sure that he would do for Emma!

"Oh, Joe didn't think I should drive the car back. I'll get a lift and bring it back tomorrow," Emma said worriedly.

"We'll sort that out tomorrow love, go and get your bath, and I'll make you some tea." Robert Smyth said with a smile, he was glad to be able to do something for his daughter, who always seemed to be rushing around after everyone else.

"I could have driven the car back with Emma beside me," Jimmy said in disgust, "but Joe said that would have made her feel even worse."

"It would too, you know that after a couple of tries we didn't get on with *me* teaching *you*, that was because you wouldn't listen, and you terrified me." Emma moved up the stairs, with Jason just a stair in front. She turned, "They say that a husband or wife shouldn't teach the other to drive, it is equally true for a brother and sister."

After a long soak in the bath Emma came downstairs enjoying the warmth of her fine fleecy leisure suit. She stepped over Jason at the bottom, where he had curled up comfortably. There was a very interesting smell coming from the kitchen, and she realised how hungry she was. She smiled in resignation, as she dealt with the plastic bag and rucksack that she had handed to her dad together with Joe's waterproof. They were residing exactly where he had immediately put them down in the hallway! She sorted out the wet things and took them into the kitchen and put them in the washer.

"Something smells good Dad you must have been busy." She walked into the small dining area off the living-room, to discover her dad, Jimmy and Joe taking off the covers of a selection of Chinese food. She hung Joe's waterproof outside the back door to dry.

"Yes love, busy getting Jimmy to order the food, and driving him into town to collect it. I've asked Joe to join us, as he did save you all from a miserable wait for help, and the unwanted publicity that would have caused." Robert Smyth agreed, he patted Joe's shoulder companionably.

"Yes he did take Jeremy and Charlotte up to the top of the crag," she answered, and received an enigmatic stare from Joe.

"Oh Jeremy Morton rang whilst you were in the bath. I said you would ring back sometime," Jimmy said, putting an obscene amount of fried rice on his plate, and then scrutinising the various delightful dishes to go with it!

"OK, I'll ring back later, or in the morning. Oh, I've just thought about the car, what if somebody reports it to the police in case someone has gone missing?" Emma said worriedly.

"Don't worry, I rang and explained everything to the police," Joe answered.

"I should have realised you would Joe," she replied, and helped herself to a portion of food. Jeremy must now be feeling embarrassed at first thinking a buzzard was an eagle, and then refusing to stop when Emma asked him. She would be sure to tell him it wasn't his fault that he suffered from vertigo.

After the meal, Robert Smyth decided to watch the news on the television, and Jimmy made his way upstairs to listen to music, and ring his friend Tom. Emma warned him that both she and Charlotte would be after him if he told anyone about them getting lost in the mist, and Jeremy could be upset if he thought anyone was talking about him! She glanced across at Joe who had a rueful expression on his face, and he slightly shook his head at Jimmy. Jimmy shrugged and made his way upstairs.

"Thank you, I bet he wouldn't have taken any notice of my objections to him chatting about today on the 'phone." Emma said to Joe, as she started to clear the table as quietly as possible as her dad was fast asleep in front of the television.

Joe turned the sound down a little on the television, and collected what was left on the table, and followed Emma into the kitchen.

"I can manage Joe, there's not much to go into the dishwasher, and the containers and wrapping will all be recycled."

"I thought we might have a cup of coffee, whilst we have a chat."

"We don't *chat* Joe, we always have an argument these days," she hoped that Joe could not hear the way she was hurting in her voice.

"Alright then, let's have an argument. That is what you seem to want," his voice was harsh, he felt like shaking her, but that was out of bounds!

"I was surprised when you didn't bring me up too. Why did you have to get those other people involved? I was not in a hurry you could have rested for a while. In fact, I could have come up on my own." Emma sounded angry, but was really put out that he had not wanted to bring her up, as he had the others.

"For heavens sake Emma what a stupid thing to say, the others were also climbing on Dow Crags, and we always help each other whatever happens. Jimmy and I were the first down and therefore the first to find you. I brought Jeremy up first because he was obviously in a bit of a state. Charlotte next, because I knew you could cope with being left, but she might have panicked being left on her own. You were wet through with the mist having given Charlotte your waterproof. You needed to be brought up quickly. Anyway you didn't seem to have any complaints about being brought up by Bill Bancroft. Very friendly indeed, at least Jeremy and Charlotte didn't make a spectacle of kissing me although *they* did thank me!" He sounded angry.

"It's a wonder Charlotte didn't, she has been trying to get your attention for months, but you don't see it."

"That is plain stupid Emma, and not worth a reply, although that may be true of her feelings for Jimmy. I think we've had our argument now. I came over to apologise to you, and then you're father asked me to stay for a meal. I wish I hadn't bothered, but I thought I might have upset you, and I didn't mean to." He turned away from her as if to leave by the kitchen door.

"You did upset me, blaming me for the whole stupid situation, and you were obviously disappointed in me and angry. It wasn't my fault, not entirely Joe."

"I know, Jeremy and Charlotte explained everything to me whilst Bill was bringing you up the crag. Charlotte said she borrowed your trainers, as you wouldn't let her come in

250

her heels. She also said you gave her your waterproof as she hadn't got anything and was cold, and *you* ended up wet and cold. Jeremy explained his stupid mistakes, and also said that when you set off none of you knew where you were going to watch birds! I had been climbing for a few hours when you telephoned. By the time I had brought up Jeremy and Charlotte I was exhausted. I thought it would be safer to get one of the others to fetch you up, and Jimmy although willing has not got the experience. I'm sorry Emma."

"I am sorry too Joe, we always seem to be having misunderstandings. I do accept that you were getting exhausted, and I guess I'm just being bloody minded. Was Mary upset when you took Jeremy home, I expect you being there made all the difference, I hadn't realised he suffered from vertigo, he was quite dizzy and upset."

"Mary is a very good and understanding person, and there was no hassle, she was just pleased that you were all home safe and sound. She had been getting worried when she thought it was getting a bit late, and was thinking of ringing your dad - as you know Jeremy is the last person to be inconsiderate."

"Meaning I am, I suppose. I agree Jeremy is definitely the very last person to be inconsiderate. I do hope you don't think we are corrupting him." Emma said angrily.

"Grow up Emma, you had better not act like that in front of Bill Bancroft or he will think you are much too young for him. You can stamp your foot now, I think we are finished." He stared into her angry eyes, dark blue with emotion and the exact same blue as her fleecy outfit. He saw her lip tremble, and he took a step towards her, but he was interrupted.

251

"Sorry to fall asleep on you both, any chance of a cup of coffee Emma?" Robert Smyth said from the doorway, as he yawned and stretched a little.

"I'll put the kettle on Dad, I believe Joe was just leaving," and then realised that her dad would think she was being very rude to Joe!

"I would like a cup of coffee with you Robert, but I'll make it just as you like it. I think Emma is overtired and should have an early night," Joe said quietly.

She was near to tears as Joe gently moved her aside to get to the back door, which he opened invitingly. "Come on Jason you can go into the garden whilst I make the coffee," Joe said as Jason looked up at him with trusting eyes and wagged his tail. Jason went outside without a glance, and Emma felt that even the dog was deserting her.

Emma kissed her dad and whispered 'goodnight,' as he made his way back into the living-room and the television set.

Emma went slowly upstairs feeling exhausted, was Joe trying to take over all of her family, as well as the dog, together with Mary and Jeremy Morton? She was well aware that he cared for Mary and Jeremy, and her dad and Jimmy, and that had also included herself in the past!

CHAPTER SIX

Emma spoke with Jeremy the next morning when he called at the house. She provided him with coffee and shortbread biscuits. Later she agreed to go bird-watching once more, but she suggested that there were more than enough lakes and tarns with large populations of birds to watch without venturing onto the high fells.

Jeremy apologised for what had happened, explaining that he hadn't really known that he suffered from vertigo, it had only happened once before, and as he had not been as high and exposed it had soon passed. He was relieved when he was told to forget what had happened, it could happen to anybody. After telling him this, she felt obliged to go out with him at least once more!

During the next three weeks Emma was invited to go climbing with Bill Bancroft and his partner Jed, and a couple of new rookies like herself. They were a newly married couple, John and Megan Warner - just moved to the

Lakes, and a whole lot of fun. The weather was good, and the evenings were still quite long, and they managed a number of evenings climbing.

After arriving home from climbing one Sunday evening, Emma could hear music coming from upstairs, and walked into the kitchen to put on the kettle. She stopped abruptly. Her dad was slumped across the living room table, with one hand clutching his right arm. She thought that she stopped breathing for a few seconds, he looked terrible and she feared the worst! She put her fingers to his neck tentatively, and then her heart started to thump. His face was scrunched up in pain, and his lips looked pale, and he was sweating. She brought an aspirin tablet from the cupboard, and put it under his tongue. She rushed to the stairs and shouted for Jimmy.

He came down jumping two steps at a time, and cannoned into her in the hallway. "Good God Emma, what are you screaming for?"

"Its Dad, ring for an ambulance. Do we put him in the recovery position or what? Joe will know." She ran through the kitchen door, then the hedge, and pounded on Joe's back door. Why did he have to have it locked tonight? Her heart dropped as she watched him come towards the door, with Mary beside him. If she had interrupted a tender moment, then it was just too bad.

"Emma, whatever is wrong?" Joe asked as he steadied her with his arm around her shoulders. They all heard Jason whining hauntingly, and Emma's heart nearly stopped – had her father stopped breathing, dogs were known to have a great empathy with their owners, or was it just an old wives tale?

"It's Dad, Jimmy is ringing for an ambulance. I've put an aspirin in his mouth, he is sweating and is dreadfully pale, what do I do now Joe?" She looked up at Joe, and followed his eyes as he gripped her shoulders, as they both watched Mary pushing her way through the fence, regardless of her clothes and hair, and then going into the kitchen next door. Emma was astounded, she had no idea that Mary could move so fast. She seemed so sedate and immaculate normally, without a hair out of place, and Emma didn't mean that thought unkindly.

Joe went over the fence which was nearly two metres high, and Emma through, and by the time they had reached the living-room, Mary had, (with Jimmy's help) moved their dad to an almost upright armchair. Mary put a cushion behind his shoulders, and put her head down towards his, trying to hear what he was trying to say.

"Robert says the crushing feeling on his chest is easing a little. He has a shortage of breath. Can you get a bowl Emma I think he is feeling a bit nauseous. If the ambulance doesn't arrive soon, we'll try another aspirin."

Emma arrived with the bowl from the kitchen, and looked at Jimmy, who looked quite grey in the face with shock, but he was watching Mary with respect and awe. Emma sighed deeply, and admitted to herself that she was glad that Mary was here.

Mary put her hand out to Joe in an appealing movement. "Joe, do you think we should lay him down on the settee?"

A decision did not have to be made, as the front door was pushed open as a paramedic came inside, and came directly to Robert Smyth.

"Can you give me a little space please, and young man, can you keep a look out for the ambulance, it should be here soon. My name is Ben and I'm here to help you and make you more comfortable, what's your name?" He listened to the weak reply. "Robert, you are lucky, I was just watching the sunset on a viewpoint not a mile away."

Jimmy gave a loud sigh of relief, it was good to have a professional here, and he moved quickly outside to the garden. A couple of neighbours were already on the street, worried by the appearance of the paramedic, and Jimmy explained to them what was happening, knowing that they were genuinely worried, and wanted to help if at all possible.

Emma watched with tears running down her cheeks, as she sat in an armchair as her dad was attended to and then put into the ambulance. Jason was whining quietly aware that something was terribly wrong and she stroked his head, as Joe comfortingly took her hand in his.

"Emma is that you love?" the paramedic enquired, "Your Dad wants you to go in the ambulance with him." The plump and fatherly ambulance man said bracingly. "We are taking your dad to Lancaster."

"Oh Joe, we'll need his things." Emma said in a tired voice.

"Don't worry Emma you go with your dad. Jimmy and Mary will get your dad's things together, and I'll go and get out my car ready to follow you. See you soon," Joe said and lightly kissed her on the forehead.

"Jason?" She patted his head, as he leaned against her, his soulful eyes gazing at her trustingly.

"Jason can come in the car with us. He is just as worried as we are!" Joe said bracingly.

Emma climbed into the ambulance, and was allowed to hold her dad's hand, as his condition was monitored with various appliances, the ambulance man was busy explaining everything to both her dad and herself, but she couldn't take it in. She was terrified of losing her dad, it was less than three years since she and Jimmy had lost their mother, and she couldn't bear to think about what might happen. The roads were very busy, and it was over an hour before they reached the hospital. Emma still held her dad's hand, and wished she could do more for him!

The Accident and Emergency Doctor explained that a second electrocardiogram would be taken shortly, and a blood test to detect abnormal levels of certain enzymes in the bloodstream. Emma didn't mind what they did as long as they did it quickly, and it helped her dad who was still in considerable pain, but much calmer than earlier.

Later Emma was waiting outside the Coronary Unit, as her dad was the subject of yet more tests, when the others arrived. She was a little surprised.

"It's very good of you to come here Mary." Emma said, and noted that Mary still looked very upset.

"Of course Mary wanted to be here Emma. We are all worried about Robert. We do all work together every day," Joe said with a frown.

"You work at the accountants Mrs Morton?"

"Emma, my name is Mary, and yes I have for the last three years, and I couldn't have two better employers." She gave Joe a wan smile, and clasped his hand, and he drew her close for a comforting hug.

Good heavens, did they have to display their feelings for each other so blatantly, given the circumstances Emma would have thought they could be more circumspect! She immediately felt guilty for having such thoughts, and she clasped Jimmy's hand, hoping the contact would bring him some comfort, he looked quite grey and his eyes were haunted.

"I'm sorry Mary I didn't know. Dad, Joe, Jimmy or Jeremy probably assumed that I already knew." Emma said, and sat down on the uncomfortable hospital chair. She knew that she felt in an odd way let down and lonely, but just for the moment she could only think of her dad.

The Doctor came back and looked directly at Emma and Jimmy. "Your father will be staying here for the night, and tomorrow he will be taken to Blackpool for a by-pass operation. You can all see him for a few minutes, and then I suggest you go home for the night as your father will be sedated and monitored, and he needs to rest. Try not to worry he will have the best of care, and before you leave you will be provided with the telephone number to call in the morning. Sister will let you know exactly what is happening, and when and where you can visit."

They all went in to say goodnight to Robert Smyth. Mary quickly went up to the bed and took his hand in hers, and then she left the room looking really upset, Jimmy looked as if he didn't know what to say or do, so to help him out Emma kissed their dad on the forehead promising they would see him in the morning, and Jimmy just touched his dad's hand, and they left the room. Joe stayed a couple of minutes and then joined them outside the ward.

"Right we'd better make tracks, tomorrow is another day. The car isn't too far away, and when we find some grass we'll take Jason out for a few minutes." Joe said leading the way to the car park. Once there he settled Mary in the front of the car. "I thought Emma and Jimmy might like some time to themselves," he said opening the back door for Emma to slip inside, whilst Jimmy walked around

258

to the other side, and they both received a warm but subdued welcome from Jason. The journey home was about three quarters of an hour, and everyone seemed deep in thought. Joe walked Mary to her bungalow door, and opened the door with her key. He shouted for Jeremy, who came to meet them, and then he hugged Mary and kissed her forehead, and returned to the car.

Emma wasn't sure how she felt about this, just that she also needed something, and she wasn't sure what it was, besides her dad making a full recovery of course.

Her mobile went, and she had a text from Charlotte, saying she had heard what had happened, and would be coming over to the house, just in case they were back.

"That's nice, Charlotte is coming over she has heard what has happened to dad." Emma said almost with relief. Maybe Charlotte could cheer up Jimmy, whilst Emma made them all something to eat. They drove into Joe's driveway, and Joe switched off the engine and pulled on the handbrake with a sigh.

"Are you eating with us Joe," she asked. "We have a cooked chicken, and I'll prepare a salad, we must eat to be strong for dad."

"No thank you Emma, I need to go over to the Office, there are things that need to be done, and then I can take you to the hospital tomorrow."

"I intend to drive there myself. Jimmy will be coming with me." Emma replied quickly, in her minds eye she saw Mary and Joe at Mary's doorway a few minutes ago. That had been very touching and caring.

"Nonsense Emma I promised your dad I would be there with you both. That's an end of the matter – deal with it." Joe said brusquely. Emma stared at his familiar handsome face which looked drawn and pale. She suddenly realised that this wasn't only about herself and Jimmy. Joe was also a special friend and colleague of Robert Smyth, as Mary seemed to be, and the others who worked in the Office. Of course, they would all be affected by what happened in the next days and weeks, and they would all be very upset too!

"Come on in Emma, *I* would rather Joe came with us, and so would Dad." Jimmy said, looking slightly more cheerful as he saw Charlotte waiting in the front garden of Laurel Cottage next door.

Emma sat in the car for a moment, watching Joe, and felt like crying, she was a selfish pig. "Thank you Joe," she said quietly as she climbed out. He glanced over the back of the seat and put his hand out. She took it and he squeezed her hand. "Don't work too hard Joe, see you in the morning. I'll ring early in the morning and then let you know how Dad is." She let his hand go reluctantly, she had never seen Joe so upset, his eyes looked extremely tired, and his usually tanned face seemed sallow. She realised that not only had his friend become seriously ill, but his partner would not be around for quite some time, and the buck would rest with him.

Emma went into the house to find Charlotte and Jimmy watching the news on television. "It's chicken and salad for tea."

"I don't feel like eating," Jimmy said miserably.

"Make me a sandwich please," Charlotte said with a glance at Emma, "And one for Jimmy we'll have them here, if that's alright Emma?"

"Fine, a sandwich will do for me too. It won't be long." Emma smiled at Charlotte with a little nod, she was dressed as normal in designer jeans and a sparkly T-shirt, and Emma appreciated her friend keeping Jimmy occupied, and hopefully, she would persuade him to eat something.

Emma thought she hadn't had much sleep that night, but realised she had not seen all the hours pass on the alarm clock. She decided to ring the hospital, after waiting until eight o'clock. The Ward Sister informed her that her dad had spent a comfortable night, but would be on his way to Blackpool within minutes. An operation was scheduled for Tuesday morning, and they would be able to visit him in Blackpool today, during the afternoon.

After informing Jimmy of the details, regretting that she had to wake him up, she rang Joe, but there was no reply and she wondered if he had had a very late night, working at the Office. She tried again later, but there was still no reply, so she rang the office, and Mary answered the 'phone. Emma realised that she had spoken with Mary many times in the past, but had not known!

"Good morning Emma, yes Joe is here, I'll put you through. I expect Joe will tell me how Robert is later." Mary's tone was a little curt, and Emma was surprised.

"Emma, what news do you have?" Joe sounded very tired.

She quickly explained what the Sister had told her, and there was a silence on the other end of the 'phone. "Joe, have you been working all night?"

"At least they are getting on with things, and your dad is not on a waiting list. I'll pick you and Jimmy up about noon. I did manage to get a few hours sleep Emma. I'll let your dad's colleagues know what is happening, they will be relieved. See you later Emma."

Emma rang the College, and informed them that she would not be in for at least a few days. They understood and

261

reminded her that the Final Examinations would be taking place very shortly, as would the end of the course year!

Robert Smyth looked much better when they visited, and he was surprised but quite pleased when Emma informed him that she had decided to stay in Blackpool so that she could spend more time at the hospital with him, particularly after his operation the next day. Jimmy decided to stay, and it was a subdued Joe that made his way back home that evening, after promising to take Jason into his own house for the time being, providing Jason was willing.

That evening, after spending most of the afternoon with their dad, Emma and Jimmy walked to the small flat that they had managed to acquire for the next two days, or longer if necessary. There were three similar flats which were for the use of patient's families. They had a ready meal, which was surprisingly good, purchased with tea, coffee, and milk at a nearby corner shop. Jimmy was watching television, and seemed reasonably engrossed. She didn't want to disturb him but felt she needed some reassurance.

"I'm having an early night Jimmy, don't stay up too late." Emma said, wondering how he could concentrate on the television programme.

"OK Sis. It's good you're having an early night, you'll look much better tomorrow," he answered with a weak smile.

She threw a cushion at him because it was expected, and made them both feel better, then moved into her small but nicely furnished bedroom.

Half an hour later she had showered and was in bed fingering her mobile 'phone. Should she ring, he might wonder why she had bothered to ring him, but he might be as worried, or almost, as she and Jimmy were!

"Hello." His voice seemed uninterested in whoever was on the other end of the 'phone and she guessed he was working.

"Joe its Emma, I thought I'd let you know that when we left dad a couple of hours ago he was quite comfortable. I also wanted to know if Jason was being a good boy."

"Emma," he was surprised. "I rang the Sister on the Ward a little while ago, she told me your dad was comfortable, and he was pleased that you and Jimmy had decided to stay. How long do you think you'll be staying?"

It was so good to hear Joe's voice, and Emma felt a whole lot better already.

"Two nights, and then hopefully it won't be long before Dad is home, if the operation goes to plan."

"Right, but will you ring me as soon as they come to see you after the operation? The Sister has met me, but the surgeons won't give information to anyone but family."

"Of course I will Joe. Jason?"

"He's here beside me, with his head on my knee, missing you all. I'm working at home. We had a long walk, and he's been fed, but he didn't want me to leave your house. I was tempted to sleep over there, but I need my computer over here for work, I think he'll settle down alright."

Emma had the strangest feeling, where would Joe have chosen to sleep in Laurel Cottage? She took a couple of deep breaths. Soon the phone call was over, and she was left with jumbled thoughts and chaotic feelings.

Emma and Jimmy arrived at the hospital early, but even then they could only spend half an hour with their dad, as his pre-med was already in operation. Emma felt a sinking feeling as she walked back to the waiting room with Jimmy.

Their dad's last words had been "The sooner we get through this operation, the sooner I will be fit and well again. See you both in an hour or two." Emma had kissed him on the forehead, and Jimmy had firmly held his dad's hand for a few seconds.

They did as the Sister suggested and went out for a walk, but even with each other for company, it seemed so wrong to be taking a walk without Jason. They were soon back at the hospital, walking up and down the waiting room, each trying to think of something encouraging to say to the other, and flipping through magazines which could not hold their attention. The waiting seemed interminable, but then the door opened and Joe was there. Emma ran towards him and he caught her and gave her a very satisfactory hug to reassure her, and then shook Jimmy's hand. Jimmy's brow cleared, it would all be alright now that Joe was here.

CHAPTER SEVEN

Emma carried in the last two bags of shopping and placed them on the kitchen table with a sigh. She bent down and patted Jason on the head, how pleased he had been when they had arrived home after staying until the day after their dad's operation, and Joe had seemed quite pleased too, and Emma had felt like throwing herself into his arms for a welcome home, as she had at Joe's unexpected arrival at the hospital when they were awaiting the end of the long operation – just in time she had realised what she was doing, and more worryingly why! She was in love with Joe, and must have been for a long time. She now acknowledged her feelings of jealousy and envy, and hated herself for them. Joe and Mary were both respectable and caring people, and she should be happy for them both.

Today was the day when Robert Smyth was coming home from the hospital. The house needed a bit of attention, stocking up, and making his room easier for him to negotiate, also his bathroom. He had looked quite well yesterday when Emma had seen him in the hospital, and he would not need any special aids, but because of visiting every day things had been let slip at home.

Mrs Robinson was still doing the upstairs, giving it a special 'do' she said, and she was singing and, therefore, must be happy in her work.

Emma gazed at the bags of shopping, thinking she had probably overdone it, wanting to have whatever was necessary to cope with the number of her dad's friends, who had asked if they could pop in when Robert Smyth was home.

Joe had insisted that his car was the biggest and, therefore, there would be more room for Robert, and Jimmy would go with him to the hospital, to pick up his dad. Emma had been pleased by his offer as she had so much to do preparing for his return and she wanted everything to be just right. During the last two weeks, Joe and Mary had visited twice as Robert had insisted he must talk with them about the business, or Emma and Jimmy had visited. On one day Emma had been exhausted, and Joe had insisted that he would drive her to Blackpool as Jimmy was taking one of his A Levels. She had enjoyed the drive (knowing that her dad was improving) and it had felt really nice to be cosseted for once. He had suggested that they might stop on the way home for something to eat, and Emma had looked forward to that experience. However, she was disappointed to be awakened by Joe when they arrived home, as she had slept most of the way!

The doorbell rang and Jason beat Emma there by a couple of metres. Emma was surprised to find Mary Morton on the doorstep, looking quite lovely in a smart black trouser suit, and an immaculate white blouse.

"Hello Emma, I've come to see if you need any help. Joe said you have been rushing around like a mad thing, because of your examinations, together with visiting your dad." Emma swallowed and felt like crying, she was obviously overtired, and was quite overcome by Mary's offer of help. She had lately realised what a nice person Mary was and she deserved a nice person like Joe!

"Come on in we'll have coffee." She offered with a watery smile.

"That would be nice, but I really would like to help. Everyone at the office is looking forward to seeing Robert, and it's wonderful that he is making such a good recovery."

Mrs Robinson was putting her cleaning things away, when they went into the kitchen. "Emma luv, I've finished upstairs, if there's nothing else, I'll be on my way. I'm looking forward to seeing your dad soon." She smiled at both Emma and Mary, and went happily on her way.

"You put the shopping away Emma, and I'll make the coffee, at least I can do that," Mary suggested, and went to switch on the kettle. "It will be lovely to have your dad back in the Office, as he has been missed, by all the staff and all his clients. Of course, Joe has been working really hard, and has kept everything ticking over nicely, and all the staff have tried to help as much as we can."

Emma was stocking up the fridge, and looked at Mary, she was really a very nice person, and Emma felt guilty about the jealous thoughts she had experienced upon seeing Joe and Mary together.

"Do you love him Mary?" Emma said. God, where had that question come from, what a cheek, she fervently hoped that Mary wouldn't tell Joe that she had asked, she desperately wished that question unasked!

Mary stood stock still by the kitchen unit where she was preparing the coffee, and after a few seconds she turned to look at Emma. Emma looked as if she was in shock, but pulled herself together, and eased her grip on a packet of eggs that she was putting in the fridge. She closed the fridge door carefully. Mary sighed, this would take careful handling, but she wasn't going to lie to Emma.

"Mary I'm sorry, I had no right to ask you that, I don't know what I was thinking about, except, of course, that you look so attractive and extremely happy." Emma said and sat down at the now empty table. She should keep her mouth shut if she couldn't control what came out of it!

"You did surprise me Emma, but yes, I am very happy. I have not admitted it to myself yet, but I have realised in the last couple of weeks that I do love him, very much, and have done for months, but not realised how much." Mary answered as she placed the coffee pot and cups on the table, and sat down. "Let's have our coffee Emma as I think we both need it. Nothing will happen for months anyway, even if he feels the same way. There will be a lot of catching up to do in the business – we'll just have to wait and see."

"Please don't mention my indiscretion to Joe, Dad or Jimmy they are all so close. I would like today to be a special one for everyone, as it is something I have prayed for since Dad's heart attack." Emma said with a sigh. At Mary's nod of the head, Emma relaxed, she would be careful to hold her tongue in future, and not let her thoughts get in the way!

"Did I see you put a packet of chocolate biscuits in that tin Emma?"

Mary was still at Laurel Cottage, when Joe drove his car into the drive. A number of neighbours came to their doors, and promised to visit as soon as Robert had settled in and felt up to company. Jason ran around in circles he was so excited at having Robert Smyth home, and didn't mind who knew it.

They all had lunch together, and afterwards Robert asked if Joe and Jimmy could help him upstairs, as he felt tired, and had probably overdone it for his first day away from the hospital. He had proved to the staff at the hospital that he could manage to get upstairs alone, but a little help just now was welcome.

Emma and Mary watched as they slowly made their way upstairs, all three talking happily together. Robert turned at the top of the stairs, "I'll get into bed I think Emma, and have a little rest. Don't forget Mary, I'll want to see you tomorrow with the Johnson file."

Emma and Mary looked at each other and wiped their eyes with a tissue, and Mary looked archly at Emma.

"Perhaps before too long you will have some happy news to impart yourself? I'll be on my way home now Emma, Jeremy will wonder where I am, he hasn't seen much of me in the last few days. Can you tell Joe I'll see him tomorrow, I know he is going out tonight to see a client?" Mary smiled at Emma, and took her tissues to the bin in the kitchen with a satisfied smile.

"Yes I'll tell Joe. Goodnight Mary, and thanks for your help today." Emma said as she walked with Mary to the front door.

Emma returned to the kitchen and sat down suddenly, what had Mary meant by her last remark, and knowing look? Surely she was not of the opinion that Emma and

269

Jeremy might eventually be an item! For one thing neither of them thought about each other that way, and anyway Jeremy would be back at university very soon, and Emma hoped to make similar plans as soon as her dad was completely well again! Besides at no time had Mary given any indication that she was pleased that Jeremy and Emma seemed to get on so well together. In the meantime she meant to make use of her newly acquired secretarial skills. She really didn't mind what she did, she just knew that it was imperative that she put some distance between herself and Joe very shortly. She was fully aware that *he* quite often found her company irksome (and that had not stopped him being a tower of strength, helpful and kind during Robert Smyth's illness) and *she* herself couldn't bear to see him and Mary so happy together, it hurt too much.

Robert Smyth settled in at home with a will, a will to get well and get back to work. Most days either Joe or Mary spent time with him, going over files and trying to catch up a backlog of work. However, both Emma and Mary made sure that he didn't get overtired. It worked well, as Emma was able to leave the house, whilst Joe and Mary worked alongside her dad, to take the final few days of her Course, including the necessary examinations.

Emma was surprised one afternoon, when returning from taking Jason for a walk, she found Simon Park waiting for her. He was sitting in his car on the street, and had arrived just in time to see her heading for the woods with the dog, and waited for her to return. She sat in the front passenger seat of his car, but with the door open and Jason beside her on the pavement still on his lead.

"I have been away for a few weeks Emma, and when I got home I heard that your dad was very ill. I have been meaning to call, are you alright, and is there anything I can do to help? Maybe we can go out some evening soon." Simon surprised her with his offer of help, and she looked at him closely, and he seemed to be sincere. She had considered that they would be going their separate ways, which had seemed to be for the best. However, she now knew that she had nothing but friendship to offer him.

"Thank you Simon that is kind of you, but Dad is improving every day, and I'm in the throes of finishing off my secretarial course this week," she said with a smile, and noticed his self-deprecating grimace.

"I wish I'd tried a bit harder, I don't think I'll be going back to university now, I've messed things up. I've been away for a few weeks, as I promised my parents I'd give rehab a try. I regret I was such an idiot Emma, will you come out with me again?" Simon asked, and grasped her hand, which left her in a difficult situation with her other hand holding the dog lead. Did it really only take a few weeks to be rehabilitated she wondered?

"We'll see how you get on Simon. I'm glad you are getting everything together, and I'm sure you will be able to take some further education if all goes well. We all know you are highly intelligent, and now you are showing common sense too! I'll see you sometime after I've finished my course, and Dad is better – I have to spend a lot of time at home now."

"Thank you for giving me your time Emma. I'll see you in a week or two," Simon said, and pulled her towards him, and kissed her lightly, as she struggled out of the car, with Jason anxious to be moving towards home. She paused with Jason pulling hard, "Good Luck Simon." He still looked untidy with his long blonde hair, and she knew that at this moment he had meant everything he had said. Maybe all he needed to help him get back on track was a really good friend. He gave her a grin, his diamond earring flashed in the light, and he looked much better than he had for a long time.

She unclipped Jason's lead, and lifted her head to see Jason greeted by Joe, who was waiting in the doorway of Laurel Cottage.

"Hello Joe, have you been to see Dad," she asked, hoping that he hadn't seen Simon waiting for her. No such luck!

"Did you have a date with Simon Park Emma? You do want your dad to get well again don't you? I saw you sitting in the car with him and letting him kiss you, your dad might have seen you from the window. Why are you bothering with him when you have Jeremy and Bill Bancroft running around after you?" Joe glowered at her, although he was patting Jason, who was squirming in delight.

"Joe, thank you for everything you do for dad, but you can leave me to look after myself, as I'm not a child and can do without you interfering in my life. I did *not* have a date with Simon, and I can't help it if he parks on the street. I told him I was too busy to go out with him, but he was kind enough to offer help if I needed any. However, I'm pleased that you can recommend Jeremy *and* Bill, and I'll give the matter some thought. Now that I've almost finished my course, I might have time to indulge myself a little." She glared back at him, and noticed that he was becoming preoccupied with something happening behind her.

"Be quiet Emma. Jeremy, Jimmy and Mary are just getting out of Mary's car." Joe said in a quiet warning voice.

Is that so, Emma thought angrily, we can't have them upset can we?

"Maybe I should wait until they join us, perhaps they would also like to give me some unwanted advice, but we must not upset them must we?" She murmured, as she stormed passed him into the house, where she assumed he had been discussing business with her dad.

"Has Joe gone already Emma, I had one or two more things to discuss with him. You haven't upset him again I hope." Her Dad said with a frown.

"I never upset anyone Dad unless they upset me first," Emma said, and threw Jason's lead into his bed, thinking that *upset* was hardly the correct word to use.

Robert Smyth shook his head at his daughter, and went back into the living room with a puzzled frown. How he wished his wife was still with them, she had always coped really well through all the different stages, including the teenage years.

That evening when Charlotte called unexpectedly Emma was a bit nonplussed. She had already agreed to go climbing with Bill, together with John and Megan Warner. She was really pleased with her own progress, and that of John and Megan. The nights would soon be drawing in, and if she was to surprise Jimmy and Joe with her newly acquired climbing prowess, then time was of the essence.

"Is it OK for me to come over, you don't seem too sure? Have you got a date I don't know about?" Charlotte asked in a surprised tone of voice.

"Come on upstairs to my room, and I'll explain." Emma said, wondering if she could catch Bill and the others before they set off. They went into the bedroom, and Emma closed the door. Jimmy was playing music along the landing.

"Why so secretive Emma, and who is the new boyfriend?" Charlotte asked, sitting down on Emma's bed and picking up an old cuddly teddy-bear.

"There's no new boyfriend. I'm supposed to be getting a climbing lesson with Bill, together with John and Megan Warner. I want to show Joe and Jimmy that I can climb the next time they try to put me off climbing. Bill is teaching John and Megan, and I've been helping him, I've had quite a lot of time on the crags lately."

"Why?" Charlotte asked in a puzzled voice.

Why indeed, Emma pondered? The urgency to *show* Joe and Jimmy seemed to have waned somewhat, it had probably started because she was annoyed with Joe, for putting her off climbing on Raven Crag! Whatever the reason, or new lack of urgency, she couldn't let down Bill, he had been very good to her during the last couple of months including her with his other pupils. Besides that, she really liked John and Megan Warner. "Would you like to come and watch - I'll only be a couple of hours?"

Charlotte pondered for a moment. "I like Bill and the Warner's but I'm not into climbing, nor likely to be. Tell you what Emma, I'll listen to some music with Jimmy, and wait for you to get back." Charlotte said, placing teddy on the bed, before wandering along the landing and tapping on Jimmy's door. She opened the door and went in, then popped her head around the door her dark hair swinging and her darkly made-up eyes smiled wickedly at Emma. "Look Emma, I'm leaving the door open, Jimmy will be quite safe!"

Emma smiled at her mischievous friend, and then stopped short. Charlotte was obviously flirting with Jimmy, and Emma realised that in a couple of weeks Jimmy would be eighteen, which made him only eighteen months younger than Charlotte. Nothing to worry about there, as everyone knew that girls matured much earlier than boys, and Charlotte was on the look-out for someone quite a bit older than herself! Emma sighed, similar to her own wayward heart's preference!

When Emma opened the front door to go to meet Bill on the street, she found Mary, Jeremy and Joe coming up the driveway.

"Hello Emma," Mary said warmly, but with a query in her voice as she noticed that Emma was wearing a light fleece, and obviously going out. "We have an appointment with Robert, and I brought Jeremy along for some younger company."

"I'm sorry I am on my way out. However, Jeremy you are in luck, Jimmy and Charlotte are in listening to music, and I'll only be a couple of hours. See you later."

Emma stood back for them to come into the house, and met Joe's enigmatic grey eyes, which left hers to look into the street towards the car parked outside Laurel Cottage, making it obvious to her that he was aware that she was meeting Bill. So what! Joe knew and liked Bill, and he was one of his climbing buddies.

"Hello Emma, we'll get off and pick up John and Megan, I thought we'd go to Hodge Close today, not too far to drive, and easy to park. I saw Joe going into your home, do you think he has realised you are learning to climb, and getting plenty of crag time?"

"No I think he has other ideas about why we are meeting," Emma replied sadly.

"Pity he isn't correct," Bill said with a rueful smile as he started up his car, leaving Emma feeling slightly embarrassed. She really liked Bill, but as a friend, and had never led him to believe it could be anything else. Neither had she made it clear that her affections lay elsewhere, but for some reason Bill seemed aware of this, and accepted matters as they were. The evening was a success, it kept fine and dry, with the Warner's also in good spirits and as eager to learn as was Emma. She took the opportunity to invite them all to a barbecue at Laurel Cottage at the weekend, which she was hoping would be a good get together for Jimmy as an early birthday celebration, leaving him free to choose what he wanted to do to celebrate his actual eighteenth birthday.

Emma found it hard to ask Joe for his help, as she had done in the past. She wanted him to ask Jimmy's climbing friends, and also for the use of his Gas Barbecue. She was aware that she looked uneasy, and Joe immediately picked up on it! She was the one at fault, she was the one who had fallen in love with him, and now felt embarrassed appearing to take his help for granted! She quickly asked him, before she changed her mind, but it *was Jimmy's* birthday.

"What's wrong Emma, you must know that I'm glad to help, as always?" Joe asked his eyes interrogating. He watched her eyes slip away from his, they were deep blue which meant she was feeling some sort of emotion, but lately she had changed from the open and happy girl she had been. Had she fallen in love with Bill Bancroft with whom she seemed to spend a lot of time, or was the man in her life Jeremy? He remembered the way she had cared for Jeremy

276

when he had suffered from vertigo, and he still visited Laurel Cottage regularly?

"I hoped you would Joe, but things are not as they always were, things are changing rapidly for all of us. Dad has had a traumatic time, Jimmy and Jeremy will be off to university soon, you are busy with your work and friends, and I have some decisions to make." She glanced at Joe who stared back at her, causing her to turn away.

"Emma, you know that I will always be here for all of your family, as I have been since I joined the Accountancy Firm. Of course things have changed, as you and Jimmy have grown up a hell of a lot in the last two years since losing your mother. Let's just give Jimmy a good surprise birthday barbecue, and then *decisions* can be made. Unless you want a dressed up affair, which I don't think Jimmy will, then I suggest that I get Bill and Jed to take Jimmy climbing, with the others, and they will bring him back home and stay for the evening."

"That's sounds fine. Dad is asking everyone from the Office, and I have asked the boys in the Band who play with Jimmy. I have also asked Charlotte. You must ask anyone else that you would like Joe."

"I may do that Emma," he said enigmatically. Leaving Emma wondering who he might ask, as Mary would already be one of the guests!

CHAPTER EIGHT

The day had been warm, and the shiny grey bark and remaining yellow foliage on the silver birch tree at the bottom of the garden looked fantastic against the yellows, browns and reds of the beech, and garden shrubs. Emma had strewn all the Christmas lights she could find on the bushes and trees, and also placed large lanterns enclosing church-type candles in suitable positions, and this gave a very festive look to the garden, which she hoped would be quite atmospheric when the sky darkened.

Mary and Jeremy were helping Robert Smyth with the garden furniture, putting two tables together, and arranging the chairs around them. Joe was at the barbecue with Charlotte (who was supposed to be helping Emma with the salads and cold dishes). Tom and the other two members of the band had already managed a couple of beers each, insisting that they were all three older than Jimmy! The plan was that Bill and Jed would bring Jimmy back from climbing, telling him that they had to visit Joe next door.

Emma noticed two shadowy figures in Joe's garden next door, and hoped they wouldn't breast their way through the fence as she had been doing for years. Just lately she had been encouraging branches to grow across the breach. The doorbell rang and she hurried to answer it, warned by Jason's bark - he was in his element with so many people around to make a fuss of him. Emma welcomed John and Megan Warner, and brought them through the house to the garden, and Emma was slightly surprised to find them in climbing clothes.

"Dad, Mary, Joe I'd like you to meet some friends of mine, John and Megan Warner." Emma introduced her friends, and was surprised when Joe kissed Megan on both cheeks, and shook hands with John.

"It's a small world Emma." Joe said with a smile. "Your friends are also valued new clients of mine, and friends too I hope."

"How lovely Joe," Megan said happily. "Emma is a friend and new climbing buddy of ours." She paused, and watched two figures crawling through the hedge, making it appear rather difficult. "And here are two more new buddies."

Bill and Jed straightened up. Bill put his hand up for silence, and looked and pointed towards the kitchen doorway. A few seconds later Jimmy stood there, with dropped jaw and astonished stare, as he was welcomed by everyone singing Happy Birthday.

Much later after the consumption of lots of good food and a number of drinks, the party was quietening down, as two boys from the band strummed guitars and Jimmy sang along happily, with Charlotte draped against him. Charlotte pulled Jimmy into the middle of the lawn to dance, and they were joined by John and Megan.

Emma felt her hand grasped and tugged. "I'm tired Bill," she said and glanced up from her sitting position, and glanced around seeing Bill and Jed quite happily drinking beer and telling climbing tales, sat at the garden tables.

"Just as well it's me then," Joe said, "You owe me at least one dance."

"Where's Mary?" Emma said desperately. Joe looked relaxed and comfortable in his jeans and T-shirt, and she thought it unwise to dance with him!

"Helping your dad put away the leftover food. Don't fuss so, we have danced before, and its Jimmy's night. Before you ask, Jeremy has gone home, he couldn't keep his eyes open, and you were not giving him much encouragement."

Emma felt bemused as she was held in Joe's arms, and moved slowly across the lawn, feeling very slight in her flat toe-post sandals. Joe's hand on her back felt warm against her thin cotton T-shirt, and she strived not to show any effect from his touch.

"Bill and Jed," Emma started to speak.

"Are our really good friends, but I think you had better let Bill know where he stands with you Emma, I don't want him hurt. According to John and Megan he and Jed are teaching you all to climb. This came as a surprise to both me and Jimmy, which was probably what you expected." Joe said quietly but firmly.

"Bill does know where he stands," Emma said succinctly. "I think it's time we all went home to bed, it has been a lovely get-together, but now it is late." Joe didn't seem at all put out that she had asked someone else to teach

280

her to climb, which left her with a hollow feeling in her stomach. Her *first* climbing lesson had been on the climbing wall on the gable end of his own house, and they had often done this, but she had been about sixteen then and Jimmy fourteen. She couldn't remember being gradually pushed out of the lessons, but Jimmy was an excellent climber now, and Emma hoped she was too, with Bill and Jed's help!

"If you're tired then off you go, I'll wind up the party," Joe said waspishly, and directed her to the kitchen doorway. "Would you please tell Mary that I'll be in to help in a few minutes."

"Whatever you say Joe, as usual." Emma murmured, not expecting him to hear, as she shrugged off his hand from her shoulder. Joe took in a breath to berate her, but Robert Smyth was standing in the kitchen doorway, and although Joe was not in awe of his partner, he was Emma's Dad.

"You look tired Emma, as you've done most of the work for tonight. You get to bed and leave the rest to us." Robert said, as his daughter kissed his cheek, and moved to the stairs with a sigh of relief.

The two main men in her life had both suggested she should go to bed, obviously both of them thought of her as a child! She closed the windows in her bedroom, drew the blind and put out the lights. Now the light was out, she peeped out of the window. Jimmy, and his band members, Bill and Jed, were still talking around the tables on the lawn. Her dad watched as Joe wheeled the now cool barbecue around into his own garden. She assumed that the boys would talk well into the early hours of the morning. Thank goodness that John and Megan had offered Charlotte a lift home, otherwise she would have had to share Emma's room, and Emma didn't feel very sociable at the moment!

It was late Sunday morning when the Police arrived. Jimmy was in bed, and Emma had, as yet, been unable to move him. Robert Smyth had left the house early to play in a local golf competition. When she opened the door to the Police, Emma's heart dropped into her boots and her heart seemed to twist. Her first thought was that her dad had suffered a further heart attack.

"Emma Smyth?" The older of the two policemen asked, and consulted a pad he held before him. At Emma's nod of the head, he introduced himself as Sergeant Watts, and then the two constables he had with him. One of whom was a woman, and didn't look any older than Emma, but she didn't grasp their names.

The Sergeant looked a little worried. "Is there anyone you would like to be here with you?"

"My father is not here, but his partner Joe Grantham lives next door," Emma said indicating the house to the left. She realised they probably thought she was much younger than her actual years, and wondered if her parents were about. She should really use a little make-up in the mornings. Please go and get Joe, she thought, I'm terrified of what you are going to tell me! Didn't they usually say something like "there is nothing for you to worry about." She watched as the male Police Constable went towards Joe's house. Please don't let him be playing golf or climbing, as was usual on a Sunday morning she prayed.

"Please come into the house, the neighbours must be wondering what has happened, as am I," Emma said worriedly.

"I'm sorry Ms Smyth, but we have been given your name as someone who may be able to help us with our enquiries." Joe joined them hurriedly. "Ah, Mr Grantham, sorry to trouble you, but this young lady would like you to be present," the Sergeant said with a brief smile towards a frowning Joe, who was wearing his climbing gear and he pushed open the front door to Laurel Cottage.

"Inside I think Sergeant," Joe said holding the door open with one arm, and placing his arm across Emma's shoulder protectively.

In the living room Joe gently pressed Emma onto the settee, and sat down beside her, whilst the Sergeant sat opposite leaving the Constables standing.

"Mr and Mrs Park have informed us that their son Simon Park has gone missing. He has not been seen for over a week now, and they are extremely worried. They told us that you are his girlfriend, and we wonder if you have seen him lately, or have any idea where he might be?"

Joe jumped in immediately. "Emma is a friend of Simon, who happens to be a girl." Emma now had a couple of seconds to unscramble her thoughts.

"Is that so, Miss?" The Sergeant seemed annoyed by the interruption.

"Yes it is. I'm afraid I haven't seen Simon for a number of weeks. He called to see me when he heard my father had suffered a heart attack, and he offered to help in any way he could. He had not been in this area for a long time. He did say he would possibly be in touch when I was less busy."

"And you haven't heard anything from him since?"

"That is correct," Emma paused. "You are aware that he had been away for some sort of 'rehabilitation' suggested by his parents?" There was no way that Emma was going to mention drugs, and she hoped that Joe wouldn't. "He

seemed quite well when he called about three weeks ago."
She glanced towards Joe anxiously.

"I can confirm that Sergeant, I was here when Simon
called to see Emma."

"You probably realise that we, and his parents, are
worried that he might do himself harm. Please give the
matter some thought, and if you think of anywhere he may
have gone, please let us know. I'll leave you my card with
the number to ring." The Sergeant and constables went on
their way, Joe having a brief word with them as he showed
them out.

He walked slowly back and joined Emma on the settee.
"You look very upset Emma, are you still carrying a torch
for Simon?"

"Of course not Joe, but he is a friend, and a young man
in trouble, of course I'm upset." She dabbed her eyes with a
tissue and glared at Joe.

Joe put his hand on her shoulder and patted it. He stood
thoughtfully, and then walked on towards the kitchen.

"Are you going home Joe," she asked in surprise.

"Of course not Emma, I'm going into the garden to ring
Bill and Jed, I'm supposed to be meeting them we were
going to Gimmer Crag at Dungeon Ghyll, as it is fast drying
rock, there was a shower earlier."

"You go Joe, I'll be alright."

"I'll be back in a minute, and we'll go over everywhere
you can think of that Simon might have gone, and with
whom. You check your 'phone Emma, see if he has left any
messages or texts."

Joe came back from the garden, to find Emma crying
miserably. He handed her the box of tissues, and sat down
beside her.

"Instead of just crying Emma, think where he might have gone." Joe said, wanting to take her in his arms to comfort her. This he knew from experience was not an option. He was feeling angry with Simon who never seemed to have any common sense or thought for other people, least of all his parents who must be going through hell! Maybe he should have made more of a fuss when Simon had bumped into the back of his BMW, and possibly have got the police involved at that early stage. If the police had been hard on him, testing him for drunk driving and drugs, maybe things would have been different?

Emma blew her nose, and glared at Joe. He was an unfeeling beast. "Don't you realise Joe that if I had taken Simon back, instead of telling him I was too busy to see him and possibly giving him the impression that I had moved on, I could have helped him over this bad patch. He had spent a few weeks in rehab, and what I said may have set him back. Now he's disappeared."

"Rubbish Emma, it is not your fault, he has no-one to blame but himself. He could easily have turned up by now. Do you want a brandy or a cup of tea, you have had a shock?" Joe stood, and looked at her expectantly.

"Tea please," she said and picked up her mobile, and could find no messages or texts from Simon. She rang Charlotte, and told her what had happened, and neither of them could come up with any ideas as to where Simon might be.

Jimmy arrived downstairs yawning, and rubbing his eyes, just as Joe came out of the kitchen with a tray of tea. "Oh good, I could do with a cup. What's up Joe I thought you were going climbing?"

Joe placed the tray on the coffee table, and stared at Jimmy. "Your sister has had a shock, and you should stay with her until your dad gets back from golf. I'll be next door if you need me." He looked at Emma, and his heart ached for her, why she was blaming herself was beyond him, as Simon was an idiot. Nevertheless, Joe hoped that he would be found safe, and soon, and then this episode could be put behind them.

Emma felt guilty for asking for Joe to be present when the Police arrived - she had selfishly ruined Joe's Sunday and, as always, he had been there for the Smyth family. She had been certain there was bad news regarding her dad, and she felt a burst of contrition at getting him involved. She watched Joe walk away and her heart ached, she felt so many conflicting emotions. He would most likely spend the day with Mary and Jeremy now that Emma had spoiled his climbing engagement, at least *they* would be pleased.

"Come on Emma, what's going on," Jimmy asked.

Emma explained at length, and Jimmy went upstairs to use his mobile. At least his friends or Charlotte who he rang first, might come up with some idea of where Simon might be. Emma was a little worried, were all these people aware that Simon had been on drugs, and then into rehab? Was she the only naive one who had not had a clue before it had been pointed out by Joe?

When Robert Smyth arrived home he was late, as he had been celebrating the fact that he had come second in the golf competition, and even better than that, he had shocked all his colleagues by scoring his first hole-in-one! Jimmy was over the moon for her dad, and when Emma joined them having heard her Dad's excited chatter from upstairs, Jimmy slowly shook his head at Emma. She realised that Jimmy didn't want to spoil their dad's evening, and she nodded sagely, and left them to it. Tomorrow would be early enough to bring their dad up to date with the upsetting news of Simon.

It was about an hour after both her dad and Jimmy had come upstairs to bed, whilst she was unable to sleep, that she thought of the barn. She mulled over her thoughts, becoming more convinced all the time that it would be worth a look. If she left it until morning, could that possibly make it too late for Simon? What if he was high on drugs, maybe an overdose? She realised she was dramatising the whole situation, but time could be of the essence. Although she thought that Simon was sensible enough not to do himself any harm, what if she was wrong! If she told the police and there was nobody there, then she would feel a fool. On the other hand all these worrying thoughts were probably because it was the middle of the night, and that was always the time when any worries were multiplied and became much more harrowing than they would appear in the morning.

She slipped downstairs, patting Jason who watched her as she crept into the kitchen his tail wagging desultorily. He licked her hand, and settled down again closing his eyes with a sigh. She felt the weight of the kettle, switched it on, and then went upstairs to get dressed in warm trousers and a sweater. As she picked up the car keys the kettle switched itself off, but she ignored it and she left by the kitchen door.

She was just sliding into the driving seat of the car, when a hand fell onto her shoulder. She gasped and looked up in shock.

"What are you doing Emma, where are you going at midnight?" She sighed as she recognised Joe, and rested her shocked face on the steering wheel for a moment and then straightened up in her seat.

"I'm not a little girl Joe. What are *you* doing out at midnight?"

He paused for a while, and then said brusquely. "I was having a cigarette."

"But you don't smoke Joe," Emma was mystified.

"Someone left them in the front of my car, months ago. I needed something, I couldn't sleep. Where are you going Emma?" He left go of her shoulder, and walked around the car, and sat in the front passenger seat. "You are not going out alone at this time of night Emma, and your dad would never forgive me if I let you."

She stared at Joe, who was obviously not moving out of the passenger seat, and caught a whiff of unaccustomed smoke on his breath. She was amazed, she had never thought of Joe as vulnerable and unable to sleep! The car door was still open and she looked into his intense eyes, which suddenly turned remote. She shivered, and started up the car - now was not the time for introspection or speculation, now was the time to tell Joe what she had been thinking about, namely Simon. Joe quietly closed the door, and tested it with his weight, it was closed and no lights had come on in Laurel Cottage. Emma drove off as quietly as she could, wondering if she would be able to find the old barn that Simon had once mentioned.

"Where are we going Emma," Joe asked wearily.

"It's an old barn that Simon once mentioned. He and some friends camped there a few years ago. He said that they had a wonderful time there, miles from anywhere fending for themselves. I've never been there, but I think I can find the barn, and we turn left soon and follow the road

288

up the valley. It used to be used for storing hay, but I've never seen any hay being gathered in the valley."

"We have parked near there when we were climbing Raven Crag." He caught her glance. "Yet another Raven Crag, I think I know where you mean. A number of years ago climbers used to camp out in the barn when they came up for a weekend's climbing. Its miles from anywhere Emma, do you really think Simon might be hiding there?"

"I don't know Joe, but I couldn't sleep after thinking about it. We'll be home before one o'clock if there is no-one there. I'm not sure what I want to happen Joe – I don't think Simon would do anything stupid, but I've got to find out if he is at the barn now that I have thought of it. It was uncanny really I was thinking of something entirely different when the thought came to me."

"Do you really think it was a call for help from Simon, I never thought you were that close a couple. Pull over Emma, I'll drive. You are getting yourself too strung up."

"We were never a *couple* Joe, just friends, but you think what you like you usually do. Joe, I can drive, I need to see this damned barn to rule it out, without getting anyone else involved, but *you insisted* on getting involved. I would like you to come with me across the field to the barn please. There's a torch in the glove compartment, will you see if it's working, I don't think I've ever needed it."

"It's a bit dim, but should last long enough to get across the field to the barn and back. If not I've got a lighter, I usually keep one in the car for friends, but I used it to light that damned cigarette and it's in my pocket."

"Stupid me, I've got a head-torch in my climbing gear in the boot, Jimmy gave it to me last Christmas, and it hasn't been used."

"Good of *Bill* and Jed to let you get home before dark," Joe said blandly.

She felt like shouting at Joe, because of his sarcastic innuendo - why she bothered to spend most of the night hours thinking about this arrogant pig that did, however, seem to be around whenever she needed help, she had no idea!

Emma was now driving very slowly looking for the entrance gate to the field in which the barn stood. She found it and slowly drew the car onto the verge, as the road was very narrow. She doused the headlights leaving on the side lights, and went to the boot of the car to get the head-torch. Joe had already set off across the field, but was making slow progress as it was very uneven terrain. Having a much better light Emma soon caught him up, but when they reached the barn, he pointed to where the door was slightly ajar, and indicated that she should wait. He took her torch off her head, adjusted it and put it on his own head, and handed her the hand torch. Emma wondered why he was making sure he had both hands free! She then belatedly thought there could be a tramp, or scores of rats, or bats in there. Joe then moved slowly to the barn door, and she wanted to follow him, she didn't want to be left alone with just a dim torch! Emma wished she was at home in bed, why would Simon come here, why would anyone come here in the middle of the night in late autumn? Joe and the glow from the headlamp disappeared inside the barn, and she nervously drew in her breath. She took her mobile from her jeans back pocket, so that if she needed to make a telephone call she was ready.

Joe seemed to be taking forever, was he investigating every bale of hay?

CHAPTER NINE

Emma heard movement from inside, and she waited with bated breath, was it such a large barn it took this long to look around? Joe opened the door slightly and she stared at his pale face. Of course it was pale, as it was the middle of the night!

"Emma please get the Police on the phone and then hand it to me."

Emma pushed passed Joe, "I'm not a child Joe, let me in I might be able to help." She stopped dead in her tracks and stared.

Joe directed the head torch to his own mobile 'phone, and moved outside. Stupid girl what she was seeing would probably stay with her for the rest of her life!

"Don't disturb anything Emma, the police and ambulance will be here as soon as possible. They will see your car, and be able to find us. A paramedic might get here first. You go across to your car, I'll wait here. Simon has a faint pulse, and I'm going to check the other one."

"There is someone else?" Emma said aghast, her eyes trying to infiltrate the sinister dark recesses of the barn.

"*Emma, go to your car and wait,*" Joe spoke brusquely, and the sound shocked her, and she moved off across the field, mouthing a prayer as she went. Until today when the police had arrived and she had prayed that they would fetch Joe, she had not prayed since her father had suffered a heart attack, and she felt guilty as sin. She sat in the driver's seat and put her head on the steering wheel and closed her eyes, but she could still see the inside of the barn, and she sobbed quietly. Simon was lying on his back with one arm across his chest and the other hanging limply over the edge of a pile of straw made up into a rough and rotting bed. His face was deathly pale, his eyes closed, and his mouth slightly open. The paleness of his grubby face showed up his long blonde unkempt hair, and Emma wished with all her heart that his parents did not have to see him like this.

She shuddered as she recalled the unpleasant excess impedimenta and detritus left after sordid drug taking, and intimate sexual and bodily activity. Simon could not have been the first person to find the barn. He might have harmed himself but he would not have harmed anyone else! She wondered who the other person was, and if they were in the same state as Simon, if Joe couldn't help them then he should have come back to the car with *her*. She sobbed louder as she realised that she was being entirely selfish, needing Joe to be with *her*.

Lights and a siren were heard in the distance, and as the sounds got nearer in the valley the siren was silenced. There was very little in this valley except one farm, and farm buildings. The harsh light blinded her as she looked in the rear view mirror, as the police and ambulance vehicles arrived following a paramedic's car.

An Inspector of Police came to her car, and introduced himself. "Ms Smyth?"

At her nod, he indicated to the others to move on into the field, and thence the barn. "Stay here Ms Smyth, your job has been done, and we thank you. We will need to speak to you later. Is Mr Grantham still at the barn?" She nodded again, as she watched as the fence was pulled down, and two ambulances drove across the field, in the wake of the paramedic.

Half an hour later Emma was relieved when Joe came to join her, he looked so drawn and tired, that her heart began a gradual contraction, and she got out of the car and slipped her arms around his waist, the only reason that he was here at all was because of her! He held her tightly for a moment, and then put her at arms length. "Emma, I don't know who the other person is, and the Police wonder if you might be able to identify him. It would be helpful if they knew who he is, so that they can contact his family. He appears to be about the same age as Simon. Would you take a look please?"

"Are they both alive," Emma asked, and held her breath.

"At the moment yes Emma, don't expect too much." Joe took her hand and she walked over to the second ambulance, and she climbed in apprehensively. She took a look on the stretcher, and then almost fainted as she climbed down. Joe picked her up in his arms, and she clung to him.

"Oh no, Joe, its Charlotte's older brother Ron." She turned to the Inspector. "He is Ronald Fleming," and she gave the address of the Fleming home. "I'm alright Joe, I can walk, but I'm not sure about driving back."

The paramedic came towards them carrying with him a large bag. "I must just check over the young lady, she has had a terrible shock. You do realise don't you, that in another hour or so those boys would not have stood the slightest chance of surviving." He looked into Emma's eyes and felt her forehead. He then turned to Joe. "She shouldn't be alone tonight, and try to keep her warm."

Forty minutes later, Joe pulled up in front of Laurel Cottage, and Jason started to bark, knowing the engine sound of the small Rover car. Joe unwound his long frame from the driving seat of the small car, and walked around to help Emma out. The light came on in Robert Smyth's room, and then the stairs and hallway.

"I will take you in Emma, and you should go straight to bed. I'll explain everything to your dad. Goodness, even Jimmy has woken up, his light has come on. Keep my sweater on, as you don't want to get cold now." He suddenly pulled her towards him, and held her close for a stretched out moment, and then with a sigh released her, and she felt bereft, as they walked together to the door.

Emma slept in Joe's sweater that night, his individual scent comforted her, and she managed to get a few hours sleep. She awoke after a nightmare, and spent the rest of the night downstairs, on the settee with Jason curled up beside her.

Three days later, Mr and Mrs Park called to see her, to tell her that Simon was going to live, and they knew that Emma and Joe had been instrumental in saving his life. It remained to be seen whether he would be completely well again, his body had suffered terribly. Whatever he had taken (they did not say what) had been a bad batch, and police investigations were ongoing. They were relieved that Simon had not wanted to harm himself, but devastated that rehab had not done what they had hoped, but they had not given up hope. Simon was their only son.

It was another couple of days before Charlotte arrived, with a message from her family. Apparently Ronald Fleming was still critical, and the whole family were desperately looking for some improvement. Charlotte was very subdued, and kept talking without making much sense, but Emma realised that she was embarrassed that her older brother had been into drugs, as she had always looked up to him. From what Charlotte didn't say, she wondered if Charlotte thought he had been even deeper than Simon in that seedy under world. Charlotte had for many years relied upon her older brothers to keep *her* out of trouble, and it now looked as though she would have to look after herself.

Jeremy came with his mother to Laurel Cottage, and whilst Mary talked with Robert Smyth and Joe, Jeremy pumped Emma for any information he could get on what had happened, so much so that Emma began to wonder if the bird-watcher, photographer, star gazer, was also into writing or journalism! She decided to give Jeremy a wide berth for the time being, which wasn't difficult as he was going back to university in a week. Jimmy had also got a place on an artificial intelligence course, which surprised everyone as he was usually outdoors at every opportunity. Emma was getting depressed by the whole sorry business regarding Simon and Ronald, and had missed out on getting a place in further education for this year.

She decided to look for an office job using her new credentials, but they seemed few and far between. The ones for which she managed to get an interview, were always given to people who had already done work experience.

Robert Smyth was very worried about his daughter, she had become very introverted and quiet, not like her usual self. All the drama of the last few weeks had taken its toll, and he insisted that she came to work for him for the time being, to take her mind off other things. This was the last thing that Emma had envisioned, as she had wanted to get a job on her own merit, besides that she would have preferred to give Joe and Mary a wide berth. She hated the thought of seeing them working together every day in the Office. Of late Joe had been pleasant but distant, and Emma wondered if she had been too clingy and possibly an embarrassment, during and after the episode when she and Joe had been involved in finding Simon and Ronald. She was relieved to find that the accountancy staff, her dad, Joe and Mary all had their own offices, and she was put in the main office with two other girls, and one young man. The days were getting short now, and she enjoyed the company of other young people, now that it was too dark to go climbing or walking in the evenings, she often went to the cinema or for a drink after work. She did, however, get together with Bill, Jed and John and Megan Warner occasionally at the weekends.

It was already December, and everything was geared towards Christmas, and the office party was to be at a local hotel, comprising dinner and a dance afterwards. A number of firms jointly booked the hotel, and then filled up the places with their staff and families.

Robert Smyth took his daughter aside one afternoon at work. "Emma love, have you settled down here, are you enjoying your new job?"

"Yes Dad I am, I've enjoyed arranging the Christmas party, together with the other firms participating, and all the staff here are really nice, and I get along with them, but you knew from the beginning that this was not what I intend for my career."

"You seemed to be settling down after all that horrible business with Simon and Ronald. I understand that you will probably be moving on come the spring. Why don't you think about accountancy Emma, there would always be a place here?"

"Thank you Dad, but I am applying to Manchester University to take either history, or archaeology. Wish me luck."

"I do Emma, if that is what you really want. I'll miss you when you go away from home, as we both miss Jimmy already."

She felt dreadful realising how much her dad would miss her, but she couldn't stay around here and watch Mary and Joe either marry, or set up home together. Joe had not once sought her out in the office, and Emma now believed that he and Mary were getting serious about each other. Particularly now, that Jeremy had gone back to his university and Mary had no immediate ties.

The next night Emma was watching television by herself, as her dad had stayed late at the office to finish a case. The telephone interrupted her, and she was amazed to find that Mrs Fleming was on the other end.

"Mrs Fleming what a surprise, how is Ronald now?"

"Oh Emma, not bad, slowly improving, thank you, but it's not Ronald I rang about it's our Charlotte. She hasn't been right since all that business with our Ronald. She has left a note saying she had left home and gone to live with Jeremy Morton. From what I understand he seems a nice boy. Do you have his address I understand he spent quite a lot of time during last summer with both you and Charlotte? Did she discuss this with you Emma, you are her best friend?"

Emma was dumbfounded, Charlotte and Jeremy! She was sure that if Charlotte had a special interest in a boy, it was with Jimmy. He would be very hurt when he found out about Jeremy, but Jeremy did appear more mature than Jimmy. It worried Emma terribly that he was away from home where she couldn't be there for him.

"I'm sorry Mrs Fleming but Charlotte did *not* mention her plans to me. I don't have Jeremy's address. His mother, Mary Morton, works in Dad's office, she is working late this evening I'll give you the telephone number."

She gave the telephone number and Mrs Fleming rang off, leaving Emma wondering if she had done the right thing, but what else could she do? Had Charlotte really gone to join Jeremy or was it a ploy to get away from home without too much fuss?

It took only fifteen minutes for Joe to have learned all about this latest trouble from Mary, and he came into the kitchen of Laurel Cottage looking like a thundercloud.

"Emma what is going on, what do you know about Charlotte Fleming running away to be with Jeremy, Mary is beside herself with worry. I don't suppose Jimmy will be very pleased either."

Emma jumped up from her sitting position and stared right back into his angry grey eyes, as Jason growled half-heartedly. "I don't know anything, it is news to me, and I have never had the slightest inclination that there was anything between Jeremy and Charlotte. Don't you dare shout at me, because his mother is upset!"

"Surely it wasn't going on whilst he was going out with you?"

"I've never *gone out* with Jeremy, we were only ever friends. However, you believe what you want, you usually do."

"Have you rung Jeremy yet?" Joe asked running his hand through his hair.

"I haven't rung Jeremy since he went back after the holidays, and I'm *not* ringing him now. However, I might try and ring Charlotte just to get you off my back, and I'm only doing it for Mary's sake. Jeremy and Charlotte are both old enough to do whatever they want you know."

"I am aware of that Emma, so is Mary, but she is still worried because Jeremy has never given any indication that he was getting involved with Charlotte."

Emma sighed and shook her head at Joe. "Perhaps *Jeremy* didn't realise *he* was getting involved with Charlotte. She is quite capable of just turning up there because it suits her at this particular moment. She had a terrible shock with regard to her idol of a brother Ronald, as she really respected and loved him. She has also had a bad time lately Joe." She quickly tried Charlotte's mobile number, and after a few seconds shrugged her shoulders. "I'll try again later."

Joe stared at her for a moment, and then smiled, taking her hand in his, as they stood opposite each other, as usual when they were arguing. He squeezed her hand and kissed her lightly on the brow. "You really have matured Emma, and I think you are probably quite right about Jeremy and Charlotte. I'll go back to the office to see Mary – your Dad was getting quite upset because she was so shocked and hurt after receiving Mrs Fleming's 'phone call."

Emma stood for a while, after watching Joe walk away from the house to go and find Mary. Why did he do this to her? An argument she could cope with, but when he squeezed her hand, kissed her forehead, and was really nice to her, it was difficult to deal with the frisson his actions had set loose along her spine, together with her shortage of breath! She would *not cry*, but would ring Bill, John and Megan to see if they felt like an early Christmas drink. Jed could come too if he liked.

When Joe came into Laurel Cottage accompanying Robert Smyth an hour later, with the thought that he would apologise to Emma about his brusque behaviour earlier in the evening, she was no where to be seen. Nor had she left a note for her dad.

CHAPTER TEN

Jeremy in his second year at university, was now sharing a house with three other students, and was able to give Charlotte the use of a bed settee in their sitting room, with the approval of his house-mates, as a temporary measure. He was under the impression that she would willingly have slept with him, just to give her time away from her family. However, the gentleman that he was came to the fore, and he was unable to take advantage of her in her present state of anxiety. He wondered why she had not chosen to follow Jimmy, but then decided that Charlotte was possibly subconsciously aware that she and Jimmy might have got together for the wrong reasons! Jimmy might still be her future, and she his, but it was too soon for commitment, and he, Jeremy, was the safe option! He wondered how long that would be his role, when would he meet the girl who shared his myriad interests and would be his soul-mate? He had wondered whether that girl might be Emma, but he now had his own ideas as to why that would not have worked.

He considered that he would sort Charlotte out first, and when that was done, if the oldies, namely his mother and her colleagues, had not got their act together then he possibly would give them a hand, if only for the sake of peace and quiet whilst he followed his beloved interests.

It was four weeks before Charlotte came home to the Lake District. She was apologetic to her family, and friends, and soon settled down to help her brother Ronald get his life back to something approaching normal. Or what she remembered as his normal life! She astounded herself when she got a job helping at a school for the disabled, and she liked it so much that she decided to get the necessary qualifications to further her career in that field. For the moment she had decided that there was plenty of time for deciding on her ultimate future.

She went to see Mary Morton, to apologise for worrying her, and to inform her that her son was a gentleman, and had given her good advice, and allowed her to stay in his shared digs until she was brave enough to return to her home and face her family. Mary could have told her that she wasn't saying anything that she didn't already know, Jeremy was one of the good guys, and she was extremely proud of him! On the night that Mrs Fleming had found the note from her daughter and had got in touch with her, Mary remembered how good Joe had been in relieving her mind, only because he had passed on Emma's thoughts on the matter. Emma had been proved correct, and Mary was relieved and wondered at Emma's perspicacity, and if there was anything between her son and Emma to give her such an understanding of the situation thrust upon them by Charlotte!

Emma and the two girls from the main office of Smyth and Grantham, Chartered Accountants, spent a Saturday afternoon in Carlisle, Christmas shopping, but mainly the outing was to buy suitable evening dresses for the Christmas Party. Emma had accompanied her father the previous year, and had been tempted to wear the same dress but the girls Jill and Sarah, would not have that, and insisted that they would all wear something new. Emma drove them, and it took just over an hour and twenty minutes, so the first thing they did was have a very nice lunch, with just one glass of wine each. When they eventually arrived back at the car park, they were laden down with shopping, and the boot was full of bags, and on hangers in the rear of the car hung three very different, but gorgeous dresses.

The drive home in the dark was tiring, and Emma was very relieved to arrive home about half past six, just as it was starting to rain. She was pleased and surprised to hear music coming from Jimmy's room – the band were in full flow, she had not been expecting Jimmy to come home for Christmas so early. As always she glanced across at Joe's house, and wondered if the book she had bought for Joe's Christmas present would be to his liking. She remembered last year's Christmas party, and how wonderful Joe and her father had looked in their dinner suits. Joe had danced with Emma only once, and it was that night that she realised that the easy friendship they had always shared, was changing, and she had not understood why! Nor did she understand now, except that she preferred to keep out of his and Mary's company because it was easier. She wondered now why Mary and Jeremy had not been at that Party - Mary must have been working for the firm at that time. Mary and Jeremy had not been introduced to Jimmy and Emma until the night of the barbecue that Joe had put on during the summer months.

Emma joined her dad in the living room. He was much better since his by-pass operation, he was awake and reading the Telegraph, and did not seem tired although he had just finished almost nine hours in the Office. "Dad, have you got the list of staff and their guests for the party? I've bought small boxes of hand-made chocolates for all of the ladies, and small leather pocket diaries for next year for the men, I must name all the presents before I put them on the table."

"In my briefcase Emma, but please remember to put it back, the hotel will need a table plan, which I haven't finished yet."

Emma found the list, and snapped shut the briefcase. "You and Jimmy, and Mary and Jeremy, will have to fight over the chocolates and the diary, I only got one of each for each couple."

Robert Smyth smiled wryly. "No doubt Jimmy will get both, and Jeremy too I expect."

Emma frowned and looked down the list. Her name was last, as the newest member of the Firm. She smiled wondering if Bill Bancroft would enjoy the evening, she had asked him to thank him for all his time spent teaching her to climb. However, she doubted whether he was the dinner and dance type. She glanced through the list again. If Mary had invited Jeremy to join her, then who had Joe invited? She stared at the typed name in front of her - Melanie Banks – who was Melanie Banks? Also, was Mary aware that Joe had invited another woman! Surely he could have asked one of his climbing cronies, well maybe not!

The following Friday, Bill arrived early (by request) to pick up Emma. When she met him at the door she was very pleasantly surprised. Gone was the rough and ready climber, and in his stead was a very handsome young man in a dinner suit, looking slightly self-conscious. His long brown hair had been brushed to within an inch of its life, it went behind his ears and hung tidily down his back, she was relieved he hadn't put it in a ponytail! He also looked slightly embarrassed wondering how to greet his date, but then made up his mind, and greeted her with a kiss on both cheeks. He then stared at her blue halter neck dress (with no back), with a wide silver belt showing off her slim waist, and it draped magically to the floor. He shook his head, as his climbing pupil had suddenly grown into a beautiful woman.

"You look beautiful Emma, and your dress is the exact colour of your eyes. I hope I'm not too early, you said you had things to do to the table." He watched as she picked up a black velvet jacket, and placed it around her shoulders, and he held the door open for her. She smiled broadly at him as she realised the old Land Rover had been cleaned inside and out, and he quickly pushed back under the passenger seat a bottle of water and a screwgate carabiner!

When they arrived at the Hotel, her dad and Joe as the hosts, were already there. Joe stared at Emma – she looked really stunning – no wonder Bill looked pleased and had made such an effort with his appearance to escort her. He shook Bill's hand and welcomed him. He then greeted the two typists, Jill and Sarah and their guests, kissing both girls on the cheek and shaking the hands of their guests. Emma caught Bill's eye, and he handed her the bag of small gifts for the table – she was aware that he had noticed Joe's omission, and he directed her towards the dining room, with his arm across her shoulders. They found the name of the firm on the table, Smyth and Grantham, and duly placed the gifts around the table for twelve. There were four other tables in the large dining room, each with the name of a local small firm, for varying numbers of guests. The whole place looked very festive, and Emma laughed and joked with their party together with Bill, but underneath there was a nagging ache in her chest, as she felt slighted by the fact that Joe had purposely decided not to kiss her cheek as he had the other office girls!

After a drink at the Bar, they were requested to take their places in the dining room. Emma and Bill were opposite her dad and Jimmy, and Mary and Joe, and on the other side of Joe sat a pretty dark curly haired woman, who seemed vaguely familiar to Emma.

"Melanie I'd like you to meet Emma Smyth, my partner's daughter, and Bill Bancroft her guest, this is Melanie Banks." Joe introduced his guest. Emma stood and her fingers touched those of Melanie. However, she was surprised when Bill stood, and shook Melanie's hand with a broad smile.

"Pleased to see you again Melanie," he smiled at Emma and Joe, "I have already had the pleasure of meeting this young lady."

Young lady Emma wondered, she must be nearer Joe's age than Bill's, but Emma had to agree that she was very personable, and the other thing that worried Emma was that Melanie was wearing a wedding ring! When there was general conversation around the table, and background music, Bill explained to Emma that Melanie was Megan Warner's sister, and she assisted in the Warner's Bed and Breakfast business. Emma glanced at Melanie, that was the reason she had seemed vaguely familiar, but she caught Joe's enigmatic eye on her and wondered what he was thinking. The other thing that bothered Emma was what was Mary thinking about Joe escorting one of his client's sisters?

The meal was very good, and the whole room, with the help of a few bottles of wine, was now rowdy and very festive. Emma was rather worried when her dad spoke to the wine waiter, who then brought to the table four bottles of champagne, each cooling in an ice bucket. Nothing like this had happened at the last office Christmas party. Glasses were filled with champagne and passed around the table, and everyone looked towards Robert Smyth and Joe Grantham wondering what was going to happen next! Emma thought she might die, as she waited with bated breath. Was Joe about to announce his engagement to Mary? She glanced towards Mary who looked extremely happy, as did Jeremy, they obviously knew what was about to take place.

Robert Smyth, looking extremely well and distinguished in his evening clothes, tapped a teaspoon upon his glass to get the attention of his staff and their guests.

"Joe and I want to thank you for what you have done during the last year for the firm, and to wish you a very Happy Christmas. I would also like to thank you all for your good wishes and help during my illness. Also, I have an announcement to make which may surprise you, but I do hope you will be happy for us. I am very pleased to announce an engagement." He lifted his glass of champagne, as did everyone around the table – even Emma. "I am very pleased to say that Mary has agreed to become my wife."

Emma didn't hear the rest of his speech, but thought it was something to do with having a heart attack, and deciding that time should not be wasted. She glanced across at Jimmy, who was hugging his dad – it seemed that he was pleased by this unexpected event. Had her dad forgotten his wife and their mother already, after only three years?

"Are you alright Emma, do you want some water," Bill asked worriedly. She looked so pale and shocked, and he didn't know what to do.

Suddenly she stood up at the table, then turned and walked out towards the bar. Bill watched for a second, and then felt a hand on his shoulder pushing him back into his seat. It was Joe and *he* was following Emma. Bill didn't bother to follow Joe, as he had no idea what to say to her! He walked around the table to sit beside Melanie, it was obvious to him that they had both been left alone to fend for themselves.

Emma ran right through the bar and into the garden beside Windermere Lake. It was cold, but she didn't feel it, and her heels sank into the lawn as she hurried towards the summer house overlooking the lake. She sat on a bench, and sat with her head in her hands. What was going on tonight, her *dad* and Mary engaged? It was not even three years since her mother had died, and Jimmy had congratulated their dad! What about Joe, he must be heartbroken and terribly hurt! Had he known this was going to happen, is that why he had invited Melanie to be his guest, to put on a brave face in front of his colleagues?

Just then she felt hands on her upper arms lifting her into a standing position. From the frisson she felt along her now straight spine at his touch, she knew it was Joe. A very angry Joe!

"I'm sorry Joe, you must feel devastated." She murmured brokenly.

"Yes I do feel devastated, how could you behave like that. Get back into that room and congratulate your father and Mary before everyone realises that you ran off. Everyone is very pleased for them, and not many are surprised. Your dad's staff and their guests are all around them giving them their good wishes. Mary was wonderful with your dad whilst he was ill, and she was very good to you and Jimmy, so for them this isn't sudden. *Get back in there Emma* before the whole evening is spoiled for everyone. You are behaving like a spoiled brat - please don't spoil this moment for your dad? You should also give some thought to Bill your guest." Joe shook her, staring into her tear drenched eyes.

She pulled away from his gripping hands, and took a tissue out of her bag and carefully wiped her eyes.

"I guess if you can do it, I can." She said cryptically, without noticing Joe's eyes turn from anger to puzzlement, as she took a deep breath, and straightened her shoulders.

She walked back into the dining room and people were still milling around her dad and Mary, and she doubted if too many people had missed her. She walked up to her dad and gave him a hug.

"You were not too shocked were you Emma. Since being so ill, I had realised that none of us have as much time as we would like, are you happy for us love?" He looked at his daughter with a slight frown, and pulled her close. "I will never ever forget your mother Emma," he whispered for her ears only. Joe pushed his way through their guests and shook his partner by the hand, then kissed Mary on both cheeks. He stood back from Mary, as if making room for Emma to do the same. She did, because she had come to like Mary very much over the last few months, and would not like to hurt her in any way – but it was just so sudden and completely unexpected. She looked at her very happy Dad, and thought that he looked so handsome and distinguished, and was such a caring man. Why had she been surprised? Her surprise was only because she had believed Joe and Mary to be a couple!

Jimmy moved over to his sister, he felt that all was not well with her, and he took her hand in his.

"It looks as if we will have a stepmother and a stepbrother Emma. It's a pity our stepbrother is so very bright, we'll have to make sure he doesn't put us in the shade." Jimmy smiled at Mary and squeezed Emma's hand, giving her time to pull her self together.

"We'll be a bigger family soon, and that should make us even stronger," Emma said, and Mary wiped a tear from her eye, and put her head on Robert's shoulder as he hugged her.

Emma turned away to find Bill, but it was Joe's enigmatic look she caught, which she thought changed to one of grudging approval. Poor Joe, he was a marvellous actor, Emma didn't believe that the rest of the staff could tell how devastated and disappointed he must be feeling. Her heart ached for Joe, and she turned determinedly towards Bill. She was surprised to find that Bill was in the midst of an interesting conversation with Melanie Banks. She moved around the table to join them, putting her hand on Bill's knee and leaning across to speak to Melanie. Bill seemed pleased, but gave her a questioning grin. She then felt like a fraud, it was not Bill she was claiming, it was her true feelings for Joe that she did not want exposing, as he was taking his seat beside Melanie. Already she had been sympathising with his position to his face, just a little too much.

Half an hour later Emma went to the ladies room expecting to find that her eyes and make-up were a mess, she was right. She had almost repaired her smudged eyes, when she was joined by Mary. Mary pushed all the toilet doors to make sure that they were alone.

"Emma, I know our engagement came as a big shock to you, are you really feeling happy about it now the shock is wearing off? I am not sure why you were so shocked Emma, you will remember that you asked me if I loved him, and as I was not going to mislead you even for a few weeks, I did say *yes*."

Emma stared into the mirror and looked into Mary's eyes, and her mouth dropped open.

"When I asked you that question, Dad and Joe were both there, and I was asking if you loved Joe?" She stared at Mary's shocked face in the mirror.

"Good heavens Emma, Joe is twelve years younger than me. I do love Joe, as a colleague and a good friend. I intend to make your dad's life a very happy one Emma, and I hope you will get used to the idea. I believe that Jimmy is already very pleased for us both. There is no way that I will be coming between Robert and his children. Jeremy and I have been alone since I lost my husband and Jeremy his father ten years ago. I hope you will find room for us in your lives."

Emma smiled at Mary, and then they both hugged, and Mary went off to find her betrothed, looking happily elated, and many years younger than her age.

Emma followed shortly, and returned to the table, which had been cleared of everything except the drinks, handbags, and presents that had been opened. She saw that Bill was dancing with Melanie Banks. Bill dancing - had the

311

champagne been too much for him - she would not have believed it if she hadn't seen it with her own eyes.

"Your date has gone off with mine Emma, so I think we should dance," Joe said holding out his hand to her. After a pause she took it, and they walked onto the floor as the music changed to a slow foxtrot. Emma assumed that this was her one dance with Joe, as last year, so she was determined to enjoy it. Besides, her heart ached for him, and she began to wonder what his relationship was with Melanie. She hoped that Bill would keep Melanie occupied until at least the end of this dance with Joe. The floor was becoming crowded and Joe held her closer, setting off a whole chain of complex sensations, and she didn't want to think of anything that had happened during the evening, except this one dance. She glanced up at Joe and looked into his grey eyes, and felt a sharp pain in her chest, and wondered if that was how he was feeling too.

"You did well Emma to come back to congratulate your Dad and Mary. I'm sorry I had to bully you into it." Joe whispered.

"You didn't have to bully me Joe, as I would have come back after I got over the shock. I was of the opinion that *you* and Mary were a couple, not Dad and Mary! And I was worried that you would be devastated." Why did he have to spoil this moment? "I see you are not devastated, so I'd better let you dance with your chosen partner." Emma said. As Bill and Melanie were next to them, Emma turned into Bill's arms to his surprise, and didn't watch to see what Joe and Melanie did, although she was aware of Joe's eyes following her progress, and the feeling she got was that his look was hostile.

312

"Are you alright now Emma," Bill asked as he swung her around the floor.

"Yes thank you Bill. It was a shock, I hadn't realised how things were between Dad and Mary. And although it is only three years since we lost mum, I will get used to the idea."

"That's alright then." He negotiated them neatly between two couples, and spun her at the corner of the room.

"Bill I am surprised that you can dance, I thought you were only into climbing and outdoor pursuits."

"Ah well, after the first dance I had to go to when I made a mess of it and embarrassed myself, I decided I would get a few lessons, after all I don't like people climbing without a few lessons, do I?"

The rest of the evening passed in a sort of haze, and Emma felt tired when Bill escorted her from the taxi to her front door. She wondered if she should ask him inside, and he suddenly kissed her, and she allowed him to.

Bill stood back from her with a rueful smile. "That was very nice, but nice doesn't cut it does it Emma? I am very fond of you, but your heart isn't in it. It's not really working for us is it?"

Emma looked at her handsome escort and smiled at him. "I do love you Bill, but...."

"I know Emma, as a friend. I will still come for you to go climbing. Saturday afternoon OK?"

"Please do Bill, don't forget." Emma replied, and put her key in the door, and watched as he climbed into the taxi with a wave.

Joe crumpled up the packet of cigarettes, and put them into his dustbin, quickly followed by the lighter. He had seen the touching, and gentlemanly farewell between Bill and Emma. However, he had not heard what was said!

CHAPTER ELEVEN

Robert and Mary decided they would get married in the Spring, a matter of waiting four months or so. Both of them having very happy first marriages they wanted a second Church Wedding, and this was booked at the fifteenth century St. Martin's Church, Bowness on Windermere where the Smyth's were parishioners. Mary was elated when she visited the Church, when she was told that the font and some of the stained glass had survived from the original church which had been destroyed by fire. She smiled at Robert, and was soundly kissed when she said that she hoped their marriage would emulate the longevity of the place in which they would make their vows!

Emma was now coming to the idea that this marriage would be the best thing for her dad, for the last three years he had seemed to be in limbo, but now he was fully involved in the planning and preparation for the big day, as was Mary. He also looked years younger as he was so happy. The date for the wedding having been decided, everyone started to plan for Christmas and the New Year.

On fine weekends Emma was still managing to get in some climbing with Bill, Jed and the Warner's, and she had now decided that she was as good as she was likely to get. What she did she really enjoyed - but she was not ambitious at all and was quite content to leave the long and arduous climbs to the men. She looked at climbing as something exciting, but mostly it was a recreational sport as far as she was concerned, and she decided the outdoor exercise was much better for her than the gymnasium.

Charlotte often joined Emma and Jason, for walks on the hills. At first this had come as a surprise to Emma, but she now realised that Charlotte had changed from a girl who preferred to be out with friends for a drink and a good time every night, to someone who was content with just one or two good friends for company. Now that Jimmy was home from university for Christmas, she was enjoying singing along with his band. Unfortunately now that two of the band were in further education and away from the Lake District most of the time, namely Jimmy and Tom, that left the other two who were finding it difficult to find the time, as they were taking on much more responsibility in their jobs.

Mary and Jeremy were joining the Smyth's at Laurel Cottage for Christmas Day. Emma knew that Mary would help her with the cooking, and probably buying the provisions, but realised that this would be the last time that she would be in charge of the arrangements.

"Dad you will be inviting Joe for Christmas as usual won't you?" Emma asked worriedly. Joe had joined in their Christmas celebrations for the last five years since he had become a partner in the business, as the only family he had left was a sister and her family in Australia, and two maiden aunts who lived on the South Coast. Maybe this year he would feel differently, knowing that Mary and Jeremy would be invited also. He had always accepted her dad's invitations over the years, although he mostly had a girlfriend around, and Emma wondered if this year it might be different as he still seemed to be seeing Melanie Banks occasionally.

"Of course Emma, it wouldn't be Christmas without Joe here. I've already asked him and he said he was looking forward to Christmas with us. However, he has other plans for Boxing Day I believe."

Emma wondered if it was a case of off with the old and on with the new, regarding his love-life. Maybe he was spending Boxing Day with Melanie. However, if she remembered rightly, Boxing Day was usually a day for climbing amongst the single men, with a celebration in the evening. Maybe Jimmy would know.

Emma was amazed how Jimmy had matured since leaving home to go to university. He now was much more helpful around the house, and he even stacked used dishes in the dishwasher. This maturity was even more pronounced with regard to Charlotte. They spent quite a lot of time together, about which Jimmy said very little to his sister. However, Charlotte was much more forthcoming. She had confided in Emma, saying that she was in love with Jimmy, even though he was two years younger than her, which seemed a lot. However, she was disappointed that he would not make a commitment, but had insisted that he would finish his course before taking things any further between them. Her new style of life had made a big impact upon Jimmy, and she was much happier with herself. He had

317

always been attracted to Charlotte and in addition to that he admired and respected her, but was adamant that they should wait. Emma was surprised that Charlotte, her previously impatient and slightly selfish friend, had agreed with Jimmy's wishes!

Christmas Day arrived, and turned out to be an extremely happy occasion. The usual number had increased by two, and there was always someone with whom to play games, or enjoy conversation or even watch television upon occasion. Emma was very pleased with Joe's present to her, as it was a gold bracelet on which he had placed two charms, one of a climber and the other a St. Christopher medal. She had been overjoyed with this, and Joe has said to her, that these charms 'could be added to over the years.' Her heart had almost stopped as she assumed that he meant he would add to them, then she realised that was not the case.

During the afternoon Tom Bell and Charlotte came to the house, and the celebrations seemed to take off. Everyone was enjoying the day, and Emma heard the doorbell ring, and couldn't think who it might be on Christmas Day.

Simon Park stood on the doorstep, with an enormous bouquet of flowers.

"Are you coming in Simon," Emma asked politely. He was so thin and pale skinned that she hardly recognised him. His blonde hair had turned grey at the temples, and it had been drastically cut.

"No thank you Emma. I won't keep you long, it is Christmas Day. I would just like a word with you, but I would also like to see Joe Grantham, I thought he might be here. The flowers are for you." He thrust them towards her, and she pulled him by his arm into the hallway. Even his voice seemed to have lost its power, and seemed weaker than she remembered. She looked into his eyes and could see that he was a man on a mission, whatever he had come to say or do he was going to do it, as his mind was made up.

She placed the flowers on the hall table, and went into the living room, which was full of laughter and good spirits. She caught Joe's eye, and indicated that she wanted him to come into the hallway. This he did with a puzzled frown, and seemed equally surprised when he saw Simon's gaunt but determined appearance.

"Mr Grantham, Emma, I came to thank you both for saving my life. Because of the second chance you have given me, I intend to do everything in my power to make it worthwhile. Thank you." His eyes welled up with tears, and he turned and left the house, closing the door behind him quietly.

"Simon, please come back," Emma said, tears running down her cheeks, but Joe caught her, and pulled her into his arms, and she realised that he too was feeling very emotional. They stayed like that, until she stopped crying, and Joe looked down into her woeful face.

"Emma, I think he meant every word, and he will make it worthwhile. He is on the way up, and we should be very pleased for him. His parents were so relieved to get him back, that they will stand by him and keep him with them for as long as he needs them." Joe handed her a tissue from a box on the hall table, and watched as she wiped her eyes and nose. He reluctantly stood back from her, as the living room door opened and Jason joined them in the hallway.

"Emma, we need you to make up a four, hurry up," Jeremy's voice came from the living room. "Charlotte doesn't care whether she is winning or losing at whist. I need a good partner."

"Bill would be feeling jealous if he were here," Joe said with a grimace, and Emma wondered at his attitude. He had obviously been enamoured of Mary, and suffered a deep disappointment, even a broken heart, when he had found that her heart lay with his partner. Did he really not have a clue as to where *she* had lost her heart, as he kept going on about Simon, Jeremy and Bill? She would be mortified if he ever found out, although he probably would assume it was the return of the schoolgirl crush she had suffered five years ago!

"I realise now that Dad and Mary are engaged to be married why Mary was not too keen on Jeremy and I becoming close. She must have been hoping we might become step-brother and sister. It's a good thing we just stayed as friends," Emma said whimsically – Joe did not seem to find this amusing, and as she looked up at him she wanted to run her hands through his hair which was far too tidy, and now that his lips were in a grim line she wanted to touch them. She pulled herself together and moved away, and Joe watched her closely as she made her way into the living room.

He stayed in the hallway patting Jason who was hoping for a walk, he was sitting so still and holding his lead in his mouth, and his beseeching dark brown eyes were hard to resist. Joe's mind was on Emma, she had been very upset after Simon's call at the house, and he didn't think she still held a torch for him, but he wasn't sure. Nor was he sure of her feelings for either Jeremy or Bill. At least Mary would be around in the future to keep an eye on Emma, she probably needed a women to talk to! A woman rather than just Charlotte, whom he had to admit, did seem to be a little more grown up of late.

Joe decided he had done too much eating, and he agreed with Jason, a bit of exercise would do them both good. He stuck his head around the living room doorway, whilst Jason was jumping up at him excitedly.

"Jason has decided he needs a walk, we won't be long."

"We could all do with some exercise," Emma said hopefully, laying down her hand of cards.

"We are in the middle of a game, come on Emma don't disappear now," Jeremy said plaintively.

Emma heard the door shut behind Joe and Jason, and felt quite miffed, she would rather be out with them than playing cards. However, Joe hadn't bothered to wait for anyone else!

Joe and Jason enjoyed the quietness of Christmas Day as they jogged through the woods. Joe was feeling better for the exercise, and Jason was glad to be free. Joe imagined Jason was probably of the opinion that there were too many people around Laurel Cottage today and he had to be quick to avoid being stepped on, and Joe was wondering if he had done the right thing in inviting Melanie Banks out to dinner on Boxing Day. He had done so because she had complained that although she loved her sister and brother in law, and they were pleased to have her working with them in the Bed and Breakfast business, she didn't want to be under their feet all over the Christmas holiday. She thought John and Megan should have some time alone. Joe liked Melanie and thought she had had a raw deal in life, but to ask her out for a second time in that many weeks might look to Melanie and everyone else as though they were dating!

Late in the evening, Emma got the impression that Mary and Jeremy didn't want to go home to their quiet home, neither did her dad wish them to leave, and she started to wonder if a Spring Wedding should maybe be brought forward. She was surprised at herself, considering that only a couple of weeks ago, she had been shocked and upset at the thought of her dad marrying again!

After quite an early night following a very enjoyable evening, she had weird and upsetting dreams, and woke with a feeling of foreboding. She looked at the 'dream catcher' made with leather, together with web, beads and feathers, hanging by her bedroom window – it had a certificate of authenticity from the Navajo tribe, but it didn't seem to be working!

Boxing Day dawned to a bright, cool, but clear morning. Emma had been correct in surmising that the single men would be off climbing. It was quite early when Jimmy and Joe set off to meet their friends. Mary had asked Robert, Emma and Charlotte too to join her and Jeremy for lunch, and this was very pleasant, and nice for Emma to be waited on for a change. After lunch Jeremy retired to his room, he was under the impression that the weather would change, and he was going to work on his computer.

Charlotte and Emma thanked Mary very much, and agreed to take a drive, followed by a brisk walk, after collecting Jason from Laurel Cottage. They drove up the Langdale Valley, and started to walk from the Old Dungeon Ghyll Hotel. They were well wrapped up against the cold, and wore their walking boots, and Emma carried her trusty rucksack. Charlotte's boots had been a Christmas present, and Emma was worried that they might not be comfortable, but Charlotte assured her that they were, they fitted her like a glove. Because of the uneven terrain on the walk towards Mickleden valley, and Charlotte's new boots, they had taken the road to Stool End Farm, and from there started to climb the Band leading up to Bowfell.

"We can't go too far Charlotte, because it will be getting dusk by about four o'clock, but we can go far enough to get a good view of the Pikes. You never know the men might be climbing on Gimmer Crag. I've brought some binoculars." Emma said warning her friend that they only had a couple of hours or so.

"I'm fine Emma, we'll go as far as you decide. Who would have thought that Charlotte Fleming would be enjoying a walk in the vast outdoors." Charlotte said with a smile of derision directed at her self.

They were passed by a number of walkers coming down from Bowfell, but only one couple were on the upward climb. They caught them up, and were surprised to find that they were John and Megan Warner. They walked to the top of the Band together, and looked at the view whilst it was still visible as a cloud was above the Langdale Pikes, which looked very different as they were normally seen from Windermere, and it looked as though the weather was changing. Emma pointed out the Old Dungeon Ghyll Hotel below them where the car was parked, to Charlotte. Suddenly they heard shouts coming from the Rosset Ghyll end of Mickleden Valley.

"It sounds as though someone is climbing on Bowfell, I hope they get things sorted before it gets much darker," Emma said worriedly, and then listened with the others to the anxious shouts echoing in the valley.

"That's Jimmy's voice," Charlotte said adamantly.

Emma listened carefully, after telling Jason who had started to bark, to 'be quiet' – he too had heard Jimmy's voice.

Emma handed Jason's lead to Charlotte, and looked at the worried faces of John and Megan who were comparatively new to the hills and valleys.

"Charlotte you must go back down with John and Megan, and take Jason with you. Here are the keys to the car, you can wait there for me. I'm going along Climber's Traverse to where they are climbing, as I can do it before it gets too dark. I have my head-lamp in the rucksack, to get me back down the valley if it gets dark. The traverse is not a good footpath, as there are big drops to the valley below. I know it and will be alright as I'll take particular care. Whatever the trouble is, I'm sure they will have sent for help by now, but just in case I must go and see." Emma said. She took off her rucksack and found the headlamp, put it on and tested that it was working. "I also have a small hand torch, and my mobile. You had better set off now, and go down the way you came up."

"We should all stick together," John said worriedly, he didn't like the thought of Emma taking off on her own, although he knew that she was the only one of them that knew the way, and knew the mountains. He looked at Megan, and she saw the expression on his face and nodded her head in acceptance of what he was thinking.

"Here is my mobile Megan you take it with you. I'm going along the traverse with Emma as that is the sensible thing to do and she is not going on her own." John said, and kissed his wife, then as Emma set off he followed her closely, unaware of what was facing him!

"We should make good progress John, but maybe you should get out your walking pole, before we get to the end it may be getting darker, and you might need it to help you progress carefully forward." Emma advised him matter-of-factly.

He followed on until they came to the traverse, and took in a breath as he saw how narrow and uneven the traverse was, with obstacles to step over, and the hundreds of feet stretching below to the rocky floor of Mickleden valley. During his climbing lessons with Bill and Jed, he had enjoyed the safety of the rope, held by professional climbers but they were now missing! He realised that he was feeling a strange sense of excitement. He was pitting himself against the odds he thought and then became very serious as he looked below into the valley. He knew he was doing the right thing in accompanying Emma, and was determined not to hold her up, or impede her in any way.

This traverse was something different from an enjoyable climb, certainly a time to be extra careful. Judging by the present trouble across the valley, problems could arise for even the best of climbers. Emma was making good progress in front of him, and he noticed particularly how she placed her feet, firmly but with great care. Her headlamp was lighting her way in the dusky light, even though John reckoned it would be about forty minutes before it became really dark, but what did he know he was a comparatively new arrival in the mountains. He looked to his right and drew in a deep breath, as Emma had not exaggerated the difficulty of this traverse. She paused and handed to him the hand torch, and then continued quietly and as quickly as safety would allow, moving forward.

CHAPTER TWELVE

Bowfell buttress was usually a very good climb, with classic high crag multi-pitch routes of varied climbing. Not one of the party of climbers envisaged having any problems on a rock with various routes which they had climbed frequently.

Joe was free climbing (namely the use of a rope for safety whilst leading the climb). In reality it refers to a climber being free of pulling gear or a rope for climbing upwards, the climber is pulling on holds of rock without the aid of bolts, which are mechanical devices or the rope. However, the rope *was* secured below on two bolts, which had been used many times before.

Joe was making good progress, when there was a movement of rock above him, which came crashing down bringing with it a large piece of rock together with small stones and plants. The rock glanced against his helmet and shoulder, and then continued on down dislodging the bolt which had been anchoring the rope, and he fell about eight metres, and was mercifully held by a lower bolt. Joe was left dangling on the rope without any contact with the rock face.

Jimmy who was below and had managed to avoid the rocks crashing down near him, was holding Joe on the rope from below which was now only belayed in one place, on a bolt which had luckily held. He managed to hold the rope which was still wrapped around an outcrop of rock about eight metres above where the first bolt had been. He could see that the rope was caught around an exposed piece of rock where the rock had sheared away. That exposed piece of razor sharp rock now took the full weight of Joe hanging below. Jimmy dare not attempt to climb up towards Joe as the rope could cut through if there was any further movement on the rope.

His frantic calls to Bill and Jed could be heard all around the valley. Bill and Jed had just completed a different climb to the left on the same buttress.

Joe had obviously suffered a serious injury caused by the falling rock, but his position now was critical, and Jimmy now shouted to Bill and Jed to abseil down from the top where they had already been climbing, and where the rock was presumably safe and secure, to see what the position was.

Bill managed to abseil down to the level where the rock had fractured and dropped away, but it was too dangerous for him to continue after he put his weight against the rock and more broke away, causing his arm to crash against the rock which was so painful that he thought it must be broken. He then instructed Jed to call for the Police, who would alert the Mountain Rescue, as he could see that the bolt anchoring Joe had broken away, and the rope on a razor sharp piece of rock was unlikely to bear any more weight. He then had to rely on Jed to get him back to the top of the crags as he could only use one arm, and his legs to assist. There was no way that he could have three points of contact with the rock at one time, and he was thankful for Jed's large frame and physically honed body.

At the moment not one of the climbers had mentioned Joe's silence, and his body was in a strange position, which looked most peculiar. It was obvious that he was badly hurt but to mention it might make it true! The other problem that was not mentioned was the fact that although they were all kitted out for the winter, now that night would be falling shortly, the temperature would fall dramatically.

Bill was in a quandary, he was aware that Joe could fall at any time as the rope would eventually be cut through by the sharp edge of the sheared rock. He was unconscious, and if he came around he could start moving, and cause himself to fall, but if he didn't fall then hypothermia would be his next problem.

Bill and Jed were at the top of hundred metre crags, and Jimmy was at the bottom, all were shouting to each other to try to come up with a course of action to save Joe, and one of the problems was that they were all climbing with fifty five metre ropes. The problems would be the same even when the Mountain Rescue arrived, and they had to do something, and soon!

Emma and John made their way to the end of the traverse, and negotiated a way through a number of rocks. Jimmy turned as he saw the light, and wondered what was happening. He had been unable to take his eyes off Joe, who was suspended at a very strange angle, and who had not moved since being struck by the rock, and when his body had been stopped from the fall by the rope. Jimmy realised he was looking at his sister, and wondered how she had found them, and the last thing he wanted at the moment was to see her distress at Joe's plight.

"Emma, thank God. There is nothing I can do here to help, except hold the end of this rope. Can you go up the Big Slab and find Bill and Jed. Bill has been injured and they might need your help?" he requested, and his eyes now focused on Joe's still body. There was no way that he wanted Emma down here at the bottom of the crag, if the rope broke and the inevitable happened. He took a couple of deep breaths, he had to stay focused and optimistic, and not think about what might happen.

"What exactly is the problem Jimmy, we heard shouting. Where's Joe?" Emma asked her heart pounding. At least her brother was relatively safe which was a relief as she could see he was fit and well.

Jimmy turned to her in consternation. "Joe is up there Emma, we can't get to him. Go and see if you can help Jed and Bill, as I asked. The Mountain Rescue team are on their way. Will *you stay* with me John, and take the strain of this rope for a while. I need to get some feeling back in my arms, as I try to think of *something* I can do to secure this rope, and then you must move away when I take over again, in case any more rocks fall."

Emma stared upwards, and could just make out in the dusk the way that Joe was hanging, and his strange position. Her heart seemed to stop for a moment. Joe, please not Joe, she must get to him!

Emma turned and ran up the uneven and rock strewn path to the Big Slab which was a massive rock to the left of where they were climbing and an easier gradient up the mountain and she ended up crawling in her hurry. Then she had to slow, her heart was pounding, and she felt light-headed. This wouldn't help Joe, she must be sensible. It was about twelve minutes later when she found Bill and Jed, but it felt like a lifetime. They were shocked to see her, but then stared at each other briefly in the now dim light. They both had the same thought at the same time.

"She *could* do it, she's good enough and *light* and quick enough," Bill said to Jed, a wild hope was beginning to dawn, but it would be dangerous.

"She could, but should we let her try?" Jed said worriedly.

Emma interrupted quickly. "If you've thought of a way to get to Joe, tell me. If I'm the *she* that could possibly do it, please let me try," the almost begged.

Jed was already undoing Bill's harness, and adjusting it to the smallest setting, and then he passed it to Emma. "Can you alter Bill's helmet a bit, but it will still be too big so put his balaclava on inside. You'll have to wear the helmet, a rock fell and left Joe in the position he is in now. Jimmy is below, we don't want any more rock falls, but we have to try and get to Joe, the rope won't last much longer, it's caught on a sharp rock left after the rock fall. A bolt was released in the rock fall, and Joe fell quite a long way. Jimmy might have to tie off the rope at the bottom and get himself to safety, but he doesn't want to put any more strain on it, it could go at any time."

"What's wrong with you Bill, have you hurt yourself" Emma asked, as she realised that Jed was doing everything without Bill's help. She was taking deep breaths to try and slow down her rapid heart-rate, and blinked her eyes to try to banish the sight of Joe hanging so still on the rope, which seemed indelibly imprinted on her mind.

"I went down to get to Joe, and although I'm very agile, I'm too heavy and started to dislodge rocks, as I tried to get across to Joe. Jed had to get me back up to the top of the crag, as I think I've broken my arm. Emma you will have to be *very* careful. Go down to the left of Joe, not too near. Then try and make your way across to him. He was unconscious when I saw him, in an ungainly position. You will have to take a second rope, somehow pull him in to the rock, and then fix the new rope through the carabiner and then extricate the rope he is on now, it could go at any time. You will have two ropes through your belay plate, be very careful." Bill said, looking at her closely and swore. "No you won't have time for all that, so you must just get a rope around Joe, try and hold it around anything suitable, and fix it to your climbing gear. Then anyone below can move away to safety. You can do it Emma, I know you can, just don't panic. If you can hold Joe on this new rope, we can get Jimmy away from below and safe. Then Jed can come down to help you, or the Mountain Rescue might be here then, they will be fresh and have more gear.

"Oh, I forgot to tell you. John Warner is with Jimmy. They can both come up the Big Slab as I did. Where are the Mountain Rescue team Bill, they should be here by now?"

"You've been too busy to notice, but from the look of it they didn't use their siren the roads can't have been busy. They are already in Mickleden bottom, making their way towards Jimmy and John I guess. Do you understand everything I said Emma, you know what you're doing, just *secure Joe*?"

331

"Of course I do Bill. Let's get started, Joe needs to be made safe. We can't wait for the Mountain Rescue, as that rope might give way. You have three arms between you, and I'm only light," Emma said briskly. "As for your gear, I didn't realise how much bigger you are than me – anyway it is now as small as we can make it. Wish me luck." She moved to the edge of the buttress, and swallowed hard, and turned to where she would be facing the rock face - she had to get to Joe, safely and quickly.

She pulled on the ropes, they were secure and gave only as she walked backwards over the edge of the crag to make a slow but steady decent. She concentrated very hard on what she was doing, trying not to think about why she was doing it. If she thought too clearly about Joe she would want to scream in denial. There was no way of knowing how badly he was hurt. She felt a slight tug on the rope from above and realised that they had let out as much rope as the distance that they thought she needed. She must now traverse to the right towards Joe. She glanced across and thought her heart would break. He must be alive, she must get to him before he regained consciousness, or the rope above would surely break at his slightest movement. She was concentrating on not dislodging any stones, when she realised she was almost far enough across to reach Joe. At first she thought she had to try to pull Joe into the rock face, but then decided that would be too much movement. She had to move nearer to him, and get the second rope tied around his waist and up under his damaged shoulder, round his back over his shoulder and back around her waist. She had to hope that Jed had the ropes well and truly belayed and they would hold both her and Joe. The only light now was from the torch on the front of Bill's helmet, and she directed this to the rock, and found a good foothold without any loose stone. She climbed up slightly to get enough slack on her rope to wedge it behind a small outcrop of rock, as she had to lean out to get the second rope wrapped around Joe, and then tied it as securely as she could to her own rope, as he was still unconscious. She slowly pulled Joe back towards the crag, and managed to loop the new rope she had wound around him onto the outcrop where her own rope was held. She looked at the ropes around them, and decided that Jimmy could now leave go of the rope at the bottom of the crag. She knew that he would have secured it somehow, but would not leave until he knew that Joe was at least attached to something or someone else. She had Joe held firmly. "I've got him" she shouted, and this seemed to penetrate his brain, as he started to move and mumble. "Don't move Joe" she whispered brokenly. They were not out of the woods yet, but she had relaxed just a little, and tears were now running down her cheeks.

"Emma what's happening," Joe said, and when he would have moved she held him and he groaned loudly. "My shoulder's no good."

"Please don't move Joe. Jimmy and John, and maybe the Mountain Rescue are hopefully moving away from below us. There are loose rocks. We will be pulled up soon, stay still." His answer was to moan loudly, and she thought her heart would break.

"I'm trying to get a foothold and a good hold with my left hand. Ignore me if I moan or curse." Joe said faintly. "I've the worst hangover I've ever had," he moaned and then mercifully he lost consciousness again. She realised then that even if he was conscious there was no way that she could have helped him up the crag, but at least they were reasonably safe for the time being.

There seemed to be a lot of talking above them, and then Emma heard movement coming down from the top of the crag. They were coming down to her left, where it was less dangerous, and would be moving across to her and Joe.

Suddenly she looked up, and just above her there appeared to be a ledge and two of the Mountain Rescue team were there with a board, on which to place Joe. Emma would not let them take Joe's rope from where it was tied to her own, until Joe was safely secured on the board. She was belayed upwards with Jed's help and she and Joe arrived at the top of the crag together. There seemed to be dozens of people milling around at the top of the crag, and as Jed removed her helmet and harness, she realised that she was freezing cold, and had the humdinger of a headache.

"I'm coming to the hospital with Joe," she declared adamantly, and her teeth started to chatter.

"Yes you are going to the hospital, for a check up. You're a very brave young lady," the leader of the Mountain Rescue said briskly.

"Jimmy could you ring Charlotte and ask her to drive my car home." Emma asked, as she had just realised that she had left Charlotte, Jason and Megan, that seemed like hours ago! She moved over to her rucksack, and took out a hat and gloves, put them on and then swung her rucksack onto her back.

"No Emma, I'm going back with Bill and Jed. John is going to drive Megan and Charlotte home, as they have had a very worrying time. Mary is bringing Dad to collect your car tomorrow morning."

"Thank you for coming along the traverse with me, I was glad you were there," Emma said to John. "I hope Charlotte and Megan have not been too distressed."

"Never mind us Emma, look after yourself and Joe. I'll never know how you managed to do what you did when it was almost dark." John said shaking his head.

Four men picked up the stretcher on which Joe now resided, and he groaned loudly. "Emma" he said weakly, and she quickly moved over to take his hand, which was difficult as he was so securely wrapped, and they all paused.

"Are you fit enough to walk Emma," Jed asked, and she looked around in surprise.

"Of course Jed, we need to get Joe and Bill to hospital as soon as possible."

Bill moved towards her and kissed her on the cheek, and indicated his bandaged arm held by a sling, and she preceded him down towards the Big Slab, and the uneven terrain that awaited them before they reached the Land Rover and ambulance in the valley bottom, an exhausting hour and twenty minutes later. Even with the lights and manpower of the Mountain Rescue, it had been a very difficult and time consuming rescue.

As soon as they reached the ambulance, and she was sat inside beside Joe, she started to fret about Joe's head injury. The ambulance man was almost certain that Joe's shoulder had been dislocated, but there was no way of knowing how serious the head injury might be – thank God he had been wearing his helmet. She remembered the Sunday he had been climbing on Raven Crag with Jimmy, and they had discussed helmets. Since that day he had worn his – Jimmy had told her.

Emma had thought they would be moving away down the valley as soon as Joe was in the ambulance. They were taking a long time over Joe, and she became very worried. She heard them talking and heard air ambulance mentioned, and wondered if Joe's need was so urgent. When the doors were closing, she caught the arm of a paramedic.

"What is going on," Emma asked urgently.

"We are hoping to meet the air ambulance helicopter in Ambleside on the rugby field, but it depends on the weather. At the moment the area is covered in fog, and it is now dark. We will press on for now." He quickly closed the doors and they were soon moving along the rough cobble strewn road.

She started to shake, and weak tears ran down her cheeks, and although she was hungry and thirsty, she felt sick. She rested her head on Joe's chest, and could hear voices talking about delayed shock, and agreed that Joe could well be suffering from shock, and then she felt a niggling pain in her arm, and she felt herself slipping away quietly. They must have meant that *she* was in shock, what rubbish Joe needed her help, and she wasn't going to leave him whatever they did, then she knew no more.

CHAPTER THIRTEEN

Emma roused herself as the ambulance stopped, and she realised they were now at the hospital in Lancaster. She was helped out of the ambulance and waited whilst Joe was brought out and wheeled into Accident and Emergency. She followed closely and was caught up by Bill, Jed and Jimmy. They had followed the ambulance closely, and managed to park across the road from the Main Entrance.

Emma tried to follow the group wheeling Joe, but was stopped and told to wait to be checked over by a Doctor. She waited with Bill whilst Jed and Jimmy went to get cups of tea, and something to eat if possible. Nobody had eaten anything since around lunchtime, and now it was seven thirty, and it wasn't until they arrived at the hospital that they realised they were hungry. Maybe they could eat now that Joe was at least getting the attention he needed.

Just as the tea and sandwiches arrived, Bill was whisked off to X-ray. He arrived back feeling a bit better, as he had been told that his arm was not broken, but very badly bruised. Soon he was taken off by a nurse to get his arm attended to, and in his good hand he carried his ham sandwich. Emma had managed to drink her tea, but was unable to eat. Her eyes were on the doorway as she waited for news of Joe.

Jimmy went and brought further cups of tea, and suddenly stopped in front of his sister and Jed. His sister's hair was like a wild halo around her head, her face and hands were dirty, and she looked exhausted, and if possible, Jed looked worse. "Have you seen yourselves, what a messy group of people we are," he glanced at himself and grimaced. "I think we should at least go and wash our hands and faces."

"I quite agree," a voice said from behind Jimmy, and he turned to see his dad and Mary.

Emma jumped up and found herself held in her dad's arms, where she promptly burst into tears. After a few minutes, she felt stupid and embarrassed, and moved away from her dad.

"I believe you have been a very brave girl, and helped save Joe," Robert Smyth said quietly.

"Everyone helped to get Joe down," Emma replied. "Jimmy, Bill, Jed, the Mountain Rescue and me, all did our bit. But we don't know if Joe has been saved yet. Why don't they tell us anything?"

Robert Smyth, frowned, looked at Mary with raised eyes, and received a nod. He walked through the double doors, and twenty minutes later he came back with a doctor. It had not taken him long to explain that he was Joe's partner, and Joe had no family except two aunts in the south of the country. Nobody would be there for him but the Smyth family.

The doctor explained that Joe was still slipping in and out of consciousness, and that he was going for a scan, and that he had mentioned a name "Ems."

"That's me, and I was with him waiting for him to be rescued. He was conscious for a few minutes, and then slipped away again." Emma was relieved that he had remembered something.

"We won't know the extent of his injuries until after the scan. If you stay in case he asks for you, it might help," the doctor asked, and then looked at his watch and walked back through the swing doors.

"Thanks Dad, at least we know what is going on," Emma said and tried to avoid Bill's watchful eyes. She was gutted, Bill had obviously seen how upset she was, and had put two and two together to make five. Before Bill left the hospital, she would make sure that she had his agreement that he would keep whatever he thought he knew to himself!

Aware that Joe had people looking out for him, Bill and Jed left the hospital about nine thirty. Robert Smyth and Mary wanted to leave, but Emma was adamant that someone should be there if Joe woke up. In the end, after Emma had fallen asleep and nearly fallen off her chair, Robert sent her home with Mary and Jimmy, whilst he stayed at the hospital.

When they arrived at Laurel Cottage, Mary decided that she would stay the night, after ringing Jeremy. She was pleased she had, she had to spend most of the night with Emma who only managed three hours sleep. Jimmy's head, of course, met the pillow and they didn't hear anything else from him until morning, when Mary had decided to drive to Lancaster to bring back Robert. She wasn't allowed to move off until Emma had showered and dressed and joined her in the car. Mary started the car, and then was shocked when the passenger door opened.

"Sorry Mary, but you are going to fetch Dad. I'll take my car as it is back home, and then I can stay a while if necessary." Emma said as she vacated the car, and left Mary to run into the house to get her car keys. Luckily, Charlotte, who had been driven home by John Warner, had been back to Dungeon Ghyll with her brother this morning, and brought back Emma's car. She came back out to the car, started it up, and then realised that she would have to get petrol. She set off before Mary, who followed her and realised when she indicated she was turning into the garage, that she needed petrol.

Emma arrived at the hospital to find Mary and her dad waiting for her. The specialist would not be in until later, and the results of the scan would not finally be known until then. They were monitoring Joe in case there was any more swelling, and because he had been in and out of consciousness.

"Emma, I did see Joe for a while. They came for me because he came round, and I'm relieved to say he knew me. He managed to grip my hand, and then he was sedated so that he wouldn't move around." Robert said, and he smiled at his daughter, who had been the one who did the 'looking after' for all the family and Joe, since he had lost his wife.

"That's better news Dad. You look absolutely shattered, have you had any rest at all?"

"Yes I managed a couple of hours I believe. You go home now, and take Mary and she will leave her car for me. I will wait until after the specialist gives his verdict," he smiled at his daughter, but she didn't look too pleased by this suggestion, and he frowned. He had been informed by Bill and Jimmy about what Emma had done to make Joe safe and he was very proud of his daughter, and relieved that he had not been aware of what was happening at the time! When Charlotte had rung him, it was not to worry him, but just to let him know that they would be late home. Later, Jimmy had rung, when they were on their way to the hospital, after the traumatic event.

He was surprised when Mary took his arm. "I think *we* will go and get some tea Emma, do you want sugar in it like last night?" At Emma's shudder, Mary laughed and pulled her betrothed through the door.

Whatever Mary had said to her dad it had worked, for after they had drunk their tea, Mary and her dad left, making her promise to ring the minute there was any news.

Later the Sister came into the waiting room, and looked around expectantly.

"Ms Emma Smyth?"

"Yes, that's me," Emma replied, her heart dropped.

"Don't worry I have just come to tell you that the specialist is running late. If you would like to you could sit with Mr Grantham for a while. He is still sedated, but occasionally he rallies, and he may settle better if he sees a face he knows," the sister said briskly. Emma nodded and stood expectantly.

"If there is any change you could let us know," Sister replied, and indicated that Emma should follow her. Emma wondered if they were short staffed, but was thankful that she would be able to see Joe.

Emma sat beside Joe's bed, and when the sister left the ward she stood and kissed his forehead. He looked pale and vulnerable, and she prayed that when he awoke without sedation, he would be the old Joe, trying to tell her what to do, and disapproving of her most of the time. She could put up with anything if he would only get well again.

An hour later the specialist arrived, and Emma was asked to leave. Later the specialist came for her, and said she might again sit with Mr Grantham. The news was good, the swelling was slowly receding, and he had spoken with Mr Grantham, and he seemed quite lucid. If he carried on the same, he would be leaving hospital in a few days.

Emma returned to his room, and he had been propped up on two pillows. His eyes lit up as he saw Emma, and he put out his hand to her, which she took with a sigh of relief.

"Joe, are you feeling any better?" She wanted to hug him, but he looked pale and tired.

"Ems, thank you for what you did. The specialist says you helped save me, what happened?" He tried to turn his head to look into her eyes, but groaned and closed his eyes for a few seconds.

"I was there Joe, but Jimmy, Bill and Jed were all involved. You'll never live it down, the Mountain Rescue were also called out." She told him with a smile. Anyone living local to the mountains never wanted to be the ones who troubled the Mountain Rescue! The Mountain Rescue personnel were mostly local people, who were volunteers. Emma remembered that Joe, Bill and Jed had in the past helped them out when necessary.

"Was it as bad as all that?" Joe asked and groaned, because he was hurting or because the Mountain Rescue had been called out Emma wasn't sure.

"I'll have to go outside and give Dad a ring, he asked me to as soon as the specialist had given his verdict on your scan."

"Don't go yet Emma," Joe asked and squeezed her hand, and she wanted to kiss his lips, but restrained herself, and just pushed his hair to one side instead. She did that again and he seemed to relax, and she hoped he was sleeping and not unconscious yet again. She looked at the hospital gown he was wearing and decided she should ask her dad to bring in his pyjamas. She then realised she had no way of knowing what he wore to sleep in, if anything.

Emma heard the door open and sister came bustling in.

"How are you feeling Mr Grantham? You have another visitor, and she says she is your girlfriend." Sister smiled and held open the door.

CHAPTER FOURTEEN

Emma's hand left Joe's, and she turned and watched Melanie Banks come into the room bearing grapes, and flowers. She looked slim and attractive, and was smiling broadly at Joe.

"I had been waiting over an hour for you last night Joe, when Megan thought to give me a ring. I understand she was waiting with Charlotte and the dog in Emma's car at Dungeon Ghyll. Emma and John had taken off, to see what the problem was." She leaned over the bed and kissed Joe on the cheek, and then glanced up at Emma, across Joe's bed. "Do you know where the vases are kept Emma this room looks quite bare without any flowers?"

"Emma," Joe said weakly and tried to lift his head, but the pain was too bad.

"No but I can find out for you, Melanie. Joe I'm going outside to ring Dad and let him know the results of your scan. I promised him I would. They will all be waiting in the

344

office to find out how you are. One of us will come to visit you tomorrow." Emma said woodenly. She picked up her jacket and bag, extracted her mobile from the bag, and with a brief smile at Melanie, she left Joe's room, the Ward and then hurried to the car park.

She rang the office, and her dad and Mary were overjoyed at Joe's good news. Emma suggested to her dad, that he would probably like to come to the hospital tomorrow, and it would be a good idea if he brought with him a change of clothes for Joe, ready for when he was discharged.

Emma wiped a tear from her eye, as she moved the plastic bag full of Joe's dirty climbing clothes from the previous evening from the passenger seat to the floor. After they were washed and she had packed some clothes for her dad to bring tomorrow, she considered her job was finished. She had found one of Joe's house keys in his pocket, and thought it would be a good idea if she got Mrs Robinson to give the house a going over, before Joe got back home. She decided it would be too bitter-sweet for her to do it, as she had intended before the arrival of Melanie at the hospital.

She drove home, taking her time, as she had no intention of going to work in the office, as her dad would have expected her to stay for the afternoon with Joe, not go running off as soon as his 'girlfriend' arrived. Emma soon learned how the pain of jealousy felt when she had assumed that Joe and Mary were together, now it seemed she was to suffer it all again. It seemed that Mary's defection with regard to Robert Smyth had not been as devastating as Emma had imagined for Joe, it seems it was a case of 'off with the old and on with the new.' She had felt relief and elation when given the news by the specialist - she had to pull herself together and again portray that feeling, or she would be letting herself and Joe down. In truth, whoever Joe decided to spend his time or his life with, she was really and truly pleased that he should make a full recovery.

She remembered that her dad had said that Joe was busy on Boxing Day, but Emma has surmised he had meant he was busy climbing. His intention must have been to take Melanie out in the evening, after returning from climbing. "The best laid plans of mice and men," she thought ruefully.

When Robert Smyth arrived home from the office, he called his daughter into the living room from the kitchen.

"What is it Dad, I'm just preparing the dinner?"

"Before coming home I rang the hospital to ask how Joe was. The sister said he was upset, and needed sedating again, Joe said you went off and left him without as much as a goodbye."

"It wasn't like that Dad, I left to give you a ring, and bring home his clothes. He was fully occupied with a visitor. Melanie Banks came with grapes, and flowers. I assumed the sister would have asked me to leave, as Melanie had introduced herself as his girlfriend. Joe certainly wasn't up to seeing too many visitors."

"But Mary said that you wanted to stay with Joe, that's why I agreed to go home with her." Her dad seemed really puzzled, and then he shrugged and continued. "Bill Bancroft rang and asked if anyone was going in tonight to see Joe. I said I didn't think so as we had both seen him today. He is going to visit tonight, so Joe won't be alone this evening."

"I'm going to ask Mrs Robinson to go into Joe's house tomorrow morning, to change his bed and towels, and get things ready for whenever he comes home. I've brought his clothes home from the hospital for washing, and will pack a bag for you to take in to him tomorrow with clean clothes. The specialist said that if he continues to improve, he could be home in a few days," Emma replied, her mind in a whirl. She hadn't meant to upset Joe whilst he was so ill, but surely he wouldn't expect her to sit around whilst his girlfriend was there!

"Good idea, maybe she can sort out his refrigerator, I never thought about perishable food and stuff." Robert said, and wandered off and picked up his Telegraph, sinking into his chair with a sigh.

The next morning Emma asked Mrs Robinson to help get the house ready for Joe's return from hospital.

"I'm sorry my dear, I only have a couple of hours this morning, as I've a long standing dentist's appointment. Maybe, if I do an hour here, we could both do an hour at Mr Grantham's that should get things done?" Mrs Robinson suggested reasonably. How could Emma refuse, the fact that she would rather not be too intimately involved with Joe and his home under the present circumstances, didn't count for anything!

Emma rang the office, and left a message for her dad, to the effect that she would have Joe's clothes ready for the hospital, and that she would be at least an hour late in the office. She took Joe's house key, and rubbed her finger over the name of the house as she went in the front door. She sorted out the post which was mostly junk mail. Presumably Joe got most of his letters sent to his office. His home was nicely furnished, but had not been altered much since he had moved in. She looked around and thought of little things that might make it seem much more homely, and welcoming. She then rushed upstairs to strip the bed, and collect towels from his bathroom, as she remembered that

Melanie would probably do exactly the same when she came here, if she had not already been to Joe's home!

She already had the first load of washing in when Mrs Robinson joined her. Mrs Robinson looked around the house with interest, opening doors, and then gave her opinion.

"Obviously a bachelor! What a waste of a lovely home, garden, and a gorgeous hunk of manhood. When will he be home again? They were talking in the post office about the climbing accident, when I called in there on my way to work. Such a lovely man is Mr Grantham."

"Yes, well Mrs Robinson, we'd better get on, we don't want you to be late at the dentist's. Now that you've got a National Health dentist you won't want to be struck off his list." Emma said, trying to change the subject. Over the last few weeks Mrs Robinson had spoken at length about her difficulty in finding a dentist.

Mrs Robinson, still investigating every room, opened a door and pulled out of the airing cupboard, a double sheet and duvet cover with pillowcases, and a bath and hand towel, all in brown. "Why do men like brown Emma, other than brown the only colour in that airing cupboard is white!"

Emma didn't reply to that, but had a thought. "Mrs Robinson, why does everyone call you that, don't you care for your first name?"

"Well dear, I was so proud to be Mrs Robinson when I wed my Nigel, that I didn't answer unless people said Mrs Robinson, and it stuck. There's only my mother who calls me Janie. You can if you like Emma. I've been coming to you for over three years now, since before your lovely mother died."

"Thank you Mrs er Janie, but I'll probably forget and still say Mrs Robinson." Emma said, and stood back to look at the now pristine bed, and watched as "Janie" dusted around. "It's alright if you go now, I've just got to put in another load of washing, and then I'll vacuum around a bit." Emma said, and watched as Mrs Robinson slipped into her coat, and started to rub at her lips with a tissue.

"I don't want lipstick all over the dentist's hands do I dear?"

Emma imagined that he would probably wear rubber gloves.

When Emma was alone in the house, she wandered around a little, touching things that Joe must have touched. She looked at the Christmas Cards on the mantelpiece, and found her own which she had chosen so carefully, so that Joe would not know that she had pondered over her choice. It was a simple manger scene and Joe would never have guessed it meant something special to her! Enough daydreaming, as if anyone came they would think she was acting strangely, so she quickly put the first load of washing in the dryer, and loaded up Joe's climbing gear to be washed, and left the house forgetting to vacuum.

She went home, and decided not to go into the office, as she would take Jason for a nice long walk because that was when she mostly did her thinking. A walk would do them both good and help clear her mind. Jason was excited, but still had time to pick up a letter off the doormat. It was addressed to Emma, and she quickly opened it up, and stared in surprise. She had applied for a distance learning course at a university, and now discovered that her A levels were acceptable, as was she, and she could start in the spring. She didn't know what to think, did she want to stay on in her dad's accountancy firm, because she would need a job, but would have to be able to attend two or three week courses at the university at various times in the year? She had decided to try a distance learning course so that she could stay at home most of the time, but now her dad was going to marry, she might be better off doing a course like Jimmy and Jeremy, full time. Now she really did need to go walking, she needed to decide what she really wanted to do with her life. Well she did know what that was, but it wasn't going to happen, and she now had a choice. She didn't intend to stick around and make herself even more unhappy just because Joe had a girlfriend, a nice one at that!

In the Royal Infirmary in Lancaster, Robert Smyth was extremely puzzled. Joe had hardly said a word since he had arrived, merely nodded when Robert had informed him that Emma had packed some clothes that he would need when he was given permission to go home. Never before in their acquaintance had Robert and Joe found it awkward to converse, about anything.

"Are you feeling any better now Joe, and is your head still aching? We have all been so worried about you."

"A bit," Joe replied, his mind on other things.

"Emma seemed a bit disappointed when she had to come home early yesterday, as your girlfriend Melanie Banks came to see you. Was she the one you invited to the Christmas Party?"

"I got the impression Emma couldn't wait to get away," Joe replied brusquely ignoring his partner's second question.

"I don't think that can be true. She was going to take Mrs Robinson into your house to get it ready for you for when you come home. I think they will do that today, and check your refrigerator, in case it's a while before you go home. I don't think she will be going into the office, I told her not to. She did have a very frightening experience by all accounts, and I'm glad I was not aware at the time of what exactly was going on!" Robert said thinking about his daughter of whom he was very proud, now after the event, although he was certain that he did not have all the facts!

"Bill Bancroft came last night to see me. He told me exactly what Emma did on Sunday night, and soon I will tell you all about it Robert. I bet Jimmy hasn't said much." Joe mumbled distractedly. Joe swung his legs out of the bed, and reached for the bag that Robert had brought with him.

"What do you think you're doing Joe?"

"I'm coming home with you Robert," Joe murmured, as he stood up beside the bed then sat down again. "I'll just give it a couple of minutes then I'm getting dressed."

Just then his doctor and entourage came into Joe's side-room, as he was doing his ward round.

"Ah Mr Grantham, how are you feeling. Is your head aching, do you need anything for the pain or are the painkillers you are on working?" The Doctor said, and picked up the notes at the foot of his bed, after rubbing his hands with antiseptic gel. "Your blood pressure, and temperature seem to be fine, you may be able to go home tomorrow," the Doctor said peering over his glasses at Joe.

"Thank you for all you have done for me Doctor, but I am going home *today*, I'll sign whatever you want." Joe said adamantly, as the Doctor looked closely at his patient and pondered.

"I see, well that is entirely up to you Mr Grantham, but you will need to take it easy, and see your GP about getting the strapping off your shoulder. Any dizziness or headaches and you must see your GP right away. If you are determined to leave today, then the nurse will get you a form to sign.

351

Good luck." He looked at Joe with a query, and then seeing how adamant he was, he nodded and moved on.

"Are you sure about this Joe? You needn't worry about work, everything is ticking along nicely." Robert asked worriedly. Something seemed to be bothering Joe since last night. On the other hand, he was probably bored in the hospital, and they would all keep an eye on him at home.

"If I can manage to shower and get dressed, then I'm fit to come home." Joe replied, and walked slowly towards the gents shower room.

Robert watched with a sigh, and settled down to wait for Joe. Maybe there was something in the strange ideas that Mary had shared with him, and if she was right then he couldn't be happier. After his shower and getting dressed, Joe did seem to be a lot happier, however the nurse did insist on Joe being taken to the car in a wheelchair, and in the end he ruefully let her have her own way!

After a surprisingly quiet journey for about half an hour, Robert had to stop at the service station on the way home for petrol. When he returned to the car he had a bag containing milk, bacon, and bread, which he handed to Joe.

"You are welcome to come and eat with us tonight Joe, if you feel up to it," Robert invited, and handed him the plastic bag of shopping. Joe had been very quiet on the way home, but he seemed to have more colour and there was a determined air about him. Robert looked at the clock on the dashboard – another twenty minutes and they would be in Windermere.

Emma and Jason had enjoyed and long energetic walk and Jason rushed to the door as soon as he was let out of the car. Her dad must have come back from the hospital, but his car was not in the garage so he must have gone on to the office. Jason ran back to her, and then passed and into the driveway of Pillar Rock.

"Come on Jason, stop fooling around, we'll get your dinner," Emma offered. He was now scratching at the door, and Emma went to drag him away, stupid dog.

"Hello Emma, can you come in for a moment, and Jason," Joe said as he opened the door, and Jason pushed his way in anyway.

"What are you doing home Joe, you should be in hospital?" Emma asked, as her heart started to beat rapidly, her Dad must be mad bringing Joe home today!

"Come inside Emma, Bill gave me a full run down of what occurred on Boxing Day. You took a really big risk Emma, but if you hadn't I might not have been around to thank you." He paused, and she slowly moved inside, and Jason moved on towards the kitchen.

"I think Jason wants a drink Emma, can you get him one, and I'd like a drink of water in the lounge. I need to sit down for a while." Joe said, and she watched his eyes and they didn't seem to be rolling or anything as he moved slowly into the living room.

She brought him a drink of water and put it on the low table in front of his seat.

"You should be in hospital, you are not fit enough to be home yet, what are you *thinking of*, and I'm surprised that Dad brought you back. I bet you didn't tell them at the hospital that you live alone!"

"I'm *thinking* I should thank you for what you did, and I think certain things need sorting out." He drank down the glass of water and placed the glass on the coffee table, and then stood up slowly. He stepped close to her, and stared into her dark blue emotion filled eyes. Without taking his eyes off hers he pulled her close, and she thought that she stopped breathing, as she felt his hand on her arm, and then it slid around her back.

"Thank you for saving my life Emma."

"It wasn't just me ..." She didn't get any further as his lips met hers ever so gently, and she was surprised at his tenderness. Slowly the kiss turned to one of desperation, and their bodies clung together, and then he allowed them to breathe. He kissed her again and she couldn't stop herself from pouring all the love she felt for him into that kiss. Suddenly he was holding her at arms length, and then he put his arm on the back of the settee and lowered himself slowly.

"Sorry Emma, but my shoulder really hurts. Would you please sit down at the other end of the settee, and stop pretending that you didn't *feel* what I did just then." He ran his hand through his hair, and she liked the untidy way it looked, and she wanted to be close to him, but she too needed answers. A desperate need started inside her as she became certain that he couldn't kiss her like that unless she meant something special to him.

"You shouldn't have run away from the hospital when Melanie came. She only told the Sister she was my girlfriend because she didn't think they would let her in otherwise. She came to tell me that she was leaving Windermere, and going back to her home. She was married, and two years ago she lost her husband who was killed in Afghanistan. Her sister, Megan Warner, introduced us, and I felt that she has had a very raw deal. She wanted to give Megan and John some space, and I asked her to the office dinner, and she asked me out on Boxing Day to repay the favour. She is a very nice woman, but only the sister of my client."

"I see, I thought it odd that you should start to date someone else so soon after Mary. Was I wrong in thinking Mary was your girlfriend when you introduced me to her and her son Jeremy. You seemed so close?"

"Mary and I have been good friends and colleagues since she came to the office. She only had eyes for your father, but she did keep that hidden for a long time. Your father confided in me the day of the Christmas Party, and I was worried how *you* would react, and at first you didn't disappointment me, but then you put things right and you appeared to be pleased that they had become engaged to be married."

"The main thing that worried me was that you would be *terribly hurt*, I thought you and Mary had been an item. Also I couldn't believe that he had forgotten Mum, but he told me he would never forget her, but he needed to move on," Emma said regretfully.

"I have been 'terribly hurt' Emma, having to get Tom Bell to leave you alone, seeing you first with Simon Park who was not good enough for you, and then Jeremy was squiring you around. However, my biggest worry was Bill Bancroft, he was the only one that I considered was good enough for you, and you always seemed to be in his company. And you even asked *him* to teach you to climb."

"That was just to put you and Jimmy in your place, as *you* didn't seem keen to teach me any more. You were good enough to teach me when I was climbing on the gable end of your house." Emma said, unable to stop showing how hurt she had been at his defection. He stared at her for a moment, and then shook his head, as she had no idea how difficult it had been for him, because she was so young!

"For God's sake Emma, you were suddenly growing into a very desirable young woman. You were someone much too young for me, and very inexperienced. I had to keep away from you and let you enjoy your teens, and meet people of your own age. However, *everyone* you met didn't meet with my approval. Jeremy was too young, Simon Park was not suitable, and then you met Bill, and I saw him kiss you after the Christmas Party, and I decided to keep out of your way as much as possible, as I was beginning to think he must be the one for you. That was really hard to do as *I* had been waiting for years for you to grow up!"

"Yes, Bill did kiss me after the party, but he then knew that my heart wasn't in it, and it would not be going any further. He was very nice and didn't seem too surprised, and accepted that we should just be good friends." She wanted to move closer to him, but wanted to hear his explanations.

"When Bill called to see me at the hospital, he told me how you had insisted on trying to help me, and he thought then that it was more than worry for a friend that spurred you on. When he and Jed explained what was needed, he was amazed at your grasp of the situation and how very determined you were to get down the rock to me, and to make me safe. You also thought of your brother Jimmy at the bottom of the crags holding the rope which could sever at any time! At first I didn't know whether to believe him or not as we always seemed to be arguing about most things. However, when you walked out when Melanie called at the hospital. That could have been quite difficult, but I couldn't stay there any longer and had to come home as soon as your

Dad came to visit me." Joe said, and as Emma moved towards him along the settee, he put his hand up to stop her.

"Please don't come any closer Emma, unless you are going to agree to be my wife, because I've waited for years for you to grow up into the wonderful girl you are, and unless we are getting married very soon you had better stay over there out of reach, or I will never be able to ask your Dad for permission to marry you."

"I think we should get married very soon Joe, and I'm old enough to know my own mind, but are you sure you haven't asked me because of the bump on your head?"

"I think the bump on the head has made me realise I've waited long enough, I can't risk letting you find someone else. I need you to kiss me now Emma, and if that doesn't get rid of this headache, then you'd better find the tablets I brought from the hospital, then we can try again."

Emma felt her heart lift, how she loved this wonderful man. She briefly wondered if Jimmy and her Dad would be surprised by them becoming a couple, and then she moved gracefully across to join Joe, whom she loved to distraction. She must not hurt his injured shoulder, but there was plenty left of her wonderful man. She could touch his hair as she had longed to and if he kissed her again like he had a few minutes ago, then she wondered how they could possibly wait to get married as there was already one marriage in the family planned.

Jason came into the room and prodded Emma on the knee to get their attention as he was feeling left out, as he also loved Joe. Meanwhile, she would have to wait until Joe was well, and then she knew that he would teach her everything she didn't already know, which she was fast becoming aware was quite a lot!

Mary became the wife of Robert Smyth in early Spring and upon their return from honeymoon, they discovered that Joe and Emma were to be married in four weeks time at St. Martin's Church, Bowness on Windermere.

Joe's house Pillar Rock was being decorated and made into a *home* for the new bride, with lots of advice from their climbing friends and the younger members of the family. Jimmy and Jeremy maintained that two marriages in the space of a month were more than enough! However, Charlotte the beautiful and now sensible bridesmaid was quite confident that she could change that situation some time in the near future!